The Return *of the* Courtesan

The
Return
of the
Courtesan

VICTORIA BLAKE

BLACK & WHITE PUBLISHING

First published 2017
by Black & White Publishing Ltd
29 Ocean Drive, Edinburgh EH6 6JL

1 3 5 7 9 10 8 6 4 2   17 18 19 20

ISBN: 978 1 78530 125 4

Originally published in hardback as *Titian's Boatman*
by Black & White Publishing in 2017

A CIP catalogue record for this book is available from the British Library.

Typeset by Iolaire, Newtonmore
Printed and bound by CPI Group (UK) Ltd, Croydon, CR0 4YY

For Maureen
'All the better part of me'
William Shakespeare - *Sonnet 39*

ACKNOWLEDGEMENTS

Heartfelt thanks to Maureen for her steadfast encouragement and much needed love and support and to my sisters Deborah Blake and Letitia Blake. I would also like to thank all those who read earlier versions of the book and gave me feedback: Richard Collier, Francesca Howard, Rose Lamb, Keir and Louise Lusby, Faith Noonan and Jeremy Trafford. Thank you also to Nick Pole who kept me in working order through regular and sustaining shiatsu. The whole team at Black & White Publishing has been a delight to work with. So thanks in particular to Campbell Brown, Alison McBride, Chris Kydd, Thomas Ross, Lina Langlee, Janne Moller and Daiden O'Regan. Finally, many thanks to my agent Teresa Chris for keeping believing!

Gather up the fragments that remain, that nothing be lost.
– John VI, 12

Imagine you can begin anywhere. You can begin in 1576 with a boatman rowing a man into a plague-infested Venice, or in New York in 2011 with a maid cleaning an apartment on the 25th floor of a block on 6th Avenue. Imagine you can begin with an actor in London rehearsing the role of Leontes in The Winter's Tale, *a man whose lover has just left him and who is numb with grief. Imagine you can begin in 1576 with a Venetian courtesan returning from the mainland to find her home ransacked by thieving servants or with a ninety-year-old nun approaching the very end of her life. Imagine you can travel to any country and create any character. You can be a man, a woman or a child. You can be any age or any nationality. You can be gay or straight or undecided. Imagine you can go forwards or backwards in time. Imagine you can begin anywhere. How would you feel? Or perhaps the more relevant question is, where would you start? Which fragment would you bend down to retrieve? Beginnings are easy, of course. All you have to do is imagine . . .*

THE BOATMAN

Venice, 1576

Who is this man who comes in the night in the rough, brown hooded cloak of a pauper? Who scuttles onto my boat with the gleam of gold in his soft pampered hand? Who looks out into the green choppy waters of the lagoon with the round, black eyes of a greedy rat? Who is this man who demands to be taken into the heart of this funeral-pyre of a city, so many of whose citizens exist now only in the ash that floats above our heads and coats our throats. Who dares to come into this city, abandoned by people, abandoned by God? The city has been sick for over a year; a divine punishment is surely being meted out. My beloved home has been turned from a beautiful, untouched virgin into the most corrupt and diseased of whores. I, who have ferried many a person into this city of rats and swallows, have learnt how to tell one from the other, and this corpulent man who I carry in my boat knows nothing of flight. He knows nothing of

1

the sweep of a wing against the curve of an open horizon. He is familiar with baser matter. So why does he come into a place from which so many have fled? Why would he take such a risk? But now, as we draw up to the northernmost part of the city, as I steady my boat against the wharf and take his elbow to help him safely ashore, as he turns to pay me, the hood of his cloak falls open a little and I see his face. Now he realises that I know who he is and what brings him here. I can see by the expression on his face that he does not like it. His father and brother are in the ashes which swirl above our heads, blocking out the moon and the stars. The old man refused to leave this time. The elderly can be stubborn, but maybe, having fled the city so many times in the past, he decided that if God wanted him he should take him now. His eyesight was failing, I heard, and for a painter to lose his sight must be a terrible thing; it would be like a boatman losing an arm. I take hold of this man's sleeve and say in my most ingratiating manner, 'I remember Aretino, God rest his soul, telling me when your father first dressed you as a priest, when you were ten years old, that he did not think you would ever make a very good one.'

I'm hoping that if he does not want his presence known in the city he will tip me well, but instead the black sheep Pomponio, oldest son of the venerated painter Titian, wrenches his arm away from me and scurries along the alleyway that leads to his father's studio. I watch the shadows eat him up and wonder why it is that so often illustrious men produce such weakling sons. It is as if the gods are penalising them for having so much talent, their punishment dealt out in the mediocrity and corruption of their offspring. This scurvy spawn, Pomponio, scuttles towards his father's studio to see what remains, to see what can be sold. I watch him with a slight smile on my face

2

until he has disappeared from sight and then point my boat back towards the mainland, thinking of fathers and sons, greatness and mediocrity, until it is just me and the boat and the rhythm of my oars in the water and all my thoughts have vanished in the wide open expanse of the sea.

TITIAN
Two weeks earlier

Venice, 1576

He waits in the shadows of his studio for death to claim him. Surely it will come this time – this time when he invites it? As a much younger man, he had fled the city in 1527, terrified, as the bodies piled up in the streets and floated in the canals. But this time is different. He is ninety-one years old. They say that this city is the nurse of old men and it has certainly been true for him. But for a year now the plague has ravaged the city and not claimed him. He shuffles slowly to the shutters and pushes them open. Perhaps death may be carried in the air. He inhales deeply, taking in the fetid odour of disturbed mud, a noxious miasma so strong it is easy to imagine it might kill you.

Even though he invites it, there is still fear of death. An image of himself holding the dead body of Christ has been haunting him in recent days. He had painted himself as Nicodemus at

Christ's entombment. The head of Christ rested against his chest, his hand held him up under his arm. When he dies he wonders if there will be anyone to hold his body with such tenderness. There is his son, if he survives him. Surely Orazio will hold him. Once he is dead, he knows what will happen. In times of plague the bodies are burnt or wrapped in cloth and thrown into lime-strewn pits. He may lie on top of a dog, a doge, a pauper or a merchant. He will be barely touched at all. There will not be the great funeral service that he has imagined. His will be a diseased body to be feared like all the rest.

He shivers and offers up a prayer. One of the privileges of being a painter is that you can insert yourself anywhere in the picture. *The Entombment of Christ* had been painted originally for the nuns of Santa Maria degli Angeli in Murano, but they hadn't liked the price. In Venice even the nuns drive a hard bargain and he'd become so fed up with their whining he had offered it to Emperor Charles V in the hope that it might bring further commissions. It had been bait to catch a much larger fish than the penny-pinching nuns and as such it had worked very well.

The way he walks now reminds him of the emperor, stricken by gout, his feet wrapped in bandages, leaning heavily on his stick. Of course he had not painted him like that. Instead he had portrayed him in full gleaming armour on a prancing black stallion holding a spear. He had done his very best to draw attention away from that terrible Habsburg chin with the flamboyant red feathers on top of his helmet, matched by those between the horse's ears. An emperor had to be depicted riding into battle at the head of his troops not carried there in a litter because he could barely walk. He had been touched, however, by the exhaustion and vulnerability of the great man and had hoped that, along with the symbols of power, he had managed to convey something of his frailty, something of his humanity.

He peers into the distance. Far away across the plains, where he can no longer see, are the mountains of his home. Beloved Cadore, his birthplace, in the Dolomite Mountains. He had always known that as soon as he had enough money he would buy a studio here in Venice; it is not a fashionable part of the city but the only place from where he could see his home. For one who had risen so quickly, it was good to be reminded of the place of one's birth. It was good to walk to the shutters, look out and consider the humble nature of one's origins. He, who had depicted emperor and king, pope and doge, made sure that whenever possible he inserted the shimmering blue of the distant Dolomites somewhere in the background. His own birthplace thus became the backdrop to each individual portrait, a little piece of humble Cadore squeezed in behind each potentate's mighty shoulders. People had always asked him why he did not paint Venice, but this great narcissus of a city, eternally reflected in the waves which surround it, did not need him to immortalise her. Nature did that all by itself. He had known better than to compete with nature. And anyway, people paid better.

He turns away from the shutter and shuffles back across the room. Many paintings rest against the walls of his studio. In these last stages of his life he has for the first time painted simply to please himself, not to please any patron, and his painting has been different. He knows that Orazio had been worried about it. His son thought that the radical change in his style was a result of his failing eyesight, the fact that he was now going blind with the pin and the web, but that was not the only reason for the transformation. Finally, in the last years of his life, he had been given the gift of alchemy, not the ability to transform base metal into gold but that of transforming paint into feeling life. Chromatic alchemy had descended on him; this was what was happening in the flaring, bursting colours of his paintings, the paint worked sometimes with his fingers much more roughly than before. He knows Orazio thinks that these paintings will reduce his value in the marketplace. He does not want them seen. But for Titian they are the best he's ever done, they are the way forward, but he has come across it so late, so very late.

He turns one of the paintings round. Ah, he remembers this one. It's an early one, which has come in for restoration. He was much younger when he painted it, in his twenties, a little hot-headed, bursting with ambition, and on that particular day incandescent with rage.

* * *

This is not the time of year to be in Venice. It's August 1510, and the city lies suppurating in the sun like an infected wound and the mosquitoes gather to gorge on it. The heat has taken the breath from his lungs, the appetite from his mouth and sleep from his weary carcass so that he feels nothing but a burden to himself. Last night he had tossed this way and that, more like a dumb animal than a man. When he awoke, he was surprised to see that he still had flesh and bones and that those had not dissolved in the sweat he had shed in the night. There is not a single bit of coolness to be found anywhere in the city. God knows he has looked in every place he can think of. The only reason he is still here is to paint the son of a man who may be of use to him in securing the state sinecure he craves, but the young man in question, Pietro Paruta, a poet supposedly, is late and cannot be found. The shutters creak open in the hot breeze and an evil stench rises up from the canals. He steps away from the window and slams them shut. The parrot squawks in its cage; even its vivid green feathers seem dulled in the heat. Dear God, if it does not rain soon the air and the earth will burn up, along with the populace.

When he had first come to Venice as a child, one of the things he had missed most was the dawn chorus of his homeland. Here, the seagull and the pigeon reigned supreme. The only nightingales you heard were in cages in the Merceria advertising the trade of the apothecaries. But everyone knows that birds in cages do not sing in the same way. Even so, in the early days of his apprenticeship, as a child filled with homesickness, he had sometimes found his way to the jostling street where the birds were sold and, closing his eyes, tried to conjure up his family town and above all else the greenery of the Dolomites. The dream, however, was short-lived. When he opened his eyes, it was to return to the reality of this city of stone and water. There was little natural greenery in Venice, except on the rare occasions when the waters of the lagoon turned from blue to the most vivid jade.

Titian spins round. 'Where is he?' he bellows into the empty room. The door of the studio is pushed open and one of his apprentices, the youngest one, chosen to bear the brunt of his master's wrath, stands there quaking.

'We are looking for him, Master.'

'Looking? You have been looking for the last hour! *Find* him, imbecile,' he roars. 'Do you hear? Bring him to me.'

'Yes, Master.'

He busies himself with paint and brushes to stave off his feelings of irritation. Young men are the worst. Women can be bought off the street or from the balconies from which they spill their bosoms and spit to gain the attentions of clients, but young men are more headstrong, less pliable. Young men think they are immortal anyway, they do not worry about being immortalised in paint; they bore easily and know nothing of stillness. All they think of is the next

8

party they may organise. When this Pietro Paruta eventually turns up, he will make him suffer for keeping him waiting so long.

Titian is young himself, but already he knows a great deal about stillness. To really look closely, you have to be still and he can be very still indeed, as still as any predator. Genius has brought with it a sense of responsibility, a sense of destiny that in his case has brought great maturity at a young age. Since he came to the city as a young child to learn his craft, he has worked assiduously not only to build up his skills but also to learn about the politics of his trade. Both will be necessary for his success. Suddenly there is a commotion outside. Here is his apprentice again, his voice squeaking with relief.

'He is coming, Master.'

Titian turns so that his back will be towards the youth when he enters. He intends to spin round and order him out, but when he does turn round the boy is on his knees in a position of contrition. But what are these clothes he's wearing? He looks as if he's been dragged out of the canal, and he also has that lazy, sated, pleased-with-himself look that a cat has when it has spent the night keeping the whole neighbourhood awake. Now he is advancing towards him on his knees, with his hands clasped in a parody of repentance, and he is looking up at him through thick chestnut hair. Despite his irritation, Titian notes his beauty and pictures him immediately, kneeling at the foot of the cross, looking up at the crucified Christ.

He shakes the image from his mind and throws up his arms. 'What have you been doing? You were due an hour ago.'

'Ah...' Pietro sits back on his heels and names a famous courtesan. 'Anzola Trivixan.'

The painter twists his mouth a little to the side, taking in the poet's tatty breeches, his stained stockings and his dirty shirt. 'How can you afford her?'

'She does not charge me.'

Now he knows for certain it's a lie. The Venetian empire is based on trade. Venice is a city of traders. Luxury items are traded for money; a courtesan is like any other luxury item the city has to offer: glass, fine silk, perfume, spices, boats from the Arsenale. There are many courtesans in the city and one thing no courtesan can allow people to think is that she is available at no charge.

'It's true,' Pietro protests. 'I pay her in poems.'

Titian laughs. He can't help himself. 'So you pay with little pieces of your soul. A very high price indeed.'

Pietro looks somewhat downcast.

Titian thinks to himself, when I am famous I will be able to have any woman I like. Vanity and the courtesan are one, and some of them are very rich. It will not be just kings and popes he will paint. Whores will do just as well. Anyone who has the money. His curiosity gets the better of him and, even though he despises himself for asking, he enquires, 'What's she like?'

After all, the woman is notorious and there is not a man in Venice, he suspects, who has not imagined what it would be like to be buried between her legs.

Pietro Paruta is still on his knees. 'She is . . .' He pauses dramatically. 'Ex–quis–ite. You cannot imagine.'

Curiosity swiftly curdles into jealousy. 'Oh, get up. How can you expect me to paint you if you turn up looking like that?'

The poet looks down at himself a little forlornly, as if seeing himself for the first time. Titian goes to the door of the studio and shouts for his servant. 'Bring the silk doublet brought by the tailor yesterday.'

The boy comes back shortly, carrying the required item of

clothing. It is the finest blue silk, the most recent fashion. A thing of great beauty. It is in breach of the most recent sumptuary laws, which are changed almost every other day at the whim of the authorities.

Pietro holds it against himself and frowns. 'It will be much too big.'

Titian waves his hand dismissively. 'It doesn't matter. Put it on.'

Pietro shrugs but does as he is told. He is right – it swamps him. Titian spends some time arranging the doublet as he wants it and then positions Pietro, with his arm resting on a trestle brought in from outside.

'I will not be able to stay in this position for long,' the poet says. 'It's uncomfortable.'

But Titian is not listening to him. His eyes are fixed instead on the sleeve, the texture and quality of that beautiful blue sleeve. And now it comes to him. He will use this young man to pose for the sleeve, but he will not paint his face. Instead he will paint his own face; he will make this a self-portrait. There are other people he can approach about the sinecure. Someone no doubt will paint the poet one day. He is certainly pretty enough. But today he will make him stay there, standing in that awkward position, because he has come from the arms of the notorious courtesan Anzola Trivixan, because he has kept a great painter waiting, because he has made a great painter jealous. He will not immortalise this young man; he does not deserve it.

He picks up a brush and runs it gently across the palm of his hand, enjoying the sensual tickle. This idiot may have come from the arms of a courtesan, but does he know how to coax flesh from oil paint? Does he know how to bring the exquisitely fine textures of silk to life on a canvas? Titian looks intently at the thick quilting of the blue silk sleeve and then briefly at the poet's face. No, he will not waste any time on that; there's nothing there of any interest to him, nothing at all. His own face will be above this sleeve, not this young fool's. And how will he depict himself? In the same way as he approaches all his subjects, with exactly the same rigorous circumspection, and above all as someone secondary to the magnificence of this sleeve. It will be his own private joke.

He has already taken a commission from the young man's father in payment and he has already spent it, mainly on this blue doublet, but everything may be smoothed over with a little charm and he has a great deal of that. Art is a business which requires it. He knows he has great talent and he knows he has great charm but Venice has always been a highly competitive city for painters. However, Giorgione died this year and he heard that del Piombo is on his way to Rome. Only the ageing Bellini remains, and his talents are withering. Soon he, Titian, will be the pre-eminent painter in Venice and he is only twenty. He knows he is on his way, but first there is this sleeve to paint, this exquisite blue sleeve. Pietro shifts disconsolately from one leg to the other.

'Keep still,' Titian barks and dips his brush in oil paint.

Now all the discomforts of the heatwave are forgotten; a feeling of arousal and excitement pulses through him, as vivid as anything the poet has experienced between the thighs of Trivixan. The ecstasy of the artist at work. Something this licentious boy knows nothing about.

Later, Titian relents. Of course he does. No painter can afford to overlook such beauty. He paints Pietro as Saint Sebastian slumped, with bare torso, eyes raised to heaven, impaled with arrows – arrows the painter would have liked to have shot at him personally on that hot August afternoon when the beautiful boy dragged himself into his studio so late and showed such disrespect to genius. As for the blue doublet, he sends it to an influential patrician, as an inducement to sit for him, knowing that if the portrait pleases him he may recommend Titian to his rich friends and lovers. So in the end it is neither the poet nor Titian's head which sits atop the beautiful, blue silk sleeve but that of the crafty Gerolamo Barbarigo.

Aurora

New York, 2011

Aurora Lopez Famosa stood in front of the painting, feather duster in hand. She longed to clean it, but she had been told by Mr Pereira when she had first begun working there ten years before that she was not to touch it. She was not to touch it *at all*. It hung there in the hall, where no natural light could damage it. There in the hall of the apartment on the 25th floor of that block on 6th Avenue was the only place where it could hang. All the other rooms were too light. After all, when you were this rich, what else was there to buy but light and air? And art. Saint Sebastian sagged against the ropes that bound him, eyes raised to heaven, his body impaled with arrows; the expression on his face was a combination of agony and ecstasy.

On that morning in September ten years ago, when the planes had come out of a clear blue sky, Aurora had been alone in the flat, as the owners were away in St Barts. Her daughter had phoned her and she had put on the television and watched. When she had finally managed to pull herself away, she had thrown herself to her knees in front of the painting and prayed in a way that she had not prayed since she was a child.

Oh, the beauty of that face! She imagined that he watched over her as she moved around the flat, as she swabbed pubic hair from the plug hole of the shower and cleaned shit from the U-bend of the toilet, as she chased the dust across the sun-warmed, smooth wooden floors. She imagined those eyes filled with suffering, filled with love, attentive to her every single movement. One of her earliest memories was of being in her mother's arms in front of a painting of the saint in Havana cathedral, with the light of the votive candles flickering in the darkness.

'Can't we take the arrows out?' she had whispered in her mother's ear.

The subsequent years had taught her that sometimes you could, sometimes you couldn't.

'You only truly know a thing if you clean it.' It is what her mother had said to her when she was very little. 'You can own a thing but know nothing of it.'

Her mother was long dead, but she had been right about the knowledge which comes from the repeated cleaning of an object. Aurora pitied these very rich people because they had no sense of wonder at what they had; they appeared to have no sense of gratitude. Their lives were a constant state of anxiety. They had so much, yet how deeply they feared losing it and how stupid they could be. A poor person, for example, would do nothing as stupid as have plastic surgery.

A month ago, when she had arrived at the flat, she had been surprised to see Mr and Mrs Pereira both there. He had told her she would not be needed for a month but that they would pay her during that time, and he had then given her the date when she should return. They had offered no reason. That was another thing she had discovered about the very rich, they felt little need to explain themselves. She had been happy enough to take the money and go. Today was her first day back. She had been a little early and had passed Mrs Pereira going out, had seen immediately from the stretched skin and the bruising, exactly what had taken place during her month away. No, a poor person would do nothing as stupid as have plastic surgery. It was not an option.

Cleaning the enormous mirror in the bathroom, Aurora looked at her own face with some affection. Yes, there were lines at the corners of her eyes and between her eyes, and her jowls were beginning to form a little bit round her cheeks, but it was a good face, she thought, a strong face, a face she was proud to have. She did not want to alter one part of it and she wondered whether it was because her mother had so often placed both her hands against her cheeks when she was little and said to her, 'Ah, my beautiful daughter!' In the course of time, Aurora had come to believe it. It was something she made sure to say to her own daughters frequently, even though they had now reached the age when they pulled her hands away and told her not to be so stupid. She knew it wasn't stupid, certainly not as stupid as putting oneself under the knife because you feared losing your ugly rich husband. Nothing was as stupid as that.

It was, she supposed, inevitable that Mrs Pereira would do it in the end. Her husband had done what the very rich often do and had left his wife for her, a younger almost identikit version. There was no doubt she was beautiful, with curly blonde hair and a broad Scandinavian face, big breasts and a tiny wasp-like waist, but she was now in her mid-fifties and, in Aurora's opinion, blondes did not hold their looks well into old age. The fairer the beauty, the more transient it was. But really it was Mr Pereira, with his spindly legs, short back and prominent pot belly, who was the one in need of radical alteration.

Aurora had never liked him. When she had first come to the city from Florida as a young woman, she had worked for many years in hotels – long enough to give her very good instincts about which men you could be alone in a room with and which you could not. When she had first started working here, Mr Pereira had on occasion been in the flat when she was cleaning, as if sniffing the air to see if there was an opportunity there. He had suggested she might like to call him Tom. She had told him firmly but politely that she was quite happy to call him Mr Pereira, that in fact she would prefer it. On another occasion he had called her into the bedroom on the excuse of showing her something under the bed which needed cleaning. Instead of joining him immediately, she had gone and got the vacuum cleaner so she would have the security of its long metal funnel between him and her. She had made sure to work briskly, to make sure that every conversation returned to her very happy family life. She had made every effort to get out of there as swiftly as was humanly possible. After that he had never bothered her. He still dropped money around the flat and sometimes put too much money in her pay packet, but that was easy enough to deal with. Only a fool would fall for such obvious tests of honesty.

Finishing with the mirror, she walked through into the living room. One whole end of the room was dominated by a huge aquarium. She looked at the neon tetras, with their vivid blue, red and silver colours, darting back and forth in the water. They were her favourites and then after them the yellow ones with the blue edging. The black and white striped ones were also kind of smart. On her first day working here, this was the other thing she'd been told not to touch.

'I'm real particular about my fish,' Mr Pereira had said. 'So don't touch this, as well as the painting.'

Now, years later, Aurora stood, hands on hips, head cocked to one side, staring at the fish tank, still puzzled. Like a child who has been told under no circumstances to touch the surface of an iron. Why not? When it looked so harmless? She wondered, as she always did, why a man like Mr Pereira had fish at all, because he had never struck her as the type to enjoy their delicate, darting beauty. Surely he was more of a pit-bull man? And the fish tank was huge: it took up the whole of one wall and it rested on something a bit like a huge metal gurney. And why in this apartment, in which everything was just so, would you have that ugly metal gurney under your aquarium? It simply didn't make any sense.

There had been a time many years ago when she had been the fish inside the tank. She was five years old, her brother, Pablo, and cousin, Miguel, were with her inside a glass-walled room, *la pecera*. The date was 1962; the place Havana airport. Out on the runway sat the Pan Am flight to Miami, Florida, shimmering in the heat. On the far side of the glass walls were her parents, anxiously watching. A soldier opened her suitcase and pulled her doll out by its golden wool hair. The red smile, stitched onto its cream face by her grandmother, hung in the air in front of her before being tossed into the pile of other toys on the floor. Then he pointed to the gold hoops in her ears.

'Take them out.'

No, she wouldn't. He had already taken the gold bracelet from her brother's wrist.

'Take them out or you don't go. All you're allowed to take are three changes of clothes.'

She clamped her hands over her ears and began to scream. She saw his mouth moving as he talked to her brother. Pablo tried to prise her hands from her ears, but she pulled away from him and ran to where she could see her parents, hands pressed against the glass wall. Her brother was behind her and he shouted out what had happened. Surely her father would protect them, protect them from the wicked soldier who had stolen her doll, who wanted to take away her earrings?

'Take them off,' her father shouted. 'Take them off, Aurora, and give them to the soldier.'

'But it's not fair,' she wailed.

'Aurora,' he shouted. 'You must do as I tell you.'

But she was only five and her doll had just been taken away from her and her parents were on the other side of a glass wall and she didn't understand anything. She sobbed and sobbed while Pablo gently pulled the hoops from her ears.

This was to be the last time she saw her parents, her father white-faced and stern, ordering her to give up her earrings, her mother, her hand clasped over her mouth, her eyes filling with tears, as if she were the one under water, as if she were the one in the fish tank. The last thing her mother said to her was, 'We'll be on the roof. I'll open the umbrella.' She held up the red umbrella in her hand. 'We'll be on the terminal roof. Look for us from the plane.'

But in the plane, clasping the Coca-Colas they'd been given by the air stewardess, they had been seated on the wrong side of the plane to see the terminal roof. Unable to see it then, she had seen it a thousand times since in her dreams. There was the red umbrella and underneath it there was her mother, smiling and waving before disappearing forever. Not much later there was a cheer as the plane entered American airspace, but Aurora didn't cheer, she was mourning her earrings, her doll, her mother and father. She was crying, as it turned out, for a childhood that had barely got started before it was ripped away from her, in exchange for a new life in America. Her parents, frightened by the changes taking

19

place in Cuba, had decided her life would be better there, but how could it be better away from them? When her children had reached the same age that she had been when she had first come to America, Aurora had wondered all over again. How could they have sent them away? She'd been only five years old. How could they?

Later she understood the behaviour of the soldiers. She might have been a child, but as far as they were concerned, her parents were betraying the revolution. So she and all the other children should suffer, they should be made to give up their toys; their toys and their gold belonged to Castro now. If their parents wanted them out, then fine, but they would have to watch their children having their toys torn from them through the glass walls and not be able to do anything about it. That is what they had to sacrifice – their toys, their gold – if they wanted to get their children out. It was only much later that she found out that the name of the operation that organised the exodus of the children was Operation Pedro Pan. Peter Pan was the boy who never grew old. The truth was the opposite of that. They had all had to grow up much too quickly. Five years old and it was as if her childhood was gone for good.

When they landed in Miami, they had been handed a carton of milk each, but she and her brother had never seen such a thing, had no idea how to open it. Eventually, after Pablo had practically destroyed the cartons, they dumped them in a bin, watching guiltily as the white fluid drip-dripped down onto the floor. And when she had been asked if she had liked the milk she had lied and said, 'Yes, thank you. Very much indeed.'

She turned away from the aquarium and walked over to the windows. The view was spectacular, glass towers marching off into a vibrant blue sky. Over the last month she had missed this view and she had missed Saint Sebastian. She sighed and looked at her watch. It was time to be going.

Mrs Pereira was not unkind. She had left her some clothes. She did this periodically, but the items were rarely to Aurora's taste. Mr Pereira bought his wife's clothes and usually they were much too tarty. Despite their fancy labels and despite her daughters' protestations, Aurora disposed of them on eBay, sometimes for quite good prices.

She pulled on her coat and wrapped her scarf tightly round her neck, picked up her handbag and a large carrier bag containing the clothes she had been given. On the way to the front door she stopped and pushed open the door to the bedroom. An enormous, explicit painting of two women making love hung above the bed. Whenever she felt envy creeping into her heart, she made sure to look at this painting and then all her envy dissipated. If there was no respect in a relationship, it was worth nothing and that was what the woman had, Aurora thought, absolutely nothing. There was only so far skin could be stretched before it split.

TERRY

London, 2011

Colin had moved out on Wednesday, while Terry was at rehearsals, and he had done so as neatly as he had moved in ten years before. All that remained was the slight sag in the mattress on his side of the bed and the ghostly lines of dust, marking where he had removed some of his favourite posters – *The Normal Heart*, *La Cage aux Folles* – from the hall. Colin had not brought much with him when he'd moved in with Terry all those years ago and there wasn't much to take with him when he left. He'd never been one for gathering things around him. Lovers had always been abundant, but not things. It was one of the characteristics that had first drawn Terry to him, the way Colin seemed to pass through the world without material attachment. All those years ago it had seemed little short of a miracle when he had become attached to Terry. There were no gaps in the bookshelves because all the books were Terry's, Colin never having been much of a reader.

On the following Sunday, Terry woke exhausted, made himself a cup of tea and went and sat in the living room. March winds were shaking the plane trees on the opposite side of the road, and shafts of weak sunlight fell across the red rugs which covered the floor. He looked around the room. Colin had been going on at him for ages to get the walls painted, but he had resisted, unable to stand the concomitant disruption, but now that Colin wasn't here to badger him, he found himself agreeing easily with him. He'd been right; the walls were filthy. Why couldn't he just have said this before? A wave of exhaustion broke over him and he leaned his head back and closed his eyes.

Rehearsals that week had not gone well and he was beginning to regret ever having accepted the role of Leontes in *The Winter's Tale*; he had come to the conclusion that he hated the part and he hated the play. Whoever had had the bright idea of describing *The Winter's Tale* as a comedy had obviously never tried playing the jealous, paranoid tyrant Leontes. A man who wrongly accuses his wife of adultery with his best friend, puts her on trial and brings about the death of her and his son, then orders the death of his baby daughter. The man was simply intolerable. All week Terry had been struggling to string together the thoughts behind the text. He had been struggling so much that he had come to the conclusion that he simply did not want to inhabit them: the irrationality, the vindictiveness, the delusional jealous state. How did one find humanity in the heart of a tyrant? It was necessary, because if he didn't manage to evoke some kind of understanding in the audience for Leontes in the beginning of the play there would be no catharsis or redemption at the end.

Particular roles could cast poisonous shadows. He had been in the business long enough to know that. The worst had been playing Konstantin in *The Seagull*. He remembered a conversation with his mother halfway through the run. He had had rave reviews and everything was going as well as it possibly could. There was the suggestion that his performance would be prize-winning, career altering, etc. but after a monosyllabic conversation with his mother she had asked him if he was all right and he had burst into tears. She was a tough woman, a doctor, but she had been surprisingly sympathetic. 'You're playing a character in the grip of suicidal depression every day. It's not surprising that something is likely to stick. You'll be fine once the run ends.' And she'd been absolutely right. He'd got blind drunk at the closing-night party and the following afternoon he'd gone to have coffee with a friend of his who was working at the Coliseum in St Martin's Lane. Coming out of the cafe into the street, he'd looked at the traffic lights and they had seemed extraordinarily bright, blazingly red and orange and green. He'd stopped dead in the street and pointed them out to his friend, who had looked a bit puzzled. No, he'd said, they were no brighter than usual. Later he had realised that for the last three months he had actually been looking at the world through a grey filter of depression; it had affected his ability to see colours. Now those colours were bursting in on him again like fireworks, so vividly he felt transfigured by them.

Leaning on the sink this Sunday morning, looking at himself in the bathroom mirror, he did not see a tyrant. He saw an exhausted, rather overweight middle-aged man whose lover had left him and who couldn't hold his own eye in the mirror for long for fear of what he might find there.

He couldn't stay inside, battling with his regrets and memories of Colin. He pulled on some clothes, grabbed his wallet, phone and keys, and left the flat. A bus was coming along the road. He set off running, waving wildly at it to stop. Once on board he went upstairs and sat at the front, as he had done as a child, squashed against the substantial bulk of his father, nose pressed to the front windscreen, sticky hands making smeary patterns on the glass.

Things had been falling apart since his mother died. Two years ago out of the blue she had summoned her three children back to her home in Norfolk. She had not told them why she had invited them all there for the weekend. It wasn't a birthday or an anniversary. It wasn't Easter or Christmas. It wasn't any particularly significant date that any of them could work out. But obediently they had all come. Their father had been dead for a couple of years and their mother had just got on with her life. She was a very self-contained woman who had never asked anything much from them.

'It's in the pancreas,' she said, as they were nursing drinks before lunch. 'Not a very clever place to have it.'

'Cancer,' she repeated. As if they might have missed that part. 'I've got cancer of the pancreas. If I was my own patient, I would be telling myself to put my affairs in order.'

'But I thought it was jaundice,' Terry burst out.

That's what she'd told them when she came back sick from her holiday with her sister in Italy. Jaundice.

'The tumour is pressing on the bile duct. The early signs of pancreatic cancer can mimic jaundice.'

Mimic, Terry thought, seeing the cancer immediately as Rory Bremner with yellow make-up. Mimic!

'Well, I think after that you could all do with another drink,' she said. 'I'm going to baste the chicken.'

On the train on the way home with his brother, Ralph, and sister, Mary, both doctors, he'd asked them how long.

'Three months,' Ralph said.

'Six months,' Mary said, and then she'd sighed. 'At any rate, it's unlikely to be longer than a year.'

They had all gone home a lot that last year. Terry would travel down on a Sunday. He'd catch the train from Liverpool Street to Norwich and then the local train to the village where his mother lived and come back on Monday afternoon, in time for the evening performance. They were working on the track at weekends. In fact, they seemed to be working on the track every single Sunday for the next six months. After his mother died, for the rest of his life, he would regard Ingatestone with loathing and rage. A place that was preventing him from getting to his mother's side, a place forever associated with a replacement coach service, a replacement fucking coach service which seemed to add hours to the journey, not just the thirty-five minutes it was claimed.

Cancer of the pancreas.

Ingatestone.

Death.

His mother's. Thirteen months later. On 25 January, after a stroke on Boxing Day.

He had not seen someone he loved suffer before. It had altered everything. After that final month watching his mother die he felt he knew all about suffering. He was primed for Leontes, in fact; or at any rate the Leontes in the final part of the play. Yes, he should have been primed for it. But he'd not been able to pay as much attention to Colin as usual and Colin was a high maintenance sort of man. Terry had simply not had the energy or the inclination to sidestep the arguments any more. By nature, he was a defuser and a placator, but grief seemed to have replaced those qualities with an implacable stubbornness and anger. Consequently, the last few months had been filled with terrible rows and recriminations. In the end, he'd wanted to be free of Colin's constant accusations and demands for attention. But he was old enough to know that this sense of relief would not last; in its wake would come loneliness and the fear of a solitary old age, the feelings of failure that always overwhelmed him when a relationship ended badly.

He got off outside the Royal Academy to skip the interminable crawl to Piccadilly and walked to Trafalgar Square.

The pigeons had been gone for years now, but he still missed them, the grey fluttering soul of the square. He had voted for Ken Livingstone as mayor, but he had never been able to forgive him for letting loose the hawks in the centre of London. In Venice, someone had told him recently, nineteen families made their living from selling pigeon feed to tourists. That seemed an eminently sensible way to handle the problem of pigeons. Even in the sunshine, the square was grim, grey and heavily monumental. The pigeons had always softened it.

He walked slowly round the square. It was early and there were only a few tourists posing in front of the lions and taking photos of Nelson. No self-respecting Londoner was in Trafalgar Square at this time of day on a Sunday; they were reaching for their lover, their paper, their coffee. Inside the National Gallery, he let himself wander, pretending that he did not know where he was going. He went through doors without any particular regard for where he would end up. He paused in each room, glanced briefly at the walls, picked a painting – *Bathers at Asnières* by Seurat, *The Ambassadors* of Holbein, *Sunflowers* of Van Gogh – spent a few moments in front of each and then moved on. He continued in this way, knowing what painting he would end up in front of. He always did.

Ah, there he was!

He stood in front of him and stared, at the blue sleeve first, and then at the man. The man in the painting looked sideways at Terry, the expression on his face guarded, suspicious, sardonic. His eyebrows seemed to have been very heavily plucked. Terry stared and stared, noticing the way that the sleeve seemed to protrude, as if coming out of the painting towards the viewer. He wondered if this was an early advertisement for the luxury items on sale in Venice, this beautiful silk. The painting, a Renaissance version of the

27

1980s Levi's ad, with the man stripping to his underpants in the laundrette to the strains of 'Heard It Through the Grapevine'. The subject of the painting was now described as *Portrait of Gerolamo (?) Barbarigo*. Terry frowned. For many years he had known the painting simply as *The Man with the Blue Sleeve* . There had then been a period of it being titled *A Man with a Quilted Sleeve*. Hadn't there also been the suggestion at one time that it might be a self-portrait of the great Titian? He wished they would stop changing the title; he found it disconcerting. However, whoever it was, there was no doubt that the picture was an effective advertisement of his skills, painted in 1510 when Titian was only twenty years old. It was a very effective calling card. Look what I can do, it announced. Look what I can do with a blue quilted sleeve. Imagine what I might do with you, given half a chance? If it was a self-portrait, it was a very unforgiving one.

It had been in front of this painting that Terry had come out to his mother. There had been no need to come out to his brother and sister since they had known probably before he did that he was gay, but he had put off biting the bullet with his parents. Partly because neither of his parents were into exchanges of personal intimacies, partly because he didn't see why he should since neither of his siblings had had to come out as heterosexual. Brooding over it all was the simple terror of rejection.

But there had been something about this painting, the sardonic, sophisticated look on the man's face, which operated as some kind of dare. He imagined the man did not think he would have the courage to do it. So standing in front of him with his mother one day, he had found himself blurting out that there was something he needed to tell her and he didn't want her to be upset. Dear God, even now he cringed at the memory of it. It had definitely been one of the least convincing performances of his life. She hadn't said much in the gallery but later at lunch he had been on the receiving end of an extremely detailed exposition of safe sex. Beyond reassuring herself that he wouldn't put himself at risk, she had expressed little opinion. There had been no overt acceptance or rejection.

A female doctor at a time when there were very few of them, an oncologist who spent a part of each working day telling people how much longer they could expect to live, his mother was a messenger of life and death. Maybe in that context her son's sexuality was of little importance other than as something to be addressed medically. Maybe it had just been irrelevant to her. He had been puzzled and disappointed in just about equal measure. He hadn't really expected her to say anything as trite as 'I love you anyway' because that wasn't her way, but some sort of reassurance would have been nice. Maybe she just assumed that he knew he was loved and that there was no need to go through the embarrassing requirement of telling him. She had always been a difficult woman to read. She had not been in the habit of bringing her work home with her; the only sign that she might have had a difficult day was a slight tetchiness and the requirement that the gin her children or husband poured her was a *large* one.

There are worse things than loneliness.

Terry spun round. The room was entirely empty other than a security officer and another visitor, a slab-faced woman with a severe pony-tail squeezed into a tight grey suit, the colour of which matched her face. He stared at her. She frowned back. No humour lines graced the corners of her eyes and he doubted they ever would. The corners of her mouth had already begun their inevitable downward journey. She did not look like the kind of woman to impart wisdom to a stranger.

He turned back to the painting.

There is a big difference between looking and seeing. You look but you do not really see.

Terry was not impressed. If the painting was talking to him, he would prefer it to talk to him in a manner which did not mimic the most banal of self-help books and GCSE art criticism. He expected greater sophistication from a Renaissance man, perhaps some juicy gossip about Leonardo or Michelangelo. He expected a more complex appraisal of his short-comings from this sardonic dandy with plucked eyebrows. Tell me something I don't know, he thought.

You are going to die soon.

What?

Well, that got your attention.

'Are you playing with me?'

He heard a sharp intake of breath and turned to see the woman walking over to the security officer. He looked back at the painting.

Well, I am very old, you must remember. When you are five hundred years old, soon could mean fifty years hence.

Someone tapped Terry on the shoulder. 'We would like you to leave now, sir.'

He turned to see the security officer next to him.

'Sorry?'

'It would be best if you left right away.'

'What are you talking about?'

'This woman says you used obscene language towards her.'

Terry was outraged, puzzled and curious all at the same time. 'What did I say?'

The woman was red in the face now. 'Pervert,' she snapped.

As the man escorted him to the exit, he asked him again. 'What did she say I said?'

'Something about playing with yourself.'

'Oh, that...' He laughed. 'She misunderstood. I was talking to the painting.'

The security officer, a plump, kindly faced man with little hair, sighed heavily. 'Well, in that case, sir, next time I'd advise a different type of conversation.'

And then Terry was outside the gallery, in bright sunshine, with Nelson's Column rising into a capacious, clear blue sky. He had never been ejected from an art gallery before. Inside the gallery, he imagined the man with the sardonic face, the man with the heavily plucked eyebrows, was laughing at him. A cold wind was slicing across the front of the gallery. Suddenly, an awful feeling of misery washed over him. He was overwhelmed with missing his mother. He took out his phone and considered ringing Colin, and then rejected the idea; the pain of unshed tears began to build up a pulsing pressure behind his eyes. He blinked hard, turned up the collar of his coat and set off towards Soho, wondering idly if Colin had taken his cashmere scarf. Colin had always had a liking for cashmere, although he'd never shown any inclination to pay for it. Terry had lost count of the number of jumpers Colin had purloined. The trouble was, Colin looked so much better in them than Terry did. Terry was short and rather overweight but distinguished-looking, he liked to think, with short grey hair and a grey beard. Colin had been taller, thinner – younger.

What does it mean? he wondered, as he strode up Charing Cross Road. What does it mean if you start hearing voices? Was it the start of something? Was it part of the magical thinking that goes with grief? But then it wasn't exactly hearing voices, was it? The picture had talked to him. And what it had said hadn't been much of a comfort. As he pushed open the door to Patisserie Valerie's and ordered a croissant and a café au lait, he wondered whether this denoted the beginning of something or the end.

A few minutes later a rather sweet-looking boy came with his order. After putting down his cup of coffee, he took a deep breath. It was the sort of breath that Terry heard on a fairly regular basis and he readied himself to receive what was coming next.

'I would just like to say, Mr Jardine, how much I love your work.'

The poor boy was shaking, Terry noticed. He broke into a broad smile and said, 'Well, thank you so much for being so kind as to let me know. You have made a sunny day even sunnier for me.'

'It was when I saw you in *Hamlet* that I decided to be an actor. Well, I'm a waiter.'

'No,' Terry said. 'You're an actor. When I was starting out, I had about ten years of small roles and taking part-time jobs to make ends meet.'

'Do you have any advice?'

Terry sighed. 'Do classes, find ways to work so that when the opportunities come your way you can seize them. Don't give up hope and don't give in to rejection.'

The boy was frowning.

'I know,' Terry said. 'Easier said than done, right?'

The boy smiled and nodded.

'Incidentally, it was seeing Derek Jacobi in *Hamlet* that made me want to act. I'd seen him in *I, Claudius* on TV and there he'd been stuttering, lame, dribbling, and then I saw him on stage in *Hamlet*. I was about fifteen and I couldn't believe it. He was this beautiful, virile, gracious creature. I was transfixed, and I was walking up the Charing Cross Road just the other day and I was suddenly aware of him walking towards me and I opened my mouth to say something to him but I was so overwhelmed that I walked straight into a lamp post.'

The boy laughed. 'Did you manage to say anything at all?'

Terry shook his head. 'Completely lost my nerve after that. You managed much better than me. It's a lovely, generous thing to let people know you've enjoyed their work, so thank you.'

The boy left him and Terry opened up his paper and tried to concentrate on what the commentators were saying about the dire state of the British economy. On the way back to the bus stop in Piccadilly, he ducked back into the National Gallery shop and bought several postcards of *The Man with the Blue Sleeve*. When he got home, he stuck one up next to the mirror in the bathroom so that he could eye this sardonic dandy as he shaved.

In case he had anything else to say to him.

Other than the fact that he was going to die, of course.

TITIAN

Venice, 1576

Plague has come to the house across the street. Outside, there is the noise of the authorities, who have come to pick up the dead, convey the living to quarantine and take everything out of the house to burn it. Then the house will be boarded up. Titian hears the ravings of his neighbour, Giovanni Memmo.

'Don't take me to Lazzaretto Vecchio. I will die. Please don't take me. I'm not ill. Please, please . . . I can pay you.'

In truth, he does not sound that ill. He certainly has the energy to vigorously protest about what is happening to him. But he is right about the likelihood of his surviving Lazzaretto Vecchio. It would be a miracle if he returned from there. The rumours that come from the boatmen, who ferry over the ill and the dying, are terrible. The dormitories were filled with screaming and the stench of the dying; people became mad and threw themselves into the sea, were dashed on the rocks

34

and drowned. And hovering over everything were clouds from the constant burning of infected corpses.

Titian cracks open the shutters and looks down into the *calle*. Giovanni is struggling with a huge colossus of a man. The city authorities have released the prisoners from the dungeons to take on these duties; no normal citizen, however terrified by the Council of Ten, could be persuaded to take on such dirty, dangerous work. The colossus has the pallid grey-green skin of a sea monster newly emerged from the bottom of the lagoon; his face is criss-crossed with a mass of scars. Someone should try and calm Giovanni, Titian thinks. Isn't it bad enough to be ill, to be dying, without this loss of dignity? This fear in the face of death is an added humiliation. But there is no one to do it. The corpses of his wife and sons lie in the street at his feet. He is alone with the sea monster, wrestling with his fears, and in the end the man picks up Giovanni round the waist and carries him to where the boat waits. He dumps him in it.

Titian remembered sneaking into the studio of Zuccatto, the mosaicist, when he was a child, and gazing down onto the tiny bright gleaming squares; the gold-leaf layered under glass shone like the glitter of the scales of a fish in a sun-lit river. He had held his hands over the *tesserae* and seen the palms of his hands begin to glow, lit up with golden light like someone from the Bible, like Christ healing the sick, he'd thought. He had experienced a moment of ecstasy, looking down at the light pouring out of his hands, and had felt himself transfigured, believed himself to be chosen.

It was the first time he'd registered the power of this thing, the power of colour. And he'd known with every part of himself that this was what he wanted to do, that this is what he would be good at, but he did not want to be confined to constructing an image with these tiny squares. He wanted the magic, the subtlety, the curved lines that brush and paint would produce. Then Mazzo, Zuccatto's foreman, had come up behind him, told him to get his dirty paws out of the *tesserae*, cuffed him round the ear, stripped him of his breeches and given him a broom to sweep the studio floor. For the whole day he'd had to go half-naked, much to the amusement of the other apprentices. From the sublime to the ridiculous in the blink of an eye.

Even though he had painted emperors, popes and kings, his memory of this humiliation is painfully vivid. Why was it that the memory of his many triumphs blurred, yet those of humiliations remained as sharp as a porcupine's quill? He had got his revenge in the end, hadn't he? That great oaf Mazzo. He had shown him! When he had come to him many years later and asked for work, he had sent him away with a flea in his ear. Later he had stepped over him begging in the street. The feeling of humiliation, however, had never left him.

Why was he thinking of him? Why was he thinking of this man, this stupid ape who knew no better than to bully him when he was a child? Would it have been such a terrible thing to have given him a job? It is ridiculous, but he is feeling squeamish about the condition of his own soul. Maybe it's time to call the priest. The cries of Giovanni echo along the canal. *Christ have mercy.* He repeats it one more time and then there is a short, sharp scream and his words cease abruptly, not, Titian guesses, as a consequence of divine mercy but because of the sea monster's meaty fist. Silence returns to the deserted *calle*, to the empty canal. The only noise is the crackling of the bonfire which has been made of Giovanni's possessions. The smoke drifts upwards and catches in his throat. Now that the authorities have gone, people emerge from their homes to see what may be pulled from the fire. Greed triumphs over fear. He closes the shutters.

What good is a painter who cannot see? Who is he, if he cannot paint? He closes his eyes and immediately sees with awful clarity an image of the Last Judgment. He sees the Antichrist with the most dreadful and terrifying features. He sees fear in the faces of the living. He sees the sun and the moon and the stars give signs that they will blot themselves out. He sees air, earth and water breathe forth their last breath. Standing off to one side, he sees Nature sterile, shrivelled up in her old age, and Time sitting withered and trembling upon a dried-up stump. Then while the trumpets of the angels shake every heart, he sees Life and Death thrown into terrible confusion, because the first is weary of raising the dead and the second is preparing to strike down the living. He sees Hope and Despair guiding the cohorts of the good and the rabble of the damned. Then he sees the amphitheatre of the clouds lit up with the rays that come from the pure flames of heaven, and on these Christ sits enthroned, encircled with terror and with splendour. He sees his face gleaming and shining with the refulgence of a light which is both jubilant and fearful; it fills the righteous with gladness and the evil-doers with fear. He sees the ministers of the Abyss, who glorify the saints and martyrs while they deride the Caesars and Alexanders, since to have conquered oneself is very different to having conquered the world. Coming from the mouth of the Son of God is his awful sentence. His words descend like two flights of arrows, the one bringing salvation, the other damnation. Finally, he sees the lights of paradise and the furnaces of hell.

He opens his eyes. Down in the *calle* the crackle of the bonfire has grown louder. Why is he being sent these visions? It is too late. It is a painting that he will never have the opportunity to start, let alone complete. Everything is drawing to an end. He closes his eyes again, seeking gentler images, and now the colours burst and flare: golds and reds, greens and blues, bursting in on him, raining down upon him until he reaches a state close to ecstasy just as he had when, as a little boy, he had buried his hands in those tiny, brightly gleaming pieces of colour, and known that this was where his destiny lay.

POMPONIO

Venice, 1576

Pomponio, Titian's eldest son, pauses in front of the main door of his father's house in Biri Grande and looks at the large wooden cross which has been hammered into it. The cross denotes that the plague has claimed victims there. It means that the only person permitted to cross the threshold is a priest. Even someone as greedy and corrupt as Pomponio flinches at the sight of something that marks the death of his father and his brother, Orazio. His brother! Pomponio feels the child-like fury and jealousy that has haunted him his whole life when he thinks of his brother. He had thought that Orazio's death would have purged it from him, but it hasn't. His father and brother are joined in death just as they were in life; it is Pomponio who is abandoned. Again. Jealousy ripples in the pit of his stomach like an eel.

It was the mediocrity of Orazio that taunted him. Pomponio had always believed that was why his father had picked him to work with. Orazio offered no threat, no competition. Solid, dependable Orazio, who had little talent for painting but was good at managing his father's affairs and was perfectly happy to live out his life in his father's shadow. He would manage his father's assistants and apprentices, order the canvas and wood for the frames, order the pigments and the oil paint and brushes, and most importantly he would chase the money. He was a man singularly lacking in imagination but very, very good at chasing the money. In the latter respect, he was a true Venetian.

His father had been a genius, there was no doubt about that, but he had been singularly indisposed to teach and assist the talented. Unlike the great Bellini, to whom Titian had been apprenticed, Titian had absolutely no interest in nurturing the skills of others. His assistants and apprentices were there to do his bidding, that was all, and Orazio made sure they knew it. It was above all else a very family affair. As well as Orazio, he had his relatives, Marco and Cesare Vecellio, working for him as painting assistants. But no one would be allowed to grow too big in his shade. Over the years, Pomponio had seen Titian expel the most talented, including El Greco and Tintoretto, from his studio, as if wanting to cut out the competition at an early stage. One of the characteristics of a genius, Pomponio knew first-hand, was selfishness and another was ruthlessness. His father had demonstrated both in ample measure.

Pomponio is a man who has always been attracted to the magical, the alchemical, to the darker arts. He likes to think that this is the reason for his father's disapproval, that he is more like him than Orazio, that he understood him more than his brother. They were closer in temperament and his father had never tolerated closeness. He turns away from the main door and moves swiftly along the alley to the corner. He must seek the back entrance. Rounding the corner at some speed, something looms out of the darkness and collides with him. For a moment, terror seizes him by the hair and he thinks it's his bad conscience made manifest and come to drag him down to hell. He cries out and begins to strike out, his hands wrestling with black, waxed cloth and punching at the curved beak of a huge crow's head. Then a voice shouts out and he realises it's one of the city's doctors, covered by this mask to protect him from the plague-ridden airs of the city. Pomponio swears viciously and pushes the man away, waiting until he is out of sight before continuing. On turning another corner, he sees the sight he has been dreading, the splintered door of the back entrance to his father's house, hanging from one hinge. Someone has been here before him. And now what he feels is fury. What remains in the studio is *his*. It is his inheritance. He may not have had his father's love but now that he is dead he will have his paintings. He must have those.

Pomponio moves swiftly through the garden, an unrec-ognisable tangle of vegetation, and approaches the steps that lead to his father's studio at the top of the house. Here is the step he cut his head open on when he was a child. His finger moves to the scar above his eyebrow. The touch, a memory, his foot pausing on the place where it happened. This door has also been broken. As he crosses the threshold, the smells of a painter's studio so redolent of his childhood overwhelm him: wood, canvas, gesso, rabbit glue and linseed oil.

A memory of watching his father paint comes to him, of his father standing in front of a canvas, paint brush in hand. In front of him a naked woman sprawled on a sofa. Her complaints filled the air. She was too cold, she had to move, her arm had gone numb. And suddenly his father's temper was loose in the studio, a wild, dangerous animal. He shouted at everyone to leave, but Pomponio, hiding behind one of the larger paintings, stayed where he was. He wanted to know what would happen next.

'I'll warm you up, then,' his father said.

He had her by the arm, pulling her off the sofa, then he bent her over, his hand pressing down the back of her neck, and he began fumbling with his clothes. He entered her with a brutality and violence devoid of any tenderness. Peering from behind the painting, Pomponio saw the shock on the woman's face, the deadness in her eyes. When his father had finished with her, his animal grunt was reflected in the contorted, agonised expression of the woman. He remembered the silence in the studio afterwards, the look of hatred on the woman's face and his father's calm indifference as he instructed her, 'Lie back on the sofa. Place your hand like this between your legs, as if you are arousing yourself.'

The only sign that anything had happened was the snail trail against the woman's inner thigh, the livid four-finger-shaped bruise rising up on the flesh of her upper arm.

Titian had then shouted for his assistants to come back into the room, into a room so thick with unspoken hatred it was as if all the air had been sucked out of it. And Pomponio, struggling to breathe in the tainted air, had coughed suddenly and found himself dragged out from his hiding place. The last thing he remembered was his father's fist looming into view and behind it the face of the woman who had got up off the sofa and was attempting, too late, to prevent it from landing. His father had beaten him unconscious and then thrown him back into the arms of his mother, the docile Cecelia, as if he'd been a sack filled with dead kittens. He had never told his mother what he had seen. How can you tell such a thing to your mother? You can't. Not even Pomponio could do that. Also he knew that if he did it would just get him another beating, this time from his mother.

Later he'd wondered if it was this early episode which had

turned his father against him. The fact that his father knew that Pomponio had seen this darker, more dangerous side to him, the part of him which dwelt in the shadows, the part which was so different to that which he exhibited to his patrons, to the people with influence and money. That man painted pictures which made men weep; he created paintings to the glory of God and Venus. This was the same man who broke the will of a woman as casually as if it were a reed. Submission was everything to him. It was a lesson Pomponio learnt early on and perhaps it was why he fought and fought and fought. Anything not to be the dead-eyed woman.

For a moment, the ash-filled cloud had been pushed to one side and moonlight streamed into the studio. He has come too late. The place has been ransacked and only the larger paintings remain, the ones so big they are too difficult to steal. His foot catches on something, which rolls across the floor. He leans down to pick it up, a jolt passes through him as he looks down at what he has in his hand: one of his father's brushes. Hatred and love do battle within him, neither wins out. The conflict will endure until he dies.

THE BOATMAN

Venice, 1576

Oh, it is cold tonight and the storm blowing in from the sea brings strong winds in its cheeks; the water surges up the canals and the gondolas dance on the unsettled waves like horses, jerking their heads against their tethers. They need to be secured tightly or they will be smashed to pieces. My boat is safe and I do not care about the weather. Huddled deep in my cloak, I stand in the shadows of the *calle* outside Titian's house. I see the candlelight flickering behind the shutters of the studio and I imagine the scum that is Pomponio, desperately scrabbling through his father's house, trying to work out what has been stolen and the value of what remains. There are many half-finished paintings in there and I wonder what he will do with them. Will he beg those of his father's apprentices who have survived the plague to complete them? Will he pay them? He will have to, but he will not have Orazio to sweet talk them, and Pomponio has always lacked charm. He will know from the state of the place that it has been ransacked. During the day I hear he interrogates his neighbours and berates local officials, all to no avail. Finally, I have the satisfaction of a man who has waited a lifetime patiently for revenge. The plague, the death of Titian and his son Orazio, and now Pomponio's return has dropped it like a ripe plum into my hand. Now, all I need do is bite into its sweetness and allow the juices to dribble down my chin.

The door of a tavern bursts open and a slice of light falls across my feet; men fall drunk and laughing into the street and with them comes the sour smell of vomit and ale. One of them drags a woman into an alleyway, lifts her skirts and thrusts into her. The city is indeed on the way to recovery if sex is returning to its *calli*. My father is long dead, but it is of him I think as I see the flickering candlelight, as I dig my chin into the warmth of my cloak, as the wind swirls around me. My beloved father and all that he suffered at the hands of a reckless, spoilt youth who thought nothing of the consequences of his lust. It is revenge on his behalf that I have sought, that I have waited for my whole life. It is revenge that warms me. Now, let me tell you what happened. Let me take you back to 1546, when I was a boy, and Pomponio brought my family to the verge of ruin. Perhaps I have surprised you, perhaps you thought this was the story of Titian. Why is it we always think that history is the history of great men? Few of us are great, but there are more of us. A universe of fleas may live on one dog. Do we not matter? Are we really of no importance? It is my story as well as his; it is the story of Sebastiano da Canal, gondolier.

Now let me take you back to when it all began . . .

THE YOUNG BOATMAN

Venice, 1546

I heard the *maleficio* ring out across the city and immediately our household was filled with the wailing of women. The noise of it froze my heart in my chest. I had not intended to go, for I had not thought that I would be able to bear it, but the sound of the bell and the movement of the people in the *campo* below brought me to my senses. I set off, running towards the *piazza*, and all the time I was murmuring under my breath, *Mary, sweet mother of God, have mercy on him. Mary, who saw the suffering of your own son, have mercy on my father. Please, please, Mary, mother of God, save him. Let him live. Please let him live.*

There was a large throng already gathered at the place of punishment and I pushed myself to the front, enduring the oaths and blows of those who wanted the best view of what was about to happen. I saw him immediately up on the scaffold. There he was among the thieves, the murderers and the sodomites. He stood erect and proud, his body strengthened by battling the currents and tides of the lagoon every day by my side. I shouted up to him and waved so that he might see me and he turned when he heard his name spoken. His face was the colour of ash.

'Courage,' I shouted. And then, 'I am here.' Although what good I thought that might do, I don't know. There was in me the need to let him know that he was not alone, that his son stood by him.

The Blessed Virgin brought a darkness down over my eyes at the moment of punishment, but in that darkness I heard a terrible cry of agony. I imagined our Lord on the cross, but when I could see again there was my father with the blood running from his eye socket and the white bones exposed where his left hand had been. My face was wet. I thought at first with tears but then when I wiped my hand across it I realised that it was covered with blood. It trickled down my forehead into the corners of my eyes, making them smart, and then over my upper lip and down between my lips onto my tongue. It dripped off my chin down onto the ground.

The crowd drew back, leaving a space around me. They stared at me in horror. I tasted the salt of my father's blood upon my lips and let out a roar of anguish. The crowd drew back even further. They were wise to, for there was no knowing what I might have done. Then I was pushing myself forwards to reach my father, who was being roughly bundled down the steps into the *piazza,* and I was speaking to him in the same tones he had used when I was a very small boy and he had told me the tales of the founding of our great city, of how the birds had shown the people where to go by picking up their young in their beaks and flying out into the lagoon.

A man whom I did not know but to whom I would

be eternally grateful, helped me carry my father home to my mother. She screamed when she saw us. What wife wouldn't? But then she leapt into action, ordered hot water to be boiled and clean cloths to be brought, and in a very short time she had his wounds bathed and bound. When she was sure he was asleep, she took more water and sat me down near the fire; she took clean cloths and washed my father's blood from my face, she held me close as we wept. She had given my father eight children but I am their only son, and although she had never shown any one of us favour over the other, the truth is I knew that I had always had a special place in her heart.

That night we were startled by a soft knock on the door. When we opened it, we were surprised to see Master Lazaro, the famous Jewish physician. The Jews are not allowed out of the ghetto at night unless it is for their doctors to administer to the patricians. The strictest of laws govern their movement, but here he was at our door with a young boy at his side. And we were no patricians.

'Quick,' he said. 'Let me in. I have come to tend to your father.'

Shocked, I stood back to let him and the boy enter, and I quickly took him to where my father lay. My mother, however, had other ideas. She stood in front of the bed where my father slept with her arms crossed.

'We look after our own,' she said.

'Come, come, Mother,' I said. 'He is the favourite physician of the patricians.'

'We cannot pay him,' she said.

'That is dealt with,' Master Lazaro said. 'Do you wish me to look at your husband or not? I have risked my life to come here. Will you really turn me away?'

It was a clever trick because he was throwing himself on my mother's mercy and it worked. With a slight shrug, she stepped away and allowed him to draw close to my father's bedside. Although his manner was blunt, we could both see that he dealt with my father's wounds with the greatest delicacy. He talked to the boy in a low murmur, as he looked at the poor empty eye socket and carefully unravelled the bandage covering my father's stump. Having examined both wounds in the closest detail, he looked up approvingly at my mother and nodded. 'The wounds have been cleaned most effectively and must be kept so. The strike that took off his hand was a clean one and there is every chance that both wounds will heal well.'

He then took my mother to one side and talked to her at some length, showing her various unguents and bottles that he had brought with him. She insisted on knowing what was in the paste that was applied to the wounds. Egg white, oil of roses and turpentine, he replied, and I remember clearly the smell of the turpentine. He explained it would help the flesh heal. He gave her instructions and then made her repeat what he had told her until she snapped that she wasn't an idiot to be told so many times.

He laughed at that. 'Sleep,' he said, 'will help most with the healing. If he becomes agitated, give him this. The wounds must be inspected daily and if a sickly odour is detected you must send to the ghetto for me immediately.'

At the door he paused briefly and turned to me. 'You Christians accuse us of crucifying your Christ, yet what you do to each other on a daily basis, these acts of barbarity...' He shook his head and left the sentence hanging in the air. 'But I am truly sorry for the troubles that have come upon your household.' Then he stepped closer to me. 'Do not let your mother be proud, boy. If there is redness and swelling in the arm and the wounds start to smell, send for me at once. Speed will be of the essence, if we are to save him.'

I nodded and then began to thank him, but the only reply

was the noise of his and his boy's hurrying footsteps as they disappeared into the night. They vanished so swiftly that I did not have time to ask him who had paid, although I certainly had my suspicions.

TERRY

London, 2011

It happened quite suddenly when Terry was rehearsing the following day. They were working on the scene in which a statue of King Leontes' wife, Hermione, whom he thinks he has been responsible for killing sixteen years earlier, comes back to life. They had gone through it a few times, but Terry knew he was not really getting it. Then when he did it once more, when he fell to his knees and said the words, 'Let be, let be, would I were dead,' he couldn't finish the rest of it because he felt an overwhelming feeling of despair open up inside him. At first everyone thought he was acting, but when he remained doubled up on his knees, with his hand over his face, when it became clear what was happening, an uneasy silence fell in the rehearsal room, punctuated only by his ineffectual attempts to stifle his sobs. After a while he heard the low murmur of voices and the sound of feet walking away, and then he felt a hand on his back.

He looked up to see the director sitting cross-legged on the floor next to him. Ludovico Zabarella was about ten years younger than him; a man made beautiful by the long hair that streamed down his back. He had courted Terry assiduously for the part, and Terry had been flattered and charmed in just about equal measure. Although Terry was one of the biggest stars of the London stage, he was not nearly as well known in the field of TV and film, so he was quite surprised that Ludovico had even heard of him.

Terry had made some enquiries and the general view of Ludovico was that he was a good guy, fun to work with and with a clear vision of what he wanted: an actor's director. And all of that had proved to be true in the course of rehearsals. Ludovico had created a safe space for the actors, encouraged them to experiment and trust themselves, but had also given them inspiring insights into the play. Terry's desire to please and impress him had grown and grown. Well, he'd blown that now, hadn't he, he thought. Now that he'd behaved like the greenest of green actors just out of drama school, unable to draw a line between technique and real emotion. He pulled an embarrassed face as Ludovico passed him a handkerchief.

'Bad day?' Ludovico asked.

Terry nodded but was unable to reply. He looked down at the handkerchief, rather a beautiful initialled one, twisting and turning it in his hands. Then he cleared his throat. 'Bad couple of years, actually.'

Ludovico stood up. 'Right, I'm taking you to lunch.'

'No, really . . . there's no need . . .'

'I've given the rest of the cast the afternoon off. Everything's going very well, so half a day won't do any harm.'

'Really?' It was the first time Terry had ever heard a director say such a thing so early in rehearsals.

'Really. You're going to be a wonderful Leontes. With your

humanity, we already have a sure fire hit on our hands. Come on – get your coat. This afternoon you are in my hands.'

He held out one of those hands to Terry, who took it and clambered shakily to his feet.

As they crossed Hungerford Bridge, Ludovico walked close to his side, face held up to the sun and wind. He let no one come between them, Terry noticed, insisting that people get out of their way. And they did. When Terry walked across by himself, he always dodged and swerved. He may have had the talent to sell out a large London theatre for a three-month run, but off stage he was like any other diffident middle-aged Englishman, ducking, diving, trying to get by.

'Why are the English so bad at mythologising themselves and their cities?' Ludovico said. 'Why has no one done for London what Woody Allen has done for New York? God, I love this city and I love this bridge. That's what I want to do, if only the councils would make it easier to film here.'

Ludovico did not look like a man who would have any trouble mythologising anything or anyone. In fact, in his long, black velvet coat and with his tall, thin figure and hair streaming out behind him, he looked as if he'd stepped straight out of a myth himself. Terry's coat was also open and the wind blew it out so that it swirled behind him like thick grey woollen wings. Halfway across, Ludovico pulled him to a halt and stepped in front of him. His hair, blown from behind now, swirled forwards and tickled Terry's face. Ludovico pulled Terry's coat to and did up the buttons, then took the scarf, grey and very soft, from round his own neck and wrapped it round Terry's. Terry recalled his mother doing this one time to get him ready for his first day at school. He remembered the tears in her eyes and his own fear. 'Unbreeched', a word from the play came into his mind, along with the certainty that these feelings that he was experiencing now had something to do with Leontes and the play. As if sensing his upset, Ludovico slipped his arm through Terry's and they carried on across the bridge. They dodged between the buses, nose-to-tail along the Strand, and into Covent Garden, down some steps and into Joe Allen's.

They stayed there most of the afternoon. Ludovico chatted away seamlessly about his life and career. And Terry was grateful because it allowed him time to try and pull himself together. He was under no pressure and could just listen. Ludovico told him about his upbringing in a small village in the north of Italy, of his father who was a poet, of how he had come to London in the early nineties to learn English and gone from there to study drama in New York. He had then become an assistant to the artistic director of an off-Broadway theatre, The Mockingbird, right at the moment when that theatre was being rebuilt.

When the artistic director had a stroke, Ludovico had taken over from him, initially just to see the project finished, but he had then ended up staying for the next ten years; the pint-sized 250-seat theatre, with a new bar, cafe and rehearsal space, had gone on to become the hot place to go, partly because of Ludovico's ability to charm well-known film and television actors to come and perform for Actors' Equity minimums in exchange for large amounts of kudos. The intimate productions, a clever mixture of classics and new writing, had been almost universally praised and were almost impossible to get tickets for. After ten years in the theatre Ludovico's first film had won the Caméra d'Or for best first feature at Cannes and ever since then he had been dividing his time between theatre and film projects in America and England.

He was blissfully indiscreet and regaled Terry with gossip from America, about the people he had worked with; periodically he broke off to engage in animated exchanges with the Italian waiter. Terry felt the kind of awe and envy that he always did for people who could move so fluidly between languages. However, when the coffee arrived Ludovico stopped talking about himself and asked very directly what the matter was. Terry told him about his mother dying, about Colin moving out and about what had happened at the National Gallery, and Ludovico listened intently. Terry told him how he wished that Colin had been there to talk to about it, to laugh about it, to shout at the silly woman.

'I mean she was just some sour-faced woman who misunderstood, but I think it was the way she said the word. "Pervert". Of course it was just a ridiculous mistake, but I felt this awful feeling of shame.'

Ludovico leant across the table and placed his hand against the side of his face. 'Dear man,' he said. 'Dear, dear man. How ridiculous and how absolutely horrible.'

Then he waved for the bill. 'Come on,' he said, when he'd paid it, 'you're coming back to my place.'

Terry began to protest, but he was too drunk to protest very effectively. In the cab he closed his eyes, aware of Ludovico's arm round his shoulders, the warmth of his thigh against his.

Inside Ludovico's flat, Nero, an enormous black cat, wove figures of eight around their legs. Ludovico scooped him into his arms and spoke tender endearments to him in Italian. Terry, waiting awkwardly in the hall, heard the rattle of cat biscuits against a metal dish. He'd drunk too much and felt dizzy and slightly sick. What was he doing here? This was a terrible mistake. He must get home. He had reached the landing and was gripping onto the banister to start down the stairs when the steps began to wobble and rise up to greet him. He sat down heavily and closed his eyes. Ludovico's hand landed on his shoulder.

'Where are you going?' he asked.

'Home,' Terry said, but as he said the word he thought of

his mother and Colin and felt the grief rise up in him all over again.

'Stay here with me,' Ludovico said firmly and guided him back into the hall. He took Terry's coat and ushered him into a bedroom. A phone rang somewhere in the flat and Ludovico left the room. Terry curled up on the bed. In the darkness everything began to swirl and twist again. He fell asleep to the distant sound of Ludovico talking Italian.

Later, Terry woke fighting for breath and knowing he was about to be sick. He got up and lurched out of the bedroom, searching for the bathroom. He pushed open a door and Ludovico sat up in bed and turned on a side light.

'Sick,' Terry blurted and Ludovico pointed to a door off the bedroom. Terry stumbled into the bathroom, knelt in front of the loo and was violently ill. When he had retched up everything in his stomach, he flushed the loo, closed the lid and sat on it, head in hands. After a few minutes there was a knock on the door.

'Are you all right?'

The door opened and Ludovico was framed in the doorway looking at him.

'Sorry,' Terry said. 'Too much to drink.'

Ludovico nodded.

Terry rubbed his face. 'I should go.'

Ludovico made a distinctly Italian sound, denoting dissent, and pulled Terry to his feet by the lapels of his jacket. In the bedroom, he sat Terry on the side of his bed and bent down to take off his shoes and socks. He took off his jacket and shirt and trousers, and then pulled him down into the bed next to him. It was all too much for Terry, who started to stammer that he didn't think it was a good idea, that he really ought to be going home. Ludovico laughed and pulled the duvet over him.

'Be quiet,' he said and threw his arm across Terry's chest. 'Relax now. Everything will be well.'

But everything felt very far from well for Terry, lying there rigid with embarrassment.

'Hush,' Ludovico said. 'Nothing is required of you.' Terry turned against him, felt his arms around him, and heard him singing something to him in Italian, the sort of lullaby you might sing to a child.

Later, when Terry woke, confused as to where he was and who he was with, he reached out in the way that he used to reach for Colin, and before he could withdraw the caress of his hands, the touch of his lips, Ludovico was responding. Terry let out a noise somewhere between a cry and a groan.

Ludovico paused. 'Shall I stop?'

'You don't have to. I'm sorry. You probably don't really want to. It was my mistake. I thought . . . I thought you were someone else . . . Oh God, that sounds rather rude . . .'

Ludovico was leaning on his elbow, frowning.

Terry continued. 'I mean, I can't imagine that it would be a pleasure to . . .'

Ludovico began to laugh. 'Shut up,' he said, and shortly afterwards his tongue and his hands demonstrated that indeed it would be; in fact, it was a very great pleasure.

Terry woke to find the black cat standing on his chest, staring deep into his eyes. 'He's mine,' Nero seemed to be saying. 'Do you understand? Ludovico's all mine. You are a temporary blot on my landscape. As long as this is understood, we will get on just fine.'

Terry, conscious of the cat's sheathed claws on his naked chest, dangerously close to his nipples, stroked him gently under the chin with one finger and said, 'I understand perfectly.'

Ludovico came into the room and sat down on the side of the bed. 'What do you understand?'

'That you are your cat's – body and soul.'

Ludovico laughed. 'Tea or coffee?'

Terry ran his hand gently along Ludovico's arm. The sun was pouring through the window behind him and his whole body was lit up with a glowing halo. To Terry, the fact that he had made love with this gorgeous man seemed little short of a miracle. Despite having the ability to hold an audience in the palm of his hand night after night, off stage Terry was riddled with much the same insecurities about his own physical attractiveness as any other portly middle-aged man. He wondered if Ludovico slept with distressed actors in order to keep the show on the road. Was this just a pity fuck? But it had seemed to Terry a lot more intimate than that. He stopped himself. Don't tear it all to pieces, he told himself. Don't over-analyse, by-pass the frontal lobe. So instead he placed his hand behind Ludovico's neck and kissed him. A few moments later he said, 'I think it had better be coffee.'

Soon the sound of a stove-top espresso maker started to hiss and bubble through the flat. Terry got up and walked to the window. The flat was near the Oxo Tower, looking out across the Thames towards St Paul's and the Gherkin. What a flat! Ludovico wouldn't have been able to afford this if he'd stayed working in the theatre. I must get my agent to get me more TV and film work, Terry thought, looking down and pulling in his stomach. Regrettably, even when pulled in it sagged. The piece of chocolate tart he had disposed of yesterday at Joe Allen's didn't help. For the hundredth time, he thought he should do something to shift it.

He got dressed and went to find Ludovico, who was turning the gas out under the espresso maker. Terry slipped his arms around his waist and leant against his back. He would ask no questions. Ludovico poured the coffee and then turned round and handed him the cup. Terry took it and, relishing the satanic darkness of it, sipped it, looking over the top of the cup at Ludovico, this man who had taken him in his arms and soothed him, his own dark angel. Ludovico looked back smiling at him. And for the first time in a long time Terry felt the comfort of being the loved not the lover. It was the relief of new beginnings. Maybe things were going to be all right after all.

TULLIA BUFFO
The Return of the Courtesan

Venice, 1576

I. The House

Cobwebs cover the stairs, catching in the bottom of Tullia Buffo's skirts. Her maid, Elisabetta, and Elisabetta's husband trail sulkily behind her. Several weeks before, Tullia had sent ahead that she was returning so that her house in the *contrada* of San Felice might be made ready for her, but she had known as soon as she passed through the water portal and stepped out of the gondola that something was wrong. Elisabetta would not meet her eye and nor would the maid's shambling idiot of a husband, whose eyes remained fixed on the cap, rather an expensive black velvet one, that he twisted round and round in his hands.

Tullia turns round. 'I presume the Flemish paintings that hung on these walls here have been put away in storage.'

Silence. Her servants look as uncomfortable as it is possible to be and still inhabit a skin.

Tullia picks up her skirts and increases her pace up the stairs. Once in the *portego*, stripped bare of wall hangings as well as paintings, she spins round. 'So, where is everything?'

Elisabetta is a picture of defiance, hands clasped across her stomach, a substantially larger one than when Tullia saw her last, her nose thrust into the air. 'Thieves, my lady, they came and took everything.'

How has this woman become so fat on the plague? Tullia thinks and then she sees a maggot crawling over a pile of corpses. She tries to control her temper because she wants information from her.

'But I left you money to look after the house to keep everything safe.'

'You cannot imagine the chaos here. It was as if the apocalypse had occurred. They opened the prisons so that the prisoners might help with the corpses. There were murderers, thieves and rapists loose on the streets; dangerous, violent men on the canals and in the *calli*. No one was safe. Nowhere was safe. The house could not be protected.'

'Did you at least board it up?'

'Too late – we thought there was no need.'

'But at least the precious items I placed in the storage box are safe.'

'No, my lady.'

'No,' Tullia repeats incredulously.

'No.' Elisabetta is blinking rapidly. 'That too was taken.'

She is lying, of course, although Tullia is not sure how much. Maybe the thieves did ransack the house, but maybe Elisabetta invited them in, gave them a cut of the goods and sold everything off in the ghetto. As Tullia goes from room to room it is an agony to remember what is missing. It is an agony to recall the majesty of the house. She had received ambassadors, princes, even a king here.

She clears her throat. 'The painting of me by Tintoretto?'

Elisabetta shakes her head.

A brittle laugh. 'The parrot, at least?'

Another shake of the head.

'Dante?'

'That moth-eaten old cat? The authorities ordered the killing of cats and dogs when the plague struck.'

Tullia clenches her fists so hard her nails create bloody stigmata in the palms of her hands. 'Did you report the losses to the Guardians of the Night Watch?'

Elisabetta shrugs. 'The system broke down. You might report the theft one day and the man was dead the next. Some died and were not replaced.'

'When did the thefts occur?'

Elisabetta looks at her sullenly.

Tullia eyes the remarkable quality of the cloth that makes up the dress Elisabetta is wearing, the very expensive cap that her husband twists in his hands, and she repeats the question more slowly this time. 'I asked you when the thefts occurred.'

Silence.

'You must remember when. A week ago, a month, a year?'

Elisabetta pulls her shawl tightly around her, as if it were armour that might protect her from her mistress's wrath. Nose in the air, hands clasped over her fat belly, she shrugs once again. This time Tullia has had enough. She pinches Elisabetta's nose between two of her fingers and twists it hard, then grabs her throat with her other hand.

'Do you take me for a fool,' she hisses. As Elisabetta scrabbles to relieve the pressure on her throat, Tullia removes her hand, swings it back and slaps her hard. 'By the Holy Virgin Mary, by everything I hold sacred, I swear I shall find out what has happened here and if you are responsible I will pursue you to the gates of hell. Do you understand?'

But now Elisabetta is wailing. 'You left,' she says accusingly. 'You left the city. You have no idea how terrible it has been. Do you think that I know where every little thing is? Well, I don't. You were the one who left. We stayed. Thieves broke in, things were stolen.' Elisabetta speaks as if her words excuse the missing items, as if they explain everything. She thinks the fact that she stayed has delivered her into a position of unassailable moral authority. It has made her brazen. But this will not do.

'You've already said that,' Tullia says, 'but I paid you a substantial sum of money to look after my home, my possessions. I trusted you.'

'You don't know what it's been like. Do you think I could keep an eye on everything here? What about my own family? People were dying all around us ...'

Tullia holds up her hand to stop her speaking. 'Do you think I will allow you to steal from me in this way? Do you think you will get away with it? I will file a complaint with the Guardians of the Night Watch and if I get no satisfaction there I will register my case with the ecclesiastical authorities.'

Elisabetta leaves snivelling. And now, as Tullia walks through her former Paradise of Venus, more and more things are coming to mind that are lost. More and more things which are missing. It is too much to endure. In the bedroom the only things that remain are the four elegant, fluted walnut posts of her bed, with the paws of a lion carved into their base, and a torn, green damask curtain that hangs from a broken railing near the window. Her eyes are suddenly sore with unshed tears. She will need the courage of a lion to begin all over again. But what else is there to do? Unless she wants to hand her children over to an orphanage and start begging on the church steps. Or sit in a window behind a candle with her breasts on display. But she is no *meretrice*, she is no *puttana*. She is no street whore. Her mother trained her up to be a courtesan. She is now more highly educated than many of the patrician's wives. Only two years ago she had Henry III of France in her bed. Yes, she is a fit consort for a king. The Republic should be grateful to her. She mustn't forget that. But then the Republic has always been a fickle, brutal beast.

She bends down and runs her hand over the carved lion's paws. It is not just what has happened to her which is terrible. It is the state of the city, the numbers of the dead. Titian, she heard today. Of course he was a tremendous age, but to hear of the death of such a genius has affected her badly. A great, great man, and a man intrinsically bound up with the city. Many of her former clients will be dead. Maybe Elisabetta is correct, maybe she shouldn't have left. Maybe because of her flight, because of her fear, the city has delivered its own judgement upon her. It has rejected her and the wheel of fortune has turned in another's favour.

Shortly before the plague struck, Titian had asked her to go for a gondola ride with him. 'To show the world I am alive and virile,' he said. 'To make them wonder at my capacity.'

She had enjoyed the ride. It was easy money, good conversation. She had enjoyed the attention, the pointing from the bridges. He had paid well and they had spent a very pleasant morning going up and down the Grand Canal. He had been in a wistful mood, talking to her of his friends.

'The trouble with old age,' he said, 'is that all of one's friends are dead: Aretino, Sansovino . . .'

The list went on and on. He had talked to her of his childhood, of when he had first come to the city, of how he knew, even though he was homesick, that he would never leave. She had made a fuss of him. Laughed in all the right places, flattered him, teased him about the fact that he had never painted her, whereas Tintoretto had.

'Such beauty,' he said, 'could never be captured in oils. Better not even to try. One would be doomed to failure.' His assessment of Tintoretto was disdainful. 'Very quick' was all he would say of him.

Clever old fox, she had thought. Yes, a clever old fox. Was this the way he had flattered doge and pope and emperor?

But now he was dead, her house ransacked, and Elisabetta surly and defiant. 'Welcome home,' she says softly to herself, to the dusty, cobweb-ridden house. 'Welcome home.' It is an attempt to comfort herself since there is no one else to say it to her. But even if this is what she has come back to she is still glad to be home.

She remembers another thing that Titian had said:

'You and I, we are not simply citizens. We are the city.'

We – yes, he was a cunning old fox, Titian. A very cunning old fox.

Suddenly, her reverie is broken by the sound of childish laughter, the scampering of light feet. Her three sons, whom she had ordered to stay in the boat, have had enough of waiting for her. They burst into the room: the two youngest, Jacopo and Bernardo, charge straight towards her and bury their faces in her skirts; the older one, Camillo, stands looking around him, puzzled.

Hard on their heels comes the gondolier, in whose care she had left them. 'I'm sorry, my lady,' he says. 'I did my best but I had run out of tricks to entertain them.' He grabs Camillo in his strong arms and hoists him into the air. 'They were too quick for me and they wanted their mother.'

'No matter,' she says. 'As you can see' – her gesture takes in the drab empty room – 'my return home is not what I expected.'

He lowers her struggling son gently to the floor and ruffles his hair.

'Will you wait a little longer? I must throw myself on the mercy of my brother. We cannot stay here.'

'How long will you be?'

'Perhaps half an hour.'

'I will wait.'

First she must force herself to make a list of all that is missing. As the children scamper at her heels, spinning the few *soldi* she has given them on the dusty, wooden floors and chasing after the spiders, Tullia goes from room to room making a mental list of all that is lost, of all that she will need to get back in business. Finally, she must remember all that was in the storage box. Her most precious items: a silver basin, six silver spoons, a salt dish, a silver candelabrum, scissors with a silver chain, a gilt prayer book, several gold bracelets and several strings of pearls. By the end of the half-hour, she is exhausted. So much is lost she does not even have a decent string of pearls to pawn.

Back in the bedroom she finds Camillo swinging on the green damask curtain. The pole that the curtain is suspended from crashes to the ground in a cloud of dust and he is completely covered. Jacopo and Bernardo stare at her, not knowing how she will react, but she has no energy left for more bad temper. As Camillo emerges, covered in dust and cobwebs, from under the heavy green curtain, the drab, dirty room is filled with all their laughter.

She gathers her children around her. 'Now we must go and see your uncle and see if he will have us to stay.' Camillo screws up his face. She strokes his cheek. 'I know you are not fond of your cousins, but it will not be for long. You must resist their attempts to push you in the canal and as soon as possible we will be back here. I promise.'

The boatman waits for them in the bottom of the house. She gives him the address of her brother, settles her children in the open part of the boat and then closes the curtains of the *felze* around her. She does not want the children to see her tears; they are for herself alone.

When the boat reaches her brother's house, the boatman helps her onto the *fondamenta* and says gravely, 'I am sorry for your troubles, my dear lady. These are parlous times we live in.' And then while her children are tumbling up the steps to the main body of the house into her brother's arms the gondolier holds her back. 'Beware, lady, there is a new spirit abroad. The authorities are mad with fear at the moment. The plague has infected their judgement. They cast about to see who they can blame for what has befallen the city. They look for easy targets. The other day Isabella Bellocchio was publicly whipped in St Mark's Square and forced to wear the mitre for one hour with the accusations against her and stand on the Rialto Bridge. She has been banished from the city for five years. The city is turning against the courtesans. You must be very careful.'

'What were the accusations against her?'

'Witchcraft.'

'And who brought the accusations?'

'Vengeful servants who did not want what they had stolen during the plague years taken from them.'

She squeezes his hand. 'Thank you,' she says. 'Your kindness is the first nice thing that has happened to me since my return.'

'If you have need of a gondolier, lady . . .'

She looks at him more carefully. 'Do I know you?'

'Titian inherited me from Aretino.'

'Were you the gondolier Aretino wrote a letter to, advising not to marry?'

He laughs. 'I was, but that was many years ago.'

'Did you follow his advice?'

'He had another agenda and it was to save me for himself.' He shrugs. 'I was a pretty youth.'

Her eyes sparkle with amusement. 'Was he successful?'

He smiles but does not reply.

'Did you row us when I went with Titian that time?'

He nods. 'I did.'

'How strange, I was thinking about that time just now.'

'I'm afraid he is dead.'

She nods. 'I had heard. A great loss to the Republic.'

'If it is any comfort, his house and studio were also ransacked.'

'Really? How interesting, and his paintings?'

'They say many were stolen.'

'And who do they say stole them?'

He shrugs. 'The city is rife with rumours, lady.'

Her eyes crinkle in amusement. 'I'm sure it is. I too have lost a painting. It was by Tintoretto – a picture of me ...' She pauses. 'Naked to the waist.'

'Ah.'

'If you hear anything about that, I would be very grateful if you would tell me.'

He nods. 'I will see what I can find out, lady.'

'Also once I have re-established myself I might be in the market for one of Titian's paintings, if it could be found.'

'The price ...'

'I know the price will be substantial, but I would be willing to pay it.'

'I will make enquiries.'

'Perhaps the paintings were stolen away by boat.'

'Maybe a boat was used, lady.' He smiles and bows his head. 'Maybe it was.'

II. The Brother

That evening, after her sister-in-law has gone to bed, she talks with her brother. Her brother's wife will not want her here long, even though Tullia has generously supported the families of both her brothers in the past. No, his prudish bitch of a wife will be on her knees, praying, praying, praying. Probably for Tullia's soul. Probably that she will repent her wicked, whoring ways, but not just yet, not while she might still have some money to give them.

'You must be very careful,' her brother says. 'The authorities are blaming the courtesans.'

'So I have heard. Well, naturally they know all about us. I have slept with most of the Council of Ten.'

'Tullia!'

She makes a gesture that signifies she is speaking in jest.

'All I am saying is that it would do to keep a low profile for the moment.'

But the more she hears what she must do, the more furious and reckless she feels. The bloody hypocrites!

She lists the items Elisabetta has stolen from her. 'She has even taken the portrait of me by Tintoretto,' she says. 'Do you think I am going to do nothing? I needed that money to begin again. I have told you the house is stripped bare. In fact, I was going to ask you if you might loan me . . .'

'A loan?' he looks surprised.

'Oh, brother,' she says. 'How else am I to survive?'

'But I thought Domenico Venier was looking after you. Surely with one of the most important patricians of the Republic as your patron your position is secure? You must have money saved.'

Tullia flinches. 'That situation is not a reliable one. Jealousies grow among his nephews. They have written scurrilous poems against me. He is old and ill and has not yet returned to the city. I cannot rely on him for the future. His powers are on the wane and without his patronage I will be exposed to every ill-wind that blows. As for savings, I have been supporting a household for the last eighteen months and not working. My savings are spent.'

He blushes. 'I am sorry but my affairs are not in such a state that I can afford you a loan at the moment. The plague has brought commerce to a standstill. Boats I invested in have sunk.'

She sighs. She knew he would disappoint her; he always has.

'I am sorry, but . . .'

She allows him to flounder in embarrassment for a while. She quite enjoys it. Then she says lightly, 'Never mind, brother. At least you have given me a roof over my head, even if it is a roof which I bought five years ago and put in your name.' Tullia gets to her feet. 'Now I must go to bed. It has been a long day and I am exhausted.'

She bends down and kisses him on the cheek, hoping to make him feel as guilty as it is possible to feel. It doesn't really matter. She has never been able to rely on anyone other than herself. So nothing has changed.

No, nothing has changed at all. She has always been alone.

III. The List of the Dead

The following morning she summons the boatman to take her to a meeting with her landlord. She recalls how she looked when she went on that journey with Titian, bejewelled, voluptuous. But there is none of that extravagance today. She wears a black dress and a veil, flat shoes. Only one row of pearls adorns her neck. She is not raised on *zoccoli*, the high wooden platform shoes that are the fashion; her cheeks are not rouged. Her appearance is sober, almost ordinary. If it weren't for the look in her eyes, she might be a widow on the way to church. The boatman does not care. His heart rejoices. To be conveying a courtesan round the city, even one dressed as dowdily as this, seems like a blessing after the plague years. If the courtesans are returning to the city, the city must be returning to its old self. While he negotiates the canals, she talks to him.

As she runs through her list of former patrons, he replies, 'Dead ... dead ... I'm not sure ... He tried to dash himself on the rocks around Lazzaretto Vecchio and is now quite mad ... Oh, that one is locked up by his family and looked after by the monks ... Exiled for sodomy ... Dead ... I don't know ... Ah, that one is alive!'

'At last! And sane?'

'Yes, and living in the city.'

She laughs. 'Well, unfortunately he never had a very heavy purse, but at least there is one of my former clients alive and sane, even if that is hardly enough to set up my former salon.'

How will she manage, she wonders, when so many of her previous liaisons are severed?

'Weren't you afraid to stay?' she asks.

'What is a gondolier away from the city? I would be a fowl without air or a fish without water. It would have been more dangerous for me to leave the city than stay. I have never left. I believe the water of the lagoon flows through my body, not blood.'

'But with so many people dying ...'

'I did not think the plague would claim me. The city will look after its own, but it is a relief now to start to convey the living along the canals, not the dead and dying towards the islands.'

'When I am established again, will you come and work for me?' she asks.

Before he can answer her, she holds out her hand. 'I should say I have absolutely no money to pay you at the moment.'

'I have to survive, Signora.'

'We all have to do that. I will also have need of a maid, a good cook, a ...'

'Will you be able to pay them?'

'Later ... later I will be able to pay everyone very well indeed.'

He laughs 'How could I refuse such an offer, Signora?'

She smiles. 'Tell me, is the tailor Strozzi still alive?'

'He is dead, but his son survives and I hear he is nimble with flax and needle.'

'Good. I will be in need of him.'

'Here we are, Signora.'

'Right,' she says, taking a deep breath. 'Now to strike a deal with the landlord.'

He takes hold of her hand. 'Good luck!'

'Thank you,' she says and then under her breath, as she smoothes her skirts, 'I am going to need it.'

IV. Marco Martinengo – The Landlord

They have not met before. All previous dealings were done directly by Venier. So when Tullia is ushered into Martinengo's presence, it is the first time she has been face to face with him. The plague has obviously worn on the landlord, as well as the city. Despite his lupine good looks, his skin is grey and his cheeks sunken. The hair on his head and that which grows on his chin is like an unkempt garden. A muscle twitches in his jaw, as if he is grinding his teeth.

She presumes he has known the profession of the woman who has been living in his house. As she watches him, she tries to imagine what his sexual peccadilloes might be; it is a habit of hers. She runs through various scenarios in her mind, alters the positions, moves her hands then his, her body, his. She tries both sides of the coin . . .

But no, none of them seem quite right. He puzzles her. His desires are hidden from her and this makes her curious.

A solemn young Saracen stands beside him. Martinengo is looking at some documents on his desk. 'I have plans for the building,' he says.

An easy lie to spot. The sheet of paper in his hand shakes

as he moves it from one hand to the other. It is clear he is not reading it. She almost feels sorry for him.

'I am sorry to hear that,' she says, 'I have greatly enjoyed living there and the payments are up to date, I understand?'

A slight movement of his head acknowledges the truth of what she has said.

They are both Venetians; they know how to strike a deal.

'I hope your family has not been badly affected by the plague,' Tullia says. Her tone is one of tender concern. She finds it easy enough to muster because the man looks in such a very bad way. The Saracen boy flinches and shakes his head slightly, then glances anxiously at his master. Martinengo does not meet her eye. His face is cast down towards the desk. His hands fumble with the parchment there. Silence fills the space between them and then a patter like the first rain drops of a thunderstorm, heavy, slow. Tears drop on the parchment, ink words blossom under each tear, like cornflowers in a meadow. If I were not here, she thinks, the boy would comfort him, but because I am he is constrained.

Now she sees the position he needs. She holds him in her arms, she caresses his face, he weeps. She resists the impulse to step round the desk, to touch his arm, to reach out to him. She sees clearly how easily he might break. He takes several deep breaths and then clears his throat. A few seconds pass. She waits patiently for him to bring himself under control.

'Perhaps I should return another time?'

He shakes his head.

She smoothes her skirts. 'The truth is I have nothing and have come to throw myself on your mercy.'

For the first time, he looks her directly in the eyes. His are very pale blue and watery beneath the layer of tears.

'My maid, who I entrusted with certain items, has stolen from me. All the items I hoped to raise money against in the ghetto. Everything is gone. Even the portrait of me by

Tintoretto is gone.' She gestures to her pearls. 'I had to grab these from my sister-in-law's scabby neck to try and make a good impression. I came here to say I had nothing to offer you by way of rent other than myself.'

Martinengo frowns slightly and he gestures for the boy to leave them. Once they are alone, he opens his mouth as if he is about to say something, but then closes it again.

Tullia laughs, liberated by simply having spoken the truth to him. 'It is difficult for me to judge how long it will be before I am in a position to pay you. My outgoings at the beginning will be great, but if you would agree to payment in kind then after that time I would agree to pay you whatever you deem suitable. I understand that if you have other plans for the house I must make other arrangements. This is the truth of my situation that I have laid in front of you. I did not intend to be so open, but you have brought it forth in me.'

'In kind?' He talks like a man with a net across his throat that the words are struggling to escape through.

She moves closer to him and whispers, 'Come to me. You will only have to send to me and I will be available to you, for conversation, for comfort, for whatever you desire . . .'

The silence hangs in the air and now it is the turn of Martinengo to start to imagine.

'Yes,' he says, but now it is not grief catching him by the throat. 'Yes,' he repeats more clearly this time. 'I think that will be perfectly satisfactory.'

'It will take some time to restore the house to its former glory. And myself, of course. But when that has happened I will let you know I am available.'

He nods.

'Meanwhile I will be at my brother's. My sister-in-law's poisonous disdain will add wings to the speed of my restoration of the house.'

'When do you think you will be in a position to pay rent?'

Tullia sighs. 'I do not wish to lie to you. It depends on many things. How quickly the city returns to itself. Many of my clients are away or dead. My connections are broken. Time will tell. Partly it depends on how quickly people return to the city. Who is alive to help me? Patronage is everything in such matters.'

She bows, preparing to leave.

'Just one more thing,' he says. 'What you did for King Henry – will you do that for me?'

Tullia smiles, moves towards him and murmurs something in his ear. His face blushes the most ferocious red. 'Oh,' he says, 'I didn't realise ...'

'*Whatever* you desire,' she whispers. 'Whatever comfort you require will be made available to you. If that is what you desire ...'

In the boat on the way back to her brother's she says to the gondolier, 'Do you know how Martinengo was affected by the plague?'

'A terrible story, Signora. His wife, his mother, all his six children. Only he and his father survived but the old man's wits are lost. Martinengo was away when the plague struck and could not get back into the city. When he did, the bodies had already been disposed of and his father had been taken to Lazzareto Vecchio.'

'He seems in torment,' she says.

'It is said he adored his wife and children. They were everything to him. To endure such a loss must be terrible. There are rumours that he locked himself up in the house for days on end, refused food, refused all attempts to help him. He allowed only the Saracen boy near him. I am surprised he agreed to see you. It was said he couldn't endure the light. He has only recently re-emerged in society.'

'Well, I have done a deal with him. For the moment, the house is secure.'

'I am glad of it.'

'By the end of the week I should have some money for you.'

He laughs. 'I will be glad of that as well.'

When they arrive at her brother's house, he helps her from the boat and she stumbles. He grips her round the waist to stop her falling and she clings to him for a moment.

'Since I was such a young girl I have had so many people to support. My mother and brothers, my children. To start all over again ...'

'Everything will be all right, Signora. You will see. It has been a shock, returning to the city, but everything will recover. Like a peacock which has lost his tail feathers. Time will restore and heal. The city will return to its former glory, as will you.'

'You're very sweet,' she says, then reaches up and strokes the side of his face. 'You are the kindest I have come across since my return.'

She smiles wearily and slowly begins to climb the stairs to the upper part of the palazzo.

AURORA
&
ALBERTO

New York, 2011

The approach had been quite casual. A young man in jeans, sneakers and bomber jacket had come up alongside her shortly after she had left the apartment and told her that Alberto wanted to have a word with her. He'd shown her his ID and Aurora had taken it from him and given it a long hard look, which she had then transferred to his face.

'Albi?' she said. 'That piece of shit?'

Joe Sarzetto, who had had the Pereira's apartment under surveillance for some time now, had developed a firm picture in his mind about what sort of woman Aurora was – docile, domestic and not particularly bright was his take on her. So he was slightly startled by the ferocity both of her look and her manner. But he didn't let it worry him too much. He was slightly hung over from having watched the ball game with his brothers the previous night and was therefore in no mood for a fight. His job was to deliver her up to his boss, Alberto, sitting in the cafe round the corner. And so that is what he duly did a couple of minutes later.

The man waiting for them in that cafe had the shoulders and forearms of a body builder, and when he stood up it was clear he also had the paunch of a man whose wife liked to cook.

'Rory, how're you doing?'

No one had called her Rory in a very long time.

'You got old and fat,' she said, sitting down opposite him.

'Any thief needs catching, I send the kid,' he said, nodding at Joe. 'I assume a supervisory capacity.'

'So you're the one to get shot or stabbed. How you like those onions?'

Joe glanced at Aurora, frowning.

'Go get the coffees,' the older man said, sitting back down. 'Rory, you want anything?'

She shook her head. 'Maybe I wanted something ten years ago. Maybe I wanted something from you then. Maybe I thought you might have something to offer the girls ten years ago when they needed it. Now, I don't want anything.'

Joe was still standing next to the table, his frown deepening. He raised his baseball cap off his head and then settled it back down again, as if this might help him gain some insight into what was happening.

'What are you still doing there?' Alberto snapped. 'Didn't I tell you to get the coffees?'

'You tell me what you want. I'll get them.'

'Jesus! What I always have. When have you ever known me have anything different? And get take-out cups,' he shouted after him.

Alberto picked a sugar stick out of a bowl and shook it. 'I hear the girls are doing well.'

'You piece of shit.'

He closed his eyes, screwed up his face and rubbed the

knuckles of his right hand over his right eyebrow, producing a light sprinkling of dry skin down onto the red Formica table top. However, when he looked up again there was no softening of her expression.

'What you want, Albi?'

It was then it dawned on him, there was no helping it – he would have to grovel.

'I'm sorry, Rory...'

'What for?'

'I'm sorry I didn't visit more afterwards.'

'After what, Albi?'

Jesus! He could feel the pliers yank–ing his teeth out slow–ly by the roots.

Aurora was holding her bag in her lap, as if it were a protective shield. Albi, the same age her husband would have been, if he were alive. But he would never have let himself get into that kind of state. Never. He would never have turned into such a slob. She wouldn't have let him.

'Look, Rory, I'm going to put my cards on the table.' But it wasn't cards he placed on the table, it was his fat, pudgy hands. And he was staring at the backs of them, as if they were the most fascinating thing in the world. Anything to avoid her eye.

'Me and the boy are working as part of the Drug Enforcement Task Force. We've had Pereira under surveillance for a while now. We think...'

Joe came back with the coffees, put the cups on the table and sat down next to Alberto. Alberto took the plastic lid off the cup, tore the top off the sugar stick, poured it in and swished it around with an ineffectual wooden stick. Joe left the lid of his on. He took his baseball hat off and dropped it on the table.

'Take your hat off the table, kid. Show some manners,' Alberto snapped.

Joe rolled his eyes, picked it up and placed it over the top of his left knee, which was jigging up and down in that way that seemed to indicate the owner of the knee might have something pressing on his mind.

'I've been telling Rory about Pereira. You want to take over?'

And so while Alberto slurped his coffee, the kid rambled on. Every now and again Alberto glanced at Aurora to see how she was taking it.

Difficult to tell.

Aurora released and then gripped the handle of her bag. She looked down at her hands; thin purple threads of veins bisected the white bones of the knuckles.

Holding on, holding on, for so many years she'd been holding on.

And now she's somewhere else and she's looking down at another pair of hands, her husband's at the undertakers, folded across his chest, so neatly. Everything about him so neat, so unnaturally neat. She'd had to borrow a suit from his brother to lay him out in. He'd been a messy, messy man, her man. Clothes dropped on the floor of the apartment, wet towels in the bathroom. And she'd gone on and on to him, nagging. God, how she had missed that mess when he was gone. She'd never nagged her children, even when their bedrooms were knee-deep in stuff. Occasionally she'd go in and sort the dirty from the clean for the washing, but that was all. Recently her daughter had made a comment that she wasn't like other mothers. She didn't tell them off about their rooms. She'd asked her why not. The question had caught Aurora on the hop, but she hadn't had the heart to tell her why.

'Life's too short to worry about trivia,' she'd replied.

How she'd longed for his mess once it was gone, once he was gone.

'Rory?' Alberto's hand touched hers.

She jerked her hand away from his and brushed the tears from her cheeks. Her bag dropped to the floor and turned upside down. The contents scattered. She pushed back her chair and stood up. Joe was down on his knees, picking things up.

The voice that came out of her mouth was like the hiss of a snake.

'Don't you dare come near me again,' she said. 'Aren't you satisfied with having half destroyed my family? You bastards. Stay away from me.'

Alberto blinked. Joe looked up at him and then back at her.

'I have two children,' she said. 'How you got the nerve?'

She pulled her chair further back to check everything had been retrieved, found a pen against the skirting board and waved it under Alberto's nose.

'Haven't I given enough, Albi? Who's going to be there for the girls? You want to get me killed as well? You fat fuck. You haven't come near me in ten years and now you come to me with this. And you're their fucking godfather. Some godfather!'

She drew back her hand and slapped him hard across the cheek. The crack rang out in the small cafe, quietening conversation, puckering lips, swivelling heads and eyes.

'Hey, that's assaulting a police officer.' Joe was on his feet, moving round the table towards her.

'Fuck off, kid.'

Alberto grabbed his arm and pulled him back down into his seat. 'Leave it.'

Aurora turned on her heels and headed for the door.

'Jesus,' Joe said. 'What's gone on between you two?'

Alberto was rubbing his cheek thoughtfully. 'She was always fiery. I thought she might have calmed down some. Got that one wrong.'

'You going to tell me what happened?'

Alberto sighed. 'Another time, kid.'

'What we going to do?'

'Wait till she's cooled off a bit. Try again later.'

'Can't wait too long. The boss said . . .'

'I know what he said, but we got to give her time.'

Joe raised his cup to his lips. The plastic lid wasn't on tight enough and the coffee dribbled out, down his chin and onto the table and his white T-shirt. 'Shit!' He wiped his chin with his hand and grabbed some napkins from the dispenser on the table, dabbing ineffectually at his T-shirt.

Alberto looked at him. 'The state of you and I'm going to be walking around with you all day looking like a ten year old.'

The boy kept dabbing and dabbing.

Alberto pushed back his chair and stood up, 'I had a bit of a thing for Rory back in the day. She's still a handsome woman.' He turned to the boy. 'You think?'

'Come on – you got twenty years on me. She's my mother.'

Alberto sighed. 'Let's go, kid.'

As Joe followed Alberto out of the cafe, he muttered under his breath, 'You know I've got a name. It's Joe, Joe Sarzetto.'

On the pavement Alberto stood for a moment, pulling on his coat. He looked up at the sky. 'You know the trouble with this city – the sky's always too far away. It's not good for a man. And when you can see it, there's not enough of it. Yeah, there's never enough sky.'

LUDOVICO
&
ANDREA

London, 2011

Ludovico's father, Andrea, was due to fly into Heathrow that afternoon, so Ludovico's plan had been to end rehearsals early in order to be there to meet him at the airport. Unfortunately he was then waylaid by his worried set designer, so he was already running late by the time he set out for the tube. As usual when he was running a little bit late, circumstances then conspired to make him horribly late. There were delays because of a signal failure on the Piccadilly Line earlier in the day at Earl's Court and Ludovico was forced to endure a stop-start, stress-filled journey, constantly checking the time on his mobile and bemoaning the fact that his father did not have one.

Ludovico had tried several times completely unsuccessfully to persuade Andrea as to their merits. In fact, the last time he had gone back to Italy he had bought a very simple pay-as-you-go phone at the airport. On being presented with it, Andrea had peered at the device, as if it were the devil incarnate, and placed it carefully in a drawer, which contained odd pieces of string, some loose nails, a broken dog's collar, his favourite hammer (a small, beautifully balanced one that had belonged to Ludovico's grandfather) and a tube of glue. Even as Ludovico was explaining to him how to put money on it and how to charge it, he knew he was wasting his time. He imagined his father squirting glue into it, whacking it with the hammer and tying it up in string before burying it in the garden. Then someone coming across it in a couple of hundred years' time and wondering what witchcraft it was part of. But he'd had to try. His father was getting older, but he still went for walks alone far into the mountains, as he always had. Suppose, Ludovico thought, he fell and hurt his ankle. Suppose he had a stroke and was stranded far away, unable to attract help. However, the safety/emergency argument for mobile phones had no effect on his father. 'I have to die sometime,' was all he had said to his son. 'If the woods claim me, it is not such a bad place to go. Better than a hospital, better than a care home.' And then he had pointed out that the signal in the woods was non-existent anyway.

So the mobiles were always 'lost' or mislaid. Once Ludovico had phoned the number only to have it answered by a young man. For a moment, he thought it had been stolen, until he recognised the voice. It was Gino, the son of Maria, Andrea's housekeeper, who told him rather apologetically that Andrea had given it away to him.

Now, on the tube, running late to meet him, Ludovico cursed his father's old-fashioned ways. Eventually he put his own mobile in his pocket, closed his eyes and tried to calm down. His father would wait for him. It would be all right. People would take care of him, they always did. When he finally ran, sweating, into the arrivals lounge, his father's plane was already marked as having landed. He scoured the seating area and, after a nerve-racking few minutes, found his father sitting like a cuckoo in the nest of a large, garrulous Indian family.

Andrea was a man who never varied his look. Whether high in the pinewoods of the Dolomites, watching his dogs snuffling out the scent of wild pigs, or in one of the largest capital cities in the world, he wore the same things: a battered grey-green felt hat with a short brim, somewhat reminiscent of Tommy Trinder, and a thick, black-and-white hound's-tooth check overcoat. On his feet was a pair of weather-beaten, sturdy brown boots. Underneath the coat would probably be a heavily darned jumper, which may or may not have been pulled off him by Maria long enough to stitch thick leather patches over the holes in the elbows.

'Papa!' Ludovico exclaimed. He was rewarded with a welcoming smile from his father and a disapproving glare from several Indian matriarchs.

The two men shook hands and kissed each other. 'I'm sorry, Papa. I was held up. There was a problem with the tube.'

His father leant over and pinched the cheek of a chubby *putto* who was trying unsuccessfully to tear its grandmother's sari off with one hand, while wrenching her glasses off with the other. Ludovico looked down at his father's case.

'Papa!' he remonstrated.

His father shrugged apologetically. 'We have travelled everywhere together. We can't stop now. It would be a terrible betrayal.'

'But your arthritis.'

Andrea shrugged. 'When I have to change, I will. People help me with it. I talk to them and enjoy it. People are very kind.'

Ludovico picked up his father's luggage, a small

battered case with leather corners and handle which had been brand new at some point in the early 1950s; the catches had broken a long time ago and a leather belt was the only thing holding it together, as well as some old stickers denoting the countries he had travelled to shortly after the end of the war: Switzerland, France and Spain. This case was another bone of contention between them. Andrea refused to use the small, black modern case with wheels which his son had given him, accusing it of being soulless, of having no history. Last time he had visited his father, Ludovico had seen the very same case stuffed with potatoes, being dragged by Maria through the narrow streets of the village.

As he picked up this case, Ludovico knew exactly what would be in it: one pair of clean socks, a couple of pairs of underwear, one clean shirt, a pair of pyjamas. His father's shaving things and a toothbrush, and little else other than books, notebooks and his father's fountain pen and a bottle of ink, wrapped in an old black sock, in case it leaked. Andrea had always moved lightly through the world, albeit with a heavy leather case.

On the tube back into town, they talked of village gossip, of who had died, who had moved, of the birth of Maria's first grandchild, a boy. They talked of the local secondary school, where Andrea had taught for most of his life, and how it was now under threat of closure because there were so few children in the village. In an Italian restaurant in Soho, Bocca di Lupo, the conversation moved onto local politics and then to national politics, although Ludovico tried to keep that brief because his father's blood pressure was always raised by any talk of Berlusconi, or 'Lo Stronzo', as his father loudly insisted on calling him, causing some consternation amongst a group of elderly, well-dressed Italian women on the table next to them.

While they waited for their food to come, the conversation turned to *The Winter's Tale.* Andrea was curious about how it was going and interested in the Arcadian, bucolic themes since they were the well-spring of his own poetry.

'Actually, I'm worried about my leading man,' Ludovico said. 'He broke down in rehearsals the other day and I think he may be having some kind of . . .'

Andrea broke off a piece of focaccia bread, dipped it in some olive oil and popped it in his mouth. 'Hmm?'

'Crisis.' Ludovico continued. 'Yes, crisis, I think.'

'How is he in the role?'

Ludovico frowned. 'Well, it's difficult and he's struggling.'

Andrea nodded. 'Of course he is. Some roles make them bleed.'

'Yes, but if I can get him there, he will be beautiful. He is the most wonderful actor. From the moment he walks onto the stage, he holds the audience. Audiences love him. Even when he turns his back to them they are happy to stare at the back of his neck. He is one of the most generous and most intelligent I have ever worked with.'

'You always fall in love with your cast. It is the way you are made.'

'This . . .' Ludovico paused. 'This . . . Papa. I mean, he . . . Terry, that is. Well, I think this may be different.'

Andrea smiled and patted Ludovico's hand. 'Maybe it will only become clear at the end of the run.'

'Maybe.'

'Perhaps I'll come over to see him.'

'Really?'

His father shrugged. 'Why not?'

Ludovico was surprised. The play was due to open in a fortnight. The run in London was only three months long. Then it would transfer to The Mockingbird in New York.

His father did not travel very much these days, so it would be unlike him to come back over so soon.

Their food had come; Ludovico forked some thinly sliced radish into his mouth and then chased some pomegranate seeds round his plate. His father took a bite of a sage leaf filled with anchovies and murmured appreciatively.

'As well as struggling, he is also having some strange experiences with paintings,' Ludovico said, between mouthfuls.

Andrea wiped his mouth on a napkin. 'Tell me.'

Ludovico continued. 'You know the painting by Titian of *The Man With the Blue Sleeve*.'

'Mmm.'

'Yes. Well, he says it spoke to him.'

'What did it say?'

'That there are worse things than loneliness and that there is a difference between looking and seeing.'

'I like this painting!' Andrea said. 'It has wisdom, I think.'

Ludovico laughed. 'I think so too. Then it told him he was going to die soon.'

Andrea smiled slightly. 'Is he in good health?'

'A little overweight, perhaps.'

'Will he make it to the end of the run?'

'Now you're being mischievous.'

'Maybe tomorrow I will go and see this painting myself. Do you think it will speak to me?'

Ludovico shrugged. 'Why not? Maybe it will recognise a fellow inhabitant of the Veneto.'

When they had finished their meal and were on the pavement outside the restaurant, Andrea paused, tucking his scarf round his neck. 'The staff seem happy and the food is excellent. A lovely combination.' Ludovico smiled, knowing that the happiness of the staff was more important to his father than the excellence of the food. He suggested they walk back to the flat and his father agreed. An enormous full moon hung low in the night sky over the London Eye. They stopped on Hungerford Bridge and stared at it in amazement.

'It's the closest it's been to earth since 1992,' Andrea said. 'That's why it seems so huge.' Ludovico put down his father's case and leant on the railing next to him.

'Luna puella pallidula,' Ludovico said. 'Luna flora eremetica, Luna unica selenita, distonia vita traviata . . .'

Andrea smiled and patted Ludovico's arm. 'It's a good son who learns his father's poetry off by heart.'

'Do you remember you used to say it to me like a lullaby when I was a child and I couldn't sleep? I say it to myself even now. I used it the other day actually. It always works.'

'Do you know why I wrote it?'

'The Russians had made the first landing on the moon in 1959 and you were not at all happy. You wanted to give the moon back some of her mystery. Reclaim her from the scientists for the poets.'

Andrea smiled. 'That was it, yes. It is important that we allow mystery in our world, in each other.' He looked at his son and then back up into the night sky. 'I will never see it so close again.'

Ludovico glanced at him suddenly, worried that his father was talking about his son as well as the moon. On the phone the evening before he arrived, Andrea had told Ludovico there was something he wanted to tell him. Ludovico was worried, imagining all kinds of things, mainly relating to his father's health, but he knew better than to press him on the matter; he might never tell him if he did that. One of the things Ludovico loved about his father was the fact that even though he had spent his whole life in the village of his birth, he could still stand on this bridge and look out at the vast sprawl of the city with the openness and curiosity of a child. There was something about him that remained open, despite his age. Standing on this bridge with the Thames running underneath him, Andrea was exactly the same as he was walking in his beloved pinewoods. There was something solid and innocent and incorruptible about him. Ludovico wondered if he had always been like this, even as a young man. He was all too aware of his own shape-shifting abilities. Directors needed charm. Especially in the film industry, they needed a great deal of charm to persuade the money men to put them in charge, but Ludovico was also conscious of the uneasy relationship between charm and integrity, of how charm could be its enemy.

Back in the flat, he offered his father a grappa. Andrea sat down heavily on the sofa. Ludovico, seeing the almost translucent skin of his father's face and the blue-bruised marks under his eyes, realised how very tired he was and berated himself for not taking a cab from the restaurant, but then, he thought, if they'd taken a cab, they wouldn't have seen the moon. While his father sat on the sofa sipping his drink, Ludovico went into the kitchen to make some coffee and listen to the messages on his mobile phone. There was one from the set designer explaining in detail why he couldn't do what Ludovico wanted him to do, another which seemed to be dead air, then another from Terry, awkward and rather tentative, and telling him in great detail that there was no need to phone him back, that he'd see him tomorrow in rehearsals. Ludovico smiled and played the message again. When he came back into the room, with the coffee, his father was asleep, his hat resting in his lap like a shabby codpiece.

What did Ludovico see when he looked at his sleeping father? A direct descendant of Virgil, of Petrarch, of Dante, a wonderful poet. A teacher, who had lived out almost his whole life in the village of his birth and had taught in the same secondary school. Finally, he saw the man who was his father, a fragile human being who had battled with depression

90

his whole life. The inspiration of all his life and creativity had been the village of his birth. Ludovico, who was beginning to lead a highly international and more rootless existence, envied him the certainty with which he had lived out his life in one place.

It had been good to be able to talk to his father about the play; he had missed talking to him about his work. Andrea had profoundly disapproved of Ludovico moving into the film-making world and had argued fervently that he should remain working in the theatre. It was as close to having an argument as the two men had ever come. Andrea had had a fairly brutish brush with the industry when he was commissioned to write some poetry for a film as a young man. He had not liked the way his verse was used, or the film, and as a consequence had come to regard the whole world of film as a debased medium. Andrea's opinion was that cinema filled people's brains with 'bubbles and poisoned colours'. The only films he approved of were those which gave the viewer access to 'strange paths' and 'new skies'.

He did not have a television and rarely went to the cinema. If he did go, it was to see the same films over and over again, usually those by Pasolini, whom he had known as a boy. Andrea had been horrified when Ludovico had told him he was going to direct his first film and had fallen silent every time his son mentioned it. In the end Ludovico had stopped talking to him about it. He hadn't even told him of the prize one of his films had picked up at Cannes. Anyway, his father disapproved of prizes. As if the life of an artist isn't hard enough, he said, without things that pit one against the other, that encourage envy and jealousy. It is not the artist who naturally does this; artists will naturally cling to each other, take pleasure in each other. It is the marketplace which corrupts, which sets one against the other. He had always refused to allow any of his works to be entered in competitions, despite the lamentations of his publishers. Ludovico knew there was no point in banging his head against the brick wall of his father's silence. He knew how stubborn Andrea could be and also how opaque. It was his way and Ludovico had learnt to live with it.

Suddenly his father opened his eyes and stretched. 'Ah, Ludovico,' he said. 'What a lovely day. I have looked at a beautiful moon with my beautiful son and he has told me that maybe he has fallen in love.'

Ludovico laughed. 'Well, I'm not sure I said that, did I?'

'Oh yes, I think you did. Incidentally, you know that your friend is talking to himself through the painting? He is reassuring himself and frightening himself in equal measure.'

'Really?'

'I am sure of it, but I still think I will pay the painting a visit tomorrow. Just in case.'

'In case . . .?'

'In case it talks to me.'

Ludovico laughed. His father was a Gemini and had always liked to have it both ways.

After his father had gone to bed, Ludovico went into the bathroom. His father's old razor was on the glass shelf under the mirror, his battered toothbrush in the glass next to his. Ludovico looked at them for quite some time before picking up his own toothbrush, brushing his teeth and taking himself off to bed. He was worried about what his father would do tomorrow while he was in rehearsal all day. He wondered when his father would get round to telling him what was on his mind, but he also knew his father could not be hurried. It was out of his hands and in the meantime he should just enjoy having him here.

In the morning Ludovico woke to his father placing a cup of coffee on his bedside table. Ludovico rubbed his eyes and looked at his alarm clock.

'Papa,' he protested. 'Six o'clock.'

'I have made you this coffee,' Andrea replied calmly, 'even though it is a disgrace to your heritage.'

'It's Lavazza.'

'And how many times have I told you? How have I raised you, Ludovico? Illy. Illy. Illy. How many times can a man say this to his son before he listens?'

Ludovico laughed and reached for the cup. His father sat down on the bed and smiled at him.

'What are you going to do with the day?' Ludovico asked.

'I am going to go out soon for a walk to see the city waking up. Then I will go and buy you some decent coffee. Then I will have some breakfast in Soho. Then I think I will go and see the Titian. After that . . .' He shrugged his shoulders.

'Will you be all right?'

'Now, what have I told you about poets?'

'That the angels watch over them because they suffer so.'

'Exactly!'

A few moments later his father appeared again in the doorway, battered hat perched jauntily on the back of his head.

'Papa, won't you take a phone with you?'

His father glanced at the expensive one on Ludovico's bedside table with a look of disdain. 'If I carry such a thing, it will not make me safer. It will make me a target for thieves.'

'You are impossible,' Ludovico said heavily.

'No,' he said firmly. 'I am right.' He placed both his hands over his son's ears and pulled his head towards him so he could kiss him on the forehead.

'Keys, Papa,' Ludovico said.

'I may be old, son, but I am not yet senile.' He tossed a set of keys lightly in his hand. 'See you this evening. I hope rehearsals go well.'

Ludovico heard the door of the flat open and close, looked again at the time: 6.15 a.m. He groaned and lay back down and tried to sleep but the coffee thumping at the door of his heart had other ideas.

The Young
Boatman

Venice, 1546

The redness that the Jewish doctor, Master Lazaro, had spoken of was visible the following day in my father's arm, as was the deterioration in his condition. That night he fell into a raging fever and, despite my mother's protestations, I went to the ghetto to fetch the doctor. Doctors were only allowed out at night, to minister to the patrician families, but the plan that the doctor had outlined to me worked well. I presented myself to the ghetto guards as a servant from the household of Francesco Calafado and stated that my mistress had gone into labour, and Lazaro was soon by my side, along with the young boy who had accompanied him before. The *calli* were empty as we hurried back to my house, the white light from a full moon glittered cruelly down onto the black waters of the canal. Once at my father's side, Lazaro peeled back the dressings on his arm, sniffed, and murmured something to the boy. He then ordered me to hold the candle high so that he could see all the way up my father's arm to the shoulder.

'You were right to have called me. Do you see this?' he said, pointing to the flesh of his forearm. 'Infection has taken hold and unless we do something soon it will reach his body and then travel up into his brain. We must remove more of his arm.'

The thought of this appalled me. 'Surely the pain and shock will kill him?' I said.

'It may, but if we do nothing then he will be dead within the week. It is up to you, but if I do it you must find people to hold him down.'

He drew back the blanket covering my father's body, assessing his strength. 'We will need two men per leg and two per arm and one to hold down his shoulders. The mottling has spread only in his forearm, so I will sever his arm just above the elbow.'

My mother was not at all convinced. She, like many Christians, distrusted the Jews, but I became angry with her. 'If the patrician families call on him for help, who are we to think we know better?' I asked. 'We must trust him.'

In the end I managed to convince her, then I went next door to rouse my neighbours. They were not happy to be woken in this way but they came in the end, complaining vigorously while they rubbed the sleep from their eyes. When we had pinned my poor father to the bed, the doctor began. I have to confess, I closed my eyes.

We needed the nine people we had to restrain him because he bucked like a wild animal. Then he screamed twice as if possessed by demons before passing out. Lazaro progressed with the speed and dexterity of a butcher on the Rialto.

Later that night the fever did break. Unfortunately, in the weeks that followed my father seemed to have broken with it. Perhaps it was the physical suffering, perhaps it was the injustice of what had happened to him, but he fell into a darkness of spirit from which there was no raising him. He became very conscious of his appearance and would not venture out into the city. I and my mother both tried our best, but even when there was no longer any physical reason for him to be in bed he would not move. A part of me understood. He was a Venetian, he was a gondolier. He could no longer ply his trade as he once had. One arm is not enough to manage a boat on the tricky tides and winds of the lagoon. He could not do it, and if he could not do that, then what would he do? His former life had been taken from him. But I was also angry with him and frightened about what was to become of our family. When you are the only son and have seven sisters, there is a big responsibility. My father's injury had plunged us into a desperate situation. Since I was a child I had always gone out on the boats with him, but now unless I wanted to see my sisters with their breasts hanging from the balconies I would have to come up with a plan. We had been relying on the kindness of relatives and friends to support us, but now it was up to me. Unfortunately, I am not someone who finds it easy to push himself forwards. It is not in my nature to do it. However, the day came when I was driven to it by the cries of hunger from my sisters and from the desperation in my mother's eyes.

Hunger and anger are a potent mix and it was with these emotions seething in me like warring serpents that, one month after the punishment had been meted out to my father, I found myself in the north-eastern part of the city, outside Titian's house, banging on the door, demanding to be let in.

The servant who came to the door regarded me with the greatest disdain. To him I was just a grubby boy, but I dodged my way past him and ran up the stone steps to the upper parts of the house where I heard voices. I pushed myself through a door, whipped off my cap and dropped to one knee. Titian was working in front of an enormous canvas, a naked woman reclined on a sofa. She did not hurry to cover herself and from that I assumed that she was a street woman relaxed with such nudity. Titian turned round and roared so ferociously at being disturbed that I felt myself quake, but I had decided that come what may I would have my say. I waited for the storm of his anger to break and remained where I was, head bowed. When I looked up, the woman on the sofa smiled at me encouragingly and I began.

'Sire, my father is a boatman who has recently been punished by having his eye gouged out and his hand cut off. The punishment came from him taking a young man to a nunnery, for the purposes of visiting a certain young lady. He was persuaded to do this against his better judgement and has been cruelly punished. His punishment has left my family destitute. I have seven sisters and my mother to provide for and . . .'

'Stop! What has this to do with me? Any punishment meted out by the Council of Ten is just and right.'

'Your son, sire. Pomponio was the one who persuaded my father to take him there. Your son who has now fled the city . . .'

'Enough!'

He threw some *soldi* in my direction and turned back towards his canvas.

I watched the coins roll across the wooden floor but instead of gratitude I was filled with a tempest of rage. This was nothing. I had not come for him to throw money at me like a beggar. This man's son had destroyed my father's life, which was in turn destroying my family. I felt the blood drain from my cheeks and it was as if the colour drained from what I looked upon. I remained where I was, struggling to keep my temper, and the silence grew and grew. Made aware of my continuing presence by the nod of the young naked woman, Titian then swung back round.

'Get out!' he yelled, and he strode towards me and stood over me, but I had no intention of doing what he demanded. I wanted more than money; I wanted a livelihood. So, I stood my ground. Then he brought back his hand and struck me in the face, sending me sprawling. As I was spitting blood onto the floor, a big lion of a man stepped out from behind a screen and walked over to where I was kneeling.

He looked at me and growled. 'Do you know that you hold up the art of a genius with your demands?'

I looked up at him and in a voice trembling with suppressed fury and emotion I said, 'I am the only man of the family. I have a mother and seven sisters to support. My father is lying maimed in body and spirit and we do not know when or if he will be able to work again. Every Venetian is aware of the genius of the great Titian, but it is not my place to think of the needs of his genius but the needs of my mother and sisters.'

And then the man did something that took me by surprise. He stroked my cheek with the back of his bejewelled hand and said softly, 'You are barely a man, the hairs have yet to trouble the surface of your cheeks.' He looked down at me and smiled with great tenderness. And then before anyone could say anything else he was raising me to my feet by my elbow and saying quietly, 'I will take him, Vecelli. I have need of a good gondolier. His muscles will grow. Last night my gondolier tried to steal from me. He put a casket of *soldi* in his boat, then remembered he had some breeches being mended and went to retrieve them. When he returned, he found that he had himself been stolen from. The scoundrel!' He roared with laughter. Then bending down and picking up the money which Titian had thrown to the ground, he said, 'I will take this towards his first week's wages.' He handed it to me with deliberate courtesy.

It was in this manner that I first became the great Pietro Aretino's boatman. It was to gradually become clear that the reason he had done this was not purely out of pity for my plight. But whatever the reason for his initial decision, the truth was that Aretino saved us at that moment and I will always be grateful to him. A great many things have been said about him, especially after his death, when people no longer had cause to fear the violence of his pen, but one thing cannot be denied: to those less fortunate than himself, he was a man of enormous generosity. As he walked me out of Titian's studio, he said, 'You are like me. We do not scare easily.'

'Desperation gives me courage,' I said, my words somewhat muffled by the back of my hand, which was pressed to the corner of my bleeding mouth.

'You are in luck,' he continued. 'I have just come from the bed of Angela Zaffetta. When I have done my business, I am like a tree which somebody has cut down for firewood and then sees it burst out in leaves and buds. It makes me generous.' Then he looked me up and down. 'We must get you some scarlet breeches and a decent cap and doublet or the other gondoliers will pelt you with rotten fruit. Now, tell me about your sisters.'

The picture that I painted of my sisters was far from complimentary: a gaggle of half-wits and drooling frumps was the sum of it. I may have been a man of little learning, but I had heard the rumours about his household, about how courtesans came and went there and how he liked to sleep with his housemaids as much as the Zaffettas and the Zuffolinas. I had no intention of pimping my sisters for his pleasure, or tempting him with the truth about my sisters, who were all, in my own undoubtedly biased opinion, great beauties.

He listened to me with a slight smile on his face and when

I had finished he laughed and said, 'You are a good brother to your sisters. That is clear enough.' Then he threw his arm around my shoulders and drew me close. 'Do you know me, boy?'

'You are the great Pietro Aretino,' I replied.

'And what do you know of me?'

'You are a great writer,' I said.

'What else?'

'I do not listen to gossip,' I said, 'but judge a man on how he behaves towards me, and to me a desperate pauper you have been courteous, kind and extremely generous.'

He beamed. 'Now let me tell you what I will require of you as my boatman. As it happens, listening to gossip is exactly what I require you to do.'

And this was what he said to me.

'Sound moves differently over water and people behave differently on a boat to how they behave on dry land. A gondola rests you, it lulls you to sleep, your spirit is soothed, your limbs and body unwind. There is something about being so close to water, something about the lapping of waves and the sea breezes, the relaxation of being taken from one place to another in such a convivial manner. People become eager to converse, and who are they to converse with if they are by themselves? The gulls? The waves? The breeze? No, the gondolier, of course. The gondolier of a prominent man may hear all kinds of things from those grandees occupying his own boat; he is in the perfect position also to hear things from his fellow gondoliers, who know who went where when and at what time they came back again and with whom. Such is life. When you are conveying a person from one place to the other, it can make him unexpectedly garrulous, especially if he has fallen into your boat from the tavern and has been wetting his snout in hog-slaying ale.'

Aretino knew what he was talking about. He was a clever

man and he had made his living and his reputation through acquiring such gossip about people and making them pay to keep him quiet. But he was also a poet, so when he put his arm around my shoulder on that first day we met he conjured a picture of how gossip moved like a breeze, it moved up and down the *calli* and the canals, and up into the balconies and across the bedrooms of the courtesans and through respectable houses and wound its way across the *campi* and *campielli* and along the *fondamenta* and through the docks and the boats, recently returned from the east, and over to the lagoon islands, and then turned round and came back again and passed through the confessional and over the cribs of the babies in the orphanage and even made its way into the senate and the most secret meetings of the Council of Ten. He explained to me that many a man and woman had erred in thinking words spoken behind the black cloth of the *felze* of a gondola were safe. It was a mistake, he said, and this was gold to him, and I should tell him everything I heard, however trivial it might appear to me, because if one piece of information was placed against another, then it might have a story to tell.

Gossip, he said, is a mosaic. All those individual pieces may build up a complete picture of a person or an occurrence. It was simply a question of putting the whole picture together. You, he told me, are going to be picking up these *tesserae* for me and I will be making the whole picture. I understood him well enough. I also understood that he would pay me for these *tesserae*, depending on their value to him. 'You will help me complete the picture, you will carry me the red lake, the gold leaf, the lapis and the vermilion.' Venice, he said to me, is a market for glass, for paintings, for spices, for human flesh. It is also a market for secrets and that is where you come in.

Aretino's house stood on the Grand Canal. He rented it from Domenico Bolani, but he was as proud of the house as if it were his own. From its windows at any hour one might see a thousand gondolas and a thousand persons. To the right were the meat markets and the fish markets, to the left the bridge and the warehouses of the German merchants, and in the middle the marvel that is the Rialto Bridge. There were grapes in the barges and game birds in the shops and vegetables spread out upon the pavement and twenty-five sail boats laden with melons waiting to be boarded by a crowd that surged forwards sniffing and weighing to see if the cargo was of high quality or not. Although his house was as grand as a house gets in Venice, his household was not what I expected. It was more chaotic and friendlier. Naturally, there were jealousies. There was always a favoured housemaid, one who was falling into favour (or his bed) as another fell out.

The first scene that I witnessed as I arrived at his house was the scarlet enamel beads of a rosary bouncing down the steps towards us. As I scampered to retrieve them, I looked up and saw two housemaids at the top of the steps, tearing at each other's hair and bodices. Apparently an argument had ensued about some rosaries Aretino had purchased. They had caught the eye of his ladies, in the same way yew berries may attract the attention of a flock of blackbirds, but there were not enough to go round. Aretino set about the job of separating the women, swearing that he regretted ever having bought the rosaries in the first place, and then introduced me as his new boatman.

One of the ladies squeezed the muscles of my arm and made a lewd comment about my lack of hardness and I blushed as red as the beads I held in my hand. Aretino murmured something in her ear and she smiled at me and said she was sure I'd grow into a big, strong man by doing daily battle with the tides and waves of the lagoon. Then Aretino gave me my first job. To deliver a letter to the rosary maker, Biagio Spina. The order, as I discovered, was for six more, which I was to take back with me, but my master had only given me money for two, writing that he would pay the rest as soon as he could. Spina grumbled at that but handed over the amount requested and I returned with them to his household.

This was not to be the last time I had such an exchange with a grumbling merchant. My master was hopeless with money. Money that he received was like one bowl of soup set in front of twenty-five hungry friars. There were thefts from his household and a constant stream of the poor and needy to his door. He was known as the scourge of princes and a friend to courtesans, but he was also, when the mood was upon him, generous to anyone who came to his door with a sorry story, any beggar he passed in the street. Even the rogues made him laugh. Perhaps he recognised himself in them.

It was luck that I became his boatman then and not Titian's. Titian, I quickly learnt, had a reputation for meanness. Across the city there were stories of the hard bargains he drove, of the money he took and the paintings he refused to deliver, but Aretino was exactly the opposite. He was constantly in a state close to destitution and then as soon as the money came in it went out again. Everyone wanted Aretino in their boat, especially when he was drunk, because then he had to be prevented from giving away the cloak from his back to someone in need. He was a man who could make the Council of Ten quake in their shoes. He might raise you up or ruin you. I was his boatman for ten years until he died and I was devoted to him from the moment he showed such tenderness towards me as I knelt in despair in Titian's studio.

AURORA

&

ALBERTO

New York, 2011

There was more sky here in Union City, New Jersey, that was for sure, but it was night, so Alberto wasn't thinking much about it as he parked his car outside Aurora's house and grabbed the take-out bags from the front seat. What he was thinking about was whether it was safe for him to leave his car here. Back in the day it wouldn't have been. He'd have had to pay some kids to watch it for him.

He hadn't been here for a long time. He hadn't been back since they moved out of the area when he got a promotion and a pay rise. As he looked up at Aurora's battered front door, he felt the steady drip, drip of regret. He'd been a coward, that was all there was to it.

Slowly, he began to climb the steps to Aurora's house. She had stayed. Her husband had been shot dead ten years ago and since then she'd been on her own. How was she going to move out of the area? She wasn't, was she? He should have come more often, that was all there was to it.

It was a couple of weeks since he'd talked to her in the cafe and he was hoping she might have calmed down some. He rang the bell, made sure he was visible in the spy hole, made sure he looked sheepish, and then wafted the two take-out bags from Artesano's around the door frame, waiting to see if she'd let him in. He had a while to wait. He'd turned and was heading back down the steps when the door flew open.

'Piece of shit.'

'I got take-out from Arte's.'

'So you're forgiven?'

'I didn't say that – I said I got take out from Artesano's.'

She took one of the bags. 'You nuts? You got enough to feed an army.'

He shrugged. 'I can never judge. Didn't know if the girls would be home. Kids can have big appetites.'

'Girls are at their cousins'.'

'Hmm.'

She peered in the bag. 'What's in there?'

'I got beef stew, shrimp with yellow rice and fried plantains. I got shrimp in red sauce. I got sides of sweet potatoes and sweet bananas and French fries. I got desserts ... I got Cokes ...'

'Enough.' She folded her arms and stood aside for him to come into the flat.

He stood in her front room, waiting for her to get plates and cutlery, looking around him, taking in the shabbiness of the decor, the beaten-up furniture. There was no man around, that was for sure. She was getting by, but there was nothing left over for luxuries like paintwork or new sofas.

She came back into the room, put the plates down on the table, and for a moment they concentrated on removing the lids and doling out the food. When they were sitting down with full plates and she had taken a couple of mouthfuls, she said, 'I can't remember the last time I had take-out.'

'You can keep what's left over for the kids.'

She didn't say anything in response. She wasn't going to say thank you, not after how he had behaved. Not even if he'd bought the whole take-out menu to her door.

'Why you here, Albi?'

So he told her.

'You sure?' she said, when he had finished. 'Pereira seems like a pretty typical Madison Avenue lawyer to me, with a kink for girl on girl action and a typical bimbo for a wife.'

'Anything you can tell us about her?'

'Hey, I haven't said I'm doing anything for you.'

'Fair enough.'

'There's nothing in this for me, is there, Albi? Other than a whole load of trouble.'

Alberto smiled in what he hoped was an ironic way. 'Well, Rory, you get to do the right thing.'

She laughed. 'I spent my whole life doing the right thing.' She gestured at the run-down room. 'Where'd that get me? You want to offer me something else?'

Alberto reached over and scooped some more shrimp onto his rice. Aurora's eyes flickered from the piled-high plate to his stomach to his face.

'Maria let you eat like that?'

'You becoming my dietician, Rory, or what?'

'Someone needs to. Look at the size of you?'

'Jesus, you can put a man off his food, you know that?' He put the plate back on the table and pushed it a little away from him. He grabbed a napkin and wiped his mouth, then picked up his Coke. 'I'm sorry, Rory, I know I should have visited more often.'

'You got that right. You're only ten years too late with that statement.'

'I meant to.'

'Why didn't you?'

He decided to tell her the truth. 'I felt real bad about what happened.'

'And so you make it even worse by not visiting?'

'You remember Isabella Gonzales?'

'Sure – same thing happened to her as happened to me but the year before.'

He nodded. 'Well, you know I did my duty by her, visited, stayed in touch.'

'This isn't making me feel any better.'

'Well, I ended up getting a little too close to her and Maria found out.'

Aurora shook her head in disgust. 'Why're you fucking men so fucking obvious?'

'Anyway, when Maria found out she wasn't happy about me visiting the recently bereaved.'

'I wasn't the "recently bereaved". I was Rory, I was Juan Lopez Famosa's wife with two baby daughters.'

'Not to her you weren't. She wasn't having it. You know what men are like, they want an easy life.'

'She could have come with you, Albi. Ever think of that?'

He shook his head. 'I'm telling you she wouldn't have it. Our marriage wasn't in a good place. We were rowing all the time.'

'You're still a piece of shit.'

'I know – I'm not saying I'm not. I'm just saying that's the way it was, that's the way she was. I didn't behave well and I'm sorry.'

'You could have stood up to her.'

He shrugged. 'Sure. You know I've thought about you over the years.'

'Another desperate widow you missed out on?'

He shook his head. 'How you were doing – that sorta thing.'

'Thoughts come cheap, Albi.'

'I'm sorry, Rory, I am. I should have done better.'

'Even that weasel Ricco came sniffing round.'

'Did he?' Alberto appeared startled. 'He never said anything to me.'

'Why would he?'

Alberto placed an empty bottle of Coke down carefully on the coffee table in front of him and leant forwards, elbows on knees. 'You going to help us?'

'I'm not doing anything dangerous.'

'All we want is for you to keep your eyes open.'

'Don't forget, I know how these things work, Albi. First it's keep your eyes open, then it's take a look at his papers or his phone or the computer. Anyway, they're not there much. It's either the Hamptons or St Barts. They're not usually at the apartment when I'm there.'

'Well, I'll tell the boss I tried.'

Aurora rubbed the end of her nose. 'He's really particular about his fish tank.'

'What do you mean?'

'It's huge. It takes up one whole end of the lounge.'

'So?'

'He's really nervy about it. Right from the start he said I wasn't to go near it. Don't bother about it. Leave it completely alone.'

'Maybe he just loves his fish.'

'Maybe.'

'Tank got fish in it?'

'Sure it has, a whole load of Nemos. The weird thing is it's on wheels, the whole tank's on one of those trolleys, you know that you get in hospitals. It's weird. They're so particular about that apartment, but the fish tank just doesn't fit.'

'Anything else?'

'Just because I'm telling you doesn't mean I'm in.'

'Sure, I know that.'

He waited.

'She's scared of him. Few times I've seen them together she looks like a rabbit in the headlights.'

He nodded, waiting.

'And there's a painting on the wall. It's really old. When I first came, that was the other thing I was told not to touch. He's really particular about the fish tank and that painting.'

'Can you tell me about the painting?'

'It's Saint Sebastian.'

Seeing his blank face, she said, 'Young man tied up and pierced with arrows.' She paused. 'It's a beautiful painting, Albi, really beautiful.'

It was the first time he'd seen any softness in her face.

'It's the most . . .'

'Is it signed?'

'I don't know. There's some writing at the bottom but it doesn't mean anything to me.'

Alberto took a notebook out of his pocket and wrote something down.

'Those two things right from the off I was warned about. That's all I can tell you. I need to worry about this guy, Albi?'

He held his hand out flat and moved it slightly from side to side in a gesture of equivocation.

'That's a real help,' she retorted.

'Truth is we just don't know yet.' He looked down at his notebook. 'How big's this thing?'

'The tank?'

'No, the painting.'

She traced a rectangular shape in the air.

'What's that, a foot by a couple of feet?'

'Yeah, I'd say so.'

'Could you sketch it for me?'

She grabbed a piece of paper and a felt tip and a few minutes later handed it to him.

'Only two arrows?'

She nodded.

'And in that position?'

'Yeah.'

'What's all this?' he asked, indicating a whole load of swirls to the left of the saint.

'Clouds, Albi. Dark, threatening clouds.'

He glanced at her and then looked away. 'I'll show this to someone. Usually they like them small.'

She gave him a quizzical look.

'If it's stolen, it would be the right kind of size. Small paintings are easier to steal. Once the *Mona Lisa* was taken off the wall of the Louvre and tucked under someone's coat. I'm going to check this painting. Since the security in the banks got better and the laws on laundering money came in, some of the serious criminals are concentrating on art theft. Paintings are easy to steal and worth a fortune. They steal them and use them as collateral in drug deals. Then a couple of years later, after the insurance has paid out, they offer them back for the reward money.'

'Reward money? That'll be the day.'

He nodded. 'I'll check this out. If it leads to something, I'll let you know.'

'Or you'll take the money yourself.'

'Come on, Rory, you got to have some trust in someone.'

'And that someone would be you, would it? The only person I got any trust in is myself, Albi, and the girls. That's it.'

She picked up some of the take-out containers and took them into the kitchen. Alberto followed suit. He looked at some photos of the children on the fridge.

'This Constanza?'

She shook her head. 'Juaneta.'

'She takes after him, doesn't she?'

'You think?'

He looked closer and nodded. 'Really like.'

Suddenly she felt exhausted to the point of tears. She wouldn't let him see her like that. 'You need to go now, Albi.'

In the doorway, he turned. 'I'll check out the painting. If anything happens, you got my card.'

She nodded. 'Yeah, I got your card.'

She closed the door behind her and leant heavily against it, closing her eyes. On the other side, Alberto stood for a moment, eyes cast down, before slowly making his way to his car.

He hadn't told her Maria died of breast cancer eighteen months ago.

He hadn't told her his children were living with his mother because he'd started drinking.

He hadn't told her he took it one day at a time now, trying to rebuild trust with his kids.

He hadn't told her any of that.

He sat in his car thinking of all the things he hadn't told her. Wondering what might happen if he did. None of that had happened to her when she lost Juan. She'd just got on with it, working hard, raising her kids. He'd fallen to pieces. She'd been stronger than him, better than him. Women usually were.

He remembered Aurora back in the day. His first kiss, ever, with anyone, had been with her. It was the kind of thing that stayed with a man. How could it not? Your first kiss!

And then he felt an overwhelming longing to kiss her again.

He phoned his sponsor. 'Remind me why I shouldn't get into a relationship yet,' he said.

'Man, you're, only six months into your recovery. In terms of recovery, you're just a baby. Relationships bring pressures. You won't be able to handle it.'

'Oh, yeah,' he said, gloomily. 'I knew there was some sort of reason.'

He ended the call. It was beginning to rain hard. As the rain hit the windscreen, the street lights melted and bloomed, melted and bloomed.

TULLIA BUFFO

Venice, 1576

I. The Merchant

'And here I will need twenty-four chairs to line the walls of the *portego* and a pinewood dining table and three painted *banche da portego*,' Tullia says.

The merchant, Elias Alfan, trails beside her with a scribe, who is scratching down her requirements. 'Twenty-four? And why the need for benches when you will have so many chairs?'

'Three painted benches,' she repeats. 'Minimum, and of course wall sconces and ...' She looks up to the ceiling from where they will be suspended. '... cesendellos of brass and glass. Here and here and here. You can see for yourself, the place has been stripped bare.'

'Aiyee but, Signora, the cost already is ...' He plucks the parchment from the hands of the boy walking at his side, runs his finger down the list. 'The Flemish paintings on the

114

stairs and the wall hangings alone are a substantial price and we have not even reached the bedroom.'

This is a man whom she cannot offer to pay in kind. If a Jew sleeps with a Christian woman, the sentence is castration. Of course, it does happen from time to time, but it usually involves a great deal of trust or a great deal of lust. She must persuade him in a different manner. A calculated burst of temper may be called for.

They step across the threshold of the door into the bedroom. 'As you see, the only thing they left were the four posts of the bed because it could not be swiftly dismantled.'

He bends over and admires the walnut pillars with the lion feet at their base.

'Obviously here I will need mattresses – six, linen, pillows and draperies to go round the bed in red or green velvet. Red would be preferable. The pillows should be as plump and smooth as a groaning wife's belly. The linen must be immaculately white and soft. On the floor, rugs from Turkey – three by the bed and one over there by the window. The bigger the better. Maybe four would be best.'

'It is too much, Signora.'

Now is her chance. She spins round and points at the boy by his side. 'Get out!' His master jerks his head towards the door and he scurries from the room.

As she talks, she walks swiftly up and down the bedroom. 'Do you take me for a *meretrice* or a *puttana*? Do you? Do you think that I should light a candle in my balcony and spill these breasts from my bodice and spit down on the heads of any scurvy knave that passes beneath me? Do you wish me to open my quiver to every arrow, in every alleyway? Is that what you want? Because if it is, it will take you much longer to get your money back. I am no *meretrice*. I am no *puttana*. Do not mistake me. I am a courtesan. And what this means is that my abode must be a palace and I must be its Cleopatra. This room must be the Paradise of Venus. Everything in here, from the rich colours and patterned surfaces – the textiles, animal skins, woods, metals or stones – must seduce either by sight or touch. As must I. My hair must be like spun gold, my skin like milk, white and flawless. The quality of my clothes, my jewels, my scent, everything. Do you understand? There is no short-cut and I do not come cut-price. When I say I must have these things, I mean I must have them to be able to be who I must be. This apartment should be capable of welcoming a king, as I am surely capable of bedding him.'

Alfan looks startled. Naturally, he has heard of her. There was a time when every man in Venice had heard of her, but he wonders if she isn't a little past her prime. The plague has aged them all, courtesans included. He considers that what he is looking at is a parrot without its plumage. What he is looking at is a woman come to do business not a courtesan come to seduce her client. And of course it was commonly known that one could more easily compute the number of glow worms of ten summers than the years of a whore.

She has observed exactly how he is looking at her. She knows. She smiles. She holds out her arms, as she does a little pirouette, so that he may assess the credit risk he is taking. So that he may weigh her flesh with his eye. It is unfortunate she is unable to offer herself in payment. She rather likes the look of him. What he must weigh up in his wise old eyes is her desirability to other men. He is calculating what a man would be willing to pay out to bed her. It is a sensitive calculation. An abacus will not help.

He sees that her skin is clear, her eyes sparkle, her hair has lustre. He sees her tiny waist beneath the swelling breasts. He notes the sensuality of her mouth and the violet colour of her eyes, the elegant curve of her neck. He inhales her scent. He remembers the rumours. There is always the risk of the

French disease, but there are no signs of illness. He sighs, calculates, weighs her in the balance, and contemplates an interest rate. A high one.

'And so,' she says, coquettishly. 'May we continue?'

He nods.

'Good. I will need two painted *casse* – one for my clothes and one for the linen. A lute, preferably thirteen-stringed, and a spinet, and then of course books – Petrarch, Dante, Ovid, Boccaccio's *Decameron*, Plato and some Cicero wouldn't go amiss.'

'Why books, Signora?' He quickly ducks his head as if to ward off another verbal onslaught. 'If I may ask?'

'Seduction is not simply a matter of the body, sir, as I'm sure you are well aware. A woman such as myself must seduce first a man's eyes, then his mind, and finally his ears. The mind plays a crucial part.'

He shrugs. 'But Plato . . .?'

She leans over and whispers in his ear. 'To a certain kind of man, Plato can be very sexy.'

He laughs. 'I'll take your word for it, Signora.'

'And then everything for my kitchen. The cutlery must be silver and carry a coat of arms. It doesn't matter whose, but it would be good if you could let me know the name.'

They exchange a smile. Every courtesan in the city claims to be the bastard child of some noble. When they are finished, he presents her with a piece of paper. 'These are my terms, Signora.'

She reads, nods, signs. The terms are steep, but she is not in a situation to bargain. She needs what he has.

'When can everything be delivered?'

'Will this afternoon be satisfactory?'

She nods. 'I will be good for the debt. You will not regret it.'

'Do you see the slope of my shoulders, Signora? Regret is

117

something that a man cannot escape in this life. All one can do is weigh the risk and decide.'

She nods in agreement. 'It is all any of us can do.'

When he has gone, she considers the things that he cannot supply, the painting of her naked from the waist up, both breasts offered to the viewer. It had come with a black velvet curtain to cover it. Drawing aside the curtain and presenting herself to her clients in this way never failed to stimulate their interest, as did the subtle pressure of her hand. There were other more intricate etchings as well in metal frames, a man tied up in a cage, another bent over being whipped, men with men, women with women, the act of fornication presented in all its glorious variety. Such things could not be bought from the ghetto just like that, such things had to be carefully sought after, enquired into, hunted down, kept secret, revealed on the right occasion and then covered over again. She sighs and wonders who has those sketches now, wonders idly if they are enjoying them.

II. The Painter

She needs another painting, so she asks around. Who is alive? Who was talented? She finds a young man, Antonio Vassilacchi, who is being trained by Veronese and she invites him to visit her. She describes to him in some detail the portrait she wishes to have painted. He is young, very sure of himself, but his prices seem rather high.

'The painting will be covered with a curtain. It will hang on the wall near the entrance to my bedroom. Do you understand?'

He nods.

'Now then, the painting must capture the softness of my curls. My flesh should be skilfully rendered to look like snow, tinted with vermillion. It must seem animated by living pulses and warmed by the spirit of life. The lynx fur ...'

'Signora, I would not dream of telling you how to do your job, yet you insist on telling me mine.'

She clears her throat. 'You are young and rather expensive, it seems to me, and you have not yet learnt the charm which is necessary in your profession. I am paying, so it would be worth your while to pay me some attention. You understand that if the painting is successful it will be seen by rich and influential men of many nationalities. It may well lead to other commissions. Now then, perhaps you could do something on the price or perhaps you could accept payment by some other method.'

He blinks, demurs. He seems a rather prickly, prudish young man. She is not altogether happy with him, but he has come highly recommended. Perhaps he can with paint what he cannot do with his own personality. She decides that she will give him a chance and perhaps, if she deems it necessary, an erotic education.

III. The First Sitting
She comes out from behind the screen wearing nothing under the man's lynx fur-lined coat. The coat hangs open, her breasts exposed. There is an intense silence in the room, followed by the clatter of Vassilacchi's brush hitting the floor. Well, this won't do, this won't do at all. They would get nowhere if he cannot even hold his brushes in her presence. She walks over to him, bends down and picks up the brush and puts it to one side. She takes his hand and places it on her naked breast, takes him behind the screen, lies down inside her fur-lined coat and draws him to her. She unbuttons his breeches and takes him in her mouth, then guides him inside her. 'Push into me, push into me up to the hilt,' she whispers. 'Now withdraw just a little. Wait.' She takes his face in her hands and pulls him close. 'Now push back in. Slowly, slowly, all the way and look in my eyes. Look in my face. Do you see

my eyes, greedy for you, my lips offered to you, my nipples hardening for you . . .'

'So,' she says a little later, 'this is how I want you to paint me. Filled to the hilt with you, dark-eyed with desire for you, swollen with pleasure. Do you understand now?'

His voice seems a little hoarse. 'I do.'

The painting progresses very well after this. Before each session she adopts the same approach. It relaxes him at least and he stops dropping his brushes. 'Do you understand?' she says each time. And by the time the painting is completed it could safely be said he understood perfectly. The finished painting pleased her very well. In truth it slightly shocked her. He had succeeded in painting her in a state of arousal as she had demanded. The quality of the painting of the fur was also very good. One breast was visible under a film of gauzy white material, the nipple hardened against the fabric. Her right hand held one side of the coat in an ambiguous manner. Was she opening the coat to reveal more or closing it to cover herself? The uncertainty of the gesture created a mystery and increased the eroticism of the painting.

'Clever boy,' she says. She peers at her painted eyes. 'But there is no blue in them. Are they really that dark?'

'When you lie beneath me, Signora, and I am swelling inside you, there is no light in them, they are as black as the abyss.'

'How sweet,' she says, stroking his cheek with one hand, another part of him with the other.

'So you are pleased with it?'

'Oh, it will do,' she says airily, conscious of not wanting to be too enthusiastic in case it makes the price rise. In truth, she is very pleased indeed. It is fit to be placed behind a black velvet curtain. It is fit to be revealed to clients.

Her hand is working inside his breeches; one finger probed

between his buttocks pushed its way into him. His legs were beginning to buckle.

'Now then,' she whispers in his ear, 'perhaps you might see your way to doing something on the price.'

'Oh . . .

oh . . .

oh . . .' is his reply.

As to the question of the price?

A little later. . . it falls.

IV. The Lynx-Lined Coat

A week later and the house is finally ready.

The spiders and cobwebs have been swept from the stairs, the sconces have been fitted and the cesendellos suspended from the ceiling. Leather and gilt wall hangings are attached, as are paintings. Her portrait, curtained in black velvet, hangs by the door of her bedroom and the twenty-four chairs, plus the three benches, are all in place. The two painted *casse* are filled with the most exquisite fabrics and bed linen. Lavender has been sprinkled on the damask sheets.

That evening, alone in her bedroom, she puts on the lynx-lined cloak. The soft fur caresses her body. She stands in front of the mirror naked. The Paradise of Venus is now ready, but what about Venus herself? She drops the coat and moves back and forth in front of the mirror, imagining herself moving in front of her paramour. There is absolutely no point in preparing paradise unless there is a Venus to fill it.

She is not too unhappy with what she sees. She will do. A courtesan, her mother said, must appear to have arisen from the flames of desire like a phoenix. A courtesan must appear to have no past and no future. It is only the present which enchants her, the man in front of her, the man paying. What you must aim for is a powerful patron, a man who will pay well and yet not restrict your other dalliances. Such men are not easy to find.

When she had first met Domenico Venier, she had certainly not thought that he would be that man. Pity had been her overwhelming emotion. Confined to a wheelchair, crippled and swollen with gout, it had been his intelligence and his humour which had attracted her. When enquiries had been made as to whether she might visit him at home, she had readily agreed. He was a poet, patrician and publisher, a man of influence. The special services that he required had been delivered with such delicacy and sensitivity for his condition that she had quickly become his favourite. Afterwards he would talk to her about poetry, recommend her reading and lend her books. He had links to the many printers who were established in the city and published his own poems and those of his literary circle. He gave them to her to read and asked her what she thought of them. She was enchanted to be asked. Yes, of course he wanted her for sex, but he paid her not just in money but in poetry, in education, in books.

He had no children of his own and maybe this was why he took her to his heart in this way. And this was how she came to read Petrarch, Dante, Ovid, Boccaccio, Plato. He talked to her about poetic forms, he encouraged her to write. He took her writing seriously. He listened to her poetry. And this was how his nephews came to hate her. After all, there was only so much patronage to go round. Money and time spent with a courtesan was money and time not spent furthering their interests and careers. But what they hated most was the fact that he gave her a voice. He not only rated her poetry but most outrageous of all he published it!

Later, she goes out onto her balcony. Today there is proof of the return of the population to the city. An infinite multitude of boats sprawled across the Grand Canal. Two gondolas are racing each other, their excitement matched by the throng of spectators crowding the Rialto Bridge, the fish markets and the Santa Sofia ferry landing. Excitement and spectacle fill the air; slowly joy is returning to the city.

She raises her eyes to the sky. It had never seemed so beautiful, with its subtle pattern of light and shade. Some clouds seemed to touch the very roofs of the houses, others receded into the distance. On the right, others are like a poised mass of grey-black smoke. The variety of colours is extraordinary. Those near at hand burned with the flames of the sun's fire, while those in the distance had the dull glow of half-molten lead. In the distance, the sky is, in certain places, green-blue. It is a sky that deserves to be painted by a master.

As she looks at the beauty of the sky, she vows that she will never leave the city again. All that had befallen her had occurred because she had left. It was her punishment for losing faith in the city. Her city. *Terra firma* was not for her. Never again, whatever the risk, whatever the temptation. She thinks of Titian. Perhaps he had had a hand in this extraordinary spectacle. Perhaps he was up there painting the skies, demonstrating his powers to God.

That night she cannot sleep. She is trying to compose a bucolic verse describing the beauty of the villa she had stayed in at Fumane. She thinks it will be good for her to recall the languid delights of the place, especially when the realities of her own life are now so at odds with that time:

'There with their amphorae never empty or listless, the nymphs swiftly carry water so that not even a piece of crystal . . .'

BANG! go the shutters.

She returns to the parchment. Now then, what was she doing with the wretched nymphs? '. . . so that not even a piece of crystal could be so clear . . .'

BANG! go the shutters again.

Oh, damn Apollo! Damn Daphne! Damn the bloody nymphs! Damn her lazy maid who had not closed the shutters properly! She throws the parchment to one side and gets out of bed. But the shutters are not open; something is on the balcony and wants to get in. She opens them and a blur rushes into the room at foot level. She looks round and is greeted by a savage yowl.

'Dante!' Her savage beauty, her old survivor, her tiger cat.

Her old cat looks much as he always has, ragged, one eared, with half a tail. He yowls again in a way that seems to convey, 'Where have you been? For heaven's sake, where have you been?' She bends down and he shakes his head as her tears drip on his ears. He rubs his broken teeth against her toes.

'Welcome home,' she says softly. 'Welcome home.'

Dante walks over to where the parchment lies on the floor next to the bed and pushes it across the floor with his paw, stops and then pushes it some more. When she bends down to pick it up, he lashes out and scythes it down the middle. She doesn't care. The critic has spoken. Anyway, she doubts that she'd ever get the bloody nymphs to the end of the wretched verse. What matters is that her old Dante is back. Her savage old beauty has come home to her. It is the best thing that has happened since she returned. As for the poem, it will have to wait; she has a note to write. She dips her quill in ink, thinks for a moment then writes: *I am ready now. Come to me for comfort or for what you will. I will welcome you most sweetly.*

She folds it and seals it and writes the landlord's name on it. Her maid will deliver it in the morning. Before she falls asleep, she sees the pale, pale blue of his eyes blinking at her through a veil of tears and wonders if he will come.

V. Marco Martinengo

Two days later and he is there. He still looks dreadful. His eyes are red-rimmed and the skin beneath them black and pitted, but she sees that rather sweetly he has tried to tidy up his hair and beard; they are less wild than before. Suddenly she is aware of the man he once was before grief broke him; tall and slender, with broad shoulders and dark good looks. He stands in the doorway blinking. She ushers him in, but he can barely hold her eye. She offers him wine and sweetmeats and she chats to him about this and that, a little light gossip, a little bit of scandal. She tries to put him at ease. When she puts her arm in his, when she runs her hand down the inside of his arm and takes his hand in hers, he shudders. When he picks up the pewter goblet and lifts it to his mouth, his hand shakes so much wine spills onto the wooden floorboards.

She takes the goblet from him and returns it to the table. 'Will you place yourself in my hands?' she murmurs. 'I promise I will hold you most carefully. I will not spill a drop.'

His eyes dart onto hers and away again. 'I have never . . . my wife was all I . . .'

'Trust me,' she says.

He still seems uncertain, but she takes him by the hand and leads him to the bed. She kneels and takes off his shoes; she helps him off with his doublet. She must leave him some covering or he will feel too exposed. She takes off her dress and slides into bed. She holds out her hand to him and takes him in her arms. For a moment she thinks it will not work. He lies next to her as stiff as a plank of wood in the Arsenale, waiting to be knocked into the side of a ship.

'All the tears in you,' she says. 'All the grief. You can let all the tears fall now in my arms. I will not spill a drop.'

He gives a stifled cry and pulls away from her, sitting on the side of the bed with his back to her. She strokes his back and murmurs. 'There,' she says. 'There, there . . .' Her hand rests on the back of his neck.

One of his hands covers hers; it is ice cold and damp. The

fingers are long and elegant but the nails are bitten down to bloody stumps. It is the first move he has made to touch her. She draws him back to her and holds him in her arms and then quite suddenly with a gasp and a heave of his chest the dam breaks, his body convulses. Later he sleeps the sleep of the dead. He clings to her like a drowning man clinging to a rock. She sings to him, lullabies from her childhood, and strokes his head. She does not move. A rock does not move. She lies there holding him, soothing him, keeping him safe in the storm.

When he wakes, she removes more of their clothes and caresses him into life. When he enters her, he is suddenly very present with her, in the caress of his hand and the touch of his lips. He is unusual in that he looks for and waits for her pleasure and when he feels it quicken he follows its rhythm. When he comes, she does not have to pretend; unusually the pleasure is hers as well. And afterwards he holds her face and looks into her eyes. The blue is no longer watery, instead it is a vivid sky blue, intense and blazing with life and full of questions.

But these are not questions a courtesan can answer, so now it is her turn to look away. It is her back that he sees as she sits on the edge of the bed, as she pulls on the lynx fur gown, as she covers herself, as she withdraws from him into a safer place. This could become complicated, she thinks, this could become very complicated indeed.

ANDREA

London, 2011

Every city in the world smells different on the threshold of a new day. Andrea, leaning on the parapet of the Embankment, inhaled a London dawn and wondered what it might deliver him. Dawn and dusk, liminal spaces, were often the best times in which to hatch poems. There was a faint chemical smell in the air. It was misty this morning and the city lay under a thick duvet of grey cloud. Across the river only the perpendicular part of the red cranes could be seen, the arms hadn't emerged from the mist yet, only the lights on them were visible, rendered large and blurry. Andrea had read somewhere that you could tell the health of a country's economy by the number of cranes you could count in its capital city. Looking at the mass of cranes criss-crossing the London skyline, he considered that this was not a city totally on its knees, whatever the talk of recession.

The river, he thought, was charmless: too big, too brown,

too obsolete. In a city this crowded, why on earth didn't they use it as a source of transport? Then at least it would have some use; it would get back its pride and dignity. All it had was its ebb and flow, and of course the dubious pleasure of transporting tourists between the two Tates, but there was no dignity in that. The tide was going out, and down on the riverbed a lone man swung his metal detector back and forth, back and forth, in front of him. Andrea felt a strong sense of affinity with him but he suspected no treasure or poem was going to poke its head out of this drab morning. Never mind, he knew that all he could do was be ready and place himself where they might emerge. It was like waiting for owls to fly by: there were never, ever any guarantees. That was part of the joy of seeing them; those moments of grace couldn't be forced or guaranteed.

And so, pondering on moments of grace, on charmless rivers, on the beautiful semaphore of cranes, Andrea walked along the Embankment to Hungerford Bridge in search of Illy coffee, in search of a cup of coffee that could look the sun in the eye without blinking. And where could he find those things? Soho, of course

He'd been here in the fifties. He'd come over to work in a restaurant run by one of his cousins, Luigi. Italian businesses had not had a good time of it during the war. Many of the owners had been locked up as enemy aliens. But once hostilities had ceased there was a gradual return and once his cousin was re-established Andrea had come over to learn English. That was when Soho was just beginning to throw off its post-war austerity, when it was filled with pimps, prostitutes and gangsters, when it was a fertile ground for artists and writers and musicians, for people of every type. He remembered his cousin paying large sums of money to a square man in a pin-striped suit with a zigzag nose. His cousin came from Naples and was used to such things; there you had to pay everyone for everything. It was just the way it was.

Andrea hadn't lasted long. He'd managed one spring and summer and autumn, but the smogs of winter had done for him. He had bad asthma – it was one of the things that had kept him out of the army during the war – and once winter arrived he found he could barely breathe, let alone work, and had had to return home. At the time he had been profoundly disappointed. For the first time in his life, he had experienced a tribal sense of belonging and it had had nothing to do with being part of the large Italian community in Soho. It had had to do with being an outsider in a district of outsiders, albeit a district in the very centre of town. There was something in those people he liked and recognised in himself: the daring to be different, to be outside the mainstream of life; the daring to play by a different set of rules altogether. Artists and criminals shared that sensibility; the rejection of the conventional.

And what did Andrea see now, walking up Charing Cross Road towards Cambridge Circus? First a homeless man lying on cardboard boxes in the fire exit of a theatre showing *Singin' in the Rain*, next a puddle of vomit. The acrid smell of piss assaulted his nostrils as he turned into Old Compton Street. Well, the piss and the vomit were familiar enough. A cafe which had had its original 1950s fittings was no longer there. In the past he would have gone in there to talk to the owner, Lorenzo, about the old days. Now its Formica tables, red cosy booths, signed black and white photos and raspberry pink coffee machine were long gone. But when had landlords cared anything about the preservation of history? All they ever wanted was more money. No one was about. It was just him and the street cleaners on this murky, dirty London morning, and his memories. He'd been there when Gina Lollobrigida had opened the Moka Bar in 1953, which was the first coffee house to install a Gaggia espresso machine, a burbling, wheezing spluttering monster. But he knew also that his memory was selective, romanticising the past. There was plenty of piss and vomit in Soho in his day. He did his fair share of sluicing it into the gutters. It wasn't just Diana Dors and Gina L. It never was, was it? There was always everything else as well.

The stuff he wanted to forget, the stones in his soup.

Reality.

His lungs.

The London smog.

A difficult conversation he had to have with his son before he left.

He entered Bar Italia. They were just opening and he asked the young man where he might get a *La Repubblica* at this time in the morning. He pointed down the street to where a white van was disgorging papers from practically every country in the world onto the pavement in front of a news-agent. He bought himself *La Repubblica* and *The Guardian* and went back to the cafe, falling into an easy conversation with the young man serving him, Angelo, about home, about his son. Yes, he showed off a little about Ludovico. Just a little – an old man's pride. Then they talked about London, the London he knew, the Moka Bar and the London this young man worked in.

'Oh, there are crooks here too,' Angelo said.

'Yes, but not like the old days,' Andrea said. 'Not like then.'

The young man smiled. 'No, nowadays the crooks are in the banks,' he said, as he placed the espresso down at his table. 'They are the biggest thieves in the world and have got away scot free and we are all paying for their crimes.'

Andrea smiled but felt a little dispirited. He didn't like such cynicism in the young. Had he been that cynical at his age? Yes, of course he had! When he was this man's age, his country was defeated, in post-war poverty. His country had been on the wrong side of history. He remembered he had been pretty cynical about that, about leaders in general, about his country that had put a man like Mussolini into power.

He stayed in the cafe for some time, enjoying watching it fill up, enjoying overhearing the conversations, imagining himself back in his twenties, the careless chat, the welcoming of customers, the light-hearted banter, the talk of football, the flirtations. At that age he hadn't been sure about his poetic vocation, or perhaps he had been but hadn't known what to do about it. He remembered himself carefree in a way he never was again. He shook open the paper. He was never this nostalgic in his poetry. There he allowed himself very little nostalgia or sentimentality; there he was rigorous, brutal, one could say, in his pursuit of the truth. He would never dream of writing a poem about this, about an old man revisiting the places of his youth, through rose-tinted spectacles. What a cliché! But even as he thought that, he felt something catch in his imagination, like a bur caught in the coat of an old dog. Ah. Yes, he thought, I'll scratch away at that for a while and between the knot and the itch something might come of it. Maybe a year down the line, when it had lain dormant in a drawer for a while. If he was still alive. He took out his pen and notebook and scribbled down a few words here, a few lines there. When he next looked up, Angelo was standing, looking down at him, smiling, and Andrea was aware that he'd said something that he hadn't heard.

'I'm sorry,' he said. 'I was in another world.'

Angelo picked up his cup. 'Can I get you something else?' he asked.

And suddenly Andrea remembered. 'No,' he said. 'I have an appointment with a painting.'

'A painter?'

'Well, maybe, but no, what I said was a painting. A painting which has started speaking.'

The young man took his empty cup and headed back behind the counter.

Andrea picked up his papers and headed for the door. 'You'll see.' He called over his shoulder. 'When you reach my age, such things will no longer surprise you.'

'Who said I was surprised?' Angelo said. 'This is the twenty-first century. This is London. Anything can happen.'

'You know when I worked in Soho in the fifties they would ring the football results through to the bar and they would be shouted out into the street. Then we would all celebrate or drown our sorrows.'

A couple of minutes later when he was wiping the table, the young man came across a piece of paper tucked under the sugar bowl. 'For Angelo' it stated 'a man who can make a cup of coffee which can look the sun in the eye without blinking.' He turned round and walked out of the bar into the street, but the elderly man was nowhere to be found. He had disappeared like a sprite. Angelo read it again, smiled and placed the note carefully in his wallet. It was not every day he had such poetic customers. The day had begun well.

The sun was out now, blazing down, creating white lightning flashes on the wet pavement, as Andrea walked down the Charing Cross Road. For a moment he stopped dead, feeling transfigured by light from above and below. He crossed over to be on the side of the second-hand bookshops and couldn't resist a quick browse, which yielded a copy of Aldous Huxley's *Chrome Yellow* for £2.50. A bargain! He continued down the street into Trafalgar Square, but unlike Terry a few days ago it did not disappoint him. He enjoyed walking round the big black lions, admiring their massive paws, their heavy grand heads. Oh, to go through life like a lion, he thought. Wouldn't that be something?

In the National Gallery, he was a little befuddled by the large groups of tourists which thronged the main hall, but once in the rooms with the paintings he felt more relaxed. A man was giving a talk to a group of school children in front of *The Ambassadors*. He was funny, effortlessly engaging, a great performer and born communicator. He even managed to squeeze in a reference to Copernicus because some of the children were Polish. Andrea was entranced. At the end he went up to him and said, 'I have taught for over twenty years and in you I recognise a true teacher.'

The man seemed dumbfounded, then smiled broadly and thanked him. 'This is easy,' he said. 'I am not in front of a class every day. I perform and then I hand them back to their teachers.'

'You had them and me in the palm of your hand,' Andrea said. 'Could you tell me where the Titians are?'

The man nodded. 'I'll take you there. This way. Why Titian?' he asked.

'Because he is a fellow inhabitant of the Veneto,' Andrea said.

'We also have Canalettos.'

'Canalettos are for chocolate-box lids and jigsaws,' Andrea scoffed.

The man laughed. 'Here we are.'

'There is another reason I have come to see the Titians. I am told that the painting of *The Man with the Blue Sleeve* has been speaking.'

Seeing the man looking at him a little anxiously, he sought to reassure him. 'Don't worry, I'm a poet and such imaginings take my fancy.'

The man smiled. 'What did it say?'

'That there are worse things than loneliness.'

'Ah well, true, I dare say . . .'

'And that there is a difference between looking and seeing.'

They stood in front of the painting. The man folded his arms and looked at it intently.

'You know that there was once the idea that it was a self-portrait.'

'Really? A Barbarigo, I thought.'

'Yes, now that is the thinking, but the *idea* of it being a self-portrait has never quite gone away.'

Andrea leant into the painting. 'If it were a self-portrait, he would be looking at himself in the most unforgiving manner.'

'Yes,' the man said. 'Like all the best painters, he would view himself with the same pitiless gaze he casts on others.' After a while the man said, 'Can you hear anything?'

'Not a thing,' Andrea replied. 'But perhaps I will try talking to him in the Veneto dialect.'

'You know, I have heard of people being so sensitive to Titian's art that they can hear sounds in his paintings. The noise of leaves rustling in the wind, the sound of music playing, the voices of his protagonists.'

'Really? Do they ever talk to you?' Andrea asked.

The man looked down at the floor. 'On occasion, but I have to say that usually rather a heavy lunch is involved and afterwards I can never remember what they've said.'

Andrea didn't quite understand. 'Heavy?'

The man tipped an invisible glass towards his mouth.

Andrea laughed and nodded, turned back to the painting. Now then, was there anybody there, reaching out across time to talk to him?

Silence

Not a word

It made more sense to Andrea that it was a Barbarigo. This man was arrogant, powerful, clear of his position in society and a little disdainful of the man painting him. At the point this was painted Titian was about twenty years old.

Perhaps it wasn't at that time so clear that he was the genius he would later be deemed to be. This man looked as if he was condescending to have his portrait painted. This man was in charge. He did not look kind, Andrea thought. The face was too worldly, too sardonic. In fact, the more he looked at him, the less he liked him. No, he thought, this man wasn't going to talk to him. No way. And he, Andrea, wasn't going to talk to him.

Andrea wandered through some other rooms in the gallery. A child in a yellow dress threw herself at her mother's feet in a tantrum, a security officer looked down at her and yawned; a group of Americans with no chins dropped a heavy door in his face; art students peered intently at paintings and tried to reproduce them in their sketch books. A group of Spanish teenagers trooped through the gallery, chattering like starlings, more fascinated by what they saw on their mobile phones than in the extraordinary art looking down at them from the walls.

Eventually Andrea ended up on the ground floor in the espresso bar. The area was scattered with black leather-covered square seats, some of which were positioned in front of computer screens. They were presumably intended for school children not the elderly. The cappuccino he ordered was a milky slop that the chinless Americans would certainly have liked. The only place for him to sit, where he could rest his back, was in front of one of these screens, where a column was positioned behind one of the squidgy squares.

He sat down, leant back and closed his eyes, but when he opened them there was the screen inviting him to touch it. So he did. He brought up Titian and his paintings, and there he was back again staring at *The Man with the Blue Sleeve*. Then, because he could, he zoomed in on his eye and then he sat back and looked at it intently. The upper and lower lids were pink and swollen, the corner of his eye, where it met the side of the nose, was black and pitted. This man looked knackered. This man, Andrea thought, could do with a column to rest his back against. This man had had a night of it. Andrea leant back and closed his eyes. The enlarged and slightly inflamed eye of *The Man with the Blue Sleeve* stared back at him.

Suppose I could speak

Suppose I could speak of all the people who have stood in front of me over the years. Starting with the painter, of course. Imagine how many people stand in front of me in a day, a year, a decade. Imagine how many people have looked at me over the span of 500 years. Imagine if I were to speak of those I have seen. So I look impatient, sardonic, exhausted. Is it any wonder? At this moment, the moment I was being painted, let us be clear who needed who most. The painter needed the patron and the patron knew it. Titian will go on to have emperors and kings as patrons, but now he is a young man starting out and the reason I am looking at him with this expression on my face is because I know a deal is being done. I am wealthy and have influence; he is the most recent bright young thing to have come out of the studios of La Serenissima. *But now, 500 years later, no one is exactly certain who I am and yet everyone knows the painter: 500 years later the roles are reversed. And yet it is I, Barbarigo, who still looks out at the world with that weary disdain, with the carefully plucked eyebrow, with the neatly tended beard. I am no longer an advertisement for Titian's precocious talents. Now it does not matter who I am. I have become a masterpiece. A painting that changed portraiture forever. That is all you need to know. Now, go buy my postcard.*

'Excuse me, sir.'

Andrea opened his eyes. An elderly couple stood nearby.

'We were wondering if you'd finished with the screen, if we might ...'

'Oh . . .' He looked at the screen, at the eye, remembering where he was. 'Of course . . .'

He stood up, feeling the upper part of his back protest, and the couple slid onto the seats with charmless speed. They touched the screen and the eye disappeared. He sighed and lingered just long enough to see what painter they would bring up. His worst fears were confirmed – Van Gogh and his wretched sunflowers. How inevitable! In the shop he bought himself a few postcards and then stepped out into a sun-washed Trafalgar Square.

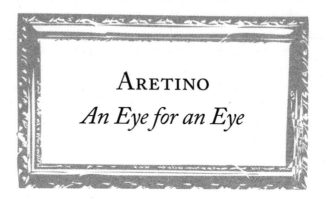

ARETINO
An Eye for an Eye

Venice, 1546

Torches burn on the bridge that links the ghetto to the city. The men guarding the bridge stamp their feet. It is bitterly cold and they long for a fire to warm their frozen limbs. Deep in the heart of the ghetto, men are gambling. The ghetto has some of the tallest buildings in the city. And why is that? Because when men are walled up, where else is there for them to go but up, up into the air above their heads. The air, after all, even in Venice, this most meretricious of cities, is free. But in this room where they gamble there is very little air. Is it hope or despair that has sucked it all out of the place? Men slouch against the walls, watching their masters. Swords have been left at the door; torches cast a flickering light on the ceiling. There is little noise but the casting of cards, the roll of dice. Servants come and go with drinks and sweetmeats. Everyone's attention is focused on four men. True gamblers register little whether they win or lose. It is only amateurs who celebrate rowdily. Not a sound comes out of these men other than the odd grunt, the odd gust of breaking wind, a slurp as they drain some wine from a pewter goblet.

Aretino is winning. He has been winning all night. He does not look particularly happy. His features are strangely impassive, as if moulded from wax. He looks at each card with the blank, indifferent killer eyes of a raptor before keeping, discarding, throwing down. The man sitting opposite him, a young French man, is losing. He has been losing all night and he does not look particularly unhappy. Something gold glitters suddenly on his face, caught by the flames that leap from the torches. Look closely and you will see that there is something odd about his right eye. The game is reaching its conclusion. The final cards are thrown.

The French man sits back and mutters something over his shoulder to one of his companions. Aretino sits back in his chair and smiles. The French man says something else and Aretino understands enough for his eyes to narrow into slits of rage. The men who have been standing around the walls of the room reach for where their swords would be if they hadn't left them outside. They then look urgently towards the door, as if wishing alone might bring the swords flying miraculously through the air and into their outstretched palms. Meanwhile Aretino, never having been one to play by the rules, has taken out a dagger, which he did not leave at the door, and he is feeling its exceptionally sharp point with the first finger of his left hand.

Their host begins to babble. 'The debt must be paid. We are all gentlemen here. Of course the debt will be paid.'

'Of course,' Aretino says. 'Of course. One way or another it will be paid. Tonight.'

Aretino has been all kinds of things in his time: pimp,

pornographer, poet as well as pugilist. He may do most of his threatening and extortion with his quill these days, but there was a time when he stood at the door of a brothel and extracted money from the unwilling, and if they had none, snapped their fingers as a reminder that they should not take what they could not pay for. He is not a man to be trifled with. This milksop with a dribble for a chin, a distant cousin of the French Ambassador, has mistaken him for someone of no consequence. Notwithstanding, Aretino knows that this situation must be handled with a certain superficial delicacy. He must not create a diplomatic incident. The honour and dignity of Venice must be upheld at all costs, otherwise he will be the one to suffer. He will not put his relationship with *La Serenissima* at risk because he loves her with his whole heart; he and the city were made for each other. He understands all too well a city that is filled with whores but worships the Virgin and he cannot imagine thriving anywhere else. He will not go back to Rome, that sewer of corruption. He's burnt his bridges in that city. So he must tread softly.

But he will be paid. One way or another, he will be paid.

He points the dagger straight at the man's face. 'I will accept that,' he says, moving the blade fractionally to the left, 'in full and final payment.'

What does he mean? Is he Salome demanding John the Baptist's head on a plate? But no, he does not mean the *whole* head. The blade of his dagger remains in the air, pointing.

Straight at the man's right eye.

There is a sharp, communal intake of breath and one of the French man's entourage starts to cough and splutter. Their host is babbling again, as if words can ward off violence, but his words are caught up in the coughing like burs in sheep's wool and the louder he speaks the more likely it seems that violence may erupt. The atmosphere in the room is thick with hostility and the other two men who have been sitting at the table, sensing danger, have pushed back their chairs and stood up. Now the only two people left sitting in the room are Aretino and the French man, staring at each other across the table.

'You owe me a substantial sum of money,' Aretino says. 'Either you pay that to me. Now. Or I will accept that in full and final payment. In the circumstances that you find yourself, it is a most generous offer.'

The man's face has flushed bright red; his mouth has formed itself into the shape of a snarl. It's the way a cornered rat looks just before a stick splits its skull. But then suddenly his face relaxes, he laughs and shrugs his shoulders. He drops his head forwards into the palm of his hand and then looks up and tosses something onto the table. It rolls slowly towards Aretino and he scoops it up and bows his head in acknowledgment.

Then he leans across the table and whispers. 'How did you lose it? Did you become so fascinated with the rotten worm between your legs that you bent down too low and it reared up and poked you in the eye?'

The group of young men at his back, the Aretines, catch each other's eye. For a man who no longer likes a physical fight, their master is adept at picking verbal fights that end in violence. Now will come the hard part.

Getting out alive.

Even though Aretino is drunk, the danger he is in sharpens his mind. In his imagination he measures the journey down the steps, across the bridge and into his waiting gondola. It suddenly seems a very long way indeed. So now he takes on an air of deliberate insouciance. He pushes back his chair and rubs his hands down the front of his chest, as if he is the most relaxed man in the world. He thanks his host and, making sure not to turn his back on the French man and his entourage, bows his way backwards towards the door.

Neither he nor his young men take their eyes off the men on the other side of the table. As he passes his host, Aretino whispers to him, 'Keep them inside, so we have time to retrieve our swords and gain some distance on them.'

Once outside the room, his air of insouciance disappears. He and his men grab their swords and move almost as one unit with great speed down the stairs. One of them has gone ahead to make sure the gates of the ghetto are open. They hurry through, across the bridge and out into the cold winter air.

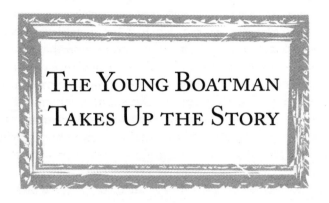

THE YOUNG BOATMAN TAKES UP THE STORY

Venice, 1546

When a gondolier takes his master to the ghetto to gamble, there is no knowing how long he will have to wait for him. I had got used to waiting for my master outside gambling dens and the salons of courtesans. Often he emerged as the mighty shoulders of the sea pushed up the golden head of the sun into a rose-coloured dawn. So that evening I was half-asleep, curled up in the cabin of the gondola, in one of Aretino's old cloaks. He had thrown it to me one day, seeing me shivering in the cold. It was much worn but it was the best cloak I had ever owned in my life, and my chin was thrust deep into the squirrel fur which lined its hood. As soon as I heard the commotion, I roused myself at once and saw a mass of torches moving over the bridge, a rush of bodies and the urgent chatter of voices. The man in the boat next to mine, Francesco, was also now awake.

'Get untied, boy,' he said. 'We're going to have to be quick.'

And then the Aretines were upon us, some jumping across my boat to get to Francesco's, others hurling themselves into mine. Aretino roaring with laughter and, uttering the most obscene of oaths, seemed indifferent to any danger. He was very, very drunk. The cold winter air had not sobered him up; it seemed to have the effect of pouring more tankards of ale down his wide open throat. A couple of his men held him upright and when they had managed to push him onto the cushions in the cabin of the gondola they urged me to get away with the utmost speed. However, my boat was trapped between the *fondamenta* and Francesco's boat, which was tied up against mine.

Now I saw more movement at the gates of the ghetto, more torches and running shadows. The men in my boat began to push the other boat away from us most urgently in order to give us room to get away, but they were too late; the other men fell upon us and soon swords were flashing white in the moonlight. I ducked and felt the air above me shiver as a sword slashed through the air, intending to make my head a stranger to my shoulders. Just when I thought we would certainly be boarded, we floated free.

The young men were breathing heavily and as frisky as a pack of dogs who have just torn a hare to pieces. They did not have blood on their muzzles – yet – but they were mighty pleased with themselves. They slapped each other's backs and relived the fight and laughed and roared. The gondola was overloaded and rocking dangerously. The danger of our situation gave me an unaccustomed authority.

'Stand still or sit down!' I roared. 'Or we will all be in the canal.'

They did calm down, although they teased me about being a young whipper-snapper ordering them what to do.

144

Meanwhile I made sure I kept to the middle of the canal and bent my back to the task of getting my unusually heavy gondola back to Aretino's house. My master meantime lay back on the cushions, his mouth open, snoring like a baby in its crib, utterly unaware of any danger. As a bitter wind blew off the lagoon, we wound our way home through the deserted canals, the air thick with the laughter and excited bellows of the young men and the steady snores of my master. Hard as the task was, it felt good that they were in my care and that I was taking them home to the warmth and safety of their beds.

Despite the bitter cold of the night, by the time we arrived at my master's house I was pouring with sweat and my legs and arms were shaking with the effort of rowing the boat. We had to rouse Aretino's servants and, between them, the young men and his maidservants carried him to bed. He had woken up and began singing more songs, with the bawdiest lyrics. I was seeing to the boat and preparing to make my way home when one of his maids told me my master was asking for me.

I climbed the stairs wearily, my legs still shaking from my exertions, and entered his bedroom, a room I had not been in before. Candlelight cast flickering shadows upon a painting on the ceiling. I stared at it aghast because it showed scenes of violence and punishment; a man's head had been severed from his body. Having almost experienced the same fate recently, my hand rose to my throat as if to confirm the connection. I wondered why on earth anyone would want such images on their bedroom ceiling. They were hardly the images to promote sweet dreams – more likely the most dreadful of nightmares.

My attention was drawn back into the room by Aretino. He lay on his bed, still fully clothed. His maid was beginning, none too gently, to pull off his hose.

'Ah, Sebastiano,' he roared when he saw me. 'You saved us from those French bastards.'

Of course I had done no such thing. It was the swords of his young men which had done that, but he ignored my protests.

'I have something for you,' he continued. He fumbled inside his clothing and then threw something towards me. 'Catch!'

It spun through the air towards me; something glittered in the candlelight. I caught it and then looked down at what I held in my hand. I let out a cry of horror and promptly dropped it. Aretino roared with laughter.

'It's glass, boy,' he yelled. 'For your father.'

The eye was rolling across the floor and I bent down to pick it up. 'I took that in exchange for three thousand ducats. The little prick thought he could get away without paying, with slinking from the city in the morning protected by the King's entourage, but I made sure I extracted something of value to him. That is the eye of a French prick and now it will rest in the infinitely more honourable socket of a deserving Venetian.'

Looking down at what I held in my hand, I saw that it was a thing of quite extraordinary beauty. It was made from enamelled gold, silver, porcelain and glass. I had never seen such a thing.

'I hope it fits,' he said and grasped his maid's breasts with great gusto.

I stuttered out my thanks and then, glancing once more at those paintings on the ceiling, did as the maid's nod towards the door bade me and turned to leave. The last thing I saw was Aretino burying his head between her ample breasts, his hand plunging greedily beneath her skirts.

The following morning I roused my father from his bed. It was hard because since his punishment he had taken to sleeping most of the day, but I was insistent and rode out his bursts of tears and anger.

'You must get up,' I insisted. 'I have something for you.'

He was very reluctant, but he did eventually get up and I brought him to the light of the window. He smelled disgusting from all the days he had spent barely moving from his bed; lice moved in his beard and matted locks. I was shocked at how wasted he had become, at how grey his face was.

I held out my hand, which contained the eye.

At first he reacted the way I had the previous night, but then he leant forwards and gave it a closer look.

'It is a thing of great value,' I said. 'My master gave it to me yesterday.'

Now my father picked it off my hand and looked at it in more detail. It was six months since his punishment and the place where his eye had been had healed.

'May I?' I said.

He nodded, so I took the eye, raised his upper lid and pushed the eye gently into the socket. The lid slid down on top of it. It fitted perfectly. I gasped and laughed out loud. The eye of a god looked back at me, next to the eye of my father, and somewhere in the depths of his living eye I saw something begin to stir – a flicker of hope? Or good humour? There was no doubt that the effect was extraordinary. I continued to look back and forth between the two eyes, and then I called my mother and sisters into the room and they all stood around my father, with their mouths open. Then I brought part of a broken mirror I had begged from Aretino's housemaid and let him see for himself. He brought his hand to his mouth and then slowly raised his hand and touched the false eye. I saw the shock and then the delight and then something that distinguished all too clearly which eye was living: tears trickled down the side of his nose. In those tears, and then the slow smile that followed, lay the beginnings of his recovery.

That afternoon for the first time in many weeks he said he wished to wash and my sister went out into the *campo* to draw water from the cistern. As we all know, it is not a good idea to wash too often, but in this case it was a sign of his return to health. He ordered us all from the room to do it, but I peered through the gap in the door. First he discarded all his clothes and kicked them to one side, then he stood for a moment, looking down at himself. He was lit up by a shaft of light which ran across the floor from the window and up his naked body. He moved himself in and out of the rays of sunlight as if discovering himself for the first time. Then he began to wash himself with great gentleness. Watching him wash was like seeing someone emerge from a baptism. Very slowly and methodically, starting with his feet and working upwards, he soaped his body. When he came to his left arm, he wept. There was still a raw strip of flesh running across the top of his stump. We still had some of the unguent recommended by the doctor and very carefully he applied this before wrapping it in strips of cloth. It was in this way, in the water and in the sunlight, I saw my father reborn. Then he called for clothes and dressed himself.

Later he went to the barber, who shaved his head and chased the lice from his beard. Finally, I gave him Aretino's cloak, which he took to with great pleasure. Like me, he had never had such a quality item of clothing.

Now, he began to leave the house again. At first we went out only at night when few people were about. Then on one of those rare days when Aretino was away from the city and his household had no need of me, I took my father out on the boat, fishing. It was a particularly beautiful day, there was a stiff breeze but the sun was out and the sea glittered in its rays. My father did not say much, sitting bundled up on the prow of the boat, head hooded, but when finally after several hours I brought the boat back to the city he sighed heavily and said, 'Oh, how I have missed the water.' I understood then that it was not just his punishment which had made him ill, but the separation from his beloved lagoon, and from that day on I took him with me everywhere on the boat. Even with one arm, he could help people on board, help tie up and steady the boat. Aretino noted that I had given him the cloak.

'You give him everything,' he observed.

'He gave me life,' was my reply. 'Isn't life everything? Don't I owe him everything?'

'You are a good son,' he remarked.

I think Aretino quite liked the presence of my father on his boat because it gave him the opportunity to regale his friends with the tale of how he came by that eye. My father did not mind. He simply smiled. After all, he now had the eye of a god and there are not many men of his status who can say that, and he liked the punchline, which was always the same.

'It looks a thousand times better in the honest face of a handsome, hard-working Venetian boatman than in the pimply, chinless visage of that pox-ridden French sodomite.' Yes, that punchline always succeeded in getting a good laugh. My father must have heard that joke more than a hundred times, but he still laughed. He laughed every time.

On other occasions Aretino would nod at my father and say to his fellow travellers, 'I have already paid the ferryman. He will make sure I get safely across the Styx. I have given him the eye of a god. How can he refuse me passage? It is a good thing too because, given my propensity for building up debts, when the time comes I'll have nothing in my pockets by way of payment, just the eye to get me across.'

The truth is he could have said anything to my father and

he would have smiled. Aretino had brought him back from the dead. If a man does that to another human being, there isn't anything he will refuse. A smile is the very least he can give him.

TULLIA BUFFO
Open for Business

Venice, 1576

Every day she waits for Marco but he does not come.

In the meantime, life must go on and soon the house is ready. Now the musicians are ordered, the harpsichord rented. Now the invitations have been sent out. Ostensibly they are for an evening of music and poetry. Poets have been tracked down and the best cooks hired. The kitchen hums with activity. Tullia stands in front of a mirror and inspects herself in minute detail. Her hair, bleached as white as possible in the sun, has been braided into the shape of a half moon, lying on its back. The tightness of her bodice raises and pushes together the two white orbs of her breasts. A stiff lace collar rises behind her head. Her dress is of red damask, embroidered with gold thread. Precious jewels have been sewn into the dress and round her neck are more jewels, this time rows of the most lustrous pearls, which also hang from her ears. The pearls are softened by the candlelight, the stones glitter back and forth in front of the mirror, the jewels and gold braid sparkle. The total value of all the rings on her fingers is well in excess of four hundred ducats. She is, of course, in breach of every sumptuary law going, which is exactly as it should be. She turns and looks at her back view. Yes, she is satisfied that everything is as it should be. Now it is time to begin all over again. Tonight no one will stay. Tonight is about showing that the shop is open, the goods are on display. The success of the evening will be counted in the enquiries that follow.

Later, when the evening is over, when the songs have been sung, the poetry recited, the food eaten, she considers her guests. She had liked the look of the Spanish Ambassador. A spy, of course – weren't they all? But he was funny and witty and had a sparkle to him that she recognised. Spies and courtesans had their similarities; neither was respectable, both were outsiders. She hoped he would be one of those who would make enquiries to seek a private appointment. She thinks they might have some fun together, if his purse were heavy enough. And then she thinks of the landlord, Marco Martinengo, of his long elegant fingers and their bloodied, bitten nails caressing her so very gently.

The following day a note arrives, tied round the neck of a live peacock:

Yours is the plumage of a peacock
The scent of the most beautiful rose
The beauty of the Madonna
The erudition and wit of Catherine de Medici.

You have bewitched me, lady.
I struggle to sleep but when I do
I dream of what may happen if I plunge
My hands beneath your feathers.
I dream and dream but obtain no rest.
It is simple. Send when I may visit you, and I will come.

She smiles. She is glad it is the Spaniard, but she hopes he is a better lover than a poet. He must be, mustn't he?

Now, then. Here he is and he's really rather beautiful. The candles in the cesendello cast a flickering light on the ceiling. They are alone.

'More wine?'

He smiles and extends his glass. She fills it and then walks round behind him. Her finger traces a path across the back of his shoulders. It is very good cloth, she notes, very black, like his pointed beard.

'I have known those who have carried their fortunes on their backs and haven't a *soldo*. The little they do own goes in oil to set a gloss upon their beards and smooth their faces.' She glances down at his feet. 'And for one pair of new shoes there are a hundred worn ones at home. I will not attach myself to a pretty doublet because in the past I have found the pretty doublets may have dribbling debts for linings.'

He stands up and begins to protest. She places one hand across his lips, another elsewhere. 'Do you have a heavy purse to match the weight of what hangs here, or is it as flat as a squeezed balloon?'

He jumps slightly, smiles, pulls her to him.

'Madam,' he says, nibbling gently at her ear, 'I can assure you I am heavy enough in both places to satisfy you.'

She gently bites his lower lip. 'Ready to plunge your hands into my plumage?' she asks.

'Oh, Madam, I am!'

Every night she waits for him but he does not come.

In the meantime, this Spaniard is fun. Of course, he would not be able to keep her, but he might recommend her to others. Word of mouth is what is required at this point to restore her good fortunes. He had known what he wanted and he had taken it, moving her body as he desired. Some of the shyer ones had to be coaxed into divulging their requirements. Coaxing could be fun, of course, a part of the erotic foreplay. A game to stimulate and explore. Everything could be turned into a game in the end. Dante lies sprawled out on his back in a patch of sun. She is the only one he will allow to ruffle his stomach. She does so, gently, and he stretches all four limbs, his face a picture of ecstasy. And something stirs in her, her own desire, her own ecstasy, and immediately she thinks of Marco's lips on her hand as he departed, those blue eyes and their long lashes and those elegant fingers that created such pleasure in her body, and she wonders when he will come again.

Every minute of every hour of every day she waits for him but still he does not come.

AURORA

New York, 2011

Oh, she was weary today. Waiting in the foyer for the lift to take her up to the apartment, Aurora felt the ache in her knees and her back, the ache in her fingers and in her wrists. She ached everywhere she could feel. Rheumatoid arthritis. That is what she suspected from looking up her symptoms on the internet. She hadn't gone to the doctor; she couldn't afford to. Maybe it wasn't, she thought. Maybe she was just coming down with the flu. Maybe there was a simpler explanation. She straightened her back, the lift doors opened and she stepped in. She closed her eyes and listened to the upwards swish of the lift, imagining herself ascending into the heavens. The end of life, death, the beginning of another life. She hoped she wouldn't be so tired in the other life. Surely God would take pity on her after all her years of toil? The door opened and she stepped out. As she did so, she caught sight of someone disappearing through the exit that led to the stairs. That would take them forever, she thought.

Maybe she should go and tell them. But they must know. Why on earth weren't they taking the lift? She pushed the key in the lock and entered the apartment. She hadn't felt comfortable here since her conversations with Alberto, but at least today she would be alone: the Pereiras were away on Long Island, so there would be no interruptions, no summons into the bedroom to look under the bed. She would be able to clean in peace and quiet. It would be her and the view and Saint Sebastian, which was how she liked it.

In the kitchen, she took off her coat and hung it on the back of the door. Then she put on her work coat, poured water into a plastic bucket, put in some disinfectant, soaked the mop and began to wash the floor. There was really no need because the floor was spotless, as was the kitchen. They never cooked, as far as Aurora could work out. They must eat out most nights and the nights they didn't they ordered take-out. There was rarely any food in the fridge. The most that she'd ever seen was some olives, a carton of milk, and bottles of white wine and champagne.

As she swept the mop over the stone floor, she wondered if she were this rich, was this what her kitchen would have looked like? No, she thought. She would miss the act of feeding herself and her children. She would miss the smell of food. It was one of the things she insisted on, sitting down to a meal with everything off: TV, phones, DS Nintendos, games, laptops. Just her and her daughters and the act of eating. She had always insisted on it. Even if they had nothing to say to each other, even then. This soulless kitchen had always unnerved her. She cleaned it because that was her job, but there was nothing to clean. It was not a normal kitchen. But here she was, cleaning it anyway, because that was what she was paid to do. She wiped down the stainless steel stools, with the white leather seats. White – that was a colour favoured by the very rich. No one on a budget would buy white leather anything, or white carpets, or a white leather three-piece suite. The only thing in this flat which wasn't white was the sheets. They were black. It was him, she thought; he chose them. He was repulsive. How could she bear him? He even liked to dress Mrs Pereira in white, like a virgin that he was going to fuck. But Aurora knew why she put up with him. Of course she did.

She paused in the hallway and made a note of the words on the bottom of the painting. She'd told Albi she'd do this and he had said something about a reward after all. Then she walked into the living room and went over to the windows and looked out at the view. This city! Her city? Yes, why not? Her city. Hers as much as anyone else's. White light poured into this white room and outside the skyscrapers marched off into the middle distance. She sighed. She liked being up in the air, floating above the city. Down below, the city whirred and throbbed, buoyed on the aspirations of its inhabitants. New York was an ant hill of aspiration and accommodation. I'm one of them, she thought wearily, an ant constantly running. In this city you had to be constantly on the move. After all, the city was.

Ten years ago, there had been the choice. Stay or flee. Well, some people had the choice. These people had. She remembered hearing them discussing it. In the end, they had stayed. It wasn't bravery, Aurora thought; it was more a question of how they would have looked to themselves and their friends if they had gone. Aurora had not had that choice. If you were poor, you didn't. In the immediate aftermath, Aurora had worked so hard to hope. It had felt like a duty to the city, a duty to her daughters. Ten years later, weariness had set in. All those years of hoping had taken their toll.

She thought of her daughters. Constanza's teacher had told her that her daughter was very clever, that if she worked hard then there would be a good chance of her going to college. College! Aurora didn't need a teacher to tell her

Constanza was clever; she'd known that for a long time. She remembered the first time she had stood up as a baby. Those steady, serious, round brown eyes watching her. And Aurora's response, every parent's response, 'Aren't you clever?'

'Yes,' those eyes seemed to reply. 'I am.'

She had taken a long time to speak but when she had, she had spoken in complete sentences. It was as if she had been listening and waiting until she could get it absolutely right and her vocabulary was extraordinary. But Aurora worried about boys; boys could derail the most intelligent of girls. She turned away from the window and the wide-open expanse of the sky and glanced quickly round the room. White walls, white sofas, wooden floors, a low glass table covered in magazines: *Vogue, Harper's, The World of Interiors*. Why, with all that money at your disposal, would you choose such a colourless home? She went into the kitchen and got some polish and a cloth, went back into the living room, removed the magazines and sprayed and polished the table, carefully replacing the magazines in exactly the same order.

She returned to the conversation she'd had with her daughter's teacher. Obviously she had been pleased, but she'd also been worried. Could she afford her daughter to be clever? There were scholarships, but the competition for those was ferocious. She wondered if her daughter would want it enough, enough to fight for it.

Aurora knew one thing for certain, though: she did not want her daughter doing this. She wanted both of them to have more choices than she'd had, than their father had had. Their father had had no choice at all. All you could do was offer more choices. If they took them or not, that was another matter. Money, she thought – in the end it all came back to money. Any child was a responsibility, but an intelligent child was a particular responsibility. And then there was the question of happiness. Aurora knew that happiness would not necessarily follow from having greater opportunities. Maybe, but not necessarily.

She finished in the living room and went back into the kitchen to clean the front of the fridge. She always left this to last. It was stainless steel and was almost as difficult to clean as the screen of a laptop. She would never have bought such a fridge. She took out two separate cloths and a special spray and began to clean it, taking care to look sideways at the front to make sure she wasn't leaving any smears. When she had finished, the fridge gleamed with an almost alien lustre. Standing back from it, she thought of her own fridge, covered in postcards from relatives in Cuba, with fridge magnets and cards from her daughters. That's what a proper family fridge should look like, she thought. It should be covered with life, love and laughter.

Later, as she was in the utilities room putting away her cleaning materials, she heard a noise in the hall, the sound of a door being quietly opened. She smelled his aftershave first, but what was he doing here? He was supposed to be in Long Island until the weekend. She called out, so that she did not startle him, and then walked into the hall. She didn't want to be alone in the apartment with him. Not now, especially not since her conversation with Alberto.

'Hello,' she shouted, as she entered the hall. 'Hello.'

It was him.

'Oh, Aurora, I'd forgotten.' He seemed distracted. 'I need the place to myself, I'm afraid. I'll pay you the same, but you need to go.'

'It's OK, I'm done here for the day. I'll get my coat from the kitchen.'

She glanced in the living room as she left. 'Goodbye, Mr Pereira, see you next week . . .'

He was standing in front of the fish tank just as she had been a few minutes earlier, hands on hips, looking at the fish.

He didn't turn his head. He didn't acknowledge her. And it was then the thought crossed her mind. *I could pretend to leave. I could make the sound of the door opening and closing but I could then tiptoe back and see what he is going to do next. I could do that. If he comes out, I could say I had forgotten something and didn't want to disturb him.*

She opened the door, remained where she was and closed it again, then she moved as quietly as possible back towards the living room. The fish tank had been moved a little away from the wall. He stood in front of a safe, a holdall at his feet, throwing something into it.

Money, bundles of money.

She turned quickly and headed for the front door, closed it softly behind her, waited for the lift, heart thumping, willing the lift to come sooner, quicker. Willing it to come now.

'Aurora?'

She turned slowly on hearing her name. He was standing in the doorway, holding out an envelope. 'I've forgotten to pay you.'

'Oh.' She moved reluctantly towards him and took the envelope.

'See you next week,' he said.

'Yes. See you then.'

She did not turn her back to him; she waited until he had closed the door. She stood with her back to the lift, watching to make sure he didn't open the door again. When she finally got into the lift and the doors closed, her breath came hissing through her teeth like gas.

Outside she phoned Alberto and told him what had happened. He suggested they meet in the same cafe as before and she agreed.

'So, now we know why he's so particular about his fish,' Alberto said, stirring the sugar in his take-out cup.

'There was a hell of a lot of it,' she said. 'Bundles.'

'Anything else?'

She shook her head, but then said, 'She's really frightened of him, Albi. Whenever they're together, she gets this smile on her face – really stretched. As if her smile can ward off his temper. It's always really tense between them.'

'I gave the details of the painting to the FBI. Anything else you can tell me about it?'

She took out a notebook, opened it to a certain page and handed it to Alberto. He glanced at what was written there:

TICIANUS FACIEBAT/MDXXII.

'Good – this'll be useful.'

'You heard anything back from them?'

'Not yet.'

'If it's stolen, you can pull him in for that, can't you?'

'No – what we're interested in are the drugs. If that falls through, we can get him for the painting, but it's really the trail to the drugs we want to follow.'

'Meanwhile, what do I do?'

'Keep your eyes open. Just keep working as usual.'

She took a breath. She didn't want to admit to the fear she'd felt when she'd smelled Mr Pereira's aftershave. When she'd known she was alone in the apartment with him.

'You all right, Rory?'

'I guess so, Albi. Guess so.'

He knew she wasn't. He knew she was frightened. And later, much later, he wished he'd asked her about it.

LUDOVICO & ANDREA

A Difficult Conversation

London, 2011

It was Andrea's last night in London. Nero sat curled up in his lap. Ludovico lay stretched out on the sofa with his eyes closed, a glass of wine within easy reach. It was now or never, Andrea thought, the last opportunity to talk to him. He had left it to the very end of his stay because he was a coward. On this particular subject he had always been something of a coward. But there would be little time in the morning and he had to be prepared to deal with his son's response. He cleared his throat and both Nero's eyes and Ludovico's opened at the same time. The cat, aware of something in the offing, jumped down onto the floor and, taking up a position equidistant between the two men, began to wash his whiskers.

'Your mother has asked to see you,' Andrea said.

Ludovico didn't move.

His mother?

'She wrote to me with her address, telephone number and

162

email and asked if I'd pass them on to you. I've written them down on here.'

He placed the card of *The Man With the Blue Sleeve* on the table and sat back in his chair, as if relieved of a heavy burden. Ludovico's eyes narrowed and then moved from the card to his father's face and back again. The silence lengthened until it became uncomfortable.

'He didn't talk to me, by the way,' Andrea said lightly. 'I wonder why he spoke to your friend.'

'I told you. Terry's very upset. His mother died recently and he's rehearsing a play in which a woman comes back from the dead.'

He spoke abruptly, impatiently. He was staring at the card with a deep frown disfiguring his face. 'This is what you came over to talk to me about?'

Andrea nodded. 'I didn't feel I could do it on the phone.'

The silence lengthened and lengthened.

'Ludovico . . .'

'My whole life you have always refused to talk to me about her. Now this? Out of the blue and you wonder if I fall silent?'

'Well, I can imagine that it's something of a shock, but she never asked to see you before.' Andrea picked up the postcard and fiddled with it. 'Will you contact her?'

'I don't know. I've only just been told she's interested in seeing me.'

'Maybe she'll finance your next film.'

Ludovico stared at his father in disbelief. It was such an unlikely and mercenary thing for him to say. 'Did she say that? What did she say?'

'She didn't *say* anything. She wrote me a letter and asked me to pass on her details. After quite a lot of consideration, I decided that I should.'

'She abandoned me as soon as I was born. Why would I, now, after all these years?'

'Look, Ludovico, when you were a child I only wanted to protect you. Now you are old enough to decide for yourself and she didn't altogether abandon you. I agreed to look after you.'

'Yes, but she had no idea what kind of father you might turn out to be. You might have been a terrible father.'

'But I wasn't, I don't think.'

'But she . . . *Puttanella!*' he shouted suddenly. '*Puttanella!*'

'Enough, Ludovico.' Hearing Andrea's rise in temper, Nero bolted for the door. 'This anger is misdirected onto the messenger. I have just one thing to say. If one's life is a puzzle, there is only one particular piece that fits the shape of one's mother. Only one. That is all. And calling your mother names helps no one.'

'Oh, so I've been walking around with some part of me missing,' Ludovico shouted, 'and somehow I never noticed.'

'Ludovico!'

Both men were now standing.

'You don't just get to suddenly talk to me about her after forty years of silence. She doesn't just get to summon me when it suits her,' Ludovico said, his voice cracking. 'She doesn't just . . .'

Andrea took a step towards him, put his hands on his upper arms and shook him gently. 'Perhaps this opportunity comes around just once. Perhaps she plucks up her courage and risks rejection just the one time. Perhaps there is no other time but this one.'

'But do you seriously think I would take a penny from her?'

A slight smile formed on his father's lips. 'Are films so easy to find funding for these days? Does £500,000 just fall out of the trees?'

'How do you know how much my last film cost? You won't even talk to me about my films. You completely disapproved.'

'Well, to be honest I had no idea you'd be so good at them.

"A film characterised by its humanity and concern for family and the elderly. A delicate and witty homage to older people. A wonderfully patient, delicately observed film." One review I read even compared you to Satyajit Ray. You see, you memorise my poems and I memorise your reviews. What can a father do in the face of such praise from the experts but lay down his objections and admit he was wrong.'

Ludovico stared at him and slowly shook his head. 'You are impossible.'

'I am sorry I was wrong about the film. An old man's pride prevented me from saying anything before. I was worried for you. My own experiences in the film industry were mixed, as you know. I read all your reviews. I kept meaning to say something but then I didn't . . . I knew this would not be easy but I felt I had to tell you that she had asked to see you. The rest is up to you. And I want you to know that I will not view it as a betrayal, if you decide to see her.'

'Do you think I should?'

Andrea drew an invisible line in the air in front of him. 'I'm not saying another word on the matter. Well, only this − if you give it some time, your curiosity may override your anger and your hurt. I am now going to hug my son and go to bed.'

And that is what he then proceeded to do, leaving Ludovico and the man with the blue sleeve eyeballing each other.

Ludovico sat for some time, looking at the postcard. He did not like what he saw; in particular, the slightly sardonic smile irritated him. He went and got a pair of scissors from the kitchen and began to cut the card into thin strips. These strips he also cut, so that soon the card was reduced to a lot of small squares. He had made sure not to look at the plain side of the card. Once he had done this, he arranged the squares in a completely different order and then sat for some time looking at the disordered mish-mash in front of him. Something needed to change. He needed to see a different picture. Looking at the neat lines of the many squares, he wondered why he hadn't just torn it up: it would have been more visceral, less clinical. The thought came to him that he could throw the pieces in the cat tray and let Nero do his worst, but he knew the thought was mere bravado. He would never do that. Tomorrow the pieces would still be lying here and he would still have a decision to make.

Puttanella!

He had been six years old, his back pressed against the August warmed stones of the wall, under the open kitchen window of his aunt's house. Three of his aunts were in there, preparing the evening meal. He smelled frying meat and heard knives chopping and water boiling. He had two large scabs on his knees. They were black and hard and beginning to itch round the edges. As he listened to his aunts gossiping, he lifted the edges of the scabs and rubbed the pale pink, healing flesh. They started talking about his mother. *Puttanella*, they said. And he knew by the way they spat out the word that it was bad. And then other snippets of conversation. *He can't know that he's his. He could be anyone's, anyone who was on the set. But he's a sweet child. Of course. And do you remember Andrea as a child – always so dreamy. Well, Ludovico's the same, isn't he? Always looking into the middle distance. Always dreaming. It's true, he is like him. And he's a beauty, that's for sure. Oh, yes. He must get that from his mother.*

And then all of them had laughed. He knew he had heard something he shouldn't. He knew he didn't understand what. Then he pulled hard at the scab on his knee. It had torn off and at its heart revealed a bloody little lake which had started to drip down his leg. He'd run into the kitchen crying and his aunts had tutted and fussed over him, as they always did, and all thoughts of what he had overheard had been temporarily obliterated.

But later that evening, while he was being tucked up in bed by his father, he had remembered.

'What's a *puttanella*?' he'd asked.

Andrea had frowned and replied, 'Where did you hear that?'

'Aunty Nicla said it.'

'Well, it's a nasty name to call a woman.'

'Why is it nasty?'

'I'll tell you when you're older. For the moment, you should know that it's not a word that you should use. It's a word that will get you into trouble.'

He'd had to test that for himself. One day when his aunt was scolding him about some minor misdemeanour he had screamed at her, '*Puttanella! Puttanella!*' He'd received a sharp slap from her. Later, when he had told his father what had happened, he'd got an 'I told you so' shrug of the shoulders. But no explanation about what the word meant. He had found that out for himself much later.

Puttanella – little whore. Whore – his mother was a whore. What exactly was he to make of that? And what did that make him?

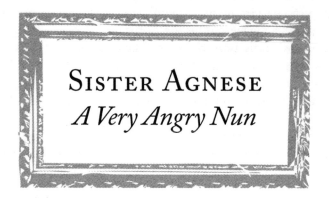

SISTER AGNESE
A Very Angry Nun

Venice, 1576

She kneels in front of me in her white satin bridal gown, glancing up at me through her long eyelashes. She is weighed down by jewellery – jewellery which should rightfully be mine. Part of my dowry hangs around her neck – a string of pearls. Part of my dowry is stitched into the dress; it glitters with gold and gleaming gemstones. My younger sister, Paola – so fair, so beautiful, her unbound hair streaming down her back also threaded with gold; she is everything I am not. The family stand arrayed behind her. Perhaps I imagine it, but I think they are holding their breath. I think they are terrified of what I, Sister Agnese, might do. This visit to the convent, where I have been locked up since I was a child, is one of many. She will be taken round all our cloistered relatives to receive their blessings. I would have thought they would have saved me from this, but ever aware of how it would look to the groom's family, here they all are, holding their breath, hoping I will behave. I utter the words of a blessing, but they are not the words I am thinking. Those are filled with bile. In my heart I wish her nothing but unhappiness, I wish her a barren womb and a sodomite husband. If she is to have children, I wish her malformed infants, only girls; I wish her death in the gush of blood from between her legs. I wish her a brutal and stupid husband. These are the things I really think as I place my hands gently on her head, as I murmur words of benediction. She looks up at me through those long eyelashes and all I see is her smug triumphalism. The stupid girl thinks she has beaten me.

The reason I am here, the reason it is me locked up in this nunnery and it is Paola who is about to get married, is simple. She is beautiful. I am ugly. My nurse used to try and comfort me by telling me that God had reached out and pulled down one side of my face to save me from the trials of marriage, but however many times she said it, I refused to be comforted. It was made clear to me from a very young age that a better marriage could be made with my fairer, younger sister and my family locked me away as a child and then placed me in the convent as soon as they decently could. It was fitting that I should be veiled. I was to be hidden; I was not to be looked upon. There was to be no money made available for my dowry. All the money would be kept for Paola; the bigger the dowry, the better the connection to be bought. In this city of markets, daughters are just another commodity to trade, another form of merchandise. Her marriage will increase our family in nobility and in political power. I know all this and I have known it all my life, but still something gnaws away at me. It gnaws and gnaws. I am the eldest. It is the unfairness of it. It is my powerlessness to alter my destiny.

Just as my family has taken a large communal sigh of relief,

I lean forwards. As I bend down and kiss Paola on the cheek, I whisper, 'Vinegar comes from wine as marriage comes from love.'

Her eyes widen. And then I repeat it louder, so that everyone in the room may hear it, and then I hook my hands into the rows of pearls round her neck and hoist her to her feet.

'These are mine,' I hiss and now I see fear in her eyes and I'm pleased.

She is glancing anxiously over her shoulder, looking for help, and I am repeating, 'These are mine.' I am tearing at them and the clasp catches in her neck and I see blood and then the necklace breaks and the pearls are rolling under the feet of my relatives and they are all scrabbling to pick them up, like beggars thrown *soldi* in the street. I still have the remains of the necklace in my hand and I throw this against my sister's dress, where it makes a bloody mark, and now I am screaming oaths that would make the devil blush and my convent sisters are dragging me from the room. The last thing I see is my sister looking down at her wedding dress, which is now splattered with blood, and the whole room scrabbling to retrieve the bloodstained pearls.

'May every pearl be a bloodstained tear that you weep,' I scream, then I begin to laugh because they all look so ridiculous, scampering after the pearls. And as I am finally ejected from the room, I shout, 'The curtain in the temple is torn; the tables of the money lenders are overturned.'

Later, locked in my cell, I think this is an end to behaving well. I have had enough of trying to compensate for my disfigurement with goodness. I will not lie on my sick bed like Sister Francesca, praying to be released from the prison of her virginity. I will not accept my fate. I decide that my face will not be my destiny. I will have a life of sensual pleasure. In this city of masks, why should I be held back?

It is on that day alone in my cell that I begin to plan my escape.

* * *

They did not keep me locked up for long. There was, of course, some sympathy towards me from my fellow sisters and also I am the only one who can calm Sister Maria. I have a talent for soothing the inconsolable, having practised for many years on myself. She called for me and when they deprived her of me she became so fretful they feared for her life. It was only a couple of days later, therefore, that I found myself forgiven and back by her side. Sister Maria is bedridden and of a tremendous age. It is thought in the nunnery that she might be ninety years old, and indeed one would think it to look at her. The wrinkles on her face are as multitudinous as the folds on the surface of the sea but, from the folds of her skin, her eyes shine out as blue as sapphires. Sister Maria had a fondness for me from the moment I entered the nunnery. She told me once that my disfigurement made her feel less ugly, which made me laugh because I rarely get such honesty in response to my face. Sometimes honesty is all one yearns for. At other times, I admit, it is the last thing one can bear to hear. Most people draw near to me from pity, but I knew in my heart that this was not what drew Sister Maria to me and I liked her the more for it. Now I believe that she recognised a difference in me that was not due simply to what lies on the surface of my face.

One night, when I was nodding by the side of her bed, she said to me, 'Sister Agnese, there is something I am going to tell you. It is a history not often told.' Perhaps I imagined it, but her eyes seemed to twinkle. 'It is the history of our disobedience.'

171

I was immediately awake because there was a colour in her cheeks and a liveliness she had not shown for many days. As the candlelight flickered against the walls, she began.

'When I first came to the convent, the Republic was in turmoil. It was five years after the Battle of Agnadello had been lost and with it all the lands that the Republic had on the mainland. With this loss came questions from its citizens. A foolish but much venerated man, Friar Timoteo, an Observant Franciscan from Lucca, had given a sermon at the Basilica of Saint Mark on Christmas Day in the presence of the doge, claiming that the loose morals of the women of the city, the Jews and the sodomites were to blame. The authorities decided that they would clamp down on what they perceived to be freedoms that we should not be allowed. The result was an attempt to interfere in the way our nunneries were run. But we were not willing to give up those freedoms lightly. Over the years that followed they tried all kinds of things to crush our spirits.'

I took the hand that she stretched out to me. In truth it was like holding a bundle of loose twigs in a soft leather pouch such was her age. She leant forwards and indicated that I should help raise her on her pillows. I smelled the sourness of her oncoming death on her breath as I helped her sit up. When she had settled herself, she continued.

'It was decided that in the interests of chastity our *parlatorio* was to be abolished. We would no longer have the right to receive visitors in an open salon, but we would be forced to receive them from behind a metal grill, as is required of Observant nuns. Now, the *parlatorio* was one of the privileges of the Conventual nuns. Did they think that we would agree to being locked up in these convents without the privileges and freedoms accorded to the daughters and sisters of patricians? We were warned that this was the intention of the Patriarch, so when his vicar came with some captains and officials, in order to install the metal grills, we were ready for them. We drew together and defended ourselves. You should have seen the expressions on their faces as the stones we threw pelted down upon their heads. We drove them away altogether and forced the Patriarch himself to come to us to explain his actions. Of course the moment of triumph was only a temporary reprieve. We sent our brothers and uncles and fathers to argue our case with the Collegio. We even managed for a while to ward them off with an appeal from the Pope.'

'It is against that background then of distrust and resentment that you must consider what I tell you now. These were years when we were incensed and filled with disgust towards the authorities. Of course the nunneries were a holding pen for the younger daughters of patricians for whom there were no dowries. But if we were to be locked up in this manner we wanted our freedoms. Well, some years later we held the sacred ceremony which attends the election of a new abbess to the convent. The doge, having the right of patronage, came to the convent to celebrate her installation. He came accompanied by the signoria and the patricians. They heard Low Mass, and then the Patriarch celebrated High Mass, and the church was most beautifully decorated, but at the end of the day, when the doge and the Patriarch had left, some young patricians and priests were secreted in the convent and after the ceremonial meal was over they danced with the nuns to a wind band until dawn and much merriment was had by all.'

My jaw had fallen open and she laughed at me, as much as she was capable. 'Come, child, you must have heard of such things.'

'No,' I gasped. And that was the plain truth. After all, who was I to have heard such things from? And my life from a young age had been the walls of this convent. Since I had been entombed here there had been no whiff of scandal either seen or heard.

'Well, that is what happened and several of the nuns fell pregnant by these young men. In those days, a word was given for those who frequented the nunneries – *muneghini*. Ah, how beautiful some of them were! Our *muneghini*! They were the very best of Venetian manhood, sons for whom there were no wives. Such lusty beauties for our delectation. At the time, the authorities were looking for any excuse to interfere in our affairs, so it was decided that this should be kept hidden in the convent and when the children were born the babies were taken into our foundling sanctuary, as if they had been left on our doorstep overnight.'

She paused and for a moment her body became wracked with coughing. Then she continued. 'Oh, how my breasts ached for my baby. The milk dripping from my breasts was a daily reproach.'

I let out a gasp. I could not help it. Sister Maria, the most holy and venerated of all our sisters, consorting with *muneghini*? Pregnant? A mother?

'I was very surprised because at the time this happened I thought my child-bearing years were almost at an end, but the child must have wanted to be born. The only thing that I could give her was a name. I called her Tullia, after my own mother. I was not allowed contact with her but I understand that she was in due course adopted. One of the sisters who worked in the sanctuary told me she became a great beauty. Although maybe she said this to soothe me ... I have always wondered what became of her. I have always wondered if she was happy.'

'Why are you telling me all this?' I asked.

She shrugged slightly. 'The abbess told me of your actions the other day. You struggle with obedience. I thought you would be a worthy recipient of my story.'

I frowned, not really understanding. 'I see.'

'My child has been much in my thoughts in recent days. And now there was something else I wanted to tell you and something I wanted to ask of you.'

She beckoned me closer.

I leant forwards and, as her soft whisper filled my ear, I found a broad smile of delight spreading slowly across my face.

Ludovico
&
Terry

London, 2011

'Are you all right?' Terry asked Ludovico, later the following evening.

'Yes, why?'

'You've been a bit off all day.'

'Off?'

'I wondered if you were sad about your father having gone back?'

Ludovico shook his head. He was sprawled disconsolately on the sofa. In rehearsals Terry had felt something was missing. It was only at the end of the day that he'd realised what it was – Ludovico's attention. Actors are very sensitive to the quality of attention they receive. Yes, Terry thought, Ludovico had been going through the motions, but his true attention had been elsewhere and it had made him feel anxious, as if there was no safety net there.

'Do you want something to drink?'

Terry shook his head and Ludovico got up and went into the kitchen. Terry glanced at the heap of squares on the table and began automatically to put them together. It was a while before he realised what it was. Ludovico came back in, carrying a bottle of white wine and two glasses – 'in case you change your mind'.

He glanced at the table. 'Oh, don't do that. Please.'

'I always liked jigsaw puzzles. I used to do them with my mother.'

Ludovico sighed and poured himself a large glass of wine. 'And don't talk to me about mothers.'

Terry sat back, leaving the half made-up postcard. 'Why did you cut him up? Did he say something to you?'

'He didn't, no, but my father wrote my mother's contact details on the back.'

'Ah.' Terry sat back and waited. 'Do you want to talk about it?' he said after a while.

Ludovico drained his glass and poured himself another. 'No ... I don't. Look, I'm sorry but ...' And then he burst out. 'If she thinks she can have absolutely nothing to do with me for the first forty-odd years of my life and then get in touch out of the blue and I'll come running. Well, she's got another thing coming. Why the hell should I? And as for my father – "Oh, she might finance your next film." What the hell does he think he's talking about?'

'Is she rich?'

'I've no idea.'

'Have you ever met her?'

Ludovico shook his head.

'Do you know why she's contacted your father now?'

He shook his head again. 'And if my father knows he's not telling.'

'Where does she live?'

Ludovico shrugged his shoulders.

'And does your father want you to meet her?'

'What's this? The bloody Spanish Inquisition?'

Terry smiled. 'Maybe you should talk to someone about it.'

'I thought I was.'

'Someone trained in this sort of thing.'

'Oh, give me a break. People who advise therapy are like people who tell you to go to the dentist. Back home they have a pair of pliers and they would rather tear out their own teeth and bleed to death than go themselves.' He leant forwards and swept the pieces of the postcard into the palm of his hand.

'What are you going to do with them?' Terry asked, not quite able to keep the anxiety out of his voice.

'Put them in the cat tray.'

'Oh, don't. Wait until morning. You may feel differently then.'

Ludovico sat back down and let the pieces dribble from his hand back onto the table. 'I hope so because at the moment I couldn't feel worse. Last night . . .' he paused. 'You know I'm ashamed to say it, but last night I wet the bed.' He laughed. 'I mean, I'm a forty-year-old man and the idea of meeting my mother is making me regress to infancy.'

He put his face in his hands.

Terry sat down on the sofa next to him and put his arm round him. 'It'll be all right,' he said.

'How do you know?'

Terry smiled and kissed him. Ludovico kissed him back.

'Make me feel differently,' Ludovico said.

'OK,' Terry said. 'I will.'

They lay sprawled against each other, hearts pounding, sweat sliding.

Terry groaned luxuriantly. 'Oh, the glory of the beast with two backs,' he said and rested his cheek against Ludovico's chest.

'Hello, beast,' Ludovico said and stroked his head.

Terry heard the steady thump, thump of Ludovico's heart. Colin had been phobic about blood and this extended to hearing a beating heart or feeling a pulse. Once when Terry had cut himself he had ended up looking after Colin, all the while attempting to staunch the blood with reams of kitchen towel. Terry, an incurable romantic, always thought it was a shame that Colin would never be able to listen to the beat of a lover's heart.

Ludovico was stroking his hair, his face. 'You have a beautiful face to play a tyrant. It's so kind, so ordinary. It's just perfect. You embody perfectly the paradox of the play. How can such a normal-looking man set about destroying his life, his kingdom, his family?'

'The banality of evil?' Terry laughed. 'Are you saying I have a banal face?'

'No, no, no,' Ludovico said, shaking his head vigorously. 'Not banal, kind and ordinary. But most especially kind.'

Terry smiled. He would settle for kind.

My dark angel, Terry thought. Why dark, though? Ludovico seemed overwhelmingly optimistic and sunny, so why dark? He had a friend who was a strict Freudian analyst. A rather tiresome man. His question, when Terry told him about new lovers, had always been, 'Where's the hate?' It was rather a depressing way of viewing people. Perhaps the darkness came from that time on the bridge heading for Joe Allen's. Ludovico's long, black velvet coat had been caught up in the wind and had blown up behind him. It wasn't just that, Terry had thought he heard something, something remarkably like the beating of wings. It was ridiculous, probably just the noise of one of the tourist boats chugging past. All noise was augmented on the water and especially under the bridge. But it was then that the phrase had popped into his mind. There was also the way Ludovico had walked next to him, refusing to allow anyone to come between them, guarding him.

The following morning was a Saturday and Terry had to leave early for a family get-together. By the time Ludovico got out of bed, it was ten o'clock. He went into the kitchen to make some coffee and then brought it through to the living room. It was a while before he saw him, carefully Sellotaped together, sardonic gaze in place, propped up against last night's empty bottle of wine. Ludovico drank his coffee and eyeballed the dandy with the blue sleeve, listening to the seagulls wheeling past his balcony.

Well, she was only his mother after all.

He flipped over the card. The first thing he saw was the name – Mariangela Acquarone. His mouth dropped open. This woman was his mother? *This* woman? No wonder his father had been anxious about him knowing her identity. Mariangela Acquarone's career had encompassed being a model, film starlet and favoured actress of a leading Italian director. For many years she had been a darling of the paparazzi, a famous beauty, who had been photographed on the arm of well-known film directors and politicians, and had even been linked with a leading member of the Mafia. One rich and powerful man had followed another before she had finally settled down with a man ten years her senior, who ran one of the top fashion houses in Milan. Since his death, she had undergone a Garbo-esque withdrawal from public life. Ludovico knew all this because every Italian knew this; for the last thirty or forty years, Mariangela Acquarone had been one of the most famous female icons of Italian cultural life.

She was his mother?

Underneath her name was an address: Venice, or, to be more precise, the island of San Clemente.

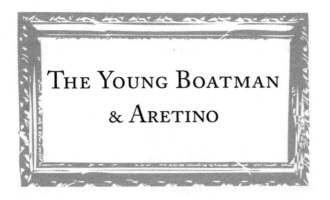

The Young Boatman
& Aretino

Venice, 1546

It was bound to happen at some time or another. My master was a man of varied and vast appetites. In such a household, filled with the young flesh of both sexes, I knew at some point I would have to make my position clear. But when the moment came I was still taken aback. It was late at night about six months after I had started working for Aretino. We had just drawn up at the bottom of the house and I had handed him out of the boat. I had taken him to the *palazzo* of the courtesan Veronica Franco, but he had not stayed and he was not in the best of tempers. The household was unnaturally quiet and I had just turned to see that the boat was properly tied up when I felt his hand slide between my legs. Then he moved me against the wall and I felt his beard against my cheek and the weight of his body pressing against mine.

I froze, uncertain how to proceed. Everything I and my family owed him flooded into my mind – my job, the golden eye. He had saved us, so how could I reject him now? He removed his hand and stood back a little, observing me.

'Relax, little one, when there is so much fruit on the point of falling, I will not reach up and tear from the tree that which isn't ripe.'

I began to stammer. 'I-I-I love you like a second father. I-I-I owe everything . . .'

'Enough – there are catamites on every corner. The city is filled with beautiful boys with an abundance of curls, laughing eyes and cheeks which are gardens of red and white roses. Such angels are all about us, with their diffident air and graceful attitudes. They float past my balcony every day and can be bought for a few *soldi*, but you . . .'

His mouth descended on mine, his hand moved. I squirmed and despite myself felt myself harden. He stood back and laughed; the stones in his rings felt cold against my cheek.

'Perhaps you are riper than I thought. But tonight I will relieve myself with one of the maids.'

He turned and, shouting for one by name, Angela, he began to climb the stairs that led to the upper reaches of the house. As I made my way home along the deserted *calli*, the noise of my master's love-making and the giggles of the maid floated out into the warm night air. 'Oh . . . oh . . . oh . . .' It could have been me spread-eagled beneath him, me with my mouth on his. My confusion was such that I wasn't sure if I envied Angela or pitied her. There is no doubt that I was frightened. The act of sodomy brought down upon the sodomite punishment. The risk was great. Banishment was likely. But what would happen to me, a boatman, if I was banished from my city? How would I survive? How would

182

my family survive? It was not a risk that a poor boatman would take, unless ...

Unless?

That was the question I was puzzling over as I reached home.

It was rumoured, of course, that the doge's two Saracen slaves delivered such services to him, but what the leaders of our Republic might get up to in the privacy of their inner chambers and what the plain citizen might do were entirely different things. In fact, the more they did such things themselves, the more likely they were to punish it in the lower classes. As if by doing this they could rid themselves of the taint of all the gossip which swirled around them.

The following morning I was worried that my behaviour would bring about an alteration in my master. But he was as jovial as ever when I picked him up to take him to Titian's studio to have his portrait painted. In fact, he was filled with goodwill towards the world and me.

'Tell me,' he said. 'What gossip do you have for me? What is the prattle among the gondoliers? What scurrilous morsels are doing the rounds?'

He lay back in the gondola and ran his hand down the black and white rectangle of his beard and smiled at me. Fortunately, I had some tittle-tattle to tell him, so by the time he was stepping out of my boat he was well pleased with me and some *soldi* rained down in recognition of my services. Much to my relief there was no indication that he was angry with me for my rejection of him the night before.

I hoped that the episode might simply be forgotten.

A month later a *festa* was taking place and the house was empty. I was asleep in the boat since I did not know if my master would want to go out or not. It was a beautiful summer evening and a warm breeze was playing over the water; the boat held me in its arms, a mother lulling her child to sleep, and I was caught between dozing and wakefulness. It was a soft velvet night, but I started awake aware that someone was watching from the shadows. I jumped up embarrassed and, trying to give the impression of alertness, said, 'Where to, Master?'

He smiled and waved his hand. 'Nowhere,' he said. 'The house is empty and I hate to dine alone. Will you attend me?'

There was nothing I could do but follow him upstairs to where dinner was laid out for him. He bade me sit down opposite him, which I did somewhat reluctantly. He began to eat. I had eaten little that night other than some bread, which the kitchen maid had given me, so as my master ate, the growls from my stomach grew louder and louder.

'How goes it?' he said, wiping the grease from his beard. 'What news?'

I racked my brain for something to entertain him with and managed to scrape up a few trifles to make him laugh. He seemed in a contemplative mood and when he began to talk it was as if he were talking to himself rather than me.

'Old age does not become me. It makes my talents grow lazy. I used to write forty stanzas of a morning. Now I can barely put together one.'

I tried to comfort him. 'But the quality of the one, Master ...'

He shook his head. 'No, I wish it were so but the quality of the one does not make up for the absence of the thirty-nine.'

He picked up a chicken leg and tore into it with his teeth. He glanced at me over the top of the leg and said, 'And love which should awake me puts me to sleep.'

My stomach let out a particularly loud growl. He laughed and pushed some platters across the table towards me.

'Eat, boy, or your stomach will drown out all conversation.'

I happily grabbed some meat and began to eat. I was sorry

to see him so downcast, but I also worried about where the conversation and his intentions were leading.

'My master lights up the city, no, the world, with his talents, his big heart and his warm nature. Everyone knows of his generosity, that he will take off the cloak from his back and give it to a beggar in need ...'

I was about to continue but he held out his hand to indicate I should stop.

'Enough. You flatter a man who knows the art too well to be pleased or deceived by it.' He assumed an oratorical position, with one hand on his breast and the other held up in the air, and began to declaim, 'Because your Majesty is more like God than any man ever was ...' He burst out laughing. 'I wrote that to the Emperor Charles in search of a pension. It didn't get me very far. Sending Titian to him produced a better result ... for Titian, at any rate.'

He pulled the napkin from under his chin and stood up. 'How's your father?'

'Very well, sir, thank you.'

He was walking behind me now and my hunger had vanished and been replaced by a feeling of tension. It seemed unwise for me to have my back to him, so I turned round. He was standing very close to me, so close that I could not push back my chair to stand up. I was trapped.

'The eye?'

'The eye of a god in a poor man's head makes the poor man half divine.'

'Be careful of what you say. A poor man divine? The authorities will hang you from a gibbet for such.'

'I meant nothing by it, sir. Just that it is a beautiful thing and it has brought my father back to us.'

He leant down and I felt his breath on my cheek. 'A man may have many types of father in his life. Is that not true?'

'Of course, my lord.'

'A father may initiate his son in many things. Is that not true?'

'Well...'

'In ancient times men took young men under their wing and taught them all the delights of the mind and the body to prepare them for adult life.'

I was at a loss how to reply. I sat trapped between table and chair, with Aretino leaning over me. I was confused by my feelings, which ran between fear and excitement. He turned the chair and placed his hands on each arm so that his face was now inches from mine and I could smell the meat he had recently eaten. He began to speak in a sort of incantation: 'Man's original body having been cut in two, each half yearned for the half from which it had been severed. When they met they threw their arms round one another and embraced, in their longing to grow together again, and they would not do anything apart...'

His mouth descended on mine. I felt his tongue push its way into my mouth. I felt as if I were drowning. My hands grasped at the air and then at him. I was not sure whether to pull him towards me or push him away. Eventually, I pulled away from him, gasping. He stood upright and stepped back frowning, 'Do you know yourself so little?' he said gently.

I did not know quite how to reply. 'I am yet young,' I said.

'You are a virgin.'

It was a statement, not a question. I felt as if my face had been set on fire. It wasn't something I could deny. I felt speechless with shame and embarrassment. I stood up quickly and the chair toppled over behind me. He grabbed hold of my arm.

'Do not think I mock you. Virginity and innocence are rare in this city.'

All I wanted was to leave the room and return to the soft velvet cradle of the night, but he still had me by the arm.

'Virginity in a maid is something of incomparable value in a city filled with courtesans, but in a male, boy, in a male it is something of an encumbrance.'

I tried to pull away from him, but he held me tight. 'Shall I tell you what I thought when I saw you asleep downstairs in the gondola? I thought usually it is only our lovers who we see sleep. I thought you were as beautiful as any woman I have seen and I have seen many a queen and courtesan in my time. I thought I wished to see you asleep, sated in my bed.' He let go of my hand. 'You have no idea of your beauty, of course, and that is part of your charm.'

I was filled with confusion. 'I do not know what to say,' I mumbled.

He raised his eyebrows. 'Either yes or no would make things plain.'

He walked back to his chair and sat down, broke off a piece of bread and placed it in his mouth. He was telling me the choice was mine; he would not take me by force. And yet he had made clear his desire for me.

I crossed to where he sat and took hold of his hand in both of mine.

Now he was the one who seemed confused and he continued his incantation.

'To give in on account of his wealth and power, either because one is frightened or because one cannot resist the material and political advantages which he confers, is neither stable nor constant. No noble friendship can be ...'

'Stop it,' I said and lowered my mouth onto his.

Later, I awoke in the night unaware at first of where I was. Then I turned and saw my master sitting up looking at me.

'My sweet boy,' he said. 'You sleep like an angel.'

Instinctively, I moved to cover myself with the sheet, but my master stopped me. 'There is no shame in the garden of Eden,' he said. 'Simply beauty.'

He put his arm around me and I rested my head against his chest. There were scars on his body from his time as a soldier and I ran my finger along the white lines that puckered his skin, then I covered them with my tongue. I moved down his body and took him in my mouth. I held him there for some time but he remained soft.

In the end he stroked my head and pulled me up to him. 'No matter, boy. Age softens the hardiest of men. I cannot go to it as I did.'

'I'm sorry,' I said.

'No matter,' he said. 'It is of no matter.' He kissed me gently on the lips and began to stroke my face. I fell asleep under the soft caress of his fingertips.

In many ways, afterwards nothing changed. My master, naturally, continued with his whoring ways but every month or so he would order me to wait for him, in case he wished to go out later that night. Then, like that first night, he would come down to where the boat was moored and he would take me into his bedchamber.

One night after he had bedded me, he said to me, 'Have you had a woman yet?'

I blushed again and shook my head.

'I will speak to one of the maids,' he said. 'They have mentioned you to me in a lusty manner.'

I was not sure how I felt about women. I had admired them, of course, as things of exquisite beauty, but I was not sure I wanted one in my bed.

'You should try everything in life,' he said and a few days later he sent Angela to me.

I tried, that is all I can say, but it was not the same. The smoothness of her skin, the smell, everything puzzled me. It was a country I did not recognise. I managed the act itself but was unsure as to whether I had given her any pleasure. Her body seemed fragile under mine and passive, and I worried about hurting her. With my master, the grooves of pleasure were worn into his body through great use. He knew his appetites and was clear about what he wanted, but the maid gave no clear indication of her desires or her pleasure and made little sound. My master roared out his pleasure in a manner which could not be mistaken.

Afterwards, he asked me about it in such indecent detail I wondered if he had been watching us. 'Did you try both sides of the coin?' he asked.

I stammered something, but then I burst out, 'No one pleases me like my master. No one could.'

'Sweet boy,' he said, as my rod hardened in his hand. 'The teeth of concupiscence bite gently and sweetly, but death is already seizing me by the hair. I would be flattered but your experience is so little. You are a great beauty and soon both men and women will be queuing for your favours.'

'But I am true to you,' I said. 'You . . .'

'To be true to one person is to bring down a heap of troubles on one's head. It will turn your life to torment, your dinner will become poisonous, your banqueting wormwood, your bed a rocky ledge . . .'

'I am yours,' I said. 'I am all yours.'

On some nights I took us out into the lagoon and under the starry night the boat rocked with our love-making and my master's laughter. I felt safest out there on the water where no one could hear or see us, and it was a relief to be in my master's arms and have the stars looking down on us and not those terrible paintings.

One time when I was declaring my undying love to him, he said, 'Make no man or woman your whole world. It is a great mistake. If you learn anything from me, remember this.'

But I thought he was truly a great man and I was young

and would not listen. I thought I knew my own mind, but he was much wiser than I could have imagined. And when I finally conveyed him for the last time to the sacristy of the church of San Luca, I remembered what he had told me and knew he had been right.

TERRY
Opening Night

London, 2011

As he checked his make-up, Terry considered that the delight of the light bulb-bordered dressing-room mirror had never really left him. He smiled at his reflection, raised his head and patted the top of two fingers against his ample double chin. All right for Falstaff, he thought, but he was still too young for the role, so it wasn't much good to him. He wouldn't be able to diet once the play was up and running. People would come and see it and he would end up going out to dinner with them afterwards. He had never been able to just go home after a performance; he'd always needed the company of people to take the buzz off or perhaps prolong it. He had hoped that pining for Colin might have taken a few pounds off, but Ludovico had come along too quickly for any pining as such. Of course Colin had been part of the problem; he

191

was a very good cook and during their years together Terry had piled on weight.

Good luck cards surrounded the mirror. There was even one from Colin. His mother had always come to opening night and he had taken the last card he had received from her and tucked it into the mirror to symbolise that she was there in spirit, if not corporeally. He checked the clock on the wall – fifteen minutes to go. He slid his hand into his trouser pocket and pulled out a leather pouch, opened it and shook the contents out into the palm of his hand. It was a solid silver bear, not more than an inch in length. He'd been ten years old and about to take on his first leading role as Scrooge in *A Christmas Carol*. On his head was a pair of his father's cream-coloured woollen underpants, which had been turned into a nightcap by his mother by the application of some judicious stitching, a bit of elastic and a cream pom-pom on the top. He had made her swear that she would not tell anyone what his hat was made of – the teasing would have been unbearable. The bear had come in a tiny, white cardboard box and when he opened the lid and lifted the soft cotton wool there it was, staring back at him. It was the most perfect present he had ever received.

'For luck,' his mother had said. 'Not that you need any,' she'd added. 'You're word perfect.'

Some of the magic of that moment, of first lifting the lid, returned to him now, as he looked at the gleaming silver bear in his hand. He rubbed its nose and placed it on the dressing-room table. He thought of the bear in the play. Ludovico had cast an irascible Scot called Jim Campbell to enact Shakespeare's most famous stage direction, 'exit pursued by a bear'. He had a good roar and the casting of his huge menacing shadow had been very effective.

From the theatre, Terry could hear waves of laughter from the audience. The pastoral scenes were taking place, when balloons were used to suggest breasts and phalluses. It sounded as if it was going well. He checked the clock on the wall: only ten minutes or so to go.

Terry held his eye in the mirror and breathed deeply. The climax of the play was approaching. He remembered what Ludovico had said in rehearsal. 'There will not be anyone in the theatre who has not lost someone, someone they wish were alive, so in the final scene when Hermione turns out to be alive, they will all be on your side, their longing will be there in the theatre. All you have to do is tap into it. They will all be rooting for you.'

Terry looked down at the silver bear. Time to go. He stood up and put his coat on. Sixteen years were supposed to have passed between the beginning of the play and his next scene. As he stood, he felt his knees stiffen, his hip ache and his body thicken. He felt the rigidity of a more elderly body come over him. He picked up a silver-topped stick and leant on it, then walked heavily across his dressing room. In the time it took him to do that, only a few seconds, sixteen years had settled over him. Waiting in the wings, he felt the longing for his mother to be alive again, in front of him, smiling, saying, 'You're word perfect.' Then he took a breath and limped slowly, heavily, grief-burdened and guilty, out onto the stage.

Back in his dressing room after the curtain call, he wiped the make-up slowly from his face. Had it gone well? The audience had certainly seemed very enthusiastic, but he had been in plays where the audience had loved it and the critics had hated it. They'd have to wait until tomorrow for the reviews to come out. They would dictate whether they were playing to full houses or not. The ending was tough. Yes, there was some form of redemption for Leontes. Yes, his family was returned to him. Yes, the kingdom could flourish again. But in the last scene, when he held out his hand to his wife and she turned and looked at him, did she or did she not take it? The audience would never know because at that point the lights went out. There had been much discussion about this moment. The actress playing Hermione had been adamant about it. He can't just have got away with it, she said. It can't be as simple as that. He has behaved abominably. One of their children has died. Terry had admired her toughness on the matter. She had argued and argued and she had got her way. His hand was not taken. The play was better for her refusal of the sentimental route. It was a tough, uncomfortable, honest ending.

Ludovico came into the dressing room. 'Bravo,' he said and kissed Terry on the cheek.

'Any notes?' Terry asked, half ironically.

People were crowding in at the door and Ludovico stood back to let them in. He'd nailed it. It had worked. Now it was a question of nailing it eight times a week for the next three months.

* * *

The following morning Terry got up late and went and bought all the papers. Although he told interviewers that he did not read his reviews, it was a lie. Of course he did and years later he could remember in forensic detail every even faintly negative thing that had been written about any of his performances. The many wonderful things, which far outweighed the criticism, he forgot almost as soon as he'd read them. He made himself some coffee, spread the papers out on the table and went through them one by one. They were almost universally ecstatic both about his performance and the production as a whole. All of them were four or five star reviews. The only faintly negative comment he could find stated, 'Terry Jardine makes a jarringly cuddly Leontes.' Terry took a deep breath and read it again: '"Cuddly... jarringly cuddly..."?' This from the same critic who never reviewed Terry's performances without getting in a sly dig about his weight. Everything the man had ever said about him over the years swam into his mind. 'It is difficult to take seriously a Hamlet who looks as if he has just come from gorging on a sticky bun' and then 'This Cassius certainly does not have "a lean and hungry look".' Terry looked down at his stomach and took a roll of it in both hands. He was suddenly filled with a wave of rage and self-loathing.

Somewhere in the bottom of his wardrobe was a tracksuit. After a bit of rummaging he located it and a pair of battered trainers. He zipped his keys into a pocket and, catching sight of the leather pouch sitting on his dressing table, pocketed that as well. After a bit of half-hearted stretching he let himself out onto the street. The park was about a five-minute walk away. He would run there and then run round it. He set off at a rather tentative trot, but as the words of the critic ricocheted inside his head he found his trot turning into something faster. Each time he brought his foot down, he imagined it coming down on the critic's face and in this way the trot became a jog became a sprint. By the time he charged into the park, the sweat was flying off him and he had worked up quite a head of steam.

TULLIA BUFFO

Venice, 1576

Every night she waits for him but he does not come.

When Tullia looked up, she saw the beautiful, red cut-velvet draperies which hung round the bed; when she looked down, it was onto the head of the young man buried between her legs. His long, black hair was spread over her upper thighs and stomach, creating a delightful tickle, which augmented the delights of what he was doing with his tongue. He was one of the poets she had invited to her salon opening.

'Stop!' she said and pulled him up so that he could enter her. Then she rolled him over so that she straddled him, rocking back and forth, laughing, her hands running over her own body, tracing a path from her lips, over her breasts and then down between her legs.

Soon the only noise in the room was that of their breathing, coming faster and faster, until they lay sprawled across each other like those who have dragged themselves from a ship-wreck onto the shore. He ran his hands through her golden tresses, settled his mouth over one of her breasts and sucked. His appetite for her was never ending. As soon as he had finished he wanted to begin all over again. She pulled his mouth from her breast, as if he were a greedy infant, and sat on the side of the bed, sweeping her hair into some sort of order.

'And where are the poems you promised me?'

'Ah, my darling Tullia.' He fell back against the pillows. 'Have patience.'

She glanced between his legs, 'And do you – does it – have patience? I think not. Otherwise you will have to pay like everyone else.'

'Poetry is a hard taskmaster and unlike a virgin it cannot be forced.'

'And what would you know of forcing virgins? You who came to my bed such an innocent himself.'

He blushed. 'Have I not learnt to your satisfaction?'

Her slight smile turned into a laugh of acknowledgment. 'Any wife of yours will find you pleasingly well-trained, but don't expect her to serve you as well as I do.'

'Wait a minute, I feel the Muse descend.' He cleared his throat dramatically:

> *Of ladies, knights, of passions and of battles*
> *Of courtliness and of valiant deeds I sing*
> *That took place in that era when the Moors*
> *Crossed the sea from Africa to bring*
> *Such troubles to France ...*

'Oh, for heaven's sake,' she said. 'How boring! Stories for young brats with wooden swords. You'll have to do better than that before you get to lie between my legs again.' She stood up and swept a black velvet shawl round her shoulders. 'I will be a more ferocious critic than was that scourge of princes, Pietro Aretino. Only the very best rhymes will satisfy me.'

'But what about rhythms?' he said. 'Don't my rhythms satisfy?'

She raised her eyebrows. 'Your rhythms are so-so.'

'My cruel mistress,' the young man said. 'So, so cruel.' He closed his eyes for a moment. 'How about this?

> *Orlando, as well, I'll celebrate, setting down*
> *What has not yet been told in verse and prose –*
> *How love drove him insane, who had been known*
> *Before as wise and prudent (like me, God knows,*
> *Until I too went half mad with my own*
> *love folly that makes it so hard to compose*
> *in ottava rima). I pray I find the strength*
> *to write this story in detail and at length.*

'Fool,' she said. 'Do you insult me by presuming that I am ignorant of *Orlando Furioso*? It gets worse and worse!' But she could not keep the smile from her mouth.

'Talking of hard lengths,' he said. 'I believe I have one to hand.'

'Well, that's where it will have to stay. In your hand. I have things to do.'

'And what might they be?'

'Matters to attend to.'

'Matters? Other men?'

'That is no concern of yours.'

'My goddess,' he murmured. 'You pretend the pleasure is all mine, but I know that some of the pleasure . . .'

He slid behind her and ran his hands over her breasts and

then down between her legs. Her body arched backwards against his momentarily, but it was not him she was thinking of. She pushed him away sharply with her elbows and he fell back on the bed.

'Enough,' she snapped. 'I have business to attend to.'

'Ah, business, the great God of Venice. I must not hold you back from that. It is rumoured that the taxes from the courtesans keep twelve galleys afloat. It is no surprise that the authorities allow you freedom to ply your trade.'

She considered him through slightly narrowed eyes. 'You are very young . . .'

'Younger certainly than all those old, soft men you take between your legs.'

'The ducats they have in their purses are hard enough for me.' She knocked her hand against the wall. 'These bricks are hard enough for me.'

'Money makes money as lice make lice. You are a Venetian and so money is your second blood. For me, a poet first, love is my second blood.'

'And what will you do when your father tires of your airs and graces? When he decides to withdraw the money he gives you because he suspects you spend it on courtesans? What will you do then? Do you think your poems will feed you? Do you think I will? Or will you give in and end up working for your father's business like every other younger son in this city?'

The expression on the young man's face had turned sulky. He got off the bed and began to pull on his clothes. He got dressed in silence and stalked out of the room, laces hanging loose from his doublet, his hose baggy at the knee. She listened to his footsteps echoing down the stone staircase.

She sighed and considered her reflection in the mirror. The reason that she was distracting herself with this young man was to keep her mind from Marco, who had not contacted her since that first visit. She had not been able to get him out of her mind or the memory of him out of her body. And so she tormented this young man in order to try and feel in control of a situation which related to another man altogether.

Love was not part of her trade. Seduction and sex, of course, but not love. If Marco was not going to visit her, at least she might satisfy herself with this poet, although satisfaction was not really what she experienced, especially when all she saw when she closed her eyes were Marco's blue eyes gazing down on her and all she felt was the way he filled her body.

Never mind, she had business to attend to at the quay; that would distract her. She shouted for her maid, Cornelia, to come and dress her. Her mind would be distracted by spices and silks, carpets and perfumes, pepper and sugar loaves. Down at the quay she would forget her yearning and for the time being would be lost in the wonders of the Orient.

A few moments later she swore at Cornelia. 'You are being particularly clumsy today,' she said. 'My hair is attached to my scalp, you know?'

Cornelia murmured an apology. A plump, maternal-looking woman, she was becoming used to her mistress's moods. She had herself started out as a street whore in the public brothels of the Rialto; there wasn't much she didn't know about the business her mistress was in. Oh dear, she thought, Tullia had fallen hard for this young man. She had been ensnared by a snivel-nosed young brat whose mouth still stunk of milk. Now his rod and olives had her behaving like the cats which rubbed their rumps on the roofs in January. It was no surprise: he was certainly a beauty. Trouble was coming to the household and they had all better be ready for it. When sex and seduction fought love and romance, the battlefield would always be bloody.

'And don't pull that pursey face,' Tullia said. 'It is singularly unattractive.'

Singularly – well, there was a fancy word. Usually she talked to her in the Veneto dialect unless she was putting on airs and graces, unless she was picking a fight.

These damned mirrors were the work of the devil, Cornelia thought; she kept forgetting her mistress could see her when she was standing behind her. Yes, trouble was coming as inevitably as the tides that rose and fell each day. She sighed and applied herself to her mistress's hair, her face a mask of servile obedience.

Suddenly, Tullia leant forwards with her head in her hands and groaned. 'What am I going to do, Cornelia?' she said. 'Each thrust of his spear had me seeing a thousand candles.' She looked at her maid's reflection in the mirror and they both burst out laughing. 'What on earth am I going to do?'

'He is not lost to you, Mistress. I saw him outside just now, standing like a mouse drowned in oil, with his head bent down upon his chest looking most forlorn. He will be back and you will work out what to do, you always do.'

Tullia looked up, frowning. 'Not him,' she said. 'It's Marco Martinengo.'

'Not the boy?'

She waved her hand in the air. 'He is but a well-hung distraction.'

'Well-hung or not, Mistress, you should ensure that he pays or he will let it be known all around town that you are giving it away for free.'

Tullia nodded. 'And then people will be making sport of my simplicity and queuing down the street.'

Cornelia continued her brushing. For a moment there was

silence in the room, the only noise being the rhythmic stroke of the brush pulled through Tullia's hair.

Tullia looked at Cornelia's reflection in the mirror. 'Why doesn't he come? He has an open invitation. What man doesn't come when he has an open invitation to visit a courtesan?'

Cornelia raised an eyebrow. 'A very unusual one.'

'I am paying no rent. I told him it would take some time before I was in a position to. I told him that in the meantime he could come to me.'

Cornelia put down the brush and now stroked her mistress's head with her hand. 'Mistress . . .' she said.

Tullia leaned back against her maid's ample stomach. 'The worst of it is that I know there is nothing more pitiable than a courtesan caught up in love's thorns. It is like a doctor who goes down with an incurable disease.'

'No one escapes love's thorns, Mistress. No one.'

'It is revenge,' Tullia said. 'For all those men I have tormented. God has his revenge on me. Every night I wait for him but he does not come.'

'If he comes to you, then perhaps he thinks you have no choice in the matter. If he comes to you, you are rent. Perhaps that is why he does not come. Perhaps he waits for you, Mistress. Perhaps it is the only way for him to think that you can give yourself freely to him. Every night he does not come, he asks nothing of you, not even rent. He makes the choice yours.'

Tullia turned round in her chair. 'How did you become so wise?'

Cornelia picked up the brush. 'Through tending to the broken hearts of a hundred whores. Through having my own heart broken a hundred times.'

'What do you know of him?'

'That he adored his wife and children, that he is a good master to his servants. He is well liked and respected, Mistress.'

'So, I must go to him?'

'Perhaps it is the only way he can know how you truly feel.'

But do I want him to know how I feel? Tullia thought. Can I bear to be so vulnerable? And then she thought of him crying a world of tears into her arms and felt ashamed of herself.

The following morning she wrote a note to him. *May I come to you?*

But no message was returned.

And as the days passed, she felt more and more of a fool and secretly cursed Cornelia, who had advised her to expose herself so openly. As the days turned into weeks and then months, she tried to banish all thoughts of him. She concentrated on running her household, on hiring a tutor for her three sons, on re-establishing her reputation and her salon. She distracted herself with her poet, who was very much in love with her, or at any rate with the idea of being in love and had taken to writing her love letters.

My Darling Tullia,
May these few lines, these simple words dictated by my sighs, written with my tears be set in paradise in the hands of the Sun. Your brow is purer than the sky, your eyebrows of ebony are made, your cheeks shame milk and cream, your teeth are two rows of pearls, your lips pomegranate blossoms, your voice does not differ from the canticle 'Gloria in Excelsis' and coming to your bosom it is two hard apples as balls of snow. Slipping down to the well of delight how unworthily I have drunk thereat, the taste is distilled nectar and the moss surrounding it is of silk. Of the reverse of the medal I can say not a word, deeming it would be necessary to raise Burchiello from the dead to sing the merest part of its marvels. He that liveth

in thy lovely bodice straightened by too much love thus
writes to you.
Your devoted poet

Reading this letter, Tullia sighed and then tucked it inside her bodice. This letter came from the wrong man. How was she to free herself from him? What was she to do with him? What was she to do with herself? What indeed!

Tullia's maid, Cornelia, stood in the door, arms folded. 'He is here again, Mistress.'

The 'again' was stated with a heavier than usual emphasis. Tullia lay in her bed, her golden hair spread across her scented pillow, a vision of petulant beauty.

'Well, turn him away *again*.' She mimicked Cornelia's emphasis.

'But I am not sure he will take no for an answer.' Cornelia was interrupted by the noise of shouting and running steps. The maid stood to one side as the poet, hotly pursued by one of the serving boys, flew past her and threw himself down by the side of Tullia's bed.

'My darling,' he said, 'why do you treat me so abominably? Is it to test my resolve?'

Tullia gestured with her head towards the door, and Cornelia and the servant left the room. Tullia looked down on him. She had some compassion for him. How he felt for her was how she felt for Marco. However hard she tried, she knew that her passion for Marco was a fire which had not yet run its course, the sparks were still in the walls, waiting to break out at any time. She had been trying to keep all thoughts of him from her mind, but in fact she yearned for him. Now, what was she to say to this boy? He did look genuinely pale and ill. Had she done this to him? Of course, she had. She immediately felt her resolve weaken.

'Hush,' she said and patted the bed, indicating he should join her.

He lay beside her. 'Why do you torment me by keeping me from your side? Why?'

She put her arms around him and comforted him as if he were a feverish child. He closed his eyes and rested against her. Looking down at him, she thought he was so very young. Their actual ages were quite close, but Tullia knew that she was so much older in experience. In experience she was his mother, his grandmother even.

Her own childhood had barely existed. Chosen from the orphanage by her mother, another courtesan, she had been trained from a young age in her occupation; she had been trained so that as the beauty of her mother was fading she, Tullia, would be making enough money to support her. Her mother had died last year, ravaged by the French disease. She had died a terrible death. Is that what she was going to do? Wait until the disease had embroidered her own face and hung from her neck, until she had to cover her face with white lead and rouge and hide it behind a fan, until she had to try unsuccessfully to cover over the stench of her rotting body with strong perfumes. Was this life which her mother had chosen for her as an infant to be her destiny? In the final stages, her mother had become quite mad; she had raved, as if possessed by demons, and nothing would calm her. Was she really going to wait until the same fate befell her?

Her rise had been vertiginous. Hieronimo di Angeli, her first patron before Domenico Venier, had helped of course. The fact that she had roused what had been unarousable at the latter stages of his life had rendered him inordinately grateful. She remembered one night after he had performed the act for the first time in many months she had asked him about his business. He came from a famous merchant family renowned for their benevolence.

'We Venetians are foxes, not lions. In business we look for the short-term gain, for the immediate opportunity. To Venice come the wines of Crete, the cinnamon of the Indies, the carpets of Alexandria, the caviar of Caffa, the sugar of Cyprus and the dates of Palestine. It is like any kind of sale. It is like the sale of your own sweet flesh. With some truth and a few lies we sell our merchandise.'

He had then gone on to tell her that cheese became lighter when it dried out and should always be weighed at the end of a voyage before being bought. This had made her laugh, for some reason. Perhaps it was the earnestness with which he said it, combined with his nudity and the subject matter. He had become furious with her. It is upon those kinds of details that a successful business rests. It was no laughing matter, he said. She had remembered that – the cheese, her laughter and his scolding. Detail. But how was a woman like her to learn such details? How could a man learn the details of the life of a courtesan?

There was no doubt she had sent Hieronimo to his grave a happy man and she had met Venier shortly afterwards. Her business interests, however, had been at a precarious stage when the plague had broken out. Her return had never been sufficient to give her confidence to give up her profession and anyway there were things she would miss: the power she wielded and conversation with intelligent men.

She had the kind of public life that no patrician's wife would ever have. She did not want to be cloistered away in a family house and only allowed out for mass on Sunday or the odd family wedding. She liked testing her wits against those of men of refinement and influence and intelligence.

Of course, such a man might say any number of things in the throes of passion and these things were often of interest to the authorities. They trusted her. When ambassadors were in town, they were guided in her direction, to her salon, into her arms. She passed on whatever might be said and often the authorities rewarded her by overlooking a tax payment or two or three. It could amount to a great deal of money. The authorities would not want her to quit her profession. In fact, they would be horrified. Looking down at the young man lying next to her, she thought he knew nothing of this. He was as transparent as the lagoon. Things were simple and clear to him. This was part of his attraction to her, of course, his innocence. He turned against her and his hand found her breast and began to caress her. She allowed her body to respond, allowed her body to surrender to his tender caresses.

Afterwards he lay sprawled on his front, dozing. With her eye, she traced the indentation of his spine down to the swell of his buttocks, across the backs of his thighs and to the soles of his feet. How ironic, then, that all she could see in her mind's eye were Marco's long flat fingers, his torn and bleeding fingernails. Now all she felt was how much she yearned to kiss them.

Her mother would have been horrified. A more hard-bitten whore it was difficult to imagine. It is business, she said, simply business. Never let it become anything else.

'But what of love?' Tullia had once asked.

Her face had rocked with the slap her mother delivered. 'That has no place in your life,' she had replied. 'Not now. Not ever. Life is about survival, not love.'

At the time she had been too young to understand, but she understood now. Love made everything too complicated. Love had no place in this business. Love delivered too much pain.

Love was an open wound.

Love was a dangerous business, a very dangerous business indeed.

Would she end up doing as her mother had done, and pluck

an orphan child from the nuns so that, as her looks faded, as her body began to stink, she would have someone to support her in her rotting old age? Would that cycle repeat itself all over again? Would she die a raving lunatic? Or would she take her fate in her hands and decide on a different outcome? She leant over the bed and gently lowered her head until her hair was tickling the soles of the poet's feet and he stirred.

The following day word came that Marco had been away seeing to properties he owned on *terra firma*. And hard on the heels of that information came a letter from him in a beautiful curling script. *Come to me tonight. Come to me. Every night away from you has been a torment.* Reading this, Tullia was suddenly breathless and shivering with desire.

LUDOVICO

London, 2011

Ludovico sat on a bench on the South Bank looking out at the Thames, April sunshine barely warming his face. He'd just read the reviews of *The Winter's Tale* and it was clear they had a hit on their hands. He hadn't managed to get hold of Terry yet to congratulate him but presumed he might be sleeping late after the opening night party. On the bench next to him was a book of short stories about Venice that Terry had given him. Short stories were not really his sort of thing – he'd never really found them meaty enough – but because he was thinking about Venice, and wondering if he might visit his mother, he opened the book and began to read a story called 'The Mermaid and the Drunk'.

The Mermaid and the Drunk

She waits out in the lagoon for night to descend on the city and remove all traces of humanity from the square. The waters are too busy to risk coming into the lagoon during the day. So many boats and ferries pass back and forth between Venice and the islands and the Lido. The risk of discovery is much too great, but just occasionally the city tempts her. How could it not? This city – her city, as she thinks of it.

Of course in the olden days they had known of her kind. The last time she had come here it had been a disaster: despite maximum discretion, she had been seen, and not just by anyone – by the sculptors Pietro, Tullio and Antonio Lombardo. Soon images of her kind had proliferated all over the city. There wasn't a tomb which did not have a scaly tail curled round the bottom of it. Fish tails, tritons and putti were suddenly everywhere. Yes, the whole thing had been an absolute disaster. That was the last time she had raised her head above the waves and taken a look at Venice. Over five hundred years ago.

She is reaching the end of her time, but before she goes she longs to see it once more. She had waited for the new moon, for darkness. Just the stars show their brightness in the night sky as she swims up the Giudecca Canal. She is the last of her kind and has been out at sea for a long, long time. She approaches St Mark's Square, slowly popping her head up and down as she goes like a seal, checking that no one is about. The red eye of the charging bull, Taurus glows red in the sky above her. That is where she will return to when her time comes, back to the stars. No one is moving across the square or along the sea front. There is just the sound of the ropes of numerous boats tugging against their moorings. Stars, but no moon. Tomorrow the young moon will be holding the old moon in her arms. She wishes for some kind of touch. She has no one to hold her in their arms. When you are the last of your kind, there is this terrible loneliness to endure. With a quick flick of her tail, she is sitting on the quay looking around her. Of course it was her kind who helped build the city in the first place. Way back when people first fled out into the marshes to make their homes in safety.

She closes her eyes for a moment and raises her face to the stars. Above her tower the two pillars of St Mark (the lion) and St Theodore (subduing the crocodile) which guard the holy space of the piazza. She remembers when executions and punishments took place between them, when the screams and cries of those suffering could be heard at the very bottom of the sea. The noise was sometimes so terrible that she and her kind buried their heads in the mud of the lagoon and stayed there until it had stopped. At least these days there are not these noises to endure. And yet here is an unwelcome sound. A noise suddenly very close, a man stumbling out of the shadows directly in front of her. She freezes, perhaps he will think she's a statue, a work of art, if she stays very still.

But no, it is too late.

'Oh no,' he says and rubs his eyes, a parody of a man who cannot believe what he is seeing. His mouth hangs open.

For heaven's sake, she thinks. For the first time in so many years she has come up for air and this fool, this drunken fool, has interrupted her star-bathing. Please God, I hope he's not a sculptor.

But it is getting worse. Now he is staggering away from her, his eyes as round as an owl's. He does not see the metal mooring; he does not see the rope. There is a soft plop and he has tumbled backwards into the lagoon, floundering down and down.

Just for a moment, observing the bubbles rising to the surface of the sea, she considers letting him drown. Suppose he is another sculptor. It would be a disaster! The moment passes, she sighs and slides back into the water. Down she goes and gets him under the arms and with a robust flick of her tail they are both on the quay again. She places him on his front and with another flick of the tail wallops his back, sending the water gushing from his lungs. He chokes and chokes and then falls unconscious.

Only when she can see clearly that he is breathing does she take a final look around her and slide back into the sea. It was a mistake to have come. She was filled with a longing for some sort of contact, but the only embrace she has had is with this grappa-soaked fool. She sinks down and down and sets off for the open sea, for the depths of the ocean to live out what remains of her life alone.

And what of the man? As he sank down under the waves, as he saw the bubbles from his gasping lungs rising to the surface of the sea, he cried out to God. If I am saved, I will go to mass. If I am saved, I will go to mass. He remembered the moment of being saved, the power of her arms around him, his head against her breasts, her hair trailing over his face and finally the tremendous power as she thrust both him and her out of the water into the square.

When the police find him wet and bedraggled and raving, they take him off to the station to sleep it off. He keeps saying to them, 'I was saved by a mermaid. I was – why won't you believe me?' The following morning when he's released he goes straight to confession. Inside the church, Santa Maria dei Miracoli, he stops and looks at the carvings. My God, they are everywhere, writhing round the plinths which support the arch which leads into the presbytery. Why hasn't he noticed this before? Pagan sea-hybrids coil and twist. Here a naked mermaid tries to push a fat putto off her scaly tail, there a young woman with a tail and wings places one hand under her right breast and another between her legs in a gesture that seems startlingly immodest for a church. And over there a double-tailed child triton holds up the leafy ends of his tail with delicately carved splayed hands. Of course, they have always been there.

In the confessional, he admits it is so long he can't remember when he last confessed. 'Father, I'm a drunk,' he says. 'But yesterday I fell in the lagoon and was saved by a mermaid.'

The priest smiles. Over many years he has heard every sort of thing in confession, but this is a first.

'A mermaid?'

'She saved me,' the man repeats.

'So why are you here?'

'Because when I was drowning I prayed and said if I was saved I would come to mass. So here I am.'

'Well, I'm glad,' the priest says. 'Welcome back.'

'You don't believe me, do you?'

'I didn't say that.'

'Come out and look at me.'

'But ...'

'No, you must, Father. I insist.'

The priest thinks he should humour him, that if he does then maybe the man may be brought back to God. He pulls back the curtain and steps outside.

In the church the man points to the stone carvings. 'Look,' he says, 'she looked exactly like that. Exactly.'

The priest nods.

'You still don't believe me, do you? Look, I've got a piece of her hair. As she rescued me, I clung to her. Look, I'll show it to you.'

As a sharp beam of light breaks through the glass windows and illuminates this extraordinary jewel-box of a church, he digs in his pocket and pulls something out. The two men stand, staring down at what he holds in his hand.

'Come and sit down,' the priest says. When they are seated in a pew, he begins. 'Do you know the origins of the church, my son?'

The man shakes his head, looking down sadly at the piece of seaweed in his hand.

'It was built to house that painting which hangs over the

213

altar and which was credited with miracle after life-saving miracle. So if your life has been saved, you have come to the right church. Maybe it was the Virgin who saved you?'

The man remembered being held in her arms, in the arms of something ancient and sensual, something powerfully erotic. In that moment he had felt everything, her irritation, her longing. He looks at the priest but is too embarrassed to reveal this. Instead he says, 'Whoever carved those sculptures knew exactly what I am talking about, Father.' He stands up, the piece of seaweed trailing from his pocket. 'But I can tell you one thing for certain, whoever it was that saved me from the sea was no virgin.'

He begins to walk towards the entrance of the church.

'Will I see you at mass?' the priest calls.

The man does not turn round but waves his hand high in the air in a gesture which could best be interpreted as a 'maybe', tipping over into a 'probably not'.

The sun is lighting up his back and his jacket, a black one, suddenly starts to quiver with iridescent light, the sort of light you might see reflected on the scales of a fish. The priest frowns and watches him all the way to the exit. Then he gets up and goes and looks closer at the sea-hybrid sculptures. It was easy in life to begin to take for granted the beauties and complexities of things you saw every day right in front of your nose. Of course these were carvings of unbridled sensuality and the reason they had been placed at the bottom of the columns was to indicate the Virgin's triumph over the sins of the flesh. A verse that he had learnt as a boy returns to him:

> *Virgin, flowering branch that saves,*
> *Harbour rare beyond the waves*
> *Drive off Scylla and the sirens,*

Cleanse our minds and loins of sin,
Plant the seeds of good within.

One could never tell what would save a man's soul. If it was a mermaid, so be it. He had learnt that it was best not to question the miracles that God could bring about, but he doubts he will see that man again. He doubts it very much indeed.

Ludovico laughed and closed the book. He liked it. Maybe short stories were all right after all. He took his phone out of his pocket to see if he'd missed a call from Terry but no message had been left.

* * *

Jim Campbell's face was covered in a thick layer of cold cream and he was wiping off his make-up with what seemed to Ludovico an alarming lack of regard for the skin underneath. Ludovico was leaning on the back of his chair and making eye contact with him in the mirror. He was trying to remain calm, even though he was filled with a crushing sense of anxiety about what might have happened to Terry. It was simply unheard of for an actor of Terry's experience to fail to turn up for a performance.

'Where the fuck is the little prick, then?' Campbell asked.

It had been a long day and Ludovico was aware of a pulse starting up under his right eye. It felt so strong that it must be visible to the naked eye but he hoped fervently that it wasn't. He didn't want Jim Campbell to think that he was intimidated by him, although why wouldn't he be? The man in front of him was bull-chested with a red face (beginning to emerge from under the cream) and small blue eyes, and

215

he had a cap of short, thick white hair on his head. He was squat and square. Any bear would have appreciated his low centre of gravity.

Ludovico took a deep breath. 'We don't know. He's not answering his phone. We've phoned his family and his friends. We've no idea. As far as I know he's never failed to turn up for a performance before. Are you going to be OK for tomorrow?'

There was a grunt, which Ludovico assumed was a 'yes'.

'So what are we looking at here? A couple of days, a week, the whole run? What?'

'I'm sorry, Jim. We don't know yet.'

'Is it a Stephen Fry?

He shook his head. 'Again, we just don't know.'

'Or a Daniel Day Lewis?'

'Err . . .'

'You know I was on stage when Ian Holm cracked up in *The Iceman Cometh.*'

Ludovico shook his head, wondering vaguely if Jim was going to go through every English stage actor who had had some kind of nervous crisis in the last thirty years.

'That was a very nasty business. Iceman? More like a puddle of sweat on the stage. Mine. I was playing Rocky and I was supposed to be polishing the glasses. By the end of it you've never seen such clear glasses in your fucking life. They looked like bloody crystal. We kept feeding him his lines. You know. "I think you were going to say . . . ", but there's that very long soliloquy at the end and we could see that looming and no one was going to be able to save him from that. Aiyee, that was a very nasty business, poor bugger.'

'I think tonight went very well in the circumstances.'

'In the circumstances,' he repeated slowly. 'Don't bullshit me, boy. Tonight was OK, little more. The others just about covered the cracks of my arse.'

'You got a standing ovation.'

'Ach, that doesn't mean anything. It was just so the audience could feel better about being cheated of the man they wanted to see. If they make out I'm extraordinary, it makes them feel better about their disappointment. The blessing of the part is that I can bone up on the last act while they're all arsing about with balloons in Bohemia.'

'I think you deserved the standing ovation,' Ludovico said. 'It was a very powerful performance.'

Campbell snorted dismissively, but there was the suggestion of a rather pleased smile on his face. 'So where do you think he's got to? Something happen?'

Ludovico shook his head. 'I don't know.'

'Lovers' tiff?'

Ludovico didn't reply and Campbell continued removing his make-up.

'Bear wasn't up to much tonight, I didn't think. You should have a word.'

Ludovico laughed. 'I've had other things on my mind.'

Campbell had finished removing his make-up and Ludovico began to move towards the door.

'Before you go, do you mind if I ask you something?'

'What?'

'Why did you hire me for the job?'

Ludovico looked down at the ground for a few moments. 'Because you're the best man for the part.'

'But you must have heard about my troubles – the divorce and the drinking I mean, word gets about. You were taking a risk.'

Ludovico shrugged. 'You're an actor I've always liked and I hadn't seen you in anything for a while and thought I might . . .' He hesitated, not wanting to hurt the pride of the man in front of him.

But there was no need to have worried. Campbell was

217

searching his face. 'You thought you'd give me a second chance, boy. Is that it?'

Ludovico began to stammer. 'No, I wouldn't say that. I mean I didn't see you as someone who needed ...'

'Well, I did and you've given it to me and I won't let you down and I won't forget. No one's been willing to hire me since the red tops got a hold of me. It's the longest period of time I've had out of work since I left the Citizens Theatre in Glasgow in the seventies.' He got up, took a sudden step towards Ludovico and enveloped him in a fierce embrace. Ludovico felt the tension he'd been feeling in the last few hours suddenly soften and escape in a loud sob. Campbell held his hand against the back of Ludovico's neck for a moment before gently releasing him.

'I owe you,' he said. 'But make sure you have a word with the new bear. It's the most famous stage instruction in Shakespeare, for God's sake.'

TERRY

Bishop's Park, Putney, London, 2011

Consciousness came to him slowly, like a camera on the end of a crane, swooping down towards where he lay. First there was an awareness of his own shape, a sprawl on the ground, and then there was the smell of earth and the taste of grit in his mouth, finally a crushing pain in his head. He licked his lips and a couple of crumbs of earth dropped from them. His mouth was parched. He sat upright and now the pain was loose in his jaw and in his back. He coughed, then retched. He looked down at his body. He was a portly, middle-aged man. His hands moved up to his face. He had a moustache and a beard. He was not wearing glasses. He was wearing a grubby tracksuit. What did he look like? What was his name? He didn't have a clue.

Slowly he stood up and immediately felt the world tilt. He bent over, hands on his knees, waiting for it to stabilise. When the world stopped spinning, he looked around him. He was surrounded by bushes. He pushed his way through

219

them and now he saw an urban park, a path, a bench. He collapsed onto the bench, forcing himself to take regular breaths, breathing as deeply as the pain would allow and that was not very deep at all. He breathed like a stone skipping the surface of the sea. It was all he could bear. He was bitterly, bitterly cold.

Terry smelled the man first – the smell was of alcohol, with hints of a body that had not been washed in a very long time. Then he heard him, or rather the rustling of plastic bags. The man was talking to himself, a monologue that could not be interrupted. It was nonsense, just a babble of words. But there was something about the rustling and the babble of words that Terry knew he must get away from. He looked up and the dying rays of sun began to flicker through the branches of the plane trees above him. Now it was even worse. If he didn't move away from here, something terrible would happen. He needed darkness. He needed silence. He needed somewhere quiet where he could try and put the pieces of himself back together. He stood up and began to walk away from the man.

'Fuck you,' the man muttered. 'Fuck you. Who do you think you are?'

Terry had no idea.

He looked down at himself and thought, I am portly and middle-aged. Maybe I am some kind of middle-rank civil servant or a teacher. The shouts of 'fuck you' followed him along a path, which led him to a pond. He got down on his hands and knees and leant over so that amongst the algae and the urban detritus of floating fag ends and Coke cans he might see his own reflection.

Ah, there he was. He had a kind, rather worried face. He was glad he liked his face.

A voice spoke behind him. 'Have you lost something, sir?'

He turned round. A policeman and a policewoman were

standing there, bulky in their anti-stab vests and equipment.

'I don't know who I am,' Terry said.

As he stood up, he felt faint and began to sway. One of them grabbed him by the arm.

'Take it easy, sir,' she said. 'Do you know where you are?'

'London,' he replied.

'Do you know where this is?'

He shook his head.

'Do you know who the Prime Minister is?'

He saw a man with a ghastly smile waving his hand in the air. 'Things are going to get better?' he said, hesitantly.

The police officers glanced at each other. 'That was a while ago and they didn't,' the woman said. 'They got a whole load worse.'

'Do you know what year it is?'

He looked down at the ground and shook his head.

'Have you got anything in your pockets which would identify you?'

Of course. How stupid of him not to have done that before!

He fumbled in his pockets, one by one. The end result of his search was a bunch of keys and one small leather pouch. He handed them over to the police.

'That's it? No mobile, no wallet?'

He shook his head. The female police officer opened the leather pouch and took out the small silver bear. 'Does this mean anything to you?'

An awful feeling of anguish tore through him. Now it was as if the world was breaking up into small squares and underneath there was nothing but white light. He buried his face in his hands.

'All right, sir. We're going to get you some help.'

He felt an arm round his waist, heard someone on a phone requesting an ambulance. Felt himself drifting towards the white light, felt himself falling. The last thing he was aware of was someone gently lowering his head to the ground.

He floats above himself, back with the camera on the end of the crane. He does not feel the lips on his lips, the breath being blown into his lungs, or the hands pumping down on his heart in chest compressions. But he hears the call for the ambulance.

He hears its sirens. Who is that for, he thinks? Someone's in trouble.

He hears one of the paramedics. 'Have we got a name?'

'The policeman said he'd lost his memory and there's nothing on him to identify him.'

His sweatshirt and T-shirt are being cut off. Something is being pushed into his arm. He feels a warm hand on his forehead. 'Hold on a minute. I know who he is. He's the actor Terry Jardine. Terry, can you hear me? Stay with us, Terry. We're almost there.'

The squares stop falling now. There is only the white light.

He is an actor! His name is Terry Jardine!

'Terry? Can you hear me? We're almost there.'

'I think we're losing him.'

That hand on his forehead again. 'Terry. Stay with us, mate.'

The pull of the white light is getting stronger. But there is someone here who won't let him go. Someone who knows his name. *Oh, why don't they let me go? All I want is peace and quiet.* Now there in the middle of the white light is the silver bear waiting for him. He moves towards him.

'Check him for rings and piercings. I'm going to shock him.'

Rings are pulled from his fingers; he hears a whirring noise and then a beep.

'Clear.'

Now all the squares are torn off and only white light

remains. And in the middle of it is Terry, twisting and turning, falling, always falling, down and down and down.

He is freezing, freezing cold. A Winter's Tale indeed! Terry sees himself spread out, naked in the Arctic. Oh, he is so cold he can't stop shivering. His hands are restricted in some way, so he can't even try and rub himself warm. On the peripheries of his vision he sees a white bear walking towards him. Well, now he really is in trouble, isn't he? He struggles but can't move at all. All he can do is wait. The bear walks all the way round him. He sniffs him and then nudges his lips with his nose.

'What are you doing here?' he says.

Voices break in: 'What's that playing?'

'He was an actor. It's a CD of him as *Hamlet*.'

Was? Is he dead then?

'I can't make head nor tail of it. Can you?'

'Some guy who can't make up his mind whether to off himself or not: "To be or not to be".'

'Well, that's just what we need. Just what he needs.' The voice seems to come closer. 'Be, do you hear me, mate. This is all about being. No, not to be. Be.'

'Also, at the end of it, they're all dead.'

'Hmm. Well, we don't want that either.'

'He's well-known, apparently.'

'Famous or not, they all look much the same when they're in ICU.'

'It's a leveller, that's for sure.'

'How much longer are we going to be applying therapeutic hypothermia?'

Therapeutic hypothermia? What the hell is that?

Now the man with the blue sleeve is standing in front of him. 'I told you, you were going to die soon, didn't I?'

Trickster, the bloody trickster.

The bear is walking away from him, but he has left him with a terrible itch on the end of his nose. 'Wait,' he shouts. 'Could you just . . .?'

The bear stops, turns round and comes back. He rubs Terry's nose with his own nose. 'You've got into terrible shape. You're too fat for *Hamlet* and not old enough for Falstaff.'

What is going on? Abuse is coming from all directions, from the bear, from that bloody man with the blue sleeve.

'Terry?'

Oh, let me sleep.

'Terry.' Louder now.

It's no good, he can't sleep, they won't let him. He might as well open his eyes. But are these eyes? They feel like ping-pong balls that have been covered in glue and rolled in grit. He tries again. Now the white light has gone, the squares are no longer falling. The picture has stabilised. Some faces swim into view. His brother Ralph, Ludovico, and with his recognition of those two men his knowledge of himself returns to him in a huge wave and with it his remembrance of *The Winter's Tale.*

'The play,' he croaks.

'That's all OK,' Ludovico says. 'You mustn't worry about that. You have to concentrate on getting better.'

His brother Ralph is crying. Ralph never cries. Not even when he gave him Chinese burns as a boy and whipped his legs with nettles. Did he really do that? The fact his brother is crying worries Terry more than anything. His brother is a surgeon who has sewn men together who have been blown apart by IEDs. Terry closes his eyes, looking for the white light, the silver bear, even the man with the blue sleeve, but none of them is there. Now when he closes his eyes it is dark, not light, certainly not white light, and in the darkness is the sound of his brother struggling to

224

control himself, the warmth of Ludovico's hand gripping his.

Ludovico comes as often as he can manage.

'How's the play going?' Terry asks.

'It's going OK.'

'I hear Jim is very good in the role.'

'He's managing much better than I expected.'

Oh, she's warm. Inside him are all those performances, eight performances a week for three months. All those performances lie stillborn inside him, all those opportunities to bring his mother back from the dead – lost. How can he get rid of them? How can he move on? Now he's like an abattoir filled with rotting meat. He torments himself with asking Ludovico about the play. Torment upon torment. Until Ludovico says, 'We'll do it again. You were too young for the part anyway. It'll be much better when you're older and then we'll do it again.'

'You never told me you thought I was too young before.'

People tire him and he becomes irritable and tearful quickly. He's fed up with them gazing at him in wonderment, as if he's Jesus Christ come back from the dead. But people will keep coming. At night he wakes to see someone on their knees in the corner of the room praying. It's exhausting being a source of wonder. The person he really wants to talk to is the paramedic who worked on him in the back of the ambulance. He comes ten days later and sits down next to his bed in his green uniform, looking a little uncomfortable.

'I hear you're doing very well,' he says.

Terry stares at him. 'You saved my life.'

The man shakes his head. 'That was the defibrillator. Shocked you back to life, mate.'

'The fact you knew my name. I was heading for the light, you know. You brought me back.'

But he's not having it. 'No, you decided to come back. You brought yourself back. I was just doing my job.'

Terry doesn't believe it. He stares at him for some time. 'Nothing more?'

The man shakes his head. 'I just did my job.'

'Thank you,' Terry says and holds out his hand.

The man smiles and takes it awkwardly in his own.

It was as simple as that. One man had done his job properly and another man's life had been saved.

In time the bear visits. He seems a little shamefaced. He glows with success. Terry hates him.

'I'm sorry about what's happened,' Jim says, 'but it's a great part and I love doing it.'

'I hear you're doing really well,' Terry says and after a beat adds. 'You complete bastard.'

Jim looks a bit startled and then bursts out laughing. 'One man's tragedy is another man's opportunity.'

It breaks the ice and Jim goes on to regale him with gossip from the play, gossip about other actors he's worked with. He's funny and irreverent and he doesn't stay too long.

At the end he says, 'I'm really sorry about what's happened to you, but I'm so glad of the role. It's turning my life around. I can feel it every day.'

Terry nods. He understands. Of course he does. Some roles are like that. You don't necessarily have to be a success in them, but they do change you.

At night he stares into the darkness of the ward. It's like the bloody M25 in here. You have to get out of hospital in order to get a decent night's sleep, in order to get a decent meal. That's the cliché, but it's true. He closes his eyes. Here is the man with the blue sleeve. Oh, and here is the bear at his side. And for once they're not saying anything. Here they are, looking down at him. The man with the blue sleeve is

226

looking somewhat less sardonic. The bear – well, the bear is looking at him in the same way as he did before, as if he were something he is considering eating. How long are they going to keep doing this, Terry wonders? How long are they going to be there every time I close my eyes? What are they waiting for? Are they a comfort or a warning sign of something yet to come?

AURORA

New York, 2011

Aurora heard the front door open, but today it was perfume she smelled not aftershave. She came out of the kitchen, drying her hands on a kitchen towel. Mrs Pereira was standing in the hall. Geisha-like make-up covered her face, annihilating all the natural lustre of the skin. But maybe the skin would have no lustre. Maybe underneath the mask her face was grey.

'I've just finished, Madam,' Aurora said. 'I hope you had a good break.'

Mrs Pereira didn't reply. She placed her handbag on the hall table with great deliberateness. She blinked. Between them on the wall Saint Sebastian's pierced body slumped against the ropes that bound him. What was going on here? Aurora thought. Was the woman on drugs? Then suddenly Mrs Pereira staggered and grabbed hold of the table, her bag fell to the ground. A sob escaped her. Startled, Aurora moved towards her. Mrs Pereira's coat had fallen open. Now white was no longer the only colour in the apartment. Here was red – red blotches, red drips, a red spray across her pristine white dress.

'Help me,' Mrs Pereira said. 'Please help me.'

Aurora was not sure whether she was talking to her or Saint Sebastian, but one thing was certain, it was into her arms that she collapsed. It was to her that Mrs Pereira repeated, 'You are going to have to help me. Please.'

Aurora caught her by the elbows. She stared at those blood-red stains on the white dress; she looked up at the white mask of geisha make-up covering the stretched skin of Mrs Pereira's face, the red slash of lipstick. There was only so far that skin could be stretched before it tore. Something had torn. A mask threatened to slip. Saint Sebastian, slumped and pierced, looked down at them from the wall, his expression impassive. Despair was a great leveller. Mrs Pereira was no longer her employer. All that had gone. She was simply someone who needed her help. Something had happened to change everything.

'Are you hurt?'

Mrs Pereira shook her head.

'Come and sit down,' Aurora said, supporting her into the kitchen and perching her on one of the white leather stools. She tried not to look at the stains on the dress. Mrs Pereira let out a gasp and put her hand over her mouth. A thin wail started to come out of her. The sound was almost disembodied. There was something terrifying about it and Aurora frowned.

'Stop that,' she said firmly, talking to her as if she were a child who was about to make itself hysterical.

Mrs Pereira did stop, but she began to hiccup instead. Aurora went to the sink and got her some water. She stood close to her to reassure her and resisted with every cell of her being uttering the words that she knew would get her into all kinds of trouble: 'Tell me what happened.'

Mrs Pereira gulped down the water and Aurora refilled the glass and handed it back to her. It was as if all the unspoken words had crowded into the room and were pressing down, leaning over their shoulders, waiting for their opportunity.

'Will you help me?' Mrs Pereira said again.

And with a barely noticeable nod Aurora sealed her fate.

'But I don't want to know what has happened.'

Teetering on the chrome and white leather stool, Mrs Pereira gulped at her, the mask of her face quivered. For a moment, Aurora thought the skin of her face was going to split open, from the corners of her mouth to the tips of her ears, in a grotesque parody of the Joker.

'You should take off that dress,' Aurora said. 'You should change your clothes.'

Mrs Pereira was beginning to shake. Aurora visualised the inside of the bathroom cabinet stuffed with pills. 'Is there anything I can get you from the bathroom?'

She nodded, named a drug.

In the bathroom Aurora checked the names on the bottles before finding the right one, took it back to the kitchen and handed it to her. Mrs Pereira shook a couple of pills into her hand and swallowed.

'Your clothes,' Aurora said.

She nodded and there in the kitchen kicked off her shoes, removed her dress and coat. Aurora bundled them into a bin bag, which she then placed in a large Ralph Lauren bag. Mrs Pereira walked out of the kitchen towards the bedroom, walking on the tips of her toes as if she was still wearing heels. Aurora wondered if she had to follow her, wondered if she was going to do something stupid, but a few minutes later she returned wearing a pair of black jeans and a cream oversize jumper, which hung off one of her shoulders, showing her black bra strap. Now she looked about fifteen years younger, almost like one of Aurora's kids. She had tidied up her face, so the big black panda eyes were gone.

'He . . .' she began.

Aurora held out her hand, warning her to stop. And for a moment Mrs Pereira did stop. But then she said, 'All I was going to say is, he's not coming back.'

Aurora absorbed that piece of information in silence.

'Did you come through the front entrance?'

She shook her head. 'I waited until one of the janitors came out of the back entrance and then walked up a few flights before getting in the lift.'

So, Aurora thought, she was not so out of it that she was unable to think about what the best thing to do was. Her opinion of her shifted slightly.

'You will not be wanting me again,' Aurora said.

Mrs Pereira shook her head.

'If anyone asks, I will say that I haven't seen you.'

Suddenly she seized Aurora in a shockingly fierce hug.

When she had disentangled herself, Aurora said, 'I'll take these away with me and get rid of them. You must give me some other clothes, so that I can dispose of them on eBay.'

Mrs Pereira nodded and went into the bedroom and came back with a pair of trousers and a dress.

'Is there anything else that needs disposing of?'

The woman glanced down at the bag at her feet. It was made of pale leather and had a thick fringe that dropped from halfway up to the bottom. It was the type of fringe you might see on the back of a cowboy's jacket. She seemed reluctant to look inside.

Aurora knew better than to touch it. 'Look inside it,' she said, 'and decide what needs to be got rid of.'

Mrs Pereira opened the bag warily, as if something might jump out at her. She took various items out and placed them

231

on a drying-up cloth – keys, to the house and a car, a wallet, a purse, an address book. The wallet appeared to be coated with something. Then she zipped up the bag and looked at Aurora. 'Everything else in there should go,' she said.

Aurora nodded. She emptied the Ralph Lauren bag, placed the handbag at the bottom and then put the clothes back on top of it.

'Right,' she said and picked her coat off the back of the kitchen door.

'Wait a minute.' The woman walked out of the kitchen and a few moments later came back with large bundles of cash in her hands.

'Here,' she said.

'No,' Aurora replied.

Mrs Pereira looked down at the bundles of money, as if she now had no idea what to do with them.

'Will you stay here?' Aurora asked.

'I can't.'

They moved back into the hall, Aurora and Mrs Pereira. Aurora glanced at the painting of Saint Sebastian. If she was not coming back, this would be the last time she would see him. She muttered a prayer under her breath in Spanish. Mrs Pereira looked puzzled, looked at the painting and then at Aurora.

'Take it,' she said suddenly.

'But . . .'

'I'm serious.'

'I won't be able to get it out of here without it being seen.'

'If it is out of the frame, it can be rolled up.'

'But isn't it . . .'

'Look, I'll show you.'

She went into the kitchen and came back with a hammer and a screwdriver. Four brief sharp taps later and the frame was in four pieces, the painting loose. Aurora looked at her in amazement. Nothing in her appearance would make you think she could wield a hammer and screwdriver with such dexterity. Seeing the expression on Aurora's face, Mrs Pereira laughed, 'I was a daddy's girl. Always hanging around in the yard. Picked up a few things.'

Not for the first time Aurora wondered what journey this woman had come on in her life that had delivered her up to where she was right now. What disguise she had adopted to survive.

Saint Sebastian lay on the ground without the protection of his frame. The painting looked everyday now like a judge who had stepped outside the court without his wig or gown and had become an everyman lost in the crowd.

Mrs Pereira went and got a cardboard paper roll, the kind they gave you if you bought a poster from an art shop. She took the painting and rolled it up and placed it inside. 'It will fit in the bag,' she said and handed it to Aurora.

She was right, it did.

'You must go now.'

She hugged Aurora again and said, 'You always seemed so kind.'

Then Aurora was out in the hall. It was only as she was walking through the foyer and waving goodbye to the receptionist that she realised what she had colluded in. She was out of a job, a good job, but she could always go back to the agency that had first placed her. I have him, she thought, as she stepped out onto the street. Saint Sebastian is all mine.

But the truth was Aurora had no idea what she had. No idea at all.

TULLIA BUFFO

Venice, 1576

Oh, how she has yearned for him

It is dangerous for women to move around the city at night. Rape is widespread but ignored. Fire, on the other hand, terrifies everyone. If a woman is attacked, she shouts 'fire' because she knows that will bring people out into the street. Why cry rape when no one will come? Tullia wants no one to know where she is going. She writes another note, telling Marco the circumstances in which she will come to him. She waits until the household is asleep and then changes into the clothing she has had her maid set aside. Before the plague struck one of her clients had required that she dress up as a boy under her normal garb. He would then tear off her female clothing and rub himself against her, while muttering obscenities. It was easy money, as far as she was concerned, although she didn't know why the man didn't pay one of the gondoliers for a similar service; it would have been cheaper than coming to her. Perhaps it was because he let it be known that he visited her and thus hoped to disguise his true sexual predilections.

She looks at herself in the mirror. Her hair is tied up and tucked under a black velvet cap, which has a lynx fur trim. She wears black velvet breeches and a black doublet with slashes in the sleeves which reveal cream silk. Her cloak is of the blackest of black cloth, her shoes of the softest leather. Her client had insisted on sending his tailor to her, so the clothes are of the finest quality and fit her perfectly. She fastens a belt holding a dagger round her waist. Now she is ready.

Quietly she lets herself out into the *calle*. It is late and the taverns are closed for the night. The city lies still under a crescent moon and the cold light of winter stars. Off in the northern part of the city a dog howls. She moves swiftly through the streets, keeping to the back alleys as much as possible, her hat pulled down at an angle over her face. If she is challenged, her disguise will easily be seen through. Even dressed like this she does not make a very believable man. Her face is altogether too feminine, her voice too high to escape detection. She will not pass, not even as a boy. She hurries onwards, frightened and excited in equal measure, towards the rendezvous they have agreed.

At first she thinks he hasn't come. She looks around, becoming increasingly worried and upset, but then he appears from the shadows, walking swiftly towards her. It is not just her stomach which lurches at the sight of him, it is her whole body. The first thing he does is kneel at her feet and press his face against her stomach. She strokes his head, then she takes his hands and kisses the end of each finger.

Oh, how she has yearned for him. How she has longed for him to come to her.

Tears drip down her face onto his. He stands up and kisses her. She looks up as a shred of cloud passes across the face of the crescent moon, as the city is plunged briefly into darkness, as he begins to ease open her clothing, as she feels his hands stroking her, as he enters her, as their cries spiral upwards into the arms of the crescent moon and the glittering winter stars.

Neither of them has spoken a word.

Nothing changes; everything changes.

Everything changes; nothing changes.

That is what love does. It tears everything down and reconstructs a new world. And then life goes on.

Marco asks nothing of her. He does not ask her to cease from her profession. In fact, he is not a man of many words at all. He assumes, rightly, that she will have heard them all before. So he remains silent. He does not write her poems. He communicates mainly with his body. It is enough for her. Oh, it is quite enough. Their relationship seems to exist in a different realm altogether. Whenever she asks to meet him, wherever she suggests, he comes.

Everyday life goes on much as usual. Tullia had not forgotten about the goods that had been stolen from her. As she had promised, she registered a complaint with the Guardians of the Night Watch and then with the ecclesiastical authorities. No one came forward within the nine allotted days to give any information to the Cancelleria Patriarcha. All the precious items, all the money remained lost. And because she could not be absolutely certain of her guilt, when Elisabetta came to her and begged for her job she gave it back to her. There was a shortage of good servants and at least they knew each other's ways. And there was always the hope that she might repent and that the items would reappear. It was a very faint hope, but Tullia held onto it.

And then a few months later it happened again; this time it was money from under her mattress, a pair of scissors on a silver chain and a gilt prayer book. This time Tullia acted. She withheld all her servants' wages: the cook's, the maid's, and her children's tutor's. She called them all together and told them that if the items did not reappear forthwith, she would withhold their wages to the sum of the items and money which had gone missing. Then she went out to mass, leaving them to fester.

When she came back, she was immediately seized by Elisabetta and dragged into the kitchen. It was packed with people and stifling. A dog sniffed the floor, looking for scraps. All her servants were there and in addition a woman who lived in the next-door house with six children, three boys and three girls. They were standing round the kitchen table, peering at a bowl of water, as if it contained serpents that might reach out and strike them. As soon as Tullia entered the room, they turned their frightened gaze on her.

'What is the meaning of this?'

'The children are performing the *inghistera*, lady.'

She was suddenly aware of Redolpho Vanitelli, the children's tutor, lounging in the doorway behind her, absorbing it all, in the way black cloth absorbs light. His hard little eyes taking in everything: the bowl of holy water, the holy branch, the sacred candles, the faces of the terrified children.

'Go on, go on,' the woman urged. 'Say the words after me. "Holy Angel, White Angel, by your holiness and by our virginity, show us who took the things which are lost."'

The thin, reedy voices of the terrified children filled the air.

'Now,' the woman said, 'look into the bowl.'

Slowly, the six children leant forwards. One screamed piercingly. Another fainted. The other four leaped backwards from the table in unison. One stood on the paw of the dog, which yelped and ran for the door. Pandemonium ensued.

'Stop this!' Tullia roared. 'Everyone be quiet. I will not have such acts performed under my roof. Is that clear? This is superstitious nonsense and it will not produce the swift return of your wages. All it does is terrify innocent children. None of you will be paid until what has been stolen is returned.'

There was silence in the kitchen, apart from the snivelling of children. The cook picked up the bowl and the neighbour removed the wedding ring which had been placed underneath it. Candles, sacred bough, blessed water and sacred candles were all removed, along with the near hysterical weeping children. Vanitelli was the last to leave, lounging in the doorway as the others pushed past him.

Up in her bedroom Tullia found she was shaking. She sat down and tried to calm herself. As a child, her mother had made her perform this ritual when a coat went missing. She had made her repeat the same incantation, and when Tullia had looked into the bowl there was her father's face, as clear as a bell, looking back at her. She had not wanted to get her father into trouble and so she had lied to her mother and said that she had seen nothing. Her mother had not believed her and had beaten her until she confessed. A terrible row had then ensued between her mother and father and that had been the last time she had seen him. It was shortly after this happened that her mother had told her that she would follow her into the same profession.

The following week Vanitelli 'found' the prayer book for sale in a bookshop in the Merceria, but still she refused to budge. She would not pay them until everything was returned. She was adamant and it was then that they turned against her and she received an order to appear at the Inquisition Courts.

Someone had accused her of witchcraft.

She immediately ceased all communication with Marco. She did not want any taint of suspicion to fall on him because of his connection to her.

'I am terrified,' she says. 'What will happen if they find me guilty?'

'They won't.'

Her old patron, Domenico Venier, has finally returned to the city. He has already been investigated by the Inquisition and come out triumphant; he has insisted that she come and see him. He sits twisted by gout in his wheelchair. She knows he is in constant pain. When she tends to him, she has to be very gentle indeed. She must put no pressure on his joints. She must minister to him with great delicacy. She throws herself down by the side of his chair and weeps.

'Tullia!' He strokes her head very gently. 'You know it is a sign of the times. As long as you denounce the water ritual as superstition, that is all they need to hear.'

'I will be whipped like Isabella. I will be put on public display at the Rialto. I will be burnt . . .'

'Stop it! The authorities are all too aware that many of these accusations originate in petty squabbles. Most of these cases are dropped after a few hearings. Very few are sentenced. I will help you. They came after me too, don't forget, and I won. You will win. We will plan your victory together. There is nothing to fear.'

'But it's the Inquisition!' She shivers involuntarily. 'The city is turning against the courtesans. It blames us for the plague. It blames us for everything bad that has befallen it!'

'In a climate of fear people are quick to denounce others because they fear otherwise that they themselves will be denounced. Our Republic is strong. It does not take kindly to interference from the Inquisitors. It is a question of authority. But of course they have to pay lip service to Rome.

Together we will go through the questions they will ask you. Together we will prepare your defence. Take heart. I will not allow anything to happen to you.' The skin of his hand is as dry as parchment, the knuckles of his fingers swollen and twisted. She holds his hand softly against her face and then kisses the palm.

He sighs; the touch of her lips is exquisite. It creates a shiver through his body of pain. And pleasure. Abruptly he gestures for his servants to leave the room.

Later, they go through it again and again.

'Repeat what I have told you,' he says.

'I must not lose my composure. I must not become angry. I must respond obediently to the Inquisitor's questions. I must stick to the facts.'

'And what will you stress?'

'I did not allow the ceremony. The ceremony was conducted by my servants and neighbours. When I saw what was happening, I tried to bring it to an end. I left the room. I do not believe in the ceremony. It was Vanitelli who urged the others to perform the ceremony because my servants' wages had been stopped and he wished to prove that he was innocent of the thefts.'

'And you will not get angry.'

'No, I will be as meek as a lamb.'

'And when they say it was wrong of you to allow such a ritual to take place in your house, what will you say?'

'I will say I recognise that I have erred and beg to be pardoned for it.'

'But isn't it true that you have devised other invocations to the devil to make men fall in love with you?'

'What? Do I look as if I need the devil's help?'

'Tullia, is that really your version of being meek as a lamb?'

She blushes. 'You were tricking me?'

240

'Whatever they say to you, Tullia, you must appear obedient, meek and mild. You must under no circumstances get angry. You must keep your composure. You must use your mind.'

'My servants steal from me and yet it is I who am on trial.'

'But they will not win if you do as I say. Do not let them win. Keep your composure and be obedient to the Inquisitor and everything will turn out for the best.'

She nods.

'Now then, what is this I hear about you eating meat on a Friday?'

'What are you talking about?'

Suddenly he is shouting at her. 'Is it true that you have been seen eating meat on a Friday?'

Tullia adopts a demure expression, her hands clasped in front of her. 'Sire, I have given birth six times. Unfortunately three of the children did not survive, God rest their souls. But all the births were on a Friday. The only circumstances that I can think of in which I may have partaken of cheese or eggs were in circumstances when I was much in need of sustenance because of the exertions of the births. I would under no other circumstances have partaken of forbidden foods.'

Her patron nods. 'Better,' he says. 'Smarter. Much, much smarter. Now you are using this.' He taps his forehead.

Tullia smiles, unclasps her hands and puts her hands on her hips. 'I think I'm beginning to get the hang of this,' she says.

'Good. So let's go through it one more time. Now then, do you believe that the *inghistera* can summon the devil?'

'I do not.'

'Now name your enemies.'

'My enemies . . . ?' She reels off a list of names.

'Perhaps without so much zeal,' Domenico says. 'Perhaps with more sadness, Tullia, and less certainty.'

'Oh yes, yes. . . .'

She clears her throat and repeats the list much more hesitantly and with some sorrow in her tone.

'Better,' he says. 'Yes, that is much better.'

TERRY
&
LUDOVICO

London, 2011

Eventually, after fitting his heart with an ICD, which would shock him back to life if the same thing happened again, the doctors let him go home. Terry felt exhausted, depressed, as if he had no skin. He could feel the metal disc of the device in his shoulder above his heart. It was summer. He sat at the window, staring out at the plane tree on the other side of the road, thinking of his mother, and wept. He touched the disc. 'Beam me up, Scotty,' he said. 'No, beam me back to before the cardiac arrest. To before.' What was life playing at? *Like flies to wanton boys are we to the gods; they kill us for their sport.*

Kill him and, in his case, bring him back to life. Now he was the wife, not the tyrant king.

But why? And for how long?

The play lies rotting in him. In his dreams he returned to the Arctic wastes, the white bear and the man with the blue sleeve. Every night they were there in various combinations. He didn't know if the depression he was experiencing was a product of his almost having died or something else.

In the end Ludovico persuaded him to go and talk to someone – a therapist – just a few sessions to process what had happened to him.

In the first session he was barely articulate.

In the second he cried.

By the third, he could talk about the Arctic wastes, the bear and the man with the blue sleeve, the dreams he had every night.

'I wake up shivering,' he said. 'I can't get warm. At night, lines from the play . . .'

'Which play is that?'

'*The Winter's Tale.*'

The therapist smiled slightly. 'Really?'

'Well, yes, it was the play I was rehearsing when . . . didn't I tell you that last time?'

'You may have.'

'Are you listening to me?' Terry said angrily.

'You're angry with me.'

'Yes,' Terry said. 'I bloody well am. I'm paying you to listen to me. If you're not going to listen, I want my money back. I almost died and you don't even have the decency to remember which play I was in.'

'I'm very sorry,' the therapist said. 'Please sit back down and continue to tell me about your dream.'

Terry did sit back down. Suddenly he felt very upset. 'I feel as if I'm never going to feel warm again in my life. You know, they have to give you drugs to stop you shivering when they apply therapeutic hypothermia. I feel like all the shivering I might have done if I could have has become trapped in my system. They have to come out. So now all I do is shiver. They're all backed up.'

'Is that what it's called – therapeutic hypothermia?'

'Yes.'

'Gosh,' the therapist said.

Gosh was not what Terry was looking for. Gosh didn't cut it somehow.

The fourth session, he cancelled. Instead he went for a very slow walk around the park.

It is a beautiful summer day. Here there are bees and birds and grass and cornflowers and poppies. He sits on a bench and looks out at a meadow of grass and flowers. The sky is a clear vivid blue. Planes fly over on the flight path to Heathrow. As soon as one is overhead, the lights of the next one are visible on the horizon. There is something mesmerising about it. He sits watching them, finding the regularity of the flight path therapeutic. He dozes, the bees buzz around him and the squirrels run along the brick wall behind him, jumping from there onto the low hanging branches of an oak.

The man with the blue sleeve leans on the wall looking at him. His arms are folded in front of him, his eyes red and puffy.

'You're lucky,' he says. 'You've got a second chance. Lots of people don't get that.'

Lucky?

Yes, he is.

The bear rolls in the meadow. He extends his front paws as far above his head as he can. He lies there stretched out, the sun blazing down on him. 'I'm hot,' he says.

Terry wakes. The planes are still droning overhead. The sun is shining on him. He *is* hot. In front of him in the meadow is a large flattened space. A woman and her two children are walking away from him towards the exit to the walled garden. She is folding a rug; a sweet wrapper glints on the flattened area. He gets heavily to his feet, picks up the sweet wrapper and puts it in his pocket, then slowly makes his way home.

The therapist phones. Terry explains he's decided to stop. He's OK about it, doesn't try and persuade him differently, and then at the end he says, 'A friend's just come back from holiday in Canada. There's a place there where they have white bears. They're not polar bears but a breed of black bear but with white coats. They're called spirit bears. When he told me, I thought of your white bear. You didn't describe it as a polar bear, did you?'

'No, it wasn't, isn't a polar bear.'

'Spirit bear – the name jumped out at me.'

'Yes, thank you.'

Spirit bears – gosh!

TERRY

&

LUDOVICO

London, 2011

The London and New York runs of *The Winter's Tale* had finished and there was a three-week break before the cast went on their travels again to Spain, Germany and Greece. Ludovico and Terry sat in Terry's front room with the Sunday papers scattered around them. Glancing at Ludovico, absorbed in the review section of the *Sunday Times*, Terry wondered how he would have managed without him. Ludovico had been steadily supportive through all the ups and downs of his convalescence, through the times when Terry was so tired and depressed he could barely communicate, and also the times when he was angry and ragingly upset. Over the last three months Ludovico had flown back frequently from New York to be with him.

Ludovico stood up and stretched. He'd been in an odd,

jumpy mood all afternoon. 'Come to Venice with me next weekend,' he said.

'Err,' Terry replied. Usually he needed about six months to contemplate going away. He mainly associated holidays with tremendous levels of stress. Holidays with Colin had always been dreadful because they simply emphasised their differences. In the end they'd given up going. Colin was a sun bunny; he could lie like a lizard on a beach quite happily for hours. If Terry did that, he ended up the colour of salami, covered in a rash with a blinding headache. He had the reverse of SAD. Intense sun depressed him. In hot countries he was only really happy once the sun had gone down.

'Err?' Ludovico said, mimicking him. 'I have lots of air miles. It won't cost you anything. We can stay in the apartment of a friend.'

'Have you finally decided to go and see your mother?'

'Perhaps. Come on. Come.'

'I don't think so.'

'What is it?'

'Holidays with Colin were rarely successful. Each time we came back I thought we would split up. Colin hated how I was on holiday. He said it brought the worst aspects of my personality to the fore.'

'Ah, I see. You're worried I will hate you if we go on holiday together?'

'Perhaps,' Terry conceded. 'I usually hate myself.'

'And if I promise not to hate you?'

'It's not a promise you can really make, is it?'

Ludovico leant forwards and kissed him. 'Trust me,' he said. 'Come.'

Terry kissed him back. 'Don't look now,' he said.

'At what?'

'No, the film. *Don't Look Now*, when they go to Venice. It doesn't end well.'

Ludovico burst out laughing. 'I promise you it won't be anything like that.'

'And then there's *Death in Venice*, of course' Terry said. 'It might be tempting fate after my recent brush with the grim reaper.'

'Don't be ridiculous. It will do you good.'

'Also I'm not sure I can go through the security gates at the airport with the ICD.'

'Nonsense, I've read all that stuff on the internet and you just tell them and they let you go around the gate and frisk you by hand. It'll be fine.'

'And I'll have to get myself some clothes.'

'Your clothes are fine.'

'But it's Italy, the country of the *bella figura*. It's Venice, one of the most beautiful cities on earth. I'm too fat and not well dressed enough. You know how they stare at you.'

Ludovico shook his head. 'You're an actor. You're used to being stared at. And do you seriously think there are no fat, badly dressed Italians?'

'I'm used to being stared at *in character on a stage*. That is a very important distinction. And I know for a fact that there are no gay, fat, badly dressed Italians in Venice. I know it and Colin has taken every item of cashmere clothing I had. Well, all the cashmere that the moths hadn't claimed.'

Ludovico sat down on the sofa next to Terry, took hold of his face and began to kiss him. A while later, he came up for air. 'I am going to keep kissing you until you say yes.'

Terry laughed. 'There's absolutely no incentive for me to agree then.'

TERRY
Don't Look Now

Venice, 2011

In Venice, how could one not look? In fact, how could one not gawp in utter amazement?

Terry, standing in St Mark's Basilica, dressed in a smart new coat and thick grey cashmere scarf, gazed up at the ceiling and stared at the mass of gold mosaic shimmering above him and tried to imagine how it was that the creator of that ceiling had planned how to get that effect with all those tiny pieces of stone, or *tesserae*, as he now knew they were called, having read something about it in a guide. How on earth could you imagine what the impact would be from down here, looking up? Gold was the overwhelming colour, gold upon gold, cascading down on him, a gold that appeared to turn the light in the cathedral almost green like the waters of the lagoon. Terry was not particularly religious, but he was filled with something close to awe – awe at the creators of this extraordinary shimmering ceiling, awe at the act of collective imagination that had gone into this building. It, like the whole of Venice, was simply astonishing.

He had first come here at the age of ten, the second place he had ever been abroad, the first being Florence at the age of seven. Before they had come he had not been able to understand how a city could have no cars. What about roads? he'd said. How do people get about? They'd come in the Easter holidays; it had rained heavily and he remembered running across the wooden boards put down over the flood waters. He'd loved that rather more than his parents had. His father, rather like a cat, liked to keep his feet dry and had suffered somewhat because he had failed to bring any wellington boots. He remembered his father's attachment to an unusual shaped guidebook, *Venice for Pleasure* by J.G. Links, which he had read religiously from cover to cover, leading them on the walks denoted therein even when they ended up in what seemed to Terry the most charmless, most obscure parts of Venice possible.

He had found himself thinking about his parents a lot since he'd been here. But in such a city, a city where the ghosts muscled out the living, maybe that wasn't so surprising. He'd seen his father leaning against a wall, *Links* in hand, glasses perched on the end of his nose. He'd even heard him in the carrying tones of an elderly Englishman, thinking that if he spoke English more loudly and deliberately somehow an Italian would be able to understand him.

He looked down at the ornate patterns under his feet, across at the swirling patterns of the marble columns and then up at that ravishing golden ceiling. Where could one look without feeling overwhelmed, without being astounded?

By the time he stepped out of the cathedral back into the misty square, back to the flutter of pigeons and the groups of tourists huddled round their guides, he felt as if he might burst. What could he possibly do now? The famous cafe, Florian's, was close by, but it would make him feel too like a tourist and this is what he hated most about holidays, this feeling of being outside looking in at something one could never have access to. So instead he walked across the square and looked out at the lagoon. The sea calmed him and the mist, which seemed to be thickening into a fog, chilled him. The combination encouraged him not to take himself so seriously and he strolled back across the square into Florian's and ordered himself a staggeringly expensive hot chocolate to warm himself up. Sitting on red velvet seating in front of a white marble table, for once he luxuriated in being the audience to the white-jacketed waiters, as they floated round the tourists with an air of ineffable superiority, exquisite players against the most magnificent of backdrops. In a city like Venice you were never going to be more than a passing shadow on the wall, but these young men were certainly very beautiful shadows. While he watched them, he wondered how things were going for Ludovico.

On the way back to the apartment Terry paused for a moment, looking down at a group of gondolas tethered together. Not much business today; it was too foggy and damp for anyone other than the extremely hardy to wish to take to one of those. Business was slow. No self-respecting Venetian, he suspected, would be seen dead in a gondola. The boats, like Florian's, like the city itself, had become the most beautiful and exquisite of tourist traps. The gondoliers were doing what taxi drivers do in every country when business is slow; they were smoking and gossiping, and complaining about the lack of customers and those bastards in the local council who were making their lives hell through overregulation and business taxes.

LUDOVICO

Venice, 2011

The island of San Clemente emerged slowly out of the fog that had been lying across the lagoon since the start of the day. Shivering on deck, the damp seeping through his coat and his trousers, Ludovico stared at it blankly. He had come out here to escape the questions of the boatman, who seemed a damned sight too inquisitive about who he was and what brought him here. Using the excuse of needing a cigarette, he had given up the warmth of the man's cabin and was now precariously balanced on the bow, peering into the mist, holding his coat collar together with one hand and a cigarette in the other. The pier emerged suddenly out of the fog and, as the boat bumped up against it, Ludovico was hurled onto his knees and his cigarette disappeared into the swirling, fog-covered waters. He swore: it was his last one and God knows he was in need of the solace of cigarettes to calm his nerves. The boatman's boy jumped ashore and held out his hand to help Ludovico from boat to land. Ludovico turned round and said something to the boatman and he nodded. The boy jumped back on board and soon the boat had disappeared into the fog, the throb of its engine the only indication of its presence.

Ludovico stood shivering on the pier. The only communication he had had with his mother was an exchange of emails. From him: Yes, he would like to meet and this is when he would be in Venice. From her: Great. Get this boat. Come at this time to this place.

He had been told to wait here to be picked up. He looked out to sea and he looked towards the interior of the island. In both directions the view was the same: thick fog. He thought back to the conversation he'd had with his father at the airport, when his father was about to fly home.

'After all,' Andrea said, 'it's only your mother.'

'Only!' He'd looked at his father and seen by the smile on his face that he was teasing him.

'Only your mother,' his father had repeated, but he had accompanied his words with a silent scream and raised hands, a mock parody of someone in a silent horror movie.

Ludovico had burst out laughing. 'Yes, and you are only my father,' he said as he gripped him in his arms.

'But, of course,' Andrea said. 'And anyway, my duties were over a long time ago. Now I hope we are friends.'

That conversation had taken place before he knew his mother was Mariangela Acquarone. Since then he had had several phone calls with his father. 'Because of who she is,' Andrea had said, 'I thought it was very important that you were established in your own personality, in your own career, before you knew. Fame and celebrity are vacuous, pernicious things. I did not want you dragged into something you could not handle, something that was corrupting. I wanted you to be someone in your own right, to have your own confidence.

Not to be "the son of Mariangela Acquarone". I did not want that for you at all. This was partly why I was upset when you went into the film industry. I was frightened of what would become of you. But you have carved that out all by yourself, for yourself, so now I am very proud of you.'

Ludovico flipped up the collar of his coat and nestled his chin more deeply into his scarf. When he had told his father that he was going to meet his mother, Andrea had uttered one word, 'good', and then changed the subject. He shivered. It was as if the cold was slim, icy fingers which could find their way into every opening, however small, finding gaps between neck and scarf, trousers and ankles, cuff and wrist. He began to walk up and down the pier, partly to keep warm, partly to steady his nerves. This is a mistake, he thought. I shouldn't have come. I had a choice in the matter. I did not have to come just because she asked. I did not have to do this. But now he was on an island in the middle of the Venetian lagoon in a fog. It was too late, much too late for such thoughts.

'Signor Zabarella. A pleasure to meet you. My name is Paolo.'

A figure emerged out of the fog. He looked like the maitre d' of a smart restaurant. He held out his hand. 'I greatly admired your recent film, especially the part where . . .'

He went into some detail, describing the part of the film that Ludovico himself was most proud of. Ludovico took his hand, feeling flattered and suspicious in just about equal measure. The man held his very cold hand in both his own warm ones.

'We must get you in from the cold,' he said. 'The weather is most inhospitable.'

He led the way, chatting away amiably to Ludovico about the history of the island and the hotel and the vagaries of Venice in the autumn. He was told that his mother had an apartment on the top floor of the hotel and eventually he was led into a room in which an enormous fire was roaring. A couple of grand French-style chairs, upholstered in white linen, stood either side of the fire. They looked like they deserved to be occupied by corpulent red-faced men in big wigs and women with oversized bustles. The room was empty other than three dogs that were lying in front of the fire. They immediately got up and came towards the visitors, wriggling their bodies and wagging their tails.

'She'll be along shortly,' Paolo said and left the room.

Ludovico petted the dogs until they got bored and went and threw themselves down once more in front of the fire. He followed them and stood in front of it, gazing into the flames. It was a proper fire, he noted, not one of those fake gas ones with blue flames. A proper live fire. It was the dogs which alerted him to the fact someone had come into the room. He turned round and saw her.

My God, he thought, she's still beautiful.

'I was so nervous I thought I'd let the dogs greet you first, and Paolo of course. I thought maybe if you liked the dogs ... Thank you so much for coming. I wasn't sure that you would, but I'm so very glad that you have.'

He was in such a state he was barely able to take her in. Although she was there and he was here, it was as if they were in two different films playing against the same wall. It was as if they were in different mediums altogether. The dogs, which had got to their feet and were wriggling their way towards her and then back to him, seemed the only thing that was connecting them.

What had he been expecting? He didn't know until that moment that it wasn't this. It was a bit like seeing a film of a beloved cartoon you have only ever read and experienced on the printed page. It was OK until the characters began to speak and then you knew that wasn't how they were supposed to sound. Asterix didn't have a squeaky voice. You had given every character your own voice, so you just knew it was wrong because they had always sounded like you. And what had he made of his mother in his head? How had she looked and sounded? Not like this, nothing like this. Not like Mariangela Acquarone. For one thing, this woman looked in no way maternal.

She walked across the rug-covered floor and held out her hand to him. He took it.

'It's very cold out there,' she remarked, looking down at the top of his hand. 'But you know I prefer Venice like this, when you can't see it, to midsummer when you can't move for tourists. I like the mystery.'

Ludovico was fed up with mysteries. His father's, his mother's, the moon's.

Fuck mysteries, he thought. Fuck them all.

She walked over to the window. 'Usually you get the most beautiful view of the city,' she said. 'But not today.'

No, Ludovico thought, nothing was visible today.

'This building has been all kinds of things, a monastery, a quarantine station, an army barracks and even a lunatic asylum.'

Ludovico wasn't really listening, he'd already had the history lesson from Paolo. He leant down and patted one of the dogs.

'Please sit down,' she said, gesturing to the oversized chair.

The chair was too short and too deep in the seat for him to be able to sit in it comfortably. In the end, he sat back as far as he could and stretched his legs straight out in front of him, feeling a bit like a plank of wood leaning against a trestle. His mother kicked off her shoes and curled up in the chair opposite in a way that reminded Ludovico of Nero. That was obviously the way to do it. The fire began to heat up one side of his face, the other side stayed resolutely chilly. He felt a pulse of pain begin to throb in his temple. He should never have come. This whole thing was a huge mistake. This woman wasn't his mother; she was a stranger. He had wanted to please his father, but it was a mistake. Now it was a question of how he could get out of here as quickly as possible.

She was looking into the fire. He glanced around the room. This was a hotel, but this room did not look like a hotel suite, there were too many personal items present, photos and paintings. Was this really her home?

'What do you think of the place?' she said in slightly self-mocking tones.

He shrugged, refusing to be impressed.

'Why now?' he asked. 'Why now, after all these years?'

A slight smile formed on her lips, 'Well, there was never really going to be a good time, was there?' She paused. 'But I saw your film.'

He didn't say anything.

'I think seeing the film made me curious to meet you.'

Ludovico wondered if that was why his father had been so hostile to his film. Had he known that it would flush his mother out into the open? Maybe that had been his real dislike of it, not the 'poisonous bubbles' but his poisonous mother.

'I very much admired it,' she said. 'I found it very touching.'

Ludovico felt his face stiffen. 'First films are like babies playing with their own shit,' he said, being deliberately coarse. 'You've no idea what you're doing.'

Who was this woman? he thought. I don't know anything about her, not a thing, and I refuse to make this easy for her.

He stood up. 'I'm sorry, I shouldn't have come. It's too much . . . I must go. I have someone waiting for me.'

'A girl?'

He didn't reply. His private life was none of her business.

'You can use the hotel boat – it runs every ten minutes or so to St Mark's Square. Paolo will show you where to get it.'

As they parted, she handed him her card. 'I would very much like to keep in touch,' she said. 'I am so glad you came.'

He glanced briefly at the card and pocketed it, then followed Paolo out of the hotel and down to the pier.

'The Signora has been so looking forward to meeting you,' he said. 'She knew it would be difficult. She's been so very nervous.'

Ludovico felt like crying. He gripped the top of his nose and said, 'I'm sorry, but it's hard . . .'

Paolo held out his hand and Ludovico took it. 'I hope next time it will be easier. Are you staying long?'

'Just over the weekend.'

'My family run a restaurant in the city. It is off the beaten track. Venetians eat in it, not tourists.' He took out a note-book and scribbled down some details. 'Mention my name and you will be well looked after'. He tore off the piece of paper and handed it to Ludovico. A rather fancy boat was approaching the pier and Ludovico joined the line of people who were queuing to board it. As the boat nudged its way through the fog towards St Mark's Square, he considered that he had never felt in so much need of a drink in his life.

THE BOATMAN

Venice, 1576

I hold my father's eye in the palm of my hand. It is a beautiful thing; the most valuable thing I own. There have been many times over the years when I have been tempted to sell it. Many times when I have been on the verge of taking it into the ghetto to see what I could get for it. But each time something has happened to render the sale unnecessary. Towards the end of his life, it pained my father to wear it and he replaced it with an eye patch. One day I will take it to one of the merchants who deal in precious metals, but for the moment I haven't the heart. It is all I have left of him. When I hold it in the palm of my hand, it is him I see looking back at me. It was the nuns who were to blame for my poor father's punishment. Whenever ill fortune strikes the city, the authorities will do everything to divert the blame away from themselves, from their soldiers and sailors. Always the same cry goes up. Corruption! It is the same in times of plague. It is the corruption of the city that has brought this bad fortune down upon us. And who do they blame? The Jews, the sodomites, the corruption of the nunneries. But the corruption of the nunneries was caused by the patricians themselves. They cannot afford the dowries to marry off all their daughters and so, not wishing to dissipate their wealth, those who are not the first-born are placed in the nunneries, and they have become little better than bordellos. Everyone in the city knows this, but nothing is done. There is even a name given for the young men who 'visit' them – *muneghini*. When I was a young man, I used to believe that the rooting out of corruption would make fortune shine upon us again, but now as an older man I know that fortune comes and goes as regularly as the tides. I know a Jew may be as decent and kind a man as a Christian and a Saracen, that one thing that happens as regularly as the tides is that people in power will do everything to divert attention away from their own shortcomings.

My poor father was an innocent victim of one of the city's periodic fits of morality. He was an innocent victim, while the real perpetrator got away with barely a rap on his soft, fat knuckles. Of course the moral of the tale is that it does not do to get caught between a young priest's lust and a nun's open legs. That is a very dangerous thing to do. It is enough to lose you an eye and a hand, especially if you are only a poor boatman, especially if you are not in holy orders and cannot call on the church courts to protect you, especially if you do not have a rich, famous father and the city wants to make an example of you. Pomponio is still in the city, still ferreting around for his father's paintings. Tormented by what he imagines has been stolen from him.

Now Tullia Buffo is also at risk. Here she comes dressed in black, veiled, demure. As I hand her into the boat, she stumbles. I catch her round the waist and feel her whole body trembling with fear. As well she might – our destination, the Court of the Inquisition. The accusation against her is witchcraft. I, too, would tremble if that was where I was summoned. I would tremble into pieces.

TULLIA BUFFO

Venice, 1576

Here in the Venetian Tribunal, she is allowed no lawyer to defend her; her fate lies in her own hands. She forces herself to look at those present in the court. Here is Girolamo Foscarini, Domenico Priuli, Alberto Bolognetti, the papal legate, and finally the Venetian Patriarch Giovanni Trevisan. Two of them she has had in her bed. She is the only woman present. Now here is the Inquisitor, dressed in black with a sharp black beard and surprisingly kind eyes. He is the one she must convince.

She folds her hands in front of her. She remembers the tap of Venier's fingers against her forehead. Use this. Do not get angry. Be humble. Be helpful. Apologise for the fact that the ceremony took place in your house. Do not be proud. Do not be arrogant. Now she will discover exactly what the charges are and who has accused her. She takes a deep breath and steadies herself. She must focus her mind. There will no doubt be the usual insult-throwing, which will be neither here nor there, but then there will be the accusation which has brought her here, the accusation of heretical belief or actions. The more self-righteous and venomous the tone of the accusations, the more demure and sorrowful she must be. The Inquisitor begins to read the charges:

She is a woman at war with good health. A sea swarming with illness. The woman who came into the world with the crow. The woman who makes the present century blind and contaminates it. She plays prohibited games and entices honest men into gambling. She has not once been to mass in two and a half months. She is constantly involved in dishonest and illicit dealings with her lovers and other men. She wears pearls specifically prohibited to courtesans by the sumptuary laws. She has performed various martelli – invocations that make certain Germans who have been frequenting her house fall in love with her. She was seen performing one ritual involving the devil card in the tarot. A candle was lit by the card and prayers addressed to it at a certain time of day. The heart of a man was hammered away at by the devil, forcing him to return.

But this is ridiculous! These are the practices of street whores. She has no need of such rituals. She does not need the devil to make a man fall in love with her.

So far, so what? she thinks. The Inquisitor draws breath.

It is said that she encouraged the performing of the inghistera ritual after the theft of various objects from her house.

Now she knows what she is fighting. Now it is clear. She engages her mind for the battle with the Inquisitor.

'Is it true,' he says, 'that for the purpose of finding lost things you had virginal children chant some prayers and look into a basin full of water?'

'It is only partly true, Signore,' she says. 'May I explain?'

The gesture of his hand takes in all the space and time she may need to hang herself.

263

TERRY
&
LUDOVICO

Venice, 2011

Ludovico stood, hands plunged into his pockets, staring out of the window down into the canal. There was a tilt to his head and a hardness to his face that Terry had not seen before. He had returned twenty minutes before and had barely said a word. Terry's various conversational opening gambits had fallen on decidedly stony ground and in the end he had given up, defeated by the strength of Ludovico's mood. Now he felt that his worst fears about this holiday were about to be realised. Here he was, stuck in this damp stone city with a moody lover who had shut down all communication. It didn't surprise him. Some cities were almost impossible to live up to. Well, at least there was only one day to go. He picked up *Links* and began flicking through it.

Ludovico sighed dramatically and spun round. 'Let's go out,' he said. 'Someone told me of a decent restaurant that's just opened. Rare for Venice. Most of the decent restaurants are hidden down the back alleys, so only the Venetians can enjoy them.'

'OK,' Terry said.

As they were shrugging on their coats, Terry said, 'I'm sorry.'

'What for?'

'You seem so upset.'

They walked swiftly through the dark alleyways of Venice. For the most part, they walked in silence, interrupted occasionally by a muffled 'Sorry' from Ludovico when he led them down an alley which ended in the soft slap of the sea against stone steps. Eventually they came to a restaurant called La Zucca. As they pushed their way inside, Terry's glasses steamed up. While he took them off and rubbed them clear with a handkerchief, Ludovico went to the front of the queue and began to talk to the maitre d'.

He returned and took Terry's elbow. 'There's a bar next door. A table will be ready in twenty minutes. They'll come and get us.'

'What did you say to him?' Terry asked.

'I mentioned a name and tipped him.'

'What name?'

'Someone I met at my mother's.'

The tilt of the head again; the shut-down face. This was going to be a fun evening. They ordered some drinks. Ludovico stared into the bottom of his glass.

'Any answers in there?' Terry asked.

Ludovico looked at him for the first time since he had come back. The whole of his face seemed cast in shadows. Terry picked up a packet of sugar and shook it.

'When I was here as a child, these packets had pictures of famous buildings and paintings, and I loved collecting them. Later, when there was a sugar shortage, we used them. My mother was very careful not to damage the pictures when she opened them, but they meant nothing to me without the sugar in them.'

Ludovico frowned at him. 'What are you talking about?'

Terry laughed. 'My childhood ... but mainly, to be honest, I'm filling the silence until you're ready to tell me what happened. I find silence uncomfortable. It makes me more garrulous than usual.' He reached across the table and put his hand over Ludovico's. 'Are you going to tell me what happened?'

Ludovico had opened his mouth to speak, but at that moment a waiter from the restaurant next door came into the bar and gestured at them.

Ludovico drained his glass. 'Our table's ready,' he said.

The food was excellent and the wine seemed to ease Ludovico's mood. In the buzzy, noisy restaurant some of his charm and humour returned. Walking back to the apartment after the meal, they came out of the maze of alleyways into St Mark's Square. In the middle of the square, Ludovico took him in his arms and kissed him. Terry's head swirled with images from the day – the marble columns and mosaics of the basilica, the waters of the lagoon lapping against stone steps, the stately grandeur of the white-jacketed waiters at Florian's. All the images of the day melded together and spun up into the air like a flock of pigeons. A strong feeling of déjà vu filled him, the feeling that he had been taken in a different pair of arms, in a different time altogether.

As an actor he could appreciate the gesture on this most extraordinary of stages, but as a human being he felt the artifice of it. He felt the effort to repair something that would only be repaired when Ludovico trusted him or himself enough to talk to him about how he was feeling. Later that night sex rebuilt some of the lost connection between them but in the morning Ludovico's silence returned. And that remained on the water-taxi ride to the airport and on the flight back. So when they parted at the airport to go to their respective homes, Terry felt an overwhelming feeling of relief, to be alone in his own amiable silence and not to be oppressed by the undertow of someone else's.

Well, he thought, as he pushed the door to his flat open and picked up the mail and pressed the message button of his answer phone, there was a dark angel there after all. He'd sensed him from the very beginning under all that charm and lightness. Now he'd met him. Terry wasn't good with moody people; he no longer wanted to tiptoe around on eggshells, playing guessing games about what might have happened or what he might have done wrong. He'd had enough of that with Colin. Perhaps we should split up, he thought. But then he remembered how moody and temperamental he had been after his cardiac arrest. How Ludovico had taken all his irritability and fear. How he had somehow absorbed it all with good humour and he felt ashamed of himself. Being ill had made him self-obsessed and narcissistic. This thing with Ludovico's mother will blow over, he thought. Things will settle down. He will get things in perspective. It's simply a matter of time. He walked into his front room and pulled up the blinds. God, he was happy to be home!

Venice, 1576

He should never have forced Pomponio into the priesthood. He knows that now. Of course he does. He sees painfully clearly all the mistakes he made with his children. Perhaps things would have been different if their mother, Cecelia, had survived. Perhaps she would have warned him of the consequences. Even so, he might not have listened. Back then all he could see was that the benefices he might collect for Pomponio would secure the family fortunes. And they might have done if Pomponio had been a different sort of man. He goes to the bookshelves and pulls out a volume: *Aretino's Letters*. He opens the book and then gets a magnifying glass from his desk and places it over the page. Aretino wrote two letters about his sons. He reads the first one.

Venice, November 26, 1537
Your father, Titian, has just brought me the greetings you

sent, and they pleased me hardly less than the two grouse that came with them. I gave the latter to myself – he told me to present them to a deserving gentleman.

And now that you have seen how big hearted I am, let me pay you back 'a thousand thousand times and sing this all night long', as the saying goes, requesting that you give the leanest of my gifts to your brother, Orazio, since he has forgotten to tell me what his latest fancy is for spending this world and the next. Your thrift is a better way of getting worldly goods and since you are to be a priest I don't believe that you will ever have to depart from Melchizedek's habit of collecting tithes.

And so good health to you – which is what I started out to say.

But now some bad news. It is time to get back to your studies, and since as far as I know there are no schools in the country, the city is the place to keep snug in this winter.

So, get going, for I want your twelve-year-old ability and a few tries at Hebrew, Latin, and Greek to drive all the learned doctors in this silly world to despair, just as the fine things your papa does drives mad all the painters in Italy.

That is all.

Now keep warm and a good appetite to you.

Only twelve years old and Pomponio had already made his feelings clear to his father by fleeing to Cadore. But Titian had refused to listen. He was determined that Pomponio would do what he wanted. He was determined to bend the boy to his will. And look where that had got him.

* * *

Now, here is Pomponio in his father's studio. The book of letters and the magnifying glass lie on the floor. There is nothing here to suggest that his father was thinking about him in the last days of his life. His father and brother are dead, Aretino is long dead. Here is Pomponio going through the paintings that remain, searching for what? He doesn't know. Just searching for anything, any sign perhaps that his father had not entirely forgotten him. A genius has died and his son is left looking at his paintings. He picks one up and brings it into the light. Frowns and stares hard at it. This does not look like his father's work. It's nothing like it. Who painted this, he wonders? What is this exactly? He turns his head slightly.

A shiver of horror runs through him.

Oh, now he understands. It is a man being flayed alive.

And here in the middle of the painting, with his chin resting on his hand, is his father, watching it happen, with the same terrifying detachment he always had. The overwhelming question being not what can I do to make it stop, the pressing question always being how to show what is happening?

ALBERTO

New York, 2011

There was a leaving-do for a retiring detective. Joe didn't know him and Alberto didn't want to put himself in the way of alcohol, so they were amongst the skeleton staff left in the station. Alberto had his feet up on his desk and was reading the sports pages when Joe came over, piece of paper in hand.

'That painting,' Joe said to Alberto. 'You know, *St Sebastian?*'

Alberto nodded.

'I just got this email from the FBI. They think it's something.'

'What kind of something?'

'Apparently there was a famous robbery in Boston in the nineties.' He looked at the piece of paper in his hand. 'Place called the Arabella Howard Granger Museum. Mean anything to you?'

Alberto shook his head.

'Anyway, apparently it took place on St Patrick's Day. Couple of guys dressed in Boston police uniforms and false moustaches...'

'The false moustaches were a nice touch.'

Joe laughed. 'Anyway, they turn up saying there's been a commotion nearby and they want to check everything's all right. They tie up the night guards, a couple of college kids, and have the place to themselves for ninety minutes. They cut out the paintings, grab what they're interested in and then leave. None of the items or paintings has ever been recovered. Oh, and they leave a card that reads: *Thanks for the poor security.*'

'Another nice touch.'

'Apparently, it's the most valuable art theft in history. So this painting. They think it's a Titian – apparently he's a big thing in the art world. Renaissance painter.'

Alberto looked up from his paper. 'Is there a reward for it?'

'In 1997 there was a reward put up of $5 million.'

Albert slowly lowered his paper.

'You're shitting me, right?'

Joe shook his head slowly back and forth. 'Nope.'

'Does that still stand today?'

'I don't know.'

'You got a contact there?'

'Sure – it's on here.'

Alberto stood up and took the piece of paper, scanned it and picked up the phone.

Aurora
&
Saint Sebastian

New York, 2011

The painting lies flat on the kitchen table. It is odd to see it like this as opposed to hanging on the wall. It is odd to look down on it; it makes her feel a little giddy. Her daughters are back earlier than she expected and she has not had time to remove the painting before they are chattering through the door and hurling their school bags in the hall.

Constanza looks at the painting and says, 'What's that?'

'Nothing,' Aurora says. 'Just something I picked up at a flea market.' She's never talked to her daughters about the painting. She's never talked to anyone about it other than Alberto.

Her daughter frowns. 'What flea market?'

'One down town.' Her daughter has always been difficult to lie to.

'It's old, isn't it?'

'Yes, I think so.'

Constanza stands there, hands on hips, staring down at it.

'It's pancakes for dinner,' Aurora says, hoping to divert Constanza's attention.

Her daughter looks at her and then back at the painting. Her frown deepens. 'Who is he?'

'Saint Sebastian.'

'Why do you want a picture of a man impaled with arrows?' Constanza says. 'That's sick.'

You're too young to understand, Aurora thinks, but does not say. She picks up the painting gingerly by its edges and takes it into her bedroom, away from her daughters' prying eyes. She places it flat on the bed and looks down at it. She used to take her children to mass every Sunday. She had taken them to Sunday school and made sure they took their first communion, but she had always told herself that when they reached their teens if they didn't want to go she wouldn't force them. She herself had had periods away from the church, when she was younger, but she had returned. You had to trust God and trust your children. At least she had given them something they could come back to. At least she had given them that. The other day Constanza had raised the old argument, if God exists, then why did he allow 9/11? Why did he allow babies to die? Why did he allow poverty, tsunamis? If God was all powerful, why did these things happen?

What was she to say to her? Aurora had no answers for her clever daughter.

Shortly afterwards, Constanza had stopped going to church. Her youngest, Juanita, still came, but only to keep her company, Aurora suspected. She had tried to explain that faith could be a comfort, but Constanza had replied, how can a lie be a comfort? Aurora had smiled at that. Constanza was young and had much to learn. Sometimes a lie was all one had to keep one going – the lie that things would surely get better, the lie that everything was for the best, the lie that there was someone up there looking after you, loving you.

Saint Sebastian looked back at her from the bed, impaled, serene, dying. Aurora believed in God because she had to have something to believe in. When Juan had been shot dead ten years ago, there hadn't been anyone around to help her but God. It was as simple and as complicated as that, but that wasn't something she could explain to her daughter. Teenage logic wouldn't buy it. Teenage logic didn't buy much.

She was worried that she might have damaged him, but there's no damage that she can make out on the surface of the painting. She has to have somewhere she can hide him. Under the bed – that's the only place she can think of. She gets down on her knees and begins to pull out shoes and plastic storage boxes. She goes and gets a broom. When she's sure it's clean enough, she places him flat under the bed and then goes and makes herself a coffee.

She has him. But what now? What on earth happens next? Her phone begins to vibrate in her pocket. She takes it out and looks at the screen – Alberto. She lets it ring until it goes to voicemail. She can't speak to him right now. She has to get her story straight. What is she going to say? What on earth is she going to say?

TERRY

London, 2011

Mr Richards, the consultant, a cadaverous man with grey hedgehog hair, steepled his elegant fingers and looked at Terry over the top of his black-rimmed glasses. They were halfway into a conversation about whether it would be OK for Terry to go back to work.

'Do you suffer much from stage fright?'

Terry pictured himself standing in the wings on opening night, waiting to go on. His heart is racing, his hands are sweating, he feels as if he might pass out or be violently sick.

'No,' he said, 'I'm lucky. It doesn't really affect me that badly.'

Mr Richards sat back in his chair. 'I have heard that the stress some actors endure on opening night is equivalent to being in a head-on car crash.'

Yes, Terry thought, that's about the gist of it. 'Really?' he said. 'Well, in that case I've been very lucky.'

Mr Richards cleared his throat and clasped his hands together, then rested them on the desk in front of him. 'I had a footballer who had a similar condition to you. I told him if he didn't go back and play football, he had a 1 per cent chance of dying. If he did, that would rise fourfold.'

'But football is an intense physical activity. That's rather different, isn't it?'

'There are always beta blockers.'

'I would not be able to act on them,' Terry said. 'They muffle feelings. It would be impossible. When I act, I have to be able to access my emotions. That's the whole point of it.'

Mr Richards smiled. 'You could specialise in playing very calm people.'

'Do you know what drama is?' Terry snapped. 'It's conflict.'

The consultant cleared his throat, stood up and walked over to the window. He turned round and rested against the windowsill. 'I believe I read an interview with you some time ago in which you said that you had always suffered very badly from stage fright.'

Terry blushed furiously. 'I was probably exaggerating to give the interviewer a story or to make him like me.'

'Well . . .' he said. 'Ultimately, of course, it's up to you, but it's worth considering that a fourfold increase in your risk of dying is quite substantial.'

'What did the footballer do?'

'He quit professional football, but a couple of years later he was having a five-a-side kickaround with his mates and he dropped dead.'

Terry stood up and grabbed his coat. 'And telling me that is supposed to help me how exactly?'

Mr Richards looked at him over the top of his glasses. 'I'm sorry,' he said, 'but I have to inform you of the risks.'

Terry began to push his arms into his coat. The winder of his watch got caught in a thread in the lining of one of the sleeves. Mr Richards moved to help him and an awkward dance ensued between the two of them.

'Perhaps it would be better if you take your arm out and start again,' he said.

'Perhaps it would be better if you took my heart out and started again.'

The man frowned. 'You don't need a transplant.'

Terry withdrew his hand from the sleeve and disentangled himself from the winder. The consultant held the coat for him, so he could put it back on. When he had got his arms into the sleeves, he felt a gentle pat on his back. It was a kindly gesture that caught him off guard. Terry leant down to pick up his bag. In the doorway, he turned round.

'I'm an actor,' he said. 'If I can't act, I might as well be dead. I don't like to work, I *need* to work. Without acting I simply . . . do not exist. I'm not just going to go off and play golf.'

The consultant blinked and frowned. 'Awful game. Well, within those parameters we'll have to see what is safe and achievable.'

The South Bank – Benugo's bar. Ludovico and Terry were sitting next to each other on one of the brightly covered sofas that Terry had secretly coveted ever since this part of the BFI was done up. He was stroking the puce velvet stripes. From the slightly strained conversations taking place all around them, it appeared that this venue was a favourite for internet dating.

'And with that parting shot,' Terry said, 'I flounced out.'

'You'll be fine,' Ludovico said. 'You just need a bit of time.'

'No one will ever employ me again.'

'Don't be ridiculous.'

Terry took hold of Ludovico's hand and slid it under his shirt until it was over the ICD. 'Can you feel it?'

He nodded.

'I don't feel human any more. I feel like a bloody robot. What happens if I can never get back the emotional range I had?'

'Enough,' Ludovico said. 'Film – you need to get into film. There's less pressure. You won't have to carry the whole thing. You can do retakes and it pays better.'

'Film?' Terry said heavily. 'Who's going to give me a part in a film?'

'Have you spoken to your agent?'

Terry shook his head. 'I don't want to do film. In a play the performance is in my hands, it's in the cast's hands. In a film it's made by the editor, by the director. And there's no live audience. There's no immediate gratification.'

'Well, make sure you work with a director you trust. It'll put you under much less pressure and it'll give you the chance to flex your muscles a bit.'

'I don't know who I am any more,' Terry said. 'If I'm not acting . . .'

Ludovico put his arched hand on his chest and in a dramatic voice said, 'I don't know who I am any more.'

Terry laughed and punched him lightly on the upper arm. 'Come on. You know what I mean.'

'There's all the rest of your life. Your life isn't simply acting.'

Terry sighed and looked at the strained face of a woman whose date was obviously not going as planned and then at the young man opposite her who reeked of desperation. 'There's not much hinterland with me, actually. There really isn't. Each cast. Each play. It's another family. It's . . .'

The young woman was looking at her watch. 'Oh, is that the time? I'll have to go soon.'

Terry looked down. 'It's where I love.'

'But you had Colin?'

'He always used to say that all my intimacy needs were

met by my relationships with fellow cast members. That he always came off second best, and he was right in a way. You know what it's like.'

'But a cast disbands at the end of the run.'

'Yes, and then another comes along – thank God. Or it did, anyway.'

'You're bound to be feeling depressed after what's happened to you. It's a huge shock to the system. You almost died. You just need to give yourself time.'

'Time . . .'

The young woman was giving her date no time at all. She was gathering her things together, her coat was shrugged on, her bag was picked up. She held out her hand. 'Nice to have met you.' Although it obviously hadn't been. The young man shook her hand and smiled a disappointed smile.

Poor boy, Terry thought, and contemplated giving him an acting lesson, a lesson in how to appear confident, on how to appear relaxed. It wasn't rocket science, after all. And then he thought it was a lesson he needed to give himself. He looked at Ludovico across the rim of his glass and felt a prickle of anxiety. They hadn't been together very long when he'd become ill. Was Ludovico still happy with him? It was difficult to dump a man who had almost died. Maybe they needed to have a conversation about . . .

'Actually,' Ludovico said. 'I was thinking of asking you . . .'

Terry was looking at the boy, who was looking at his bottle of beer. He wanted to comfort him but was worried that, if he did, it would only increase the boy's feelings of humiliation, or even worse he would think he was hitting on him.

'Terry?'

'Yes, sorry . . .'

'Well, I've been in email communication with my mother.

She suggested I do something in the gardens of the hotel next year. I wondered if you'd like to be involved in some way.'

'What, dress up as a harlequin and entertain the punters? A pantaloon, perhaps? Back to the days when directors would only cast me as fops, freaks and fuck-ups?'

'Actually, I was thinking of putting on a performance of *Othello* in the gardens of the hotel on San Clemente and having you play Iago.'

Terry spluttered into his wine glass. 'Iago!'

Ludovico laughed.

'What was all that about giving myself time and getting small parts in films?'

'You've never done Iago, have you?'

'You know I haven't.'

'Well, it was just a thought.'

'Iago!'

'Well, it would certainly test out your heart. It's one of the longest parts in Shakespeare.'

'Are you serious?'

'Fourth longest, apparently.'

'No, no, I don't mean about that. I mean about putting it on with me in it.'

'Absolutely.'

'But you were just talking about me doing film . . .'

Ludovico leant forwards. 'Tell me you're not already thinking about how you'd play it. Tell me your imagination hasn't immediately locked into it . . .'

Terry cleared his throat. 'Yes, but what if I die?'

'You're not going to die. Trust me, you're going to be fine.'

'What? Trust me, I'm a director?'

Ludovico laughed. 'Yes – something like that.'

'Who would play Othello?'

Ludovico named a well-known black American actor.

'I was thinking of making it a joint American–English company.'

Is Ludovico my dark angel? Terry thought. Is this where the dark angel comes in, tempting me towards the edge of the cliff and pushing me off? Iago is as dark as they come.

'Will you at least think about it?'

Terry nodded. Suddenly he thought of *The Man with the Blue Sleeve*. He was only a short walk away, across the bridge and into Trafalgar Square. What would he have to say about this? Perhaps he should find out.

Perhaps he would give him some tips about Iago.

On the other hand, perhaps this man *was* Iago.

Terry twisted his head slightly, like a crow sitting on a branch looking down at something edible on the pavement. Here he was – *The Man with the Blue Sleeve*. Given the fact that the last time he'd been here the portrait had announced his death, he felt rather nervous standing in front of it now. He wondered if the man would mind being defined purely by his doublet, by his sleeve. Perhaps he would cherish his anonymity in the face of all this staring. He did not look like a man who cared at all about the opinions of others. Lucky sod.

Iago – an absolute bastard, if ever there was one.

A large group of people gathered around the painting and Terry mingled with them, waiting to see what their guide would tell them. After an introduction which did not tell Terry anything he didn't know the guide ended, 'The sleeve, you know, the doublet, was almost certainly in breach of the sumptuary laws of the time. It's a sign of his status, you see, that he could wear it anyway and could get away with it. He had the money to pay the fine.'

This was obviously the last painting of the tour and the group began to break up.

Terry went up to the guide and asked, 'If he was Gerolamo Barbarigo, what was he like?'

'Very rich, part of the patrician class, which was the top five per cent of the population. Almost certainly homosexual.'

'Really?'

'Yes, there's always been the suggestion that the painting has a strong homoerotic undertow.'

'How strange,' Terry said.

'You don't think so?'

Terry laughed. 'You know, it never crossed my mind.'

'You're Terry Jardine, aren't you?'

Terry nodded.

'I can't tell you how much pleasure you've given me over the years.'

'Oh,' Terry said blushing. 'Well, thank you very much.'

'What's your next role?'

'Well, I'm thinking of playing Iago in Venice.'

'Ahh,' the man said. 'How wonderful. Is it fun playing someone so unremittingly evil?'

'It can be – but it can also be quite debilitating.'

'But to play it in Venice . . .!'

'Yes,' Terry said. 'I've only just been asked. I thought I'd come here and see what he had to say on the matter.' He nodded at the painting.

'Are you all right? There was something in the paper . . .'

'I've not been well, actually. It's taken me longer than I thought to get back on my feet.'

'There are a lot of nasty things going around.'

Terry smiled. 'Yes – it's the time of year.'

He didn't mention his heart. He was bored of talking about it. I mean, what was the point? And then he saw himself as Iago, wearing a doublet made of this blue watered silk. He saw himself addressing the audience in one of the soliloquies and he knew at once that he was the man with the blue sleeve. It was himself he was looking at when he looked at the painting. It was, in fact, a self-portrait. *The Man With the Blue Sleeve* had come home to himself. Why had it taken him so long to realise that?

A couple of hours later, when he'd got home, he phoned Ludovico.

'Yes,' he said, 'I'll do it. But on one condition. At some point in the play, I get to wear a doublet of blue watered silk.'

Ludovico laughed. 'But he's a soldier. I'm not sure that would be altogether . . .'

'It's not negotiable.'

'OK, then.' There was a pause. 'Well, in that case, you'll get to wear it.'

Terry went and got *Othello* off his shelves and opened it at the first page.

ALBERTO
&
AURORA

New York, 2011

Alberto stood in front of the fish tank, wrinkling his nose. The tank had been yanked away from the wall; its oxygen supply had been disconnected. The water was beginning to smell. Some fish had already died; others were looking decidedly lacklustre. The safe stood open – empty. A team of people were moving through the apartment, going from room to room. Alberto had already done that and it was quite clear to him that the painting, the reason why they had been able to get the warrant in the first place, was missing. He went and stood where Aurora had stood a month ago, looking out at the view. The Pereiras had disappeared and so had the painting. He thought of the soft look on Aurora's face when she talked about Saint Sebastian. He'd found the four pieces of wood that made up the frame in the kitchen cupboard behind the vacuum cleaner. He wasn't quite sure what to do next. She wasn't returning his calls. His first instinct was to protect her. His second was to protect himself. They would have to settle on a story because if there was any suggestion that she had stolen it, then she would be in a great deal of trouble. And if there was any suggestion he had helped her, he would be as well. He stood there, looking out of the window, wondering what the hell he should do, but the towers of New York were delivering no answers and in the end he turned back into the room and went to look for Joe. They needed to get their story straight as well.

His phone rang and he answered it. It was his boss. 'Pereira's just been dragged out of the Hudson.'

Now it had become a murder enquiry.

'You again.' Aurora said. 'You keep turning up like a bad smell.'

'Well, if you won't answer your phone, you get me on your doorstep. Can I come in?'

She stood to one side. He hitched up his trousers and stepped into the hall. In the front room, she eyed him across folded arms.

'Some things I need to tell you.'

She didn't say anything.

'Today we got a warrant to search the Pereiras' apartment. We got the warrant on the basis of your description of the painting. Turns out it's by someone who counts. It was stolen from the Arabella Howard Granger Museum in Boston in the nineties. Turns out there's a substantial reward for information leading to its return.'

Aurora's head jerked back, as if she'd been slapped.

'Thing is, we get to the apartment and there's no painting and the safe's standing open and empty.'

'So?'

'Well, the way we look at it is any number of things may have happened. The people who have the painting may know

286

what they have, but suppose someone has it and they don't know. Suppose that were the case? We found the pieces of the frame in the broom cupboard in the kitchen. And if they don't know its value, they won't know that people might be coming after them for it. That they might be in danger because what they have is worth a shit load of money. You see what I'm saying?'

Aurora had a sudden vivid image of Saint Sebastian lying on the floor upstairs, staring up at her bed springs. She did see what he was saying. She saw exactly what he was saying.

'And there's another thing. Pereira's been fished out of the Hudson. You know anything about that?'

'Jesus, Albi, I'm the maid. What am I going to know about that?'

'When were you last there?'

'You've had the apartment under surveillance. Why you asking me? Check the log.'

'Come on, Rory, this is serious now.'

'I'm not saying it isn't. What I'm saying is, why are you asking damn fool questions you know the answers to?'

Suddenly he was fed up with it all, fed up with everything, with being a policeman, with the antagonism between them. 'You mind if I sit down, Rory. It's been a long day.'

She gestured none too willingly towards the sofa.

'Maria died eighteen months ago from breast cancer. I've been meaning to tell you but other things kept getting in the way. I haven't been handling things well since then. It's not been . . . Well, you know how hard it is.'

Aurora unfolded her arms. 'Why'd you let me say all those nasty things about her, Albi? I wouldn't have if I'd known.'

He shook his head. 'I don't know, Rory. Recently I've decided I don't know anything any more. Not a thing.' He leant his head on the back of the sofa and closed his eyes. 'And the thing is, I'm tired, so tired of it all, all the pain, the kids are still so upset and sometimes I just think they'd be better off without me. I didn't handle it well afterwards and they still don't trust me and I don't know how I'm ever going to get them to trust me again . . .'

'What did you do?'

'Drank.'

'You got a handle on it now?'

He nodded. 'I go to the meetings, but sometimes I just can't see it getting any better. You know what I mean?' He opened his eyes. 'You know what I mean, Rory? I can't be their mother and I really let them down.'

She nodded slowly. 'I know what you mean.'

That's why she'd loved the painting so much. Somehow Saint Sebastian had given her the strength to endure it, the hopeless times, the suffering times. Somehow he'd made her feel better. It's why she felt she couldn't bear to be parted from him. She simply couldn't bear it. Not yet, anyway.

She looked back at Alberto; his mouth had fallen open and he was asleep. She sat down in the armchair opposite, watching the steady rise and fall of his chest, trying to work out what she should do next.

TULLIA BUFFO

Venice, 1576

The hearing has been going on for some time. Tullia speaks in Venetian dialect to create a bond between them. We are the city, she thinks. We. If they attack me, they attack themselves. She is explaining why she allowed the ritual to continue when she entered the house and found out what was happening. She is lying a little bit.

'Redolfo fell to his knees. He begged me to allow the mother and children to continue with their incantation.'

'And what exactly was done?'

She explains the bowl of water, the children holding candles, the cross made from two leaves of an olive branch, the ring placed under the bowl.

'And what exactly was said?'

'Holy Angel, White Angel, by your sanctity and my virginity, show me the true one and the truth. Who took that thing?'

'What do you think the words mean?'

'Well, I know that in Venice one calls a Saracen white, so I think that the white angel may also be a black angel.'

'The devil?'

'Yes, Signore.'

'And then what happened?'

'Despite my protests, once they had performed the ritual the children were unable to disclose what they had seen, one saying one thing, one another, so I gave them something to eat and sent them on their way. It was at this point that everyone turned against me because they said I was crazy not to believe in such things.'

'Have you ever taken part in this ritual before?'

'As an innocent child my mother made me do it when a coat went missing. She made me say the same incantation and then say three paternosters and three Ave Marias while looking into a basin.'

'And what happened?'

'I saw my father there because he was foolish enough to come up behind me when I was looking into the bowl.'

There is a ripple of laughter in the court.

The Inquisitor frowns. 'Have you ever devised other invocations to the devil or made men fall in love with you?'

'Signore, never and may God and the Madonna protect me. I am the most timid woman in the world when it comes to demons and the dead.'

'But it is still true that you allowed this ritual to take place in your property.'

'It is true for the reasons I have given. I was bullied into it by my servants from whom I had withheld wages. I recognise that I have erred and humbly ask to be pardoned for it.'

'Have you ever eaten meat on Friday or Saturday or other prohibited days?'

'I don't believe so. No, Signore . . .'

Shortly afterwards, the hearing comes to an end. She is told to wait while the Inquisitor speaks with the others and then she is ordered to return the following day for another hearing.

It is only as she steps out of the gondola, at the end of the day, that she realises how exhausted she is. She calls her maid to undress her and goes straight to bed. She falls asleep immediately but wakes in the night screaming, a nightmare vivid in her mind. She has been stripped naked and is being marched through the streets of Venice to the Rialto. Crowds jeer and mock and spit. All the men she has had in her bed are in the crowd; they leer at her and grab at her. They start to tear her to pieces. She cries out and her cries wake her.

She walks to the windows and opens the shutters. She has never felt so alone. She longs for Marco. The city is asleep and from the heavens the stars and the moon shine down upon her. She sighs deeply, breathing in the city, breathing in the moon and the stars. Venier was right, of course. All she has to do is show sufficient humility, apologise sincerely and everything will be all right. But still the unfairness of it eats at her. All she has ever wanted is to look after her children and her extended family. All she has ever wanted is her independence. She has treated her servants fairly, but they have turned against her, stolen from her, and denounced her when she does not deserve it. And the only reason they have done so is because she is a courtesan, because they think they can get away with it. At least her children are sons. At least she does not have a girl to protect. Yes, thank God she has only sons. A daughter, in this city, would be a terrible worry.

She thinks back to the time before the plague hit the city, to when a king came to call. A king who the Republic wanted on their side, a king who was welcomed as a most honoured guest. She closes her eyes and remembers.

'Lady, he is coming!' Her maid was beside herself, her voice squeaking with excitement.

Tullia had been forewarned and servants had been posted. A king was coming. To visit her.

Separated from his courtiers, from the panoply of power, here in her bedroom King Henry III did not look much like a king. He had a small V-shaped growth of hair clinging to his lower lip and a weak moustache. Tullia had, however, been well instructed by the Venetian ambassadors. Venice was, of course, famous for its spies, present in all the courts in Europe, even in the bedrooms of the courts. She had been briefed in the most exquisite detail, so she had an idea of what her approach would be, but after that she would have to see where her instincts directed her.

'It is an immense honour to meet you, the son of that most esteemed of women, Catherine de Medici, who is famous all over the world for the bounty of her learning.'

If that wasn't laying it on with a trowel, she did not know what was.

'Ah, my mother. Do you know what she calls me?'

She shook her head.

He laughed somewhat embarrassedly. 'Precious eyes.'

So she had heard. Mummy's boy.

'If I may,' she said, stepping closer to him so that she might look into his face. 'How fitting, my Lord.'

He swayed away from her, obviously unhappy with being approached so closely. She frowned a little at his retreating back. Men did not usually move away from her in her bedroom. He continued to walk restlessly up and down, looking at the furnishings, the wall hangings, the paintings. She could not sit down while he was still standing. She waited to see what would happen when he stopped. When one was with a king, one did not make the first move unless he suggested it. She waited and watched. She had already offered him wine and sweetmeats. If her job had honed one element in her, it was the ability to assess accurately the likely sexual appetites of her clients. And she was rarely wrong. And this man, it was beginning to dawn on her, was a rarity in this room because he appeared to have no appetite for her at all. Eventually, she thought, he will stop walking back and forth, admiring the paintings, and then she would find out if the rumours were true.

But for now she would wait and watch.

The silence, however, extended for an embarrassingly long period of time. In the end she cracked. 'My Lord, I understand you travel to France to be crowned.'

He nodded, still marching restlessly up and down.

'It is a great honour for the Republic to have you as its guest. It would be a great honour for me to offer you all of the delights that *La Serenissima* has to offer. Whatever you desire, my Lord, is available to you here. You need only . . .'

'Yes, yes . . .' He was staring hard at a rather dull Flemish painting.

'I have some sketches here, my Lord, which may interest you.' She opened a drawer and placed a series of etchings on a table.

Casually, he strolled over to look at them. He flicked through them one by one, holding one in his hand longer than the others, while the tension in the room thickened like lagoon fog.

So, the spies were right.

She bowed her head, curtsied low, took his hand and kissed his ring. He bent down to raise her up and as he did she whispered something in his ear. He nodded. He stayed with her for the next twenty-four hours. By the end of it, her wrist and arm ached from wielding the switch, and he winced slightly as he lowered himself onto the cushions of the gondola.

But that was then, when she had a king in her bed, when she was at the service of the Republic. That was when they needed her. Now, all they want to do is call her names. *Puttana. Meretrice.* Now, all they want to do is tear her to pieces.

She closes the shutters and goes back to bed. Tomorrow is the second hearing. Tomorrow it begins all over again.

TITIAN

Venice, 27th August 1576

Half-blind and toothless, Titian stumbles through his studio. The heat is insufferable. Orazio had come to him when the plague had first broken out and there was still time to leave the city. He had suggested they go to the villa in the Cenedese hills; they would have been safe there. But Titian had refused to go; it was too hot and he was too old to tolerate the journey and he had known that Orazio would not leave him. He had never left him. And there was still work to do, still so much work. He still had the *Pietà* he had promised for the church in his home town to finish. He picks up a magnifying glass and peers at the painting, worrying away at it, always unsatisfied. Death will be the thing that announces it as finished. Only death will tear it from his grasp.

Now, he peers at the shimmering golden mosaic semi-dome he has painted as a backdrop, at the pelican plucking blood from its breast to feed its young, a symbol of Christ's resurrection. He had painted it to hark back to the Byzantine domes and vaults he had first seen when he came to the city, to show his respect to Bellini, a man he had swiftly supplanted with his more daring and dynamic works. In his youth he had been in such a rush, always in such a rush to prove himself, to make money.

There is one thing he wants to finish now. At the bottom right-hand corner, there is a shield with his coat of arms, bearing the Habsburg eagle, and a tablet of himself and Orazio, kneeling in prayer in front of the celestial vision of the *Pietà*.

'Orazio,' he calls out. 'Orazio come and help me.'

When Orazio does come, he finds his father crumpled on the ground at the foot of the *Pietà*, a paintbrush in the palm of his hand.

The doctor is called. His groin and armpits are examined for the black leech-like lesions which announce the presence of plague. But there are none. In a city where thousands are dying of plague, Titian dies of a fever and his age is noted down as 103. Because of the plague, his body is rushed through the frightened streets of the city and he is interred in the Frari. For a genius, it is a very modest funeral.

One week later the plague doctors visit Orazio and he is sent to Lazzaretto Vecchio, where he dies. Titian dies without a will and Pomponio has the unenviable task of sorting everything out. Titian might have been a genius, but he leaves a mess behind him, a terrible mess for his estranged son. The *Pietà* never makes it to Cadore. It remains in Venice, where it eventually comes to rest in the Gallerie dell'Accademia.

THE BOATMAN

Venice, 1576

I was there at his funeral. I was one of the twenty or so
people who braved the plague-ridden air to see him
interred. By that time, I had been his boatman for many a
year and the injustice of what had happened to my father
was not such a sharp knife in my side. Old age softens
bitterness – a little. He was interred in the Chapel of the
Crucifixion. My bitterness was, of course, also softened by
the number of paintings I had managed to steal in the chaos
that followed Orazio's removal to Lazzaretto Vecchio. That
helped a lot. So, as the canons of St Mark's celebrated
mass, I stood there with a slight smile. I couldn't help it. I
knew my fortune was made. The city had become the city
of lost things: lost souls and lost possessions. The city was
bankrupt; they say the public debt was 5,714,439 ducats.
They say 46,721 Venetians died. Everyone was grieving,
everyone was struggling. And it was in these circumstances

that fortune shone upon me more brightly than at any other time in my life.

I only took the smaller ones. The larger ones were too difficult to get out over the garden wall without damaging them. Some were paintings which had come back for restoration – you could see the paint beginning to bubble and blister. One of the risks in this damp city of ours. Some were incomplete. Perhaps we would be able to get some of the men who worked for him to finish them. Now that Titian was dead, there would never be another painting by him. The size of the market was set and the price would surely rise. I heard that already people were making enquiries of the dealers; day-by-day, these enquiries would grow. I heard that there was great interest in the Low Countries. My fortune was made.

I had had to wait a long time, but finally my fortune was made. No wonder I couldn't keep the smile from my face, there in the shadows of the Frari, as the canon raised the host. No wonder.

LUDOVICO

London, 2012

The call came just after midnight and even before he was properly awake Ludovico's heart was thumping. No one phones with good news at that hour.

'Hello?'

It was his aunt Nicla. His father had fallen and been found by Maria and taken to hospital. Could he come out? The doctors were not sure. Well, they didn't seem to be that sure about anything.

He ended the call and sat for a few moments with his head in his hands. Then he phoned Terry. He explained what had happened and asked Terry to come out with him.

There was silence on the end of the phone. Terry considered briefly that, given what had happened to him recently, sitting at the bedside of a man who was probably dying was the last thing in the world he wanted to do. And then he said, 'Yes, of course I'll come.'

And Ludovico thanked him and said he would book the tickets and let him know what time the flight was.

The following night the two men found themselves in Andrea's house. They had gone straight from the airport to the hospital, where they had found Andrea stable but unconscious. They had stayed for a couple of hours and then, on Nicla's urgings, had come here to drop off their bags and get some food. Ludovico was going to go back to the hospital later.

Ludovico was opening and closing doors, cupboards, drawers. Terry recognised his behaviour. It had been his own after his mother had died. In every cupboard and drawer opened was a search for the person who had died. As if they might pop out at you, insisting on their vitality, and of course in one sense they did pop out at you, in letters, in their handwriting, in photos, in correspondence, in all kinds of painful ways.

Ludovico was standing at his father's desk, looking down at the contents of an open drawer. He took some pages out and dropped them on the desk, sat down in his father's battered leather chair and began to read.

> *Hills like a bear's torso*
> *Powers of bear bile*
> *Shuttle like viruses*
> *For transverse origins*
> *These dreamy spillages*
> *These scatterings of dreams*
> *In the maw fur of the bear*
> *Unravelling by dream–wolf–bear*
> *This heaping up of the dream fragments*

Oh God – what did it mean? What was a child to make of his father's writing? It was an odd way to encounter him.

Odd because the private was made public. Odd because something was revealed that had never been talked about. It was a very peculiar business, having a father who was a poet.

When his father had been in London, he had left Ludovico a volume of his most recently published poems. Ludovico hadn't read them yet, mainly because he found them almost all universally obscure. In person his father had never been as opaque as in his writing – thank God. Andrea had always been immediate, present, loving. A miracle, really, of father-liness, but reading his poems made Ludovico feel as if he did not know him at all. It was an unsettling and disorientating experience. His father had never been one to explain either. There had been times, when he was younger, when Ludovico had tried to open a conversation with him about his poetry but it had ended with Andrea becoming angry and defensive, saying, 'They are what they are. They are what you make of them. That is the end of it.'

And that *had* been the end of it.

Translating into English, he read out his father's jottings to Terry.

'"This heaping up of dream fragments" – I like that,' Terry said. 'And the bears and the wolves.'

Ludovico walked over to the sofa and sat down next to Terry. 'Thank you so much for coming here with me. I don't know what I would have done without you.'

Terry took hold of his arm and stroked it, and Ludovico leant his head against his shoulder and closed his eyes.

Unravelling by dream-wolf-bear.

Yes, that was lovely, Ludovico thought. Yes, a phrase, a poem could be lovely without one having to have the faintest idea what it meant.

Terry looked at the beeping machine and the clear plastic tubes running into Andrea's nose and down from the side of the bed into bags that he did not want to look at too closely. As an actor, he was always struck by how clichéd deathbed scenes were in comparison to real life. Ludovico sat on the other side of the bed, holding his father's hand and reading to him. They had had a discussion as to whether he should read Andrea some of his own poetry, but then decided against it. Terry had said, 'It could be a particularly awful kind of torture. When I was unconscious and they were playing me *Hamlet*, I found it unbearable. I didn't want to hear myself, anyone but...'

So, on the other side of the bed, Ludovico sat, reading out some of Petrarch's *Sonnets*, poems his father had always loved. This time Terry was the audience, Ludovico the performer. Italian must be God's language, Terry thought, as he closed his eyes and allowed the beautiful sounds to fill his heart and mind. It must be.

It was at that moment that the monitor went off; the ECG had flat-lined.

TULLIA BUFFO
The Second Hearing

Venice, 1576

She feels faint and slightly queasy. The Inquisitor is not satisfied with what she said in the first hearing. She has had to go through all the details of the ritual again.

'How can you say that the ritual is not effective,' the Inquisitor says, 'when you had the experience as a child of being able to discern who stole the coat? Weren't you, in fact, saying then that the ritual worked?'

'No, no, you misunderstood, because for every time the devil tells the truth there are a hundred times when he lies. When my maid insisted the ritual was effective, I told her it wasn't because the only image the children were able to see was their own reflections, one on top of the other.'

'And yet you allowed them to perform the ritual?'

'I was a single woman alone, surrounded by a group of hostile servants who I believe had stolen from me. What could I do? I was outnumbered. I know I should not have allowed the ritual to take place, but how could I have stopped it? I assure you I am not a woman who condones evil practices.'

'Are you able to name any of your enemies?'

'None of my servants were happy with me because I had withheld their wages – Redolpho, Borthola and perhaps Checho, the sausage maker who lives beneath me and sometimes serves me at table.'

And with a brief nod she is dismissed. 'You may go.'

It is over.

Back home she faints. Then the following morning she is violently sick. It is the stress of the hearings, she thinks. She needs a few days to recover and then everything will return to normal.

For now, she has survived.

Aurora

Miami, 1965

It was the mid-1960s. Cuba and America had signed a memorandum of understanding. Parents of children who had arrived unaccompanied in America during the early sixties were given priority to leave Cuba. Aurora and Pablo were squashed into a public telephone booth in the orphanage in Miami.

'Don't cry!' her brother hissed and she felt the pinch of his fingers on her arm and pulled away from him. On the end of the line was her mother's voice. Aurora saw her smiling up at her from under a red umbrella. She imagined running into her arms at the airport.

She forced back her tears. 'Everything is well,' she said. 'We are doing very well. Kind people are looking after us. There is no need to worry.' Her voice wobbled.

She repeated these words like a mantra. They had been drilled into her by Pablo over and over again. It was only when she was word perfect that he would let her speak to their mother. He had told her over and over: 'They are far away. They have done the best they can for us. There is no point in worrying them. If you cry, it will only upset them. You mustn't cry and you must not tell them we are in an orphanage.'

Yet when she heard the tears in her mother's voice – 'Darling, my darling daughter . . .' – she couldn't help herself. Her brother grabbed the phone.

She heard him say, 'Aurora has a bit of a cold, but she's fine. We are doing very well. Kind people are looking after us. There is no need to worry. We are both doing very well in school.'

He sounded distant, formal almost. It was the persona he had adopted to get through it all. It was the persona he adopted for the rest of his life – stoic and unemotional. Her older brother, holding it all together, forced to grow up well before his time, forced to cope. As he continued to speak to their mother, Aurora threw her arms around his waist and buried her face against his back, trying to stifle her sobs. It was then, for the first time, she saw Saint Sebastian, the image she had seen in Havana Cathedral, and with that image she felt herself back in her mother's arms. She now knew what those arrows meant. She knew what suffering meant, her removal from her mother, from her family, from everything that was familiar.

Her brother's voice broke in. 'Oh, I see. Yes, of course. Of course, I understand. Goodbye, mother.'

He turned round and hugged her. 'Mother says we are doing very well and that we are making her proud. We must continue to make her proud, mustn't we?'

'When are they coming?' she asked.

'Soon,' he said. 'As soon as they can.'

It was only much much later that he told her what her

mother had actually said, that their father had been arrested by Castro as a counter-revolutionary, that their mother was unable to come over because their grandfather had had a stroke, that they would have to manage as best they could for the time being.

It was the last conversation they had with her. They never heard from either their mother or their father again. Gradually, all their friends were reunited with their families. By mid-1966, only five hundred children were left in the Cuban Children's Program; Aurora and her brother were among them.

Shortly before her brother died he said to her, 'After that I felt we'd been dropped. We were on our own. We would just have to manage as best we could. I've never felt so alone in my life. Something in me died then. Hope. Happiness.'

Nothing was ever the same again.

Alberto shifted on the sofa and swallowed. Aurora got up and went into her bedroom, knelt down and pulled the painting out from under the bed. She pulled the duvet straight and placed it on top. If there was that kind of reward money, she had to take it. She should have been delighted, but instead she started to cry. Maybe he would hang in a public gallery again and she'd be able to go and see him, she thought. Other people should be able to see him, shouldn't they? But it wouldn't be just him and her alone any more. She was crying for her mother, her father, her brother, for Juan, for herself. She had to let him go for her children's sake. The reward money would change everything. She couldn't just keep him under the bed forever. That would be really stupid. But the tears continued to flow.

Alberto stood in the doorway. She turned away from him and wiped away her tears. He came and stood next to her, looking down at the painting.

'So, here he is,' he said.

'Mrs Pereira gave him to me. She told me to take him.'

He nodded. 'You know where she is?'

Aurora shrugged her shoulders. She ran her fingers along the edge of the painting. 'I was very careful with it,' she said. 'I don't think it's damaged.'

Alberto saw a rather dingy painting of a semi-nude man with two arrows protruding from him, his eyes raised to heaven. It didn't do much for him. He looked at Aurora, who was gazing at the painting with an expression not unlike that of Saint Sebastian on her face.

'You go to church, Albi?'

He shook his head. 'AA,' he said. 'I go to AA, that's my church. My sponsor – he's my priest.'

She nodded. 'I go,' she said. 'Through everything, I've gone. Even when I've no idea why, I've still gone.'

Alberto's phone rang. He looked at the screen but didn't answer it.

'When our parents sent us out of Cuba, it was because they didn't want us raised by Castro, they handed us over to the Catholic Church instead. But you know sometimes I wonder what the difference was.'

'You can't think that, Rory.'

She shrugged. 'Sometimes I think the only reason I go is because it makes me feel close to my mother. It's one of the few memories I got, being held in her arms in Havana Cathedral in front of a painting of Saint Sebastian.'

She reached for Alberto's hand, held it between both of hers. 'So, what do we do now? You going to arrest me?'

THE BOATMAN

Venice, 1576

Pomponio is running around like a rat that has lost his tail. Of course a man may go mad with grief. Or greed. To think that a man like Titian has died without leaving a will. It shows how foolish a genius may be. It wasn't as if he didn't know any notaries or have the money to pay them. Like many a man, maybe he thought making his will would bring his death a little closer. Or did he think he would defy death? None of us will do that. So Pomponio, the black sheep, is left with a terrible mess to sort out. Pomponio, a man who is always short of money, a man who is always in debt, now has care of his father's estate. I take him on several trips to the ghetto. He goes there in a gondola, weighed down with objects. My contacts there tell me of three gold chains, fourteen rings with rubies and diamonds, bowls of silver and of copper, two vases, twenty-five salt cellars, twelve silver spoons, six silver forks, Flemish shawls, a cross with two jewels in it. Back he comes on foot with the sides of his purse bulging a little more.

Of course a man may go mad with grief ...

Or greed ...

Or love ...

TULLIA BUFFO

Venice, 1577

She is not ill, she is pregnant. The herbs have failed her. As they have six times before. She knows she cannot get rid of the child growing in her belly. She knows this life must be born. It might be Marco's, she thinks. No, it must be his. Their love for each other has overcome any attempt to prevent life. It is only with him that she has been reckless. She sends for the midwife who helped her with her three sons.

'Did you not take the herbs?' she says severely. 'Didn't I tell you what might happen if you have another child? You almost died last time. Have you forgotten so quickly? You should end the pregnancy as quickly as possible.'

'No,' Tullia says. 'I must have this child.'

'Then you will most likely die.'

'Will you attend me?'

'And why would I want to do that? It would be like attending a blood bath.'

'Then I will have to find another.'

The woman leaves her and Tullia goes out onto the balcony. She is shaken by her hostility. Has she never made a mistake? Has she never longed to bring a life into this world? The Grand Canal is awash with boats, those containing merchandise for the markets round the Rialto and those filled with Venetians going about their daily business. It is a bright, crisp winter's day. The sun sparkles on the waters of the canal and somewhere off in the distance a musician is practising the harpsichord. Down in the *calle,* under her balcony, a jester juggles five balls, as a dog dances on its hind legs.

She is suddenly filled with a love of her life, of this life, of Venice. The woman is wrong, she thinks. It will be all right. I have not escaped the Inquisition only to be caught up in the snares of love. I cannot, I will not, get rid of this child. It must be born; it will tie me to him for all eternity, it will save him.

For the first time in many weeks, she puts quill to parchment. *There is no happiness for me except when I think and speak of you. My ardour has been heightened by these weeks apart. Come to me tonight at the usual place.*

As she dresses that night in her male clothing, her fingers fumble with laces and buttons. As she tries to tie the belt round her waist, she drops it and the dagger clatters to the floor. It is bitterly cold as she lets herself out into the *calle* and hurries to their meeting place. She cannot stop shaking, but she knows it has nothing to do with the cold.

She waits, but he does not come.

She falls asleep inside a church until a young priest shakes her by the shoulder and, looking at her curiously, asks if she has come for confession. As she makes her way home, she barely hears the *marangona* summoning the populace to work. All she can think of is how she longs for the touch of his hands on her body. All she can think of is how much she yearns for him and that he hasn't come.

LUDOVICO

Italy, 2012

Terry had flown back to London that morning. Ludovico was staying a few days longer to sort things out. He looked up at the larch and beech trees above his head. His father had loved these woods, loved to walk here. He was the first person to name the trees for him. Larch. Beech. Fir. Pine. Spring was in the air; you could smell it. He tried not to think, just to follow one step after the other on the path he had chosen. It was one he had walked many times as a child, one of his father's favourites. He felt his father at his side, with the energy he had possessed as a much younger man when he was the stronger of the two and Ludovico had struggled to keep up. He remembered the thud as Andrea planted his stick and whistled for his dog, the way he looked up at the branches of the trees, spreading over his head, absorbing everything, connected to everything around him.

Ludovico allowed himself the fantasy of imagining that

he could make a life for himself here in his home town; it lasted about thirty seconds. He remembered how desperate he'd been to get away, how as a teenager everything about the place had bored and frustrated him, how he had longed for the cosmopolitan energy of city life: longed for it, found it and then thrived on it.

And yet.

A deer lurched out onto the path and stood for a moment, staring at him, before bounding away into the undergrowth.

And yet.

Back in his father's house, he made himself some coffee and sat down on the sofa. What was he going to do with the house? He could keep it and let it out to skiers in the winter, but then he'd have to do it up. He looked round the room; there wasn't anything he wanted to change. Nothing. But if he kept it for himself, would he use it enough? He had barely made a dent on all the things he needed to do. For a start, no one seemed to know where his father's will was, or even if he had made one. Overwhelmed by it all, he closed his eyes. Just before he fell asleep it occurred to him that he should probably write and tell his mother. She'd want to know, wouldn't she? Maybe he should have told her, so that she could have come to the funeral, but the whole idea of that had been much too stressful to contemplate.

Later that evening, after he had eaten, he sat with a sheaf of papers in his lap. He had found them in a folder in the drawer to his father's desk.

Now serenity has returned; the bells ring for vespers and I listen to them with great enchantment. Why do the birds sing cheerfully in the sky? Because they know what I have forgotten. Before long it will be spring, the fields will put on their green coat and I, like a withered flower, will watch all of these marvels once more.

Tomorrow he would have to search the house for a will.

He couldn't believe his father hadn't made one. If that were the case, it would be most out of character.

The following morning Ludovico phoned his mother.

'I'm so sorry,' she said. 'Had he ... was it unexpected?'

'Yes,' Ludovico said. 'He had a stroke and then didn't regain consciousness.'

'I'm so sorry,' she said again and the shake in her voice seemed to suggest that her words were genuine. 'He was ...' she hesitated. 'He loved you very much.'

'Yes.'

'Come and see me,' she said. 'Come and see me anytime. Before you go back, if you'd like. You'd be most welcome. And we could talk about plans for *Othello*.'

As he finished the call, the bell rang and he went to open the door. Maria hugged him and then burst into tears. It was going to be a very long morning.

THE BOATMAN

Venice, 1577

When it is time for him to leave, it is I who takes Pomponio back to the mainland. It is not a comfortable journey. He sits huddled in his cloak, his humour as grey and dank as the fog which envelops us. As he stands up to disembark, he turns abruptly and grips me by the wrist, so firmly that he throws me off balance and I am in danger of dropping my oar.

'Do you know who ransacked my father's studio?'

In my most ingratiating manner, I tell him I did not realise that had happened, that I was appalled. 'Didn't the authorities board up the house?' I ask.

'Paintings are missing. I am sure of it.'

I wonder how he can tell, since he has not set foot in Venice for many years.

'In these times the world was truly turned upside down,' I say. 'The city was close to lawless for months on end. It was a thief's paradise. They knew which houses were empty. The *pizzigamorti* took Orazio away. In a world where people were disappearing every day, for a few paintings to go missing ...' I end with a shrug.

Pomponio tightens his grip on my wrist and pulls me closer, and now the salt in the air is mixed with the bitterness of his breath.

'Those paintings are not just any paintings. They are the work of a genius and they are mine,' he says, and I see the fury in his eyes and hear the crack in his voice. 'They are all I have left of him.'

There are tears in his eyes and something stirs in me that I do not expect. Pity. There it is, plucking mournful notes in my stomach; it is most unwelcome. He reaches under his cloak and produces some coins.

'Any information you may find out will be generously rewarded.' He places several *soldi* in my hand.

I puff out my cheeks. 'If you wish me to make enquiries, this will not get me or you very far.' A few more coins are placed in my hand and I nod. 'I will see what I can find out.'

Then the black rat Pomponio scuttles onto the mainland and the fog swirls around him like a magician's cloth and swallows him up.

Now he is gone from the city, I feel I can breathe more easily and am more confident in doing what I need to do. I tell Signora Buffo that there may be some items that she might find interesting if she would come with me into the ghetto. She has not been well these past days, but what I say to her pricks her interest, and so it is that a few days later we are in the house of the merchant Signor Mazod and she is leaning heavily on my arm as we ascend to the top of the house. The ghetto buildings rise higher than any others in the city, so the climb is an arduous one, but soon oil cloths are being removed from a series of paintings leaning against the wall. My lady does not look well. In recent days she has become more and more pale, almost like a ghost of herself. Either she is ill or she is pining for someone. Maybe it is merely that she is recovering from the strain of the Inquisition hearings. The light glances in through the window as she looks at each painting in turn. Mazod and I keep quiet. The only noise is that of his boy, carefully uncovering the paintings and showing them to her, one by one. I am curious to know which ones she will be interested in. Very curious indeed.

She takes a long time to look at them, asking at first for a dozen to be set to one side. Then she looks again at each one until finally there are just three left. She asks for a chair to be brought and then sits for some time, examining them all in great detail. One is of a child trying to thread flax into a needle while a little dog paws at her dress. The second is of Mary Magdalene, the penitent whore and first witness to the resurrection. The last one is of Cupid and Venus. Cupid holds a mirror for Venus, who is looking at herself, both are naked.

Finally, she seems exhausted by the intensity of her observation. She asks for a glass of water and the boy scurries away. Mazod follows him out and for the moment it is just the two of us in the room. She turns to me and sighs heavily. Looking at her more closely, I see tears in her eyes.

'Are you all right, Signora?'

'I am pregnant. My last birth nearly killed me. I have been told this one almost certainly will.'

I am dumbstruck. In recent days, I have grown fond of her. I hate to think of such a beauty being destroyed. I wonder if she is telling me this because she has a bargain to strike, but when I look more closely at her face I see that she is telling the truth.

She gestures at the paintings. 'What do you think of my choice?'

'A pretty choice, Signora .'

'The penitent whore, Love, and an innocent child.'

'The child is, I believe, Adria, Aretino's young daughter.'

'Adria – named after the city. How fitting. How much for the three?'

My mouth opens, but no sound comes out.

'What's the matter?' she smiles slightly. 'Are you unable to bargain with a dying woman?'

Usually I am as good at making a bargain as the next man, but in this case something hinders me.

She laughs at my discomfort. 'Talk to Mazod then.'

I am thinking of her three boys, of the fact that she has barely got herself back on her feet. I am thinking that she cannot afford the paintings and that we must sell them to someone else. I look at the paintings and then I look back at her. Then I think to myself. The paintings are mine to do with as I please. I stole them. I took that risk. I can do what I want and we have others. I look at her again and in her I see a child and Mary Magdalene; I see Cupid and Venus. I think the paintings are hers.

She gets wearily to her feet. 'They are the ones I would have. If you decide on a price, let me know what it is and I will see what can be done.'

The boy comes back with a glass of water and she drinks it. Mazod also returns with him and looks quizzically at me. Her face has turned grey and I have to help her down the stairs. As I row her home, I wonder why a woman like her will put herself at such risk. There are wise women, who know how to deal with these things, although of course the cure may be as dangerous as the pregnancy, and if the authorities discover her she will be back in front of the Inquisition.

The following day I arrange for the paintings to be delivered to her. She hangs them in her bedroom and covers them with curtains, not because they are obscene but because someone might recognise them as being the stolen Titians. I have absolutely no idea why, but I ask her nothing for them.

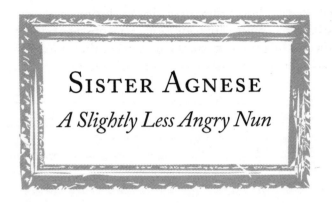

SISTER AGNESE
A Slightly Less Angry Nun

Venice, 1577

Sister Maria had told me how I might get out of the nunnery. It was very simple. It had been the way the young men had gained access at night. There was a key, a door, a staircase, and at the bottom of the staircase a boat. One night shortly after my conversation with her, she took the key from around her neck and handed it to me. I waited for a still night and then not long afterwards I took the key, I found the door, I went down the staircase and, as the waters of the lagoon lapped at my feet, I stepped into the boat and set out into the city. I was thrilled to be out in the air. When you have been enclosed as long as I had, the feeling of looking up at a night sky full of stars is unimaginable. I looked up and took a deep, deep breath.

Of course, I was frightened as well. No woman moved around the city at night without the threat of danger. There were certain dreadful and desperate villains in Venice. They wandered abroad very late, a gauntlet upon their hand with a little sharp stiletto. They lurked commonly near the waterside and if they came across any man that was worth the rifling they would stab him, strip him of his valuables and, when his plumes were thoroughly plucked, throw him in one of the canals. I knew all this from gossip with the serving maids in the nunnery, so I knew not to venture near the land. My intention was to row through the city that night, keeping as far away from the villains and the brigands as I could. I knew that if I kept to the water they would not easily be able to reach me. Wrapped up against the cold in my thick cloak, with the marten fur hood pulled well down over my head, I made my way into the coiled entrails of the city. The only noise was the slap of my oars as they dipped into the water, and the slight ripple of the water against the hull of my little boat. My aim this first time was simply to wander freely wherever my spirit took me. Before dawn I returned to the nunnery, secured the boat and made my way, content, to my room.

I had found her house.

The next part of my mission was not going to be so easy.

TULLIA BUFFO

Venice, 1577

Each day that passes brings her closer to her death. She lights candles at the foot of the painting and looks at it intently. Mary Magdalene, the penitent whore, the first witness to Christ's resurrection. Why, when there were so many people to choose from, did Christ pick her? Tullia watches as the guttering candles cast a fluctuating light over the surface of the painting. She gazes at the face of the woman and wonders who it was that Titian plucked from the streets as the model for Mary. It was well known that he had a tendency to exhaust himself with street whores. Venice was probably littered with his bastards. She feels the baby move in her womb. Does she fear hell? Of course, she does. She is not penitent. She refuses to regret the life she has lived. For a little girl raised in the foundling hospital by the nuns, she has risen to great heights. She has had a king in her bed. She smiles, imagining having that conversation with one

323

of the nuns who had looked after her as a little girl, Sister Felicita. She strokes her stomach. In the last few weeks she has started to feel the baby moving, the fluttering motion of a butterfly. Maybe that is what she will name the child if it is a girl, Farfalla. It is five months and she is still barely showing. If the midwife is correct, she has four more months of life. She must call the notary. She must make a will – she has her sons to think of. She has not told Marco. She has not seen Marco. He has disappeared and all her enquiries have produced no result. No one, it seems, has any idea where he is. Meanwhile the child grows in her belly and each day that passes brings her closer to her death.

Marco
&
Tullia

Venice, 1577

Marco, a silent man, clever enough to realise that writing poems to a courtesan who has most likely heard it all before, is not a good idea, sits at home pining for her. Silence presses in on him. Within the silence is all his grief for his children and his wife, and all his yearning for Tullia. His grief and his longing are so entwined he cannot separate one thread from the other. It is one terrible skein of grief and desire in which he is entangled. Her silence destroys him. Eventually he reaches for quill and parchment; eventually he seeks some sort of relief in words. If only for himself.

> *Lady, your absence has been to me,*
> *Your faithful servant and devoted lover,*
> *A death as cruel as it was unexpected.*
> *My soul and my enamoured heart*

Are used to living in your gentle angelic face
And in your eyes so beautiful and blessed:
These were the bright and only sun
On my days, without them sad and dark,
And full of what grieves man by far the most,
As bereaved and weak as are my eyes
In this sepulchre of life, which, without you,
Will not be restored to health.
Send for me, Tullia, and I will come.

He imagines her laughing as she reads it, putting it on a pile of many others she has received. He is one of many; there is nothing particular about him. Of course, there isn't. He has deceived himself. She has tired of him and moved on. Otherwise why doesn't she contact him? Why doesn't she? He scrunches the poem into a ball and throws it across the room. What a fool he is! She is a whore – what did he expect? Loyalty?

But Tullia is also writing:

Here before me now stands the bed
Where I first took you in my arms and which still
Preserves the imprint of our bodies, breast to breast.
In it I find now neither joy nor sleep,
But only weeping, by night and by day,
Which transforms me into a river of tears
Within this very place which once was
The cherished shelter of our joys
I now live alone in torment and in grief.
Why won't you come to me?
Please, please come.
Tonight.

She melts the wax and applies her seal. She hands it to her

servant for delivery. The servant takes it not to Marco but to the home of the young poet whose feet she had tickled with her hair. He gives him a few *soldi* and dismisses him, opens it, reads it, smiles to himself and tosses it out of the window into the lagoon. There it see-saws down to the bottom of the canal, where it joins all the other letters Tullia has written to Marco and which have never been delivered.

But there is another servant, the Saracen, a boy who Marco has educated and trained in the ways of his business. This boy is as devoted to Marco as it is possible to be. He has been at his side through all his tragic losses and loves him like a son. In the immediate aftermath of that tragedy, he slept on the floor by the side of Marco's bed, watching over him, worried that he might do something stupid. He has heard him crying in the night, crying out in his sleep for those he loved. He has been there in the morning when the cold light of dawn has brought with it the terrible realisation once more of all that he has lost. He has brought him his breakfast, cajoled him into eating. He has been alongside him, a witness to his despair. He has brought the priest to him when he feared he would do himself some violence. It is this boy who finds the scrunched up parchment. It is this boy who reads what is written there and it is this boy who goes to Tullia Buffo and asks for a private audience with her.

'Signora, I humbly beseech your pardon if what I am going to say offends, but I found this in my master's room.' He hands her the parchment and waits while she reads it.

'But why didn't he send it?'

'I do not know. All I know is that you must not, I beg you, meddle with my master's heart. He ... he was not well after the losses he incurred. His heart ...' He wrings his hands. '... is fragile, and he cannot be made sport of. I beg of you ... do not ... think you may play on him like a lute ... He will not be able to stand it.'

'But I have written many times and received no reply. I had assumed that he was no longer . . . that it was he who had . . . I sent so many times.'

The boy frowns. 'He did not receive them, Signora. Your servants must be deceiving you.'

'It was he, I thought, who was meddling with *my* heart.'

The boy gestures at the parchment she holds in her hands. 'I found that this morning, Signora. You can read there how he feels about you.'

'You are a good servant to your master. Let me tell you that I would never meddle with his heart. I know his heart is broken. I know how he mourns. It began as a business proposition because I had no rent to pay him, but it became something else. I promise you, all I seek is his . . .' She pauses. 'To soothe him in his distress. That is all.' She walks over to a desk and sits down. 'Will you wait and take this to him?'

He nods.

She tries to recollect as accurately as possible what she wrote last night. She folds it and hands it to him. 'Take this to him. Tell him what has happened.'

He nods, takes it from her and bows. As he turns to go, she touches his shoulder. 'Thank you,' she says. 'I have been tormented by his silence.'

'And he by yours.'

'From now on, I think it will be safer if you are our go-be-tween. My servants are vipers.'

'It seems so, Signora.'

He bows and is gone.

But what is she going to tell him about her condition; she cannot tell him that she will most likely die. She cannot. She goes over to the three paintings and stands in front of each one: Mary Magdalene, Cupid and Venus, the innocent child threading the needle.

If her child is a girl . . . but no, she cannot bear the thought. If her child is a girl and she is not there to protect her or look after her, she knows what will happen. Will she be able to trust Marco with her child? Will he even accept the child as his? She is going to have to think all this through very, very carefully.

LUDOVICO

Venice, 2012

Ludovico and his mother were having supper on her private roof terrace on top of the hotel. The sun was setting over the city and its dying rays were transforming the colours of the stone. His mother pulled her shawl around her and said, 'Did your father ever talk to you about the circumstances of your birth?'

Ludovico's forkful of spaghetti hovered in mid-air and then descended to his plate. He cleared his throat. 'My father would not talk to me about that at all. The only thing he said was that you both decided it would be for the best if he raised me.'

His mother's eyes slid away from his and down to her plate, onto the remnants of a spaghetti alle vongole. 'Would you like to know?'

Ludovico sighed heavily. There had been times in his life when all this had mattered so much to him. It had been practically the *only* thing that mattered to him. But now?

Now that his father was dead and could not be consulted, was he going to let his mother just tell him her version? It seemed like a betrayal. But on the other hand, Andrea had encouraged him to get in touch with her, so surely he would have known that eventually some kind of discussion like this would be likely to take place between them. The fact that she looked so cool, so in control, irritated him.

He shrugged his shoulders. 'Sure,' he said. 'If you like?'

'Let me get this straight,' Terry said, struggling to keep a straight face. It was a couple of days later and Ludovico was back in London. 'Your mother says you were conceived during the filming of Fellini's *Casanova* in Venice!'

'Well, no, not exactly. Apparently Fellini wanted my father to write some poetry for the opening scene, where the head of a black goddess is raised from the bottom of the lagoon. He knew that my father used Venetian dialect in his poetry and that's what he wanted. She said they met first when my father was staying in her family's hotel in Venice in order to get inspiration for what he was writing. She was only eighteen and working there over that summer. She was an aspiring actress and one thing led to another. Reading between the lines, I think she wanted my father to introduce her to Fellini, which he did. He took her to Rome, where the film was shot, and Fellini gave her a small role. It was the start of her film career. My father liked Fellini, but he didn't like the film and he hated the way his words were used. He hated everything about the experience.'

'You were conceived on the set of *Casanova*!'

'Oh, stop it,' Ludovico said. 'Stop saying it like that. Anyway, I'm not sure if I was conceived in Venice or Rome.'

'Well, how should I say it?' Terry adopted the portentous tones of a newsreader and said it again. 'You were conceived on the set of *Casanova*!'

Ludovico laughed. 'God, that's even worse.'

He picked up his glass and drained it. 'Anyway, she fell pregnant. My father offered to do the right thing and marry her, but apparently she didn't want that. At that time abortion was illegal in Italy, but I don't think my mother wanted an abortion, so it was agreed she would have me and that I would be adopted. But then my father changed his mind and he said he would take me, but the deal was she wouldn't seek to have any contact with me. And so that's what happened.'

'Very unusual for a man to do that then,' Terry remarked.

'My father was a very unusual man, but he was also living in a village which was home to his three sisters and their families. He knew that I would be brought up within a large extended family. You know the saying, "It takes a village to raise a child"? Well, that was me, raised by a village.'

'Seems like it did a pretty good job.'

'So that's the story of my beginnings.'

After a moment's silence, Terry said, 'It was a truly terrible film.'

Ludovico sighed and nodded. 'Good costumes, though. Very, very good costumes.'

'Interminable film,' Terry said. 'Simply interminable. Do you know what role your mother played?'

'Stop it,' Ludovico said. 'Just stop it!'

Terry laughed. 'Have you found your father's will yet?'

Ludovico shook his head. 'I don't think there is one. I've looked everywhere and his lawyer says he hasn't got it. I don't know what else I can do.'

THE BOATMAN

Venice, 1577

He cannot know. My mistress cannot have told him. If he knew, Marco Martinengo could not look so happy. Of course I understand why she hasn't. All the grief he has suffered and then the comfort she has offered him. There is something about this woman that has caught in my heart – not in the same way that she has caught in his, but she is in there all the same. It is her bravery, I think. It is perhaps that she is such a beauty. Perhaps also it is the fact that she has always been plain in her dealings with me. Of course, there is also her reputation. A man cannot help but wonder. How can he help himself? I am, I admit it, just a little bit curious to know what brought a king to her bed. This is a city of thousands of courtesans. What was it that made her so special?

After I have taken Marco Martinengo home, I am to pick up the notary and take him to her. She is making ready for her death. But after I have dropped him off I head for the ghetto,

333

not this time to see the paintings but to talk to Isaac Lazaro. He was a boy when he helped his father save my father's life, but now he is the most respected doctor in the city and I am going to him with a business proposition. I wonder what has come over me. My initial motivation in seizing the paintings was revenge, but now all I can think of is the good I might do with them. This turn of events, I confess, has surprised me. Recently I have been thinking more and more of my master, Pietro Aretino, of that moment in Titian's studio when he stroked my cheek and pulled me to my feet, when he took me under his wing. My life changed for good at that point. He had the power to do that. Perhaps it is vanity that makes me think that I can change people's lives, even save them. Perhaps it is no more than vanity, and all my plans will crumble into dust and I will see what a silly old fool I have become. Only time will tell.

TULLIA BUFFO

Venice, 1577

'My first son, Camillo, is the child of Jacomo Baballi Raguseo, my second, Bernardo, and third son, Jacopo, are the sons of Andrea Tron, son of Paolo Tron.'

The notary's notably whiskery eyebrows ripple slightly across his forehead as he scratches down what she is saying.

'The child I am bearing is the child of Marco Martinengo.' He pauses and glances up at her.

She sighs, gets to her feet and walks over to the window. 'There will be different requirements if this child is a boy or a girl.'

'Of course.'

'Also I do not know if Marco Martinengo will accept the child as his.'

'We can deal with both possibilities in the will, Signora.'

'Yes, well we will have to.' She gazes down at the canal.

She will have to talk to Marco about it before the birth and then she will be able to gauge his reaction.

'What would you do,' she asks, 'if a courtesan told you she was expecting your child?'

He sits back and sniffs. 'I would ask her how she could possibly know it was mine.'

She nods. 'And if she said she just knew and if she died and the child was orphaned?'

'I would feel under no obligation.'

'No obligation,' Tullia snaps. 'No obligation. And if that woman meant everything to you? If she had saved you from the despair you felt after the plague had wiped out almost your entire family? If you knew the woman loved you?'

He folds his arms and looks down at the floor in silence for a moment.

'Well, in that case . . .'

'Yes?'

'In that case, maybe I wouldn't mind whether the child was mine or not. Maybe I would take it on as mine out of my love for the woman. Maybe in those circumstances I might feel somewhat differently.'

She smiles. 'Yes? Would you?'

He shrugs his shoulders. 'It depends on the man, Signora,' he says, dipping his quill in the ink and looking up at her expectantly.

She places her hand on her stomach. This child was no longer a butterfly. It was kicking like a carthorse. She would have to call it Cavallo rather than Farfalla. Now then, how would she continue?

'On my death,' she says, 'I wish my executors to make an inventory of my possessions and that these should be sold and all my money should be held in trust for my three or four children . . .'

'We have not named your executors yet.'

'Oh, no.' A wave of nausea washes over her. 'I'm sorry, but I think we must leave it there for today. Can you come back in the morning?'

He nods, gathers his things together, bows and leaves.

She could not write the will without talking to Marco first. It simply wasn't possible.

After the notary has gone, Tullia draws the curtains back from the three Titians. She feels certain her child is going to be a girl. This pregnancy does not feel like the others. A girl needs more protection than a boy. She knows all too well what might happen to an unprotected girl. She doesn't want such a fate to befall any child of hers.

Marco is asleep. He lies on his front, his hand across her belly; the fingers are no longer bitten down to the quick. A slight white line is growing on the top of each nail. She caresses each finger between two of her own and thinks of the time they had made love under the crescent moon. How the moon now lives on the tip of each finger. Perhaps she should write to him. Perhaps that would be better. But suddenly she is overwhelmed with the need to know how he is going to react. Now. She must tell him now. She has to have this settled in her mind. He stirs next to her, swallows and opens his eyes.

'There is something I need to talk to you about,' she says.

He blinks and opens his eyes wide to wake himself up. He props himself on his elbow and looks at her. She has got off the bed and put on her lynx-lined cloak. She cannot have this conversation with him while she is naked. She pulls it tightly around her.

'There is something ... I am pregnant,' she says. 'I believe the child is yours. Of course, I understand that you may wonder how I could possibly know that. I understand and in response all I can say is that I believe that the strength of our love has broken through all the remedies and herbs that I take to prevent this happening. It is for this reason that I want to have the child.'

He is no longer propped up on his elbow; he is sitting on the edge of the bed, frowning.

'I am telling you because if anything happens to me I need to know what you would be willing to do. Would you accept her as yours, or would I have to make other arrangements?'

'Her?'

'You see, if she is a girl I could not bear for her to be raised by my brother and sister-in-law. My sister-in-law will punish her, I know, for her mother's profession, and I could not bear to think that she will suffer because of me. My brother is a coward and will do nothing to protect her. My sons will not suffer in the same way.'

'Her?'

'I am sure it is a girl. Also if it is a girl she will require more protection. I could not bear it if ... I ... could not ... and ...' Tears were now pouring down her cheeks.

He gets off the bed and goes to her. He takes her by the collar of her coat and shakes her gently. He looks into her eyes. 'All the things you cannot bear,' he says softly.

'You see, I ... I was given no choice,' Tullia says. 'From the moment I was taken from the orphanage, I was given no choice in what I became. My mother decided what my life should be and I was entered into a position of physical and spiritual bondage. I have made the very best of it, but I do not want this life for my daughter. It is a very dangerous way to live. I want her to marry honestly. I could not ...'

He is still holding her by the collar. 'You could not bear it ...'

'No ... I ...'

'Nothing is going to happen to you, but if it did even if

338

she were not mine I would take her. I would give her a good dowry. I would take your sons as well.'

'You would?'

'I would and because they are yours I would love them.'

'You would?'

'Tullia, do you not know this of me already?'

He falls to his knees and is kissing her belly. 'I love you,' he says. 'I will do anything for you.'

She strokes his head as a sob of relief escapes her. Of course there is one thing she had not told him, namely that she is likely to die, but now at least she could go ahead and finish her will and hopefully protect the future of her children. Then whatever the future holds she could approach it with a clear conscience and with the knowledge that they would be looked after.

AURORA

New York, 2011

Aurora was being given a grilling by Alberto's boss. There was no air in the windowless room and she felt however deeply she inhaled she could not get enough oxygen. Sweat trickled down the side of her body.

'And then what happened?'

Aurora pinched the front of her shirt and flapped it back and forth. 'She – that is Mrs Pereira – told me to take the painting. She knew I loved it because we'd talked about it over the years and she just said take it.'

'But didn't you think that was a little odd? You know, a strange thing for her to have done – suddenly, out of the blue, like that? You must have known this was a valuable painting, right?'

'I did think it odd, but I loved the painting, so I didn't ask any questions. I just took it.'

'But didn't you think that Mr Pereira might have had something to say about it?'

'Well, sure, but he wasn't there, was he?'

'But why did you take it out of its frame?'

'Mrs Pereira suggested that. She said it would be easier to carry. You'll find her prints on the hammer.'

'Easier to carry, not easier to hide?'

'Why would I want to hide it?'

'I don't know. Why would you?'

Aurora sighed and sipped from the glass of water which was on the table in front of her. She'd been going over and over it for some time now.

'When you saw her, did Mrs Pereira say anything about her husband?'

Aurora shook her head. 'Nope. Like I said, she said they weren't going to be needing my services any more.'

'Did she say why not?'

She shook her head. 'The rich don't think they have to give reasons to someone like me. They just do what they want. She said that she was sorry. She gave me some clothes of hers and then just as I was leaving she suggested I take the painting.'

'And then what happened?'

'Well, I took it home with me. I'd given a description of the painting to Alberto and he had said he was going to check up about it, so when I got it home I phoned him and he came round.'

'But that's not exactly right, is it?'

Aurora sighed but remained silent.

'First we've got no evidence of Mrs Pereira being in the building on the day you say. Second, if she was there on the day you say and you took the painting, then how come it took you two days to phone Alberto?'

'I don't care if you haven't got evidence of her being there.

Maybe she came up the back way because she didn't want to be caught on camera.'

'And why would that be?'

'I don't know. All I know is that she was there on the Tuesday, like I said. As for the two days, well...' She suddenly felt exhausted by the whole thing. 'I...'

The interview room door opened and Alberto came in and sat down. 'So,' he said, 'where we got to?'

The other man frowned. 'I was just wanting Aurora here to explain to me why it was there was a two-day gap between her taking the painting and her phoning you about it?'

'There wasn't.'

'There wasn't?'

She phoned me that evening and left me a message. That night Pereira was pulled out of the Hudson and all hell broke loose. It was only later that I remembered, so the delay was my fault. She'd let me know on the day.'

'Oh she did, did she?'

'Sure she did.'

'And you didn't tell anyone?'

'It kind of slipped my mind. I knew the painting would be safe with her and there were other things to deal with.'

Aurora rubbed her forehead. 'How much longer's this going to go on? I need to get home and feed my kids.'

'Shall we wrap this up?' Alberto said. 'You got everything you need?'

'Yeah,' he said, glancing back and forth between Aurora and Alberto. 'I think I got the long and short of it.' He closed the folder and got to his feet.

In the car on the way home, Aurora said, 'If you hadn't come in, I was going to tell him the truth, you know. That the reason I didn't phone was because I couldn't bear to let go of him. I just wanted him all to myself for a few days to see if he could make the pain go away.'

Alberto pulled up outside her home. 'I'm so sorry about how I behaved after Juan died, Rory. That was no way for a man to behave.'

Aurora shook her head in a gesture of exhaustion. 'It's water under the bridge, Albi.' She opened the door and stepped out onto the sidewalk. She turned towards the house and then hesitated. 'You want to come in. Meet the kids?'

'You not too tired?'

'Sure I'm tired, but it's good for them to meet people who knew their father. You want to come in and watch me fry some pancakes, I'm not stopping you. You don't get to eat any, mind,' she said, glancing at his stomach. 'We got to do something about that.'

He smiled, climbed out of the car, hitched up his trousers and followed her slowly up the path to her front door. *We*, he was thinking as the smile spread across his face – she said *we*.

TULLIA,
SISTER AGNESE
& SISTER MARIA

Venice, 1577

Sister Maria is reaching the end of her time on this earth.
She has become fretful, urgent in her requests that she may
see her child, Tullia, once before she dies. I have not told her
of her child's profession. I send a letter via one of the serving
maids. I do not tell the full story, but I say that I urgently
need to see her. She must ask for me. I tell the abbess that
this woman must come and see Sister Maria before she
dies. I say it is very important. She is wise enough to ask no
questions. And this is how Tullia Buffo comes to be sitting
at the bedside of her mother one day later. The sick room
smells of Sister Maria's impending death, despite my best
efforts to cover the smell with sweet smelling herbs, and I see
her flinch as she enters. I have just told her that Sister Maria
believes her to be her child.

'Tullia?'

Sister Maria's voice is thin and quavers. She reaches out her hand and Tullia steps forward and takes it. She has come very simply dressed and is covered in a black hooded cloak. She casts the hood back from her face and I see at once what a beauty she is, but also that she is very, very pale. I expected a harder, tougher face because of her profession but all I see is her fragility, her vulnerability, the elegance of her neck. I wonder if this is what draws men to her, this feeling that she might break under them if they handle her too roughly.

'Will you forgive me, child?'

'There is nothing to forgive. Nothing.'

'I prayed for you. Every day of my life I have prayed for you. You were in my heart every moment of every day. Lean closer.'

She leans forwards so that her face is lit by the candle that sits on the table next to Sister Maria's bed.

'Ahh,' a smile spreads across her face. 'You are a great beauty. Look at you!' Maria reaches out and strokes the side of her face. There is a moment of silence and then Tullia bursts into a storm of weeping. She holds her mother's hand against her face and sobs and sobs. 'Hush, child. Nothing is lost. I am here now.'

She weeps and she weeps. I move across from where I have been standing and place my hand on her shoulder to steady her.

'I prayed so much that you would be happy.'

Tullia glances up at me and I see the question in her eyes. I lean down and whisper. 'She knows nothing of your life.'

I see the relief in her face and she nods. 'My life has been most blessed. I made an honest marriage. I have three children and . . . ' – she pulls back the cloak to reveal that she is heavily pregnant – 'will soon have another. Will you bless me and my child?' she asks.

Sister Maria reaches out and places her hand on her belly.

The low murmur of her prayer soon fills the room. The prayer seems to soothe her and soon afterwards Sister Maria falls asleep.

Tullia looks up at me. 'May I sit with her for a time?' she asks.

'Of course,' I say. 'I will wait outside.'

She reaches out and takes my hand. 'No,' she says. 'Would you stay with me, please?'

So I do.

When she leaves, she takes my hand and says to me, 'I have three children by two different men and this one is by a third. I am not married. You know my profession?'

I nod.

'Tell me. Will God forgive my lies to a dying woman?'

'I think He will. You lied to comfort her. You did not want to make her feel guilty for what became of you. Your feelings were all for her.'

Tears begin to fill her eyes again. 'They say I am most likely to die with this child, but I love the man who gave it me so ...'

'So you are willing to give your life for another?'

'It seems that I must.'

I continue, 'Maybe they are wrong. Maybe God has a different plan for you.'

She laughs. 'An honest marriage, perhaps?' She shakes her head. 'No one escapes from this life that easily. No one. My ... the woman who took me from the foundling hospital, the woman who decided what I would become, she died recently from the French disease. It was a terrible, terrible death.'

As she steps into the gondola, she says, 'How long do you think?'

I shrug. 'She has already outlived her time. Maybe now that she has seen you and asked your forgiveness she will be able to leave us.'

'Will you send for me if she worsens?'

'I will.'

'Thank you. You have brought my life round in a circle. If I am to die with this child, at least I will go to my grave with my mother's blessing freshly upon me. I will know that she prayed for my happiness every single day. I will know that she did not forget me.'

'Sister Maria is greatly loved,' I say. 'We are taking good care of her.'

She nods. 'I see it,' she says. 'I see that you love her. I know that she is in good hands.'

I am about to leave when she says, 'How did you find me? How did you know?'

'There were records in the foundling hospital and Sister Maria told me the name that she had given you. We had the name of the woman who took you, the same surname you still use. Your name is … well, it is quite well known in the city.'

She laughs. 'You mean I am notorious? Well, I am glad that my notoriety helped you find me and also that it had not reached my mother's ears.'

She settles herself on the cushions of the gondola and draws the curtain around her. I catch the eye of the gondolier and I see him take in the damaged half of my face. He looks at me curiously and then smiles warmly. As the gondola sets off I hear her sobs drifting across the water towards me. There are other things I must tell her – like who her father is – but now is not the time. She has had enough to break her already.

THE BOATMAN

Venice, 1577

I had told Signora Buffo's maid to come to me when my mistress's waters broke. And so it was that I was rudely shaken awake at three in the morning one bitterly cold night in the middle of winter. I made my way straight to the ghetto on foot because the canals were frozen and using the same ruse that I had used all those many years ago when the infection had spread up my father's arm, I informed the guards that my mistress (I gave the name of a patrician who I knew was heavily pregnant) was in labour and that Isaac Lazaro must be summoned. Then I took him to my mistress's house as fast as I could. Her cries of agony could be heard echoing round the *campiello* as we approached her home. I had not told her what I intended to do because I did not think that she would agree, so she looked alarmed when we both entered her bedroom. I quickly told her of Isaac's skill and she agreed that he could examine her. I left the room and waited outside like any anxious father but a few moments later he was at the door. His sleeves were rolled up and his hands were covered in blood.

'Bring me ice,' he said. 'As much as you can.'

'Ice?'

'Ice, man. It is vital. God knows there is enough in the canals. Break it up. As quick as you can. And bring it to me.'

I ran downstairs and banged on the door of Checho, the sausage maker, and quickly told him what I needed. Although grumpy to start with, he then took on some of my urgency and to the accompaniment of Tullia's groans we used some of his tools to gouge ice from the surface of the canal. I wondered what possible use Isaac could make of it. When I had a bucket full, I ran back into the house and into the bedroom.

He glanced in the pail. 'Too big. It needs to be smashed into small pieces.'

I took the dagger from my belt and began to set about it. When it was in smaller pieces, he picked up a pillowcase which was on the end of the bed and scooped the ice into it and then laid this across the top of my mistress's stomach.

She yelled out a series of most filthy oaths. 'Am I not in enough agony? Are you now trying to freeze me to death?'

'The baby needs to turn. It is coming down feet first. It may turn away from the cold. Now then, damp down the fire. Do not let it go out completely. All of you go and stand in front of the fire. I want as much of the light extinguished as possible and hand me all the candles we have and blow out those on the cesendellos and those over there by the door.'

And so I stood in front of the fire with the sausage maker and the two maids and between us we blocked out almost all the light. I was very wet and my breeches began to steam because of their close proximity to the fire. Now the room was in almost complete darkness other than the candles that were in the hands of the doctor. One of the maids gripped my arm, 'Is this necromancy?' she whispered. 'Is he . . .'

'Be quiet,' I said. 'He has seen more babies born than our mistress has had men between her legs. He knows his trade. He is the doctor the patricians ask for. He is a man of learning. This is not necromancy. This is wisdom. We will ask him when it is all over.'

'But what is he doing with the candles? Why does he hold them between our lady's . . .?' She was clutching onto my arm in terror. 'What is he doing?'

I had absolutely no idea and I could see why the maid was frightened. It was an eerie scene. What with the steam rising off me and the sausage maker, and the groans of my lady, and the flickering light of the candles showing the bloodstained sheets. We all seemed to be frozen in this way for a long time and then Isaac gave a short grunt of satisfaction. He turned towards us.

'Stand away from the fire and stoke it up.' He threw the ice-filled pillowcase towards us. 'Get that out of here. Light back up the cesendellos and place these candles back where they came from. Bring me clean water and clean cloths. Lots of both.'

'There now,' he said, moving to my mistress's head and stroking her forehead. 'There now. Everything will be all right. The baby has turned. His head is in the right direction. You have nothing to worry about now. Everything will be well.'

I had an image of Isaac, as a young boy, standing fearlessly by his father's side during the amputation. Now here he was, a confident, wise man, a healer who could save lives with his skill. I envied him since I did not have the same sense of progress in my own life.

Two hours later my mistress gave birth to a baby daughter.

When it was all over, I accompanied Isaac back to the ghetto. We had an appointment to keep. Thick cloud lay over the city. Every canal was a solid green path and children were sliding and slithering here and there. It was bitterly, bitterly cold. Isaac began to shake, although whether with cold or exhaustion I was uncertain. I took off my own cloak and threw it over his shoulders.

'It is not the quality you are used to,' I said, 'but it will get you home warmer than if you were without it.'

He smiled ruefully in acknowledgment and paused for a moment. 'She was lucky to survive.'

'She had you to see to her, so luck did not come into it.'

'If the baby had not turned . . .'

'Could you tell me about the ice and the candles?'

He glanced sideways at me and smiled. 'What, and give away my secrets? The patricians pay good money for my knowledge.'

'I promise not to tell a soul.'

He shrugged. 'Babies are like plants, they like light and warmth. The ice at the top of the bump is on top of their heads. They want to be warm, so they may turn to get away from the cold. It has also been known for them to turn towards a bright light.'

'Ice and light!'

'At any rate it seemed to work today, thank God, or they would both probably have died.'

Inside the ghetto we climbed the stairs to the room with the paintings. A chair was brought and a bowl of soup. He sipped his soup as the paintings were shown to him. It was difficult to measure his response to what he was seeing. Maybe he was simply too exhausted to respond in any way. Mazod and I left the room for a moment and when we stepped back in we found Isaac fast asleep, nodding over the bowl he held in his lap. The paintings appeared to be looking at him reproachfully, but he had saved two lives that night: he deserved his rest. They would have to wait for a later, fuller appreciation of their merits. We let him sleep.

TERRY

Venice, 2012

Another set of light bulbs around another mirror. Another country. Another play. Another time. Terry looked at himself in the mirror. He'd had a savage crew cut for the part; soft and cuddly he was not. He scratched his head. *I am not what I am.* A line that most actors understood all too well. *I am not what I am.* Outside, the murmur of the audience, that anticipatory hum. There was a knock on the door and Frederico, his dresser, a beautiful, rather excitable young man, wearing suffocating amounts of aftershave, came in carrying a blue silk doublet. With a flourish, he took it off its hanger and held it out so that Terry could slide his arms into the sleeves. Then he stood in front of him, lacing it up. When he'd finished, he ran both his hands lightly down Terry's chest. 'Bellissimo,' he said and looked up, smiling. Terry assumed he meant the doublet not himself. *I am not what I am.*

No, now he was no longer Terry Jardine, he was the man with the blue sleeve. And out there in the gardens of San Clemente his audience awaited the arrival of Iago.

TULLIA

Venice, 1577

Since the birth of her daughter, Tullia has been unable to stop crying. The tears fall from her eyes like raindrops from the sky. She wonders if this storm will ever stop.

At first she thinks they are tears of gratitude for her child, for her life, for the love of Marco. But then shortly after the birth and when she has been given strict instructions that she is not to move from her bed, that it could be life-threatening, news comes from the nunnery of her mother's death. So then tears of gratitude are mixed with those of grief.

Sometimes she does not know why – all she knows is that she is crying and crying. She cries when Marco visits; she cries when he takes the baby in his arms. She cries when she tells him that her mother has died and that she has not been allowed to go to the funeral because of her condition. She cries when he takes her in his arms and holds her, and she cries when he tells her he wants to marry her. It is as if every tear she has refused to shed in her life is queuing up, demanding to get out.

There is nothing she can do but allow the tempest to roar through her. She cannot understand it. Her life has always been so hard. It has been something to fight for, to endure. But now when there seems to be the chance of true happiness all she feels is this storm of grief. For so long all she has had is hope. Now her love for Marco, the birth of her child and the death of her mother seem to have cracked her wide open.

As she weeps, she wonders if all the prayers her mother had said on her behalf during her long and holy life had finally been heard, that her mother was in heaven arguing her case. And this thought makes her weep even harder.

TERRY
&
LUDOVICO

Venice, 2012

After the performance Terry and Ludovico went out for a meal with some of the cast and people who had been working on the production.

Ludovico leant against Terry and said, 'So, how is it becoming the man with the blue sleeve?'

Terry shrugged. 'I love the doublet. It even makes Frederico want to stroke me.'

The two men glanced down the table to where Frederico was caressing his very beautiful girlfriend. They both laughed.

Ludovico picked up his glass and raised it to his lips. 'You know when I came to see my mother after my father's funeral.'

'You mean when you discovered that you were conceived on the set of *Casanova*?' Terry said, laughing as Ludovico made 'keep your voice down' gestures.

'Yes, then. Well, she told me something else as well. Something pretty strange, actually.'

'Oh, yeah?' Terry said, tucking into some polenta and liver.

'She said ...' Ludovico paused. 'I think maybe I'll just have to show you ... because I'm not sure if I believe her altogether. It's really, really odd.'

'Show me?'

'Yes, I'll ask my mother. Can you come to the hotel on San Clemente early tomorrow afternoon?'

'Of course.' Terry frowned. 'You've come over all mysterious all of a sudden.'

'Well, come tomorrow and you'll see why.'

'Actually,' Ludovico said, 'she's not terribly happy about you being here.' It was the following afternoon and the two men were standing in a picture-lined gallery attached to Ludovico's mother's apartment.

'Well, I'm not surprised. She doesn't know me. As far as she knows, I might go out and blab this about.'

'But you won't?'

'You know I won't.' Terry leant forwards slightly. 'And no one knows about them?'

'Apparently not.'

'Is that possible?'

'Of course it is. There's a Titian that's just been discovered in the basement of the National Gallery. Who knows what's out there in private ownership anywhere in the world.'

'But ...'

'She doesn't have any other children. I'm her heir. She said she felt she had to tell me because ... well, in case anything happened to her ... I think what she was saying was for God's sake don't let anyone value them as part of her estate. You know – make sure they're kept secret.'

'But did she tell you how the family ... I mean, how come they're here not hanging in a gallery?'

Ludovico was looking more and more worried. He shook his head. 'She didn't say.'

'God!' Terry said.

'She only said that they'd always been in the family. No one else had ever owned them. That there was an understanding in the family that they should never be sold. And there's another thing she said. She said that I'm directly related to Titian, that the ancestor who owned these paintings was a famous courtesan called Tullia Buffo who stated in her will that she was the grandchild of Titian and the child of his son, Pomponio.'

'Did your father know?'

Ludovico shrugged. 'I don't know. I just don't know.'

'Did he ever say anything?'

Ludovico shook his head. 'Never. He was very critical of Venice. He said it was no better than a Disneyland site for tourists, but I wonder now whether he wanted to protect me from ...' He waved at the paintings. 'All this.'

'Maybe he was right to.'

'Yes ...' Ludovico sat down heavily on a painted bench. 'Maybe he was, but the weird thing is that since I've been coming here more, since I've had contact with my mother, I feel at home in a way I never have before.'

'You should make a film,' Terry said. When there was no reply from Ludovico, he turned round and saw that he was holding his head in his hands as if it was being split in two by an axe.

He sat down next to him. 'Ludovico,' he said, taking his hand and placing it on his own knee and stroking his arm.

Ludovico tried to smile but only managed a sort of grimace. 'It's just a lot to take in. It just feels too much to absorb at the moment. And with my father just having

358

died, all I can think is how I'd like to talk to him about it, that he would help me make sense of it.' He leant his head against Terry's shoulder.

'You are not who you thought you were,' Terry said gently.

Ludovico laughed. 'I am not what I am. Have you got any tips for me on that front?'

Terry shook his head. 'None whatsoever, I'm afraid, just that you should give yourself time and not be too hard on yourself, but then recently that's been my answer to absolutely everything.'

Later they walked across the square, the pigeons flying up in the air in front of them. Terry stopped and gestured around them. 'You know, if you're a direct descendent it's not surprising you feel at home here. I mean he was here when the square was being built. He was here in its heyday. He was here when the myth of Venice was being founded. He was part of all that. It must have been incredible.'

Ludovico looked up and spun round, his hair dancing in the air. For a moment he looked like a whirling dervish, arms out and head back. Terry stood still, watching him, thinking how exceptionally beautiful he was. Ludovico came to a halt and turned towards him.

'You know, of course, that I'm deeply in love with you.'

Terry's mouth opened as if he were about to say something, but nothing came out.

Ludovico laughed and slid his arm through Terry's. 'Come on,' he said. 'I have to get my Iago back for his afternoon nap.'

'Let's feed the pigeons,' Terry said suddenly.

They went and bought some bags of corn and soon the two men were covered in birds: they sat along their arms, on their hands and on their shoulders. They pecked the corn from their hands and then once the corn was gone so were the pigeons, on to the next group of tourists, the next bag of grain. And then they walked slowly back to the hotel.

Imagine you can end anywhere. You can end with the boatman carrying Tullia to the party which will celebrate her marriage to Marco, or with Aurora being married to Alberto by her local priest. Suppose you can end it anywhere. With Terry and Ludovico celebrating their honeymoon in Venice two years later, or Aurora receiving the cheque which will change her and her children's lives forever. We have more choice over our endings than our beginnings. Imagine you can end this in any way you like and then imagine ...

An Art Exhibition in Venice

Two Years Later

Venice, 2014

It had been a terrible struggle getting here. When Alberto had suggested it, she had said yes, but Aurora had no idea what she was saying yes to. She had no idea of the nightmares and torrents of grief. She had not travelled so far since she was five years old and had left Cuba. Reflecting on it afterwards, she could see that her response wasn't at all surprising, but at the time she had been rocked by the strength of her reaction. She was convinced that if she left she would never get home again, that she would never see her children again, that her life would be ripped away from her. Thank God for Alberto. She lay in his arms and shook and shook until finally the terror had subsided and they had got on a plane and flown to Venice.

And now here they were in the Gallerie dell'Accademia looking at *St Sebastian* hanging in one of the largest exhibitions there had ever been of Titian's works. Paintings had been lent from all over the world, from the Prado in Madrid, from the National Gallery in London, from the Hermitage in Russia, and from the National Museum in Kromeriz in the Czech Republic. There was great excitement in particular about four paintings that had not been on public display in Venice before: one had come from London and was of the French doctor, Girolamo Fracastoro, who had named the disease syphilis, the other three from Venice itself.

A large crowd of people were gathered down one end of the gallery where these four paintings were hanging, but Aurora had eyes for *St Sebastian* alone. Oh, yes, she thought, he is so beautiful. So, so beautiful, just as I remember him. She thought back to all those years she had spent with him in the Pereiras' apartment. She thought of him lying under her bed looking up at the springs. She thought of taking hold of Alberto's hand as they both stood looking down at him. She thought of how her life had changed so much in the last few years. It was truly beyond recognition.

Alberto had left her side and moved to the next painting.

Aurora suddenly felt the need to tell someone, anyone, her story. She turned to the man standing next to her. He was short and portly with a beard. He had a warm, lively face and seemed somehow approachable.

'This painting,' she said, 'I gave the police the information about where this was. It had been stolen. It changed my life.'

Terry smiled at her. 'Really?' He had read a little about the history of the painting in the exhibition catalogue. 'So you brought him home?'

'Home?' Aurora said. 'Oh . . .' She brought her hand up to her mouth. The man had a very kind, sympathetic face. Tears pricked her eyes.

'I'm sorry,' Terry said. 'I didn't mean to upset you.'

Aurora waved her hand back and forth. 'It's not you. Recently I've been crying at everything.' She began to laugh. 'Someone holds a door open for me and I cry.'

Terry said, 'Let me show you my favourite.'

She followed him until he stopped in front of the painting of *The Man With the Blue Sleeve*. 'This is on loan from the National Gallery in London,' he said. 'Three years ago I was standing in front of it and he told me I was going to die soon.'

'Well,' Aurora said. 'He got that wrong.'

'He didn't actually. I had a cardiac arrest shortly afterwards. My heart stopped beating. Officially I did die, although only for a moment or two.'

'So,' she said, 'you had some kind of premonition.'

They stood for a moment in silence.

'Did you come to the city for the exhibition?' Aurora asked.

'Sort of, but I live part of the year here. I have a friend who keeps an apartment here.'

'This is my first time. I couldn't believe it when we arrived at the airport and looked across the sea. It didn't seem possible.'

Terry smiled in agreement.

'Well,' she said, 'I must go find my husband.'

Me too, Terry thought. 'Good luck,' he said.

'I think Saint Sebastian's granted me enough of that for one lifetime,' she said, 'but thanks anyway.'

As Aurora made her way towards the crowd at the other end of the gallery, Terry was joined by Ludovico.

'Has he got any words of wisdom for you?' Ludovico asked, nodding at the painting.

Terry shook his head. 'I mean, he could have told me I was going to fall in love that time, but instead he told me I was going to die.'

'Maybe he thought telling you you were going to die was the more urgent message. I think he looks hungover. He's had a night out on the tiles.'

Ludovico glanced down the other end of the room to where the crowd had gathered in front of the paintings which had until recently belonged to his mother.

'Have you got any regrets?' Terry asked.

Ludovico shook his head. 'Absolutely none. From the moment my mother showed them to me, I thought there was something obscene about them being in private hands. They're masterpieces and they should be able to be enjoyed by everyone. Anyway, if I want to come and see them, all I have to do is come here. That was part of the settlement when my mother died. The Gallerie dell'Accademia gets them and there's no tax on them. From the moment she showed them to me, I knew that was what I would do if I got the chance. Things like this belong to the whole world not one individual family.'

'Your father would be proud of you.'

Ludovico smiled. 'Yes, I think he would approve. My mother, on the other hand...'

'A tough cookie,' Terry said. 'Rather terrifying, actually.'

A few moments later Ludovico said, 'Have you seen enough?'

Terry nodded and they made their way outside into the warm evening air. The sun was sinking and the sky was turning the most beautiful pale green. Ludovico took a deep breath. 'How about some spaghetti alle vongole?'

'Good.'

'But you're not to have any parmesan on it this time.'

'Spoil sport.'

'I've told you, if you have parmesan with seafood the waiters will despise you.'

'But I can live with that, and anyway I need to fatten up for Falstaff.'

'You do not need to fatten up for Falstaff and it'll be bad for your liver.'

'My liver is fine. It was my heart that...'

Arm in arm and bickering gently, the two men set off into the serpentine alleyways of the city in search of their supper.

THE BOATMAN

Venice, 1578

It was the summer after my mistress got married to Marco Martinego and I had taken her sons out in my boat to go duck shooting. They were too young to have much success, but we were enjoying the sun on our shoulders and the glittering surface of the lagoon. The boys were sitting very still with their bows and arrows at the ready as I slowly edged the boat closer to some ducks sitting in the reeds. Then Jacapo sneezed and, as one group, the ducks rose from the water and flew away from us over the island. I laughed, while the older two berated their younger brother.

'Patience is everything in these matters,' I said. 'You must learn stealth and patience. These come with age.'

The youngest one was looking tearful, so I did what I usually do when there are children to be entertained, I took out my father's glass eye from the pouch which hangs at my hip and let him hold it in the palm of his hand while I rowed us back to the city. He held it very carefully in both hands, occasionally removing the covering hand to gaze at it and gaze at it, as if another world existed in its smooth surface.

After I had returned the boys to their mother, I moored the boat and walked home through the city. I am now a wealthy man, but I have no wish to advertise my wealth and I have no wish to stop working for Tullia Buffo and Marco Martinengo. I fear that if I am away from the canals and waters that I love, like my father, my appetite for life will drain away from me and death will put his arms around me and draw me into an eternal embrace.

My father's eye is a hard nudge against my hip. I have carried it ever since he died, as a reminder to myself to exact my revenge upon those who hurt him, but my father was a man who would not drown a sack of kittens; when my mother ordered that we be beaten, he would take us outside, thrash the wall with his belt and tell us to yell. Maybe it is because of this that I have sought to use the paintings in the way that I have, gently and for the good of others. My mistress still has the three that she chose and Isaac has one that he says is of a French doctor who was the first to name the French disease. He likes the lynx fur of the French man's coat and that he is a medical man. The other paintings have been sold, some to patricians, others to artists in the Low Countries.

I love her, my mistress. I know no other woman like her. In some ways she reminds me of Aretino. When she gets into my boat, she always asks after the gossip, the more scurrilous the better, although unlike my master she does not use it to blackmail others.

The day is ending. Tonight small apricot clouds scud over the city, lit up by the rays of the setting sun. My father's eye nudges against my hip. In St Mark's Square they are putting up platforms for the *festa* tomorrow. A couple of buffoons practise their acrobatics and the lament of the bagpipes drifts over from a wind band. Tomorrow night fireworks will erupt over the city. Suddenly, I know what I must do. I walk towards the pillars of St Theodore and St Mark's, between which my father's punishment was carried out. I walk between them, defying the superstition which states it is unlucky to do so. I walk to the water's edge and take the eye from my pouch. I look at it one last time and as the dying rays of the sun strike the roofs of the city, I hurl it as hard as I can out into the sea. I imagine it sinking down, down to the bottom of the lagoon. I take a deep breath as a weight I have been bearing since I was a boy lifts from my shoulders. Finally, it is over.

Slowly, as the shadows begin to lengthen, I make my way home through the *calli* of this city that I love so much. Yes, it is over. I am an old man, but now my life can truly begin.

AUTHOR'S NOTE

It's because I don't fancy being haunted by my late father's ghost that I'm writing this. He was the historian Robert Blake and the accuracy of facts mattered to him. I, on the other hand, write fiction and playing slightly fast and loose with the historical facts in order to write an entertaining story has been more of my approach. So be warned – some of the material in this book is true and some of it is not and some of it is disputed.

I feel I should also explain that the painting described here as *The Man with the Blue Sleeve* has undergone a few title changes over the years. When I first encountered it in the early eighties it had the aforementioned title. It then became *A Man with a Quilted Sleeve* and finally *Portrait of Gerolamo (?) Barbarigo*. The title I have used is the first one because it is my favourite and seems to me the most elegant. What is certain however is that it hangs (unless it is out on loan) in The National Gallery in London. Please visit him and see what he has to say to you!

If some of the matters described in *The Return of the Courtesan* have pricked your interest, below are the books that I have enjoyed reading in the course of my research and I hope you may enjoy too.

371

Peter Ackroyd – *Venice* (Vintage, 2010)

Pietro Aretino – *Selected Letters* (Penguin Classics, 1976)

Patricia Fortini Brown – *Private Lives in Renaissance Venice: Art, Architecture and the Family* (Yale University Press, 2004)

Thomas Caldecot Chubb – *The Letters of Aretino* (Archon Books, 1967)

Veronica Franco – *Poems and Selected Letters* (University of Chicago Press, 1998)

Sheila Hale – *Titian: His Life* (Harper Press, 2012)

Mark Hudson – *Titian: The Last Days* (Bloomsbury, 2009)

Jonathan Jones – *The Loves of the Artists: Art and Passion in the Renaissance* (Simon and Schuster, 2013)

Ed. Patricia H. Labalme and Laura Sanguineti White – *Venice, Città Excelentissima: Selections from the Renaissance Diaries of Marin Sanudo* (The John Hopkins University Press, 2008)

Mary Laven – *Virgins of Venice* (Penguin, 2003)

Michelle Lovric – *Venice: Tales of the City* (Abacus, 2005)

Sandy Nairne – *Art Theft* (Reaktion Books, 2011)

John Julius Norwich – *A History of Venice* (Penguin, 2003)

Carlo Ridolfi – *The Life of Titian* (Penn State Press, 1996)

Margaret F. Rosenthal – *The Honest Courtesan: Veronica Franco, Citizen and Writer in Sixteenth-Century Venice* (University of Chicago, 1992)

Victor Andres Triay – *Fleeing Castro: Operation Pedro Pan and the Cuban Children's Program* (University Press of Florida, 1998)